Fanny Beulah Bates

Between the Lights

Thoughts for the Quiet Hour

Fanny Beulah Bates

Between the Lights
Thoughts for the Quiet Hour

ISBN/EAN: 9783337254940

Printed in Europe, USA, Canada, Australia, Japan

Cover: Foto ©Andreas Hilbeck / pixelio.de

More available books at **www.hansebooks.com**

BETWEEN THE LIGHTS

Thoughts for the Quiet Hour

COMPILED AND ARRANGED

By Fanny B. Bates

" The longest day at last bends down to evening."

" A little pause in life while daylight lingers
Between the sunset and the pale moonrise,
When daily labor slips from weary fingers,
And soft gray shadows veil the aching eyes."

NEW YORK
THOMAS Y. CROWELL & CO.
PUBLISHERS

TO

The Memory

OF

MY FATHER AND MOTHER.

"They are all gone into the world of light,
  And I alone sit lingering here;
Their very memory is fair and bright,
  And my sad thoughts doth clear."

NOTE.

FOR many years gems of poetry and prose have found their way into a scrap-book, until friends, who felt a delicacy in borrowing so well-worn a volume, have urged me to give it publication.

"Between the Lights" is for the "little pause in life" at the close of the day, when the most conscientiously busy worker will steal a few moments of rest and refreshment before the lamps are lighted. In the compilation many favorite poems have, with reluctance, been omitted, on account of their length, while many have been retained whose sentiment is superior to their diction. A few quaint old things I have used as a kind of moral tonic. Some original things have been given me; and others are added because of tender associations.

In making my selections I have not been limited by any lines of party or sect; and I have chosen chiefly those which might be to others, as to myself, a helping hand in "the long way up-hill,"—a gleam of sunshine on "the path thro' the snow."

BETWEEN THE LIGHTS.

January 1.

Choose you this day whom ye will serve. — JOSHUA
xxiv. 15.

AS with doubtful hands we push away the shades and
take our first steps in the opening year, the thought
cannot fail to come to us all of how little we know what
is before us. Living, but living an uncertain life, let the
season utter its warnings. One thing is certain, that if
you desire improvement in anything, it will never come
to you accidentally. It must begin in a distinct, resolved
purpose to make a change for the better. I call on you
to give this day to a serious review of your life, of what
you have been living for, and of what you purpose henceforth to live for. Give one day to this, and let it be this
first day of the year : at least begin the year aright. Here
you stand at the parting of the ways : some road you are to
take ; and as you stand here, consider and know how it is
that you intend to live. Carry no bad habits, no corrupt-
ing associations, no enmities and strifes, into this new
year. Leave these behind, and let the dead Past bury
its dead ; leave them behind, and thank God that you
are able to leave them.

EPHRAIM PEABODY.

NEW-YEAR THOUGHTS.

FAREWELL, Old Year, the rustle of whose garment,
  Fragrant with memory, I still can hear ;
For all thy tender kindness and thy bounty
  I drop my thankful tribute on thy bier.

What is in store for me, brave New Year, hidden
  Beneath thy glistening robe of ice and snows ?
Are there sweet songs of birds, and breath of lilacs,
  And blushing blooms of June's scent-laden rose ?

1

Are there cold winds and dropping leaves of autumn,
　　Heart-searching frosts, and storm-clouds black and drear?
Is there a rainbow spanning the dark heaven?
　　Wilt thou not speak and tell me, glad New Year?

As silent art thou of the unknown future
　　As if thy days were numbered with the dead;
Yet as I enter thy wide-open portal,
　　I cross thy threshold with glad hope, not dread.

To me no pain or fear or crushing sorrow
　　Hast thou the power without *His* will to bring;
And so I fear thee not, O untried morrow!
　　For well I know my Father is thy King.

If joy thou bringest, straight to God. the giver,
　　My gratitude shall rise, for 't is His gift;
If sorrow, still, 'mid waves of Grief's deep river,
　　My trembling heart I'll to my Father lift.

If life's full cup shall be my happy portion,
　　With thankful joy I'll drink the precious draught;
If death, my waiting soul across life's ocean
　　But little sooner to my home 't will waft.

So, hope-lit New Year, with thy joys uncertain,
　　Whose unsolved mystery none may foretell,
I calmly trust my God to lift thy curtain;
　　Safe in His love, for *me* 't will all be well.

　　　　　　　　　　　　　　　　　JULIA B. CADY.

January 2.

*With my whole heart have I sought Thee: O let me not
wander from Thy commandments.* — Ps. cxix. 10.

NOW, O man, cease for a little from thy work, withdraw thyself for a while from thy stormy thoughts,
forget thy weary and burdensome struggling, give thyself
for a time to God, and rest calmly in Him. Leave all
around thee where God is not, and where thou wilt find
no help from Him; go into the inner chamber of thine
heart, and shut the door behind thee. Say then with thy
whole heart: "I seek Thy face, O Lord; teach Thou
me how and where I should seek Thee, and where and
how I shall find Thee."

　　　　　　　　　　　　　　　　SAINT ANSELM.

WITHIN AND WITHOUT.

Out ! out ! away !
Soul, in this alien house thou hast no stay !
Seek thou thy dwelling in Eternity ;
    'T is there shall be
    Thy hiding-place, thy nest,
Where nor the world nor self can break thy rest.
    Within the heart of God,
    There is thy still abode ;
There mayst thou dwell at rest and be at home,
Howe'er the body here may toil and roam.

    Within ! within, oh, turn
    Thy spirit's eyes, and learn
Thy wandering senses gently to control !
Thy dearest Friend dwells deep within thy soul,
    And asks thyself of thee
That heart and mind and sense He may make whole
    In perfect harmony.
    Doth not thy inmost spirit yield
And sink where Love stands thus revealed ?
    Be still and veil thy face ;
The Lord is here, — this is His holy place !
Then back to earth ; and 'mid its toil and throng,
One glance within will keep thee calm and strong.
And when the toil is o'er, how sweet, O God, to flee
    Within, to Thee !

GERHARD TERSTEEGEN.
Tr. by CATHERINE WINKWORTH.

———◆———

January 3.

While we look not at the things which are seen, but at the things which are not seen. — 2 COR. iv. 18.

WE speak of the snow as of an image of death. It may be that ; but it hides the everlasting life always under its robe, — the life to be revealed in due time, when all cold shadows shall melt away before the ascending sun, and we shall be, not unclothed, but clothed upon, and mortality shall be swallowed up of life.

ROBERT COLLYER

UNDER THE SNOW.

It is pleasant to think, just under the snow,
　That stretches so bleak and blank and cold,
Are beauty and warmth that we cannot know, ––
　Green fields and leaves and blossoms of gold.

Yes, under this frozen and dumb expanse,
　Ungladdened by bee or bird or flower,
A world where the leaping fountains glance,
　And the buds expand, is waiting its hour.

It is hidden now; not a glimmer breaks
　Through the hard blue ice and the sparkling drift
The world shrinks back from the downy flakes
　Which out of the folds of the night-cloud sift.

But as fair and real a world it is
　As any that rolls in the upper blue;
If you wait, you will hear its melodies,
　And see the sparkle of fount and dew.

And often now when the skies are wild,
　And hoarse and sullen the night winds blow,
And lanes and hollows with drifts are piled,
　I think of the violets under the snow;

I look in the wild-flower's tremulous eye,
　I hear the chirp of the ground bird brown;
A breath from the budding grove steals by,
　And the swallows are dipping above the town.

So there, from the outer sense concealed,
　It lies, shut in by a veil of snow:
But there, to the inward eye revealed,
　Are boughs that blossom, and flowers that glow.

The lily shines on its bending stem,
　The crocus opens its April gold,
And the rose up-tosses its diadem
　Against the floor of the winter's cold.

And that other world, to my soul I say,
　That veiled and mystic world of the dead,
Is no farther away on any day
　Than the lilies just under the snow we tread.

T. Hempstead

January 4.

*Mark the perfect man, and behold the upright; for the end
of that man is peace.* — Ps. xxxvii. 37.

SHALL we make no account of the slackened but
surer pace, the dignity, the calm, which make old
age what God intended it should be, — a sublime halt
between a conquered world and eternity?

I collect myself, O my God ! at the close of life, as at
the close of day, and bring to Thee my thoughts and my
love. The last thoughts of a heart that loves Thee are
like those last, deepest, ruddiest rays of the setting sun.
Thou hast willed, O my God ! that life should be beautiful even to the end. Make me to grow and keep my
green, and climb like the plant which lifts its head to
Thee for the last time before it drops its seed and dies.

MADAME SWETCHINE.

THE WORLD OF STARS.

OH, sweetly sinks this life of ours,
   Through age's cloudy bars, —
A fading flush on hill and sky,
   And lo, the world of stars !

We bless Thee, gracious God, for birth,
   By which we hither come ;
We bless Thee for the gate of death, —
   The good man's passage home.

We bless Thee for the heart to feel,
   And for the eye to see ;
For faith that reaches over time,
   And grasps eternity.

Oh, softly fades this life of ours,
   Through age's silver bars, —
A tender flush on hill and sky,
   And lo, the world of stars !

FROM THE ROUND TABLE

January 5.

In a little wrath I hid my face from thee for a moment; but with everlasting kindness will I have mercy on thee, saith the Lord thy Redeemer. — ISA. liv. 8.

STRANGELY do some people talk of " getting over " a great sorrow, — overleaping it, passing it by, thrusting it into oblivion. Not so. No one ever does that, — at least no nature which can be touched by the feeling of grief at all. The only way is to pass through the ocean of affliction solemnly, slowly, with humility and faith, as the Israelites passed through the sea. Then its very waves of misery will divide and become to us a wall on the right side and on the left, until the gulf narrows and narrows before our eyes, and we land safe on the opposite shore.

DINAH MULOCH CRAIK.

SORROW PAST.

THE shadow has gone by;
A peace fills all the sky;
My days are warm with quiet, sunny life,
My nights are full of rest;
Thy love is manifest;
I thank Thee Thou hast led me from the strife.

I know that toil and pain
Will come to me again;
That many shadows on my life must fall;
I know by long years past
Such quiet cannot last;
And yet I thank Thee it has come at all.

When darkness falls at length,
I shall have gathered strength
From these sweet days of pleasantness and calm;
And with sincerest heart,
When sweetest lights depart,
I may, through all, lift up my voice in psalm.

Now, with no care or fear,
Because I feel Thee near,
Because my hands were not reached out in vain,

May I from out my calm
Reach humbly out some balm,
Some peace, some light, to others in their pain.

And when at last I sleep,
May others come and reap
The harvest planted here by these weak hands ;
A harvest white for Thee
I pray it thus may be.
Show me my field ; I wait for Thy commands.

---◆---

January 6.

Peace I leave with you, my peace I give unto you ; not as the world giveth, give I unto you. Let not your heart be troubled, neither let it be afraid. — JOHN xiv. 27.

NOW I want you to think that in life troubles will come, which seem as if they never would pass away. The night and the storm look as if they would last forever, but the calm and the morning cannot be stayed ; the storm in its very nature is transient. The effort of nature, as that of the human heart, ever is to return to its repose, for God is Peace.

GEORGE MACDONALD.

THE PEACE OF GOD.

WE ask for peace, O Lord !
Thy children ask Thy peace ;
Not what the world calls rest,
That toil and care should cease,
That through bright, sunny hours
Calm life should fleet away,
And tranquil night should fade
In smiling day, —
It is not for such peace that we would pray.

We ask for peace, O Lord !
Yet not to stand secure,
Girt round with iron pride.
Contented to endure :

Crushing the gentle strings
 That human hearts should know,
Untouched by others' joy
 Or others' woe ;
Thou, O dear Lord, wilt never teach us so.

We ask Thy peace, O Lord !
 Through storm and fear and strife,
To light and guide us on,
 Through a long, struggling life ;
To lean on Thee entranced,
 In calm and perfect rest ;
Give us that peace, O Lord,
 Divine and blest,
Thou keepest for those hearts who love Thee best.

ADELAIDE A. PROCTER.

January 7.

Thou wilt show me the path of life ; in Thy presence is fulness of joy ; at Thy right hand there are pleasures forevermore. — PS. xvi. 11.

THERE is an eventide in the day, — an hour when the sun retires and the shadows fall, and when Nature assumes the appearance of soberness and silence. It is an hour from which everywhere the thoughtless fly, as peopled only in their imaginations with images of gloom ; it is the hour, on the other hand, which in every age the wise have loved, as bringing with it sentiments and affections more valuable than all the splendors of the day. Its first impression is to still all the turbulence of thought or passion which the day may have brought forth. We follow with our eye the descending sun ; we listen to the decaying sounds of labor and of toil ; and when all the fields are silent around us, we feel a kindred stillness to breathe upon our souls, and to calm them from the agitations of society. From this first impression there is a second which naturally follows it : in the day we are living with men ; in the eventide we begin to live with Nature ; we see the world withdrawn from us, the shades of night darken over the habitations of men, and we feel ourselves alone. It is an hour fitted, as it would seem, by Him who made us, to still, but with gentle hand, the throb of every unruly passion, and, while it veils for a time the world that misleads us, to awaken in our hearts those legitimate affections which the heat of the day may have dissolved. In the moments when earth is overshadowed, heaven opens to our eyes the radiance of a sublimer being; our hearts follow the successive splendors of the scene; and while we forget for a time the obscurity of earthly concerns, we feel that there are "yet greater things than these."

A. ALISON, 1757–1839.

BETWEEN THE LIGHTS.

A LITTLE pause in life, while daylight lingers
  Between the sunset and the pale moonrise,
When daily labor slips from weary fingers,
  And soft gray shadows veil the aching eyes.

Old perfumes wander back from fields of clover
  Seen in the light of suns that long have set;
Beloved ones, whose earthly toil is over,
  Draw near, as if they lived among us yet.

Old voices call me, through the dusk returning;
  I hear the echoes of departed feet;
And then I ask, with vain and troubled yearning,
  What is the charm that makes old things so sweet?

Must the old joys be evermore withholden?
  Even their memory keeps me pure and true;
And yet, from out Jerusalem the Golden
  God speaketh, saying, "I make all things new."

"Father," I cry, "the old must still be nearer,
  Stifle my love, or give me back the past!
Give me the fair old earth, whose paths are dearer
  Than all Thy shining streets and mansions vast."

Peace, peace! the Lord of earth and heaven knoweth
  The human soul in all its heat and strife;
Out of His throne no stream of Lethe floweth,
  But the clear river of eternal life.

He giveth life, aye, life in all its sweetness ;
 Old loves, old sunny scenes will He restore ;
Only the curse of sin and incompleteness
 Shall taint thine earth and vex thine heart no more.

Serve Him in daily work and earnest living,
 And faith shall lift thee to His sunlit heights ;
Then shall a psalm of gladness and thanksgiving
 Fill the calm hour that comes between the lights.

SARAH DOUDNEY

January 8.

Are they not all ministering spirits? — HEB. i. 14.
It doth not yet appear what we shall be. — 1 JOHN iii. 2.

NOT until we know all that God knows can we estimate to the full the power and the sacredness of
some one life which may seem the humblest in the world.

There is no action so slight nor so mean but it may be
done to a great purpose, and ennobled therefor ; nor is
any purpose so great but that slight actions may help it,
and may be so done as to help it much, most especially
that chief of all purposes, — the pleasing of God. We
treat God with irreverence by banishing Him from our
thoughts, not by referring to His will on slight occasions.
His is not the finite authority of intelligence which cannot
be troubled with small things.

JOHN RUSKIN

THE CELESTIAL ARMY.

I STOOD by an open casement,
 And looked upon the night,
And saw the eastward-going stars
 Pass slowly out of sight.

Slowly the bright procession
 Went down the gleaming arch,
And my soul discerned the music
 Of their long triumphal march ;

Till the great celestial army,
　Stretching far beyond the poles,
Became the eternal symbol
　Of the mighty march of souls.

Onward, forever onward,
　Red Mars led down the clan,
And the moon, like a mailèd maiden,
　Was riding in the van.

And some were bright in beauty,
　And some were faint and small ;
But these might be, in their greatest height,
　The noblest of them all.

Downward, forever downward,
　Behind earth's dusky shore,
They passed into the unknown night;
　They passed and were no more.

No more?　Oh, say not so !
　And *downward* is not just ;
For the sight is weak and the sense is dim
　That looks through heated dust.

The stars and the mailèd moon,
　Though they seem to fall and die,
Still sweep with their embattled lines
　An endless track of sky.

And though the hills of death
　May hide the bright array,
The marshalled brotherhood of souls
　Still keeps its upward way.

Upward, forever upward,
　I see their march sublime,
And hear the glorious music
　Of the conquerors of Time.

And long let me remember
　That the palest, faintest one
May to diviner vision be
　A bright and blessed sun.

THOMAS BUCHANAN READ.

January 9.

I would have you without carefulness. — 1 COR. vii. 32.

WHAT a vast proportion of our lives is spent in anxious and useless forebodings concerning the future, — either our own or those of our dear ones. Present joys, present blessings, slip by, and we miss half their sweet flavor, and all for want of faith in Him who provides for the tiniest insect in the sunbeam. Oh, when shall we learn the sweet trust in God that our little children teach us every day by their confiding faith in us? We, who are so mutable, so faulty, so irritable, so unjust; and He, who is so watchful, so pitiful, so loving, so forgiving? Why cannot we, slipping our hand into His each day, walk trustingly over that day's appointed path, thorny or flowery, crooked or straight, knowing that evening will bring us sleep, peace, and home?

PHILLIPS BROOKS

AN EVENING HYMN.

Now God be with us, for the night is closing,
The light and darkness are of His disposing ;
And 'neath His shadow here to rest we yield us,
　　　　For He will shield us.

Let evil thoughts and spirits flee before us ;
Till morning cometh, watch, O Master, o'er us ;
In soul and body Thou from harm defend us ;
　　　　Thine angels send us.

Let holy thoughts be ours when sleep o'ertakes us,
Our earliest thoughts be Thine when morning wakes us ,
All day serve Thee, in all that we are doing,
　　　　Thy praise pursuing.

As Thy belovèd, soothe the sick and weeping,
And bid the prisoner lose his griefs in sleeping ;
Widows and orphans we to Thee commend them.
　　　　Do Thou befriend them.

We have no refuge, none on earth to aid us,
Save Thee, O Father, who Thine own hast made us ;
But Thy dear presence will not leave them lonely
　　　　Who seek Thee only.

Father, Thy name be praised, Thy kingdom given,
Thy will be done on earth as 't is in heaven;
Keep us in life, forgive our sins, deliver
              Us now and ever.   Amen.

                    HYMN OF THE BOHEMIAN BRETHREN

January 10.

*For ye have need of patience, that, after ye have done the will
of God, ye might receive the promise.* — HEB. x. 36.

HEARTS weary of the woe and worry of life look
longingly to heaven with a sentiment not much
higher than that which moved a world-sick poet to cry
for a desert, " Where he might all forget the human race."
Anywhere, away from man.   Heaven! the world where
earth with all its storm and strife may be forgotten; alone
with the quiet angels, within the tranquil sphere of the
serene activity of God.   Nothing like this will be heaven.
It is the sphere in which the elect spirits who have won
the prizes in life's battles, who have come forth from the
chaos of strife trained, inured, yet pure, shall play out
their parts on a grander scale, in a wider theatre, under
the eye of a more absolute and exigent King.   All that
society aims at on earth and misses, the grand order of
human relations, the majestic procession of human activi-
ties, of which, maimed and crippled as they are on earth,
the wisest and noblest have not ceased to dream, shall
there be realized, with Christ the King visibly in the
centre of it, and the angels attendant.

                              J. BALDWIN BROWN

"CAREST THOU NOT?"

CAREST Thou not, O Thou that givest life,
    Carest Thou not, who art the love Thou teachest,
While half Thy children perish in the strife
    For lack of the sweet charity Thou preachest?
The eye that sees, the heart that longs and yearns
    For beauty, wealth, and calm of golden hours;
Or Thou, or Nature gave the brain that burns,
    The mind that chafes to use its latent powers

Caught in the bitter net of circumstance,
   We strive and faint amid each baffling fold,
While careless fingers take, or miss, the chance,
   Or idle with the precious thing they hold.
We fain would see and save and live and laugh,
   Fain would have honest heart and open hand;
Ah ! hope and love make but a breaking staff
   When 'mid our shattered dreams alone we stand.

Carest Thou not, O Lord ?   Old age creeps on,
   Blighting each lingering bloom we dare to cherish.
A little while, and the last day is done :
   Carest Thou not, O Lord, because we perish ?
Oh, stretch the right hand, strong to stay and save!
   Speak, through wild winds above, wild seas beneath !
Say, despite failing life and opening grave,
   " Why will ye doubt, O ye of little faith ?"

ALL THE YEAR ROUND.

January 11.

Lead me in Thy truth, and teach me ; for Thou art the God of my salvation ; on Thee do I wait all the day. — Ps. xxv. 5.

FAITH is truly a light in the soul, but it is a light which shines only upon duties, and not upon results or events.   It tells us what is now to be done, but it does not tell us what is to follow, and accordingly it guides us but a single step at a time and when we take that step under the guidance of faith, we advance directly into a land of surrounding shadows and darkness.   Like the patriarch, Abraham, we go, not knowing whither we go, but only that God is with us.   In man's darkness, we nevertheless walk and live in God's light.   A way of living blessed and glorious, however mysterious it may be to human vision.

THOMAS C. UPHAM.

THY WILL BE DONE.

WE see not, know not; all our way
Is night; with Thee alone is day.
From out the torrent's troubled drift,
Above the storm our prayer we lift,
           Thy will be done!

The flesh may fail, the heart may faint,
But who are we to make complaint,
Or dare to plead in times like these
The weakness of our love of ease?
           Thy will be done!

We take with solemn thankfulness
Our burden up, nor ask it less;
And count it joy that even we
May suffer, serve, or wait for Thee.
           Thy will be done!

Though dim as yet in tint and line,
We trace Thy picture's wise design,
And thank Thee that our age supplies
The dark relief of sacrifice.
           Thy will be done!

Strike, Thou the master, we thy keys,
The anthem of the destinies!
The minor of Thy loftier strain,
Our hearts shall breathe the old refrain,
           Thy will be done!

JOHN G. WHITTIER

January 12.

As one whom his mother comforteth, so will I comfort you. — Isa. lxvi. 13.

GOD has not so created the creatures that after creating He abandons them. He loves them, delights in them, is with them; moves and sustains each creature according to its kind. We Christians know that with God creating and sustaining are one thing.

LUTHER.

THE TRUE COMFORTER.

WHEN me my nearest friends forsake,
  When I am wretched and forlorn,
I refuge with the Father take,
  My pang to heaven's God is borne;
Unchained by words, my silent sigh
Steals to the Loving One on high.

What deepest, keenest, stirs the heart,
  What human lips can never speak,
What ne'er to human ear can dart,
  Hath voice to Him who shields the weak;
Its mystic force to Him unrolls,
The spirit's source, the soul of souls.

In Christ's dear name I will outpour
  My fullest bosom, Lord, to Thee;
Learn by sweet silence to adore,
  To see, by seeking not to see;
My needs shall feed Thine altar's flame,
If I them breathe in Christ's dear name.

HYMNS OF DENMARK

January 13.

Mine eyes fail for Thy word, saying, When will Thou com-
fort me ? — Ps. cxix. 82.

YOUR sacrifice is burning on the altar, and around you
the temple of life is filled with smoke, and no light
comes in through the windows, and the very walls you
cannot see, but you know where you are ; for as long as
you suffer you are nigh the altar. That you know, and
by that knowledge hold fast.   Be quiet, fear not ; and be
you sure that when your sacrifice is over, one after the
other the windows that open into the infinite — faith and
hope — will show themselves ; and the air about you will
be the clearer and the sweeter for having been so darkened awhile.

WILLIAM MOUNTFORD

THE DIVINE HELPER.

THOU that art strong to comfort, look on me !
  I sit in darkness and behold no light ;
Over my soul the waves of agony
  Have gone and left me in a rayless night.

A bruised and broken reed sustain ! sustain !
  Divinest Comforter, to Thee I fly,
To whom no soul hath ever fled in vain ;
  Support me with Thy love, or else I die !

Father, whate'er I had, it all was Thine ;
  A God of mercy Thou hast ever been ;
Oh, help me what I most love to resign,
  And if I murmur, count it not for sin !

My soul is strengthened now, and it shall bear
  All that remains, whatever it may be ;
And from the very depths of my despair
  I will look up, O God, and trust in Thee.

January 14.

The day is Thine, the night also is Thine; Thou hast pre-
pared the light and the sun. Thou hast set all the
borders of the earth: Thou hast made summer and
winter. — Ps. lxxiv. 16, 17.

WHAT fire is this that so warmeth my heart? What
light is this that so enlighteneth my soul! O fire
that always burneth, and never goeth out, kindle me! O
light which ever shineth, and art never darkened, illumi-
nate me! O that I had my heat from thee, most holy
fire! how sweetly dost thou burn!   SAINT AUGUSTINE.

ALL THINGS ARE THINE.

THOU art, O God, the life and light
　　Of all this wondrous world we see;
Its glow by day, its smile by night,
　　Are but reflections caught from Thee.
Where'er we turn, Thy glories shine,
And all things bright and fair are Thine!

When day, with farewell beam, delays
　　Among the opening clouds of even,
And we can almost think we gaze
　　Through golden vistas into heaven, —
Those hues that make the sun's decline
So soft, so radiant, Lord! are Thine.

When night, with wings of starry gloom,
　　O'ershadows all the earth and skies,
Like some dark, beauteous bird, whose plume
　　Is sparkling with unnumbered eyes, —
That sacred gloom, those fires divine,
So grand, so countless, Lord! are Thine.

When youthful spring around us breathes,
　　Thy spirit warms her fragrant sigh;
And every flower the summer wreathes
　　Is born beneath that kindling eye.
Where'er we turn, Thy glories shine,
And all things fair and bright are Thine!

THOMAS MOORE

January 15.

Whosoever liveth and believeth in me shall never die. — JOHN xi. 26.

THE departed have not ceased their communication with us, though the visible chain is broken. If they are still the same, they must still think of us. If they live there, they love there. "God is not the God of the dead, but the God of the living." Then it is true, that they live there ; and they yet speak to us. From that bright sphere, from that calm region, from the bowers of the life immortal, they speak to us. They say to us, "Sigh not in despair over the broken and defeated expectations of earth. Sorrow not as those who have no hope. Bear calmly and cheerfully thy lot. Brighten the chain of love, of sympathy ; of communion with all pure minds on earth and in heaven. Come, children of earth ! come to the bright and blessed land ! "

ORVILLE DEWEY

THE MESSENGER BIRD.

THOU art come from the spirits' land, thou bird !
 Thou art come from the spirits' land !
Through the dark pine grove let thy voice be heard,
 And tell of the shadowy band !

We know that the bowers are green and fair
 In the light of that summer shore,
And we know that the friends we have lost are there ;
 They are there, — and they weep no more !

And we know they have quenched their fever's thirst,
 From the Fountain of Youth ere now ;
For there must the stream in its freshness burst,
 Which none may find below.

And we know that they will not be lured to earth,
 From the land of deathless flowers,
By the feast, or the dance, or the song of mirth.
 Though their hearts were once with ours ;

Though they sat with us by the night-fire's blaze,
And bent with us the bow,
And heard the tales of our fathers' days,
Which are told to others now.

But tell us, thou bird of the solemn strain!
Can those who have loved forget?
We call, and they answer not again —
Do they love — do they love us yet?

We call them far through the silent night,
And they speak not from cave or hill;
We know, thou bird! that their land is bright,
But say, do they love there still?

FELECIA HEMANS

January 16.

*Have mercy upon me, O God, according to Thy loving kind-
ness; according unto the multitude of Thy tender mercies
blot out my transgressions. — Ps. li. 1.*

IN a world where there is so much to ruffle the spirit's
plumes, how needful that entering into the secret of
His pavilion, which will alone bring it back to composure
and peace! In a world where there is so much to sadden
and depress, how blessed that communion with Him in
whom is the one true source and fountain of all true gladness and abiding joy! In a world where so much is ever
seeking to unhallow our spirits, to render them common
and profane, how high the privilege of consecrating them
anew in prayer to holiness and to God!

RICHARD CHENEVIX TRENCH.

EVENING PRAYER.

TAKE unto Thyself, O Father!
This folded day of Thine,
This weary day of mine;
Its ragged corners cut me yet,
Oh, still the jar and fret!
Father, do not forget
That I am tired
With this day of Thine

Breathe Thy pure breath, watching Father,
On this marred day of Thine,
This wandering day of mine ;
Be patient with its blur and blot,
Wash it white of stain and spot,
Reproachful eyes ! remember not
That I have grieved Thee,
On this day of Thine.

ELIZABETH STUART PHELPS.

January 17.

Beloved, think it not strange concerning the fiery trial which is to try you, as though some strange thing happened unto you ; but rejoice, inasmuch as ye are partakers of Christ's sufferings ; that, when His glory shall be revealed, ye may be glad also with exceeding joy. — 1 PETER iv. 12, 13.

MANY a waiting hour was needful to enrich the harp of David, and many a waiting hour in the wilderness will gather for us a psalm of " thanksgiving, and the voice of melody," to cheer the hearts of fainting ones here below, and to make glad our Father's house on high. What was the preparation of the son of Jesse for the songs like unto which none have ever sounded on this earth ? The outrage of the wicked, which brought forth cries for God's help.   Then the faint hope in God's goodness blossomed into a song of rejoicing for His mighty deliverances and manifold mercies.   Every sorrow was another string to his harp ; every deliverance another theme for praise.   One thrill of anguish spared, one blessing unmarked or unprized, one difficulty or danger evaded, how great would have been our loss in that thrilling Psalmody in which God's people to-day find the expression of their grief or praise !   To wait for God, and to suffer His will, is to know Him in the fellowship of His sufferings, and to be conformed to the likeness of His Son.   So now, if the vessel is to be enlarged for spiritual understanding, be not affrighted at the wider sphere of suffering that awaits you. The divine capacity of sympathy will have a more extended sphere; for the breathing of the Holy Ghost in the new creation never made a stoic, but left the heart's affection tender and true.

ANNA SHIPTON.

MANY a seed of sacrifice bears its hundredfold in this life ; and those which cannot, sown in Christ's grave, shall when we are glorified with Him receive a life everlasting.

THE SOWER.

" I HAD much seed to sow," said one ; " I planned
    To fill broad furrows, and to watch it spring,
And water it with care.   But now the hand
    Of Him to whom I sought great sheaves to bring
Is laid upon His laborer, and I wait,
Weak, helpless, at His palace gate.

" Now I have nothing only day by day
    Grace to sustain me till the day is done ;
And some sweet passing glimpses by the way
    Of Him, the altogether lovely one,
And some strange things to learn, unlearned before,
That make the suffering light, if it but teach me more."

Yet, from the hush of that secluded room,
    Forth floated winged seeds of thought and prayer, —
Those, reaching many a desert place to bloom,
    And pleasant fruit an hundredfold to bear.
Those, wafted heavenward with song and sigh,
To fall again with showers of blessings from on high.

FRANCES RIDLEY HAVERGAL

January 18.

For now we see through a glass, darkly; but then face to face; now I know in part; but then shall I know even as also I am known. — 1 COR. xiii. 12.

THE most exalted idea we can form of the future state is, that it brings and joins us to God. But is not approach to this great being begun on earth? Another delightful view of heaven is, that it unites us with the good and great of our own race, and even with higher orders of beings. But this union is one of spirit, not of mere place; it is accordance of thought and feeling, not an outward relation; and does not this harmony begin even now? and is not virtuous friendship on earth essentially the pleasure which we hope hereafter? What place would be drearier than the future mansions of Christ, to one who should want sympathy with their inhabitants, who would feel himself a foreigner there, who would be taught by the joys which he could not partake his own loneliness and desolation?

THE FUTURE LIFE.

How shall I know thee in the sphere which keeps
    The disembodied spirits of the dead,
When all of thee that time could wither sleeps
    And perishes among the dust we tread?

For I shall feel the sting of ceaseless pain
    If there I meet thy gentle presence not;
Nor hear the voice I love, nor read again
    In thy serenest eyes the tender thought.

Will not thy own meek heart demand me there?
    That heart whose fondest throbs to me were given;
My name on earth was ever in thy prayer,
    And wilt thou never utter it in heaven?

In meadows fanned by heaven's life-breathing wind,
    In the resplendence of that glorious sphere,
And larger movements of the unfettered mind,
    Wilt thou forget the love that joined us here?

The love that lived through all the stormy past,
  And meekly with my harsher nature bore,
And deeper grew, and tenderer to the last,
  Shall it expire with life, and be no more?

A happier lot than mine, and larger light,
  Await thee there ; for thou hast bowed thy will
In cheerful homage to the rule of right,
  And lovest all and renderest good for ill.

For me, the sordid cares in which I dwell,
  Shrink and consume my heart; as heat the scroll,
And wrath has left its scar — that fire of hell
  Has left its frightful scar upon my soul.

Yet though thou wear'st the glory of the sky,
  Wilt thou not keep the same beloved name,
The same fair thoughtful brow, and gentle eye,
  Lovelier in heaven's sweet climate, yet the same?

Shalt thou not teach me in that calmer home
  The wisdom that I learned so ill in this —
The wisdom which is love — till I become
  Thy fit companion in that land of bliss?

WILLIAM CULLEN BRYANT

January 19.

*If we hope for that we see not, then do we with patience
wait for it.* — ROM. viii. 25.
Their strength is to sit still. — ISA. xxx. 7.

THERE are sweet surprises awaiting many a humble
soul fighting against great odds in the battle of a
seemingly commonplace life.

THERE is something prophetic in thought and in emotion. In the heart of our imperfect knowledge there is
lodged the hope of a perfect wisdom. At the end of our
broken reasonings there shines the light of a higher truth.
All our conclusions, all our theories, all our aspirations,
point forward. Our very defects are intimations of a
future development, and our limitations are but barriers
which we are gaining strength to overleap. What is it all

worth unless there be a beyond? What are the attainments and acquisitions of our threescore and ten years, unless they are to be completed and perfected and applied in a hereafter? Why struggle and toil to gather a little knowledge that will be buried in all its weakness and incompleteness in the grave? But Reason herself breaks the chains of such a despairing doctrine. She shapes her wings to fly. She looks onward and upward. An endless vista opens before her. She anticipates immortality.

H. J. Van Dyke.

WAITING.

I.

I HAVE my dreams as you do, yet for me
  There can be no fulfilment ; but to dream
  Is pleasant sometimes. Just to let these seem
Realities brings comfort. To be free
From earthly circumstance, to climb in glee
  High as my soul can reach and feel the beam
  Of glory on my brow — who does not deem
It good to sometimes dwell in Fantasy ?
O tender heart and true ! be what you will,
  Who have the power. I, though I stay below
    And watch you as you rise to heights elate,
Begrudge you nothing ; dreams that you fulfil
  I feel the beauty of. 'T is yours to grow
    Ever and ever ; mine to stand and wait.

II.

To wait: it is not wearisome ; each day
  Brings something ; newer needs, or lessons caught
  From yesterday, a stream of sunshine fraught
With gold that glitters, though it fades away
After a little. Nothing comes to stay,
  Success or suffering. To wait is naught
  When waiting means to serve. Yea, I have thought
(To stop and think, or even stop and pray,
When duty calls, is not alone unwise
  But somewhat selfish) that 't is better so
    Than to be carried upward by the swell
Of great Ambition. Ah, to wait ! there lies
  Something beyond the waiting, else I know
    I could not be content to say — 'T is well !

James Berry Bensel

January 20.

*How precious also are Thy thoughts unto me, O God! how
great is the sum of them!* — Ps. cxxxix. 17.

THERE are seasons, when, for the moment, at least,
the power of the world seems to drop. A strange
and awful sense of responsibility comes upon us. Aspirations rise up out of the soul like the morning mist kindling
in the sun as it rises from the mountain top towards
heaven. We long for a higher and holier life. The
vanity of the world, the worth of virtue, the goodness of
God, and the peace of a trusting and devout heart are
revealed to us. It is a heavenly vision open before the
soul. These hours, when the soul is freed from its bonds,
and holds communion with truth and God, and sees revealed the realities of its existence, are blessed hours —
hours of heaven — hours, which if obeyed, shall raise the
soul upward to heaven.   EPHRAIM PEABODY

MY SPIRIT TURNS TO THEE.

THOUGHTS of my soul! how swift ye go
　　Swift as the eagle's glance of fire,
Or arrows from the archer's bow —
　　To the far aim of your desire !
Thought after thought, ye thronging rise,
　　Like spring-doves from the startled wood,
Bearing like them your sacrifice
　　Of music unto God !

And shall these thoughts of joy and love
　　Come back again no more to me, —
Returning, like the Patriarch's dove,
　　Wing-weary, from the eternal sea,
To bear within my longing arms
　　The promise-bough of kindlier skies,
Plucked from the green, immortal palms
　　Which shadow Paradise ?

All-moving Spirit ! freely forth,
　　At Thy command, the strong wind goes
Its errand to the passive earth ;
　　Nor art can stay, nor strength oppose,

Until it folds its weary wing
　　Once more within the hand divine ;
So, weary of each earthly thing,
　　My spirit turns to Thine !

LAMARTINE.

---◆---

January 21.

They go from strength to strength, every one of them in Zion appeareth before God. — PS. lxxxiv. 7.

BE always displeased at what thou art, if thou desirest to attain to what thou art not ; for where thou hast pleased thyself, there thou abidest.　　SAINT AUGUSTINE.

THE CHAMBERED NAUTILUS.

THIS is the ship of pearl, which, poets feign,
　　Sails the unshadowed main, —
　　The venturous bark that flings
On the sweet summer wind its purpled wings
In gulfs enchanted, where the Siren sings,
　　And coral reefs lie bare,
Where the cold sea-maids rise to sun their streaming hair.

Its webs of living gauze no more unfurl,
　　Wrecked is the ship of pearl !
　　And every chambered cell,
Where its dim dreaming life was wont to dwell,
As the frail tenant shaped his growing shell,
　　Before thee lies revealed, —
Its irised ceiling rent, its sunless crypt unsealed !

Year after year beheld the silent toil
　　That spread his lustrous coil ;
　　Still, as the spiral grew,
He left the past year's dwelling for the new,
Stole with soft step the shining archway through,
　　Built up its idle door,
Stretched in his last-found home, and knew the old no more

Thanks for the heavenly message brought by thee,
　　Child of the wandering sea,
　　Cast from her lap, forlorn !

From thy dead lips a clearer note is born
Than ever Triton blew from wreathèd horn !
   While on mine ear it rings,
Through the deep caves of thought I hear a voice that sings:

Build thee more stately mansions, O my soul,
   As the swift seasons roll !
    Leave thy low-vaulted past !
Let each new temple, nobler than the last,
Shut thee from heaven with a dome more vast,
   Till thou at length art free,
Leaving thine outgrown shell by life's unresting sea !

OLIVER WENDELL HOLMES.

———◆———

January 22.

Then shall we know, if we follow on to know the Lord. —
HOSEA vi. 3.
Lord, increase our faith. — LUKE xvii. 5.

THERE is many a crisis in life when we need a faith
like the martyr's to support us. There are hours
in life like martyrdom, — as full of bitter anguish, as full of
utter earthly desolation ; in which life itself loses its value,
and we ask to die ; in whose dread struggle and agony,
life might drop from us and not be minded. Oh, then
must our cry, like that of Jesus, go up to the pitying
heavens for help, and nothing but the infinite and immortal can help us. Then, when the world is sinking beneath
us, must we seek the everlasting arms to bear us up, —
to bear us up to heaven. Thus was it with our great
example, and so must it be with us. " In Him was life ; "
the life of self-renunciation, the life of love, the life of
spiritual and all-conquering faith ; and that life is the light
of men. Oh, blessed light ! come to our darkness ; for
our soul is dark, our way is dark, for want of thee ; come
to our darkness and turn it into day ; and let it shine
brighter and brighter, till it mingles with the light of the
all-perfect and everlasting day !

FAITH AND SIGHT.

Thou sayst, " Take up thy cross
  O man, and follow me ; "
The night is black, the feet are slack,
  Yet we would follow Thee.

But O dear Lord, we cry,
  That we Thy face could see !
Thy blessed face one moment's space —
  Then might we follow Thee !

Dim tracts of time divide
  Those golden days from me ;
Thy voice comes strange o'er years of change
  How can I follow Thee ?

Comes faint and far Thy voice
  From vales of Galilee ;
Thy vision fades in ancient shades ;
  How should we follow Thee ?

Ah, sense-bound heart and blind !
  Is naught but what we see ?
Can time undo what once was true,
  Can we not follow Thee ?

Unchanging law binds all,
  And nature all we see ;
Thou art a star far off, too far
  That we should follow Thee !

O heavy cross — of faith,
  In what we cannot see !
As once of yore, Thyself restore,
  And help to follow Thee !

If not as once Thou cam'st
  In true humanity,
Come yet as guest within the breast
  That burns to follow Thee.

Within our heart of hearts,
  In nearest nearness be ;
Set up Thy throne within Thine own,
  Go, Lord ; we follow Thee.

FRANCIS TURNER PALGRAVE

January 23.

And where the spirit of the Lord is, there is liberty. —
2 COR. iii. 17.

THE sweetest word in the language, next to love, is
liberty. God and His angels alone respect the perfect freedom of man. It is the continual effort of the
Lord to deliver us from ourselves, our enemies, and our
friends; and to bring us into a simple, frank, and volun-
tary relation to Himself alone. This is the glorious
liberty wherewith Christ maketh free. To shake off the
yoke of sin, to put our own evil passions and falsities
under foot; to receive from others and to give to them
nothing but the reflected love and wisdom of the Lord;
to identify cordially our own wills and lives with His will
and life and with no others, — this is to know and love the
true God " whose service is perfect freedom."

LIBERTY.

WHEN linnet-like confinèd, I
  With shriller throat shall sing
The sweetness, mercy, majesty,
  And glories of my King;
When I shall voice aloud how good
  He is, how great should be,
Enlargèd winds, that curl the flood,
  Know no such liberty.

Stone walls do not a prison make,
  Nor iron bars a cage;
Minds innocent and quiet take
  That for an hermitage;
If I have freedom in my love
  And in my soul am free,
Angels alone, that soar above,
  Enjoy such liberty.
                    RICHARD LOVELACE, 1618

January 24.

And this is the promise that He hath promised us, even eternal life. — 1 JOHN ii. 25.

LIFE eternal! How shall I express my thought of it? It is not mere existence, however prolonged and free from annoyances. It is not the pleasure of the senses, however vivid. It is not peace. It is not happiness. It is not joy. But it is all these combined into one condition of spiritual perfection, — one emotion of indescribable rapture, — the peace after the storm has gone by, the soft repose after the grief is over, the joy of victory when the conflict is ended.

HILL

THE JERUSALEM THAT IS ABOVE.

BRIEF life is here our portion ;
  Brief sorrow, short-lived care ;
The life that knows no ending,
  The tearless life, is there.

Oh, happy retribution,
  Short toil, eternal rest ;
For mortals and for sinners
  A mansion with the blest.

And now we fight the battle,
  But then shall wear the crown
Of full, and everlasting,
  And passionless renown.

And now we watch and struggle,
  And now we live in hope ;
And Sion in her anguish
  With Babylon must cope ;

But He, whom now we trust in
  Shall there be seen and known ;
And they that know and see Him
  Shall have Him for their own.

The morning shall awaken,
The shadows flee away,
And each true-hearted servant
Shall shine as doth the day.

There God, our king and patron
In fulness of His grace,
Shall we behold forever,
And worship face to face.

BERNARD OF CLUNY.

January 25.

*And the city had no need of the sun, neither of the moon,
to shine in it ; for the glory of God did lighten it, and
the Lamb is the light thereof.* — REV. xxi. 23.

NOW just as the gates were opened to let in the men,
I looked in after them, and behold the city shone
like the sun ; the streets also were paved with gold ; and
in them walked many men with crowns on their heads,
palms in their hands, and golden harps, to sing praises
withal. There were also of them that had wings, and they
answered one another without intermission, saying, " Holy,
holy, holy, is the Lord ! " And after that they shut up
the gates ; which when I had seen I wished myself among
them.

PILGRIM'S PROGRESS.

For thee. O dear, dear country,
Mine eyes their vigils keep ;
For very love beholding
Thy happy name, they weep.

The mention of thy glory
Is unction to the breast.
And medicine in sickness,
And love and light and rest.

O one, O only mansion !
O Paradise of joy !
Where tears are ever banished
And smiles have no alloy ;

The Lamb is all thy splendor,
  The Crucified thy praise
His land and benediction
  Thy ransomed people praise.

With jasper glow thy bulwarks,
  Thy streets with emeralds blaze ;
The sardius and the topaz
  Unite in thee their rays.

Thine ageless walls are bounded
  With amethyst unpriced ;
The saints build up the fabric,
  And the corner-stone is Christ.

Thou hast no shore, fair ocean !
  Thou hast no time, bright day !
Dear fountain of refreshment
  To pilgrims far away !

Upon the Rock of Ages
  They raise thy holy tower ;
Thine are the victor's laurels,
  And thine the golden dower.
                              BERNARD OF CLUNY.

January 26.

*But now they desire a better country, that is, an heavenly ;
wherefore God is not ashamed to be called their God ;
for He hath prepared for them a city. — HEB. xi. 16.*

THE soul that lives, ascends frequently, and runs familiarly through the streets of the heavenly Jerusalem,
visiting the patriarchs and prophets, saluting the apostles,
and admiring the army of martyrs. So do thou lead
on thy heart, and bring it to the palace of the Great
King.   RICHARD BAXTER.

JERUSALEM the golden !
  With milk and honey blest !
Beneath thy contemplation
  Sink heart and voice opprest.

I know not, oh ! I know not
  What joys await me there ;
What radiancy of glory,
  What bliss beyond compare.

They stand, those halls of Sion,
  All jubilant with song,
And bright with many an angel,
  And all the martyr throng.

The Prince is ever in them,
  The daylight ever bright ;
The pastures of the blessed
  Are decked in glorious light ;

There is the throne of David ;
  And there from care released,
The shout of them that triumph,
  The song of them that feast ;

And they who with their Leader
  Have conquered in the fight,
Forever and forever
  Are clad in robes of white.

O sweet and blessed country,
  The home of God's elect !
O sweet and blessed country,
  That eager hearts expect !

Jesu, in mercy bring us,
  To that dear land of rest ;
Who art, with God the Father
  And Spirit, ever blest.
                    Amen.

                    BERNARD OF CLUNY.

January 27.

And there shall be no more death, neither sorrow, nor crying, neither shall there be any more pain ; for the former things are passed away. — REV. xxi. 4.

THE divine Being is that to a Christian, which home is to a weary traveller ; it is his dwelling-place, the stay, the solace, the centre and rest of his spirit ; and hence he is constantly anticipating his arrival at home.

ROBERT HALL.

THERE 's a land where those who loved when here shall meet to love again.

THE HEAVENLY LAND.

THERE is a land where beauty will not fade,
  Nor sorrow dim the eye ;
Where true hearts will not shrink nor be dismayed,
  And love will never die.
Tell me, — I fain would go,
For I am burdened with a heavy woe ;
The beautiful have left me all alone ;
The true, the tender from my path are gone ;
And I am weak, and fainting with despair ;
Where is it ? Tell me, where !

Friend, thou must trust in Him who trod before
  The desolate paths of life ;
Must bear in meekness, as He meekly bore,
  Sorrow and toil and strife.
Think how the Son of God
These thorny paths hath trod ;
Think how He longed to go,
Yet tarried out for thee th' appointed woe ;
Think of His loneliness in places dim,
When no man comforted nor cared for Him ;
Think how He prayed, unaided and alone.
In that dread agony, " Thy will be done ! "
Friend, do not thou despair,
Christ, in His heaven of heavens, will hear thy prayer.

FROM THE GERMAN OF UHLAND

January 28.

But God forbid that I should glory, save in the cross of our Lord Jesus Christ, by whom the world is crucified unto me, and I unto the world. — GAL. vi. 14.

WHEN the twilight has gone down behind the western hills, and darkness has begun to flood the streets and to cover the dwellings of men, — above, in the clear air, you have seen a gilded cross on which the sunbeams still rested, and, as you gazed on its blazing sign, you all at once became conscious, from the contrast, of the dark-ness closing around you, and also saw the visible assur-ance, that, though unseen by you, the sun was still shining with undecaying and undeclining light. So does the cross reared above the earth make us conscious of man's sins, and aware of God's mercy.

THE CROSS.

MY wave-worn bark through life's tempestuous sea
Has sped its course, and touched the crowded shore,
Where all must give account the Judge before,
And, as their actions merit, sentenced be.
At length from Fancy's wild enchantments free,
That made me Art, as some strange god, adore,
I deeply feel how vain its richest store,
Now that the one thing needful faileth me.
Vain dreams of Love! once sweet, now yield they aught,
If, earned by them, a twofold death be mine, —
This, doomed me here ; and that, beyond the grave ?
Nor painting's art, nor sculptor's skill e'er brought
Peace to the soul that seeks that Friend Divine
Who on the cross stretched out His arms to save.

MICHAEL ANGELO

January 29.

*I am the vine, ye are the branches ; he that abideth in me,
and I in him, the same bringeth forth much fruit; for
without me ye can do nothing.* — JOHN xv. 5.

IT is a painful thing, this pruning work, this cutting off
of the over-luxuriant shoots, in order to call back
the wandering juices into the healthier and more living
parts. In religion it is described thus : " Every branch
in me that beareth fruit, He purgeth it, that it may bring
forth more fruit." The keen edge of God's pruning-knife
cuts sheer through. No weak tenderness stops Him
whose love seeks goodness, not comfort, for His servants.

F. W. ROBERTSON

A LIVING BRANCH.

FATHER of heaven ! if by Thy mercy's grace
A living branch I am of that true vine
Which spreads o'er all — and would we did resign
Ourselves entire by faith to its embrace ! —
In me much drooping, Lord, Thine eye will trace,
Caused by the shade of these rank leaves of mine.
Unless in season due Thou dost refine
The humor gross, and quicken its dull pace.
So cleanse me, that abiding e'er with Thee,
I feed me hourly with the heavenly dew,
And with my falling tears refresh the root.
Thou said'st, and Thou art truth, Thou 'dst with me be.
Then willing come, that I may bear much fruit,
And worthy of the stock on which it grew.

VITTORIA COLONNA

January 30.

O send out Thy light and Thy truth ; let them lead me. —
Ps. xliii. 3.

TO follow Christ does not of necessity involve anything
new or unwonted ; to be perfect in Him does not
always need change. To " abide in the same calling

wherein we are called ; " to strive each day to do the
wonted service more perfectly ; to infuse and maintain in
every detail a purer motive ; to master each impulse, and
bring each thought under a holier discipline ; to be blameless in word ; to sacrifice self, as an habitual law, in each
sudden call to action ; to take more and more secretly
the lowest place ; to move amid constant distractions, and
above them undisturbedly ; to be content to do nothing
that attracts notice, but to do it always for the greater
glory of God ; to let each day pass seemingly as though it
were lost, bearing no manifest fruit, nothing eventful, only
the monotony of the " trivial round ; " to be ever growing in watchfulness and care, faithfully bearing the secret
unknown burden of this undistinguished destiny, drawing
every impulse and wish more and more into union with the
unseen but ever-present God, — such a course of necessity is the general lot, and is the preparation of the greater
proportion of the " cloud of witnesses." To seek with a
single eye to discern what is God's will for one's self
through the outward circumstances that encompass us
round about, is to every one the sure hope of final
peace.

THE MASTER.

BLOW, winds of God, awake and blow
   The mists of earth away.
Shine out, O Light Divine, and show
   How wide and far we stray.

Hush every lip, close every book,
   The strife of tongues forbear ;
Why forward reach, or backward look,
   For love which clasps like air ?

We may not climb the heavenly steeps
   To bring the Lord Christ down.
In vain we search the lowest deeps
   For Him no depth can drown.

In joy of inward peace, or sense
   Of sorrow over sin,
He is His own best evidence,
   His witness is within.

No fable old, nor mythic lore,
  Nor dream of bards and seers,
No dead fact stranded on the shore
  Of the oblivious years ;

But warm, sweet, tender — even yet
  A present help is He ;
And faith has still its Olivet,
  And love its Galilee.

Through Him the first fond prayers are said
  Our lips of childhood frame ;
The last low whispers of our dead
  Are burdened with His name.

O Lord and Master of us all !
  Whate'er our name or sign,
We own Thy sway, we hear Thy call,
  We test our lives by Thine.

We faintly hear, we dimly see,
  In differing phrase we pray ;
But, dim or clear, we own in Thee
  The Light, the Truth, the Way.

Apart from Thee all gain is loss,
  All labor vainly done ;
The solemn shadow of Thy Cross
  Is better than the sun.

Our Friend, our Brother, and our Lord,
  What may Thy service be ? —
Nor name, nor form, nor ritual word,
  But simply following Thee.

Deep strike Thy roots, O heavenly Vine,
  Within our earthly sod ;
Most human, and yet most divine,
  The flower of man and God.

                          JOHN G. WHITTIER

January 31.

Let us therefore come boldly unto the throne of grace, that we may obtain mercy, and find grace to help in time of need. — HEB. iv. 16.

IN all troubles and sadder accidents, let us take sanctuary in religion ; and, by innocence, cast out anchors for our souls, to keep them from shipwreck, though they be not kept from storm. The greatest evils are from within us, and from ourselves also we must look for our greatest good ; for God is the fountain of it, but reaches it to us by our own hand ; and when all things look sadly round about us, then only we shall find how excellent a fortune it is to have God to our friend ; and, of all friendships, that only is created to support us in our needs.

JEREMY TAYLOR.

HIS PRESENCE.

I LOOK to Thee in every need, and never look in vain;
I feel Thy strong and tender love, and all is well! again;
    The thought of Thee is mightier far
    Than sin and pain and sorrow are.

Discouraged in the work of life, disheartened by its load,
Shamed by its failures or its fears, I sink beside the road ;
    But let me only think of Thee,
    And then new heart springs up in me.

Thy calmness bends serene above, my restlessness to still ;
Around me flows Thy quickening life, to nerve my faltering will;
    Thy presence fills my solitude ;
    Thy providence turns all to good.

February 1.

*For whatsoever things were written aforetime were written
for our learning, that we through patience and comfort
of the scriptures might have hope.* — ROM. xv. 4.

PRAYER does not directly take away a trial or its pain,
any more than a sense of duty directly takes away
the danger of infection, but it preserves the strength of
the whole spiritual fibre, so that the trial does not pass into
temptation to sin. A sorrow comes upon you. Omit
prayer and you fall out of God's testing into the devil's
temptation; you get angry, hard of heart, reckless. But
meet the dreadful hour with prayer, cast your care on
God, claim Him as your Father, though He seem cruel, —
and the degrading, paralyzing, embittering effects of pain
and sorrow pass away, a stream of sanctifying and softening thought pours into the soul, and that which might
have wrought your fall but works in you the peaceable
fruits of righteousness. You pass from bitterness into the
courage of endurance, and from endurance into battle,
and from battle into victory, till at last the trial dignifies
and blesses your life. The answer to prayer is slow; the
force of prayer is cumulative. Not till life is over is the
whole answer given, the whole strength it has brought
understood.

STOPFORD BROOKE

PATIENT.

I WAS not patient in that olden time,
When my unchastened heart began to long
For bliss that lay beyond its reach; my prime
Was wild, impulsive, passionate, and strong.
I could not wait for happiness and love,
Heaven-sent, to come and nestle in my breast;
I could not realize how time might prove
That patient waiting would avail me best.
" Let me be happy now," my heart cried out,
" In mine own way, and with my chosen lot;
The future is too dark, and full of doubt,
For me to tarry, and I trust it not.
Take all my blessings, all I am and have,
But give that glimpse of heaven before the grave ! "

Ah me ! God heard my wayward, selfish cry,
And taking pity on my blinded heart,
He bade the angel of strong grief draw nigh,
Who pierced my bosom in its tenderest part.
I drank wrath's wine-cup to the bitter lees,
With strong amazement and a broken will;
Then, humbled, straightway fell upon my knees,
And God doth know my heart is kneeling still.

I have grown patient; seeking not to choose
Mine own blind lot, but take that God shall send,
In which, if what I long for I should lose,
I know the loss will work some blessed end,
Some better fate for mine and me than I
Could ever compass underneath the sky.

ALL THE YEAR ROUND.

February 2.

Commit thy way unto the Lord. — Ps. xxxvii. 5.

DO not believe that God offers Himself as a guide in His providence, and a guide towards a holy life by His spirit, and yet will leave the mind alone which soberly explores the dark places of truth in the hope of His aid. *How* He can aid, it is useless to ask ; but that *He can aid*, who is *truth itself, and has sure access to minds and hearts*, you must not doubt.   He may move in all silence, He may act on the soul and so on the mind indirectly, He may cause — as often happens — external things to illustrate truth in some remarkable manner.   But be assured of this, — that if, in obedience and hope, you wait on Him, He will bring you to the sunlight at last.   And then the rest, the peace of having passed through and left behind you the wilderness of doubt, will be a life-long enjoyment.

THEODORE D. WOOLSEY.

BE STILL MY HEART.

I WILL commit my way, O Lord, to Thee,
Nor doubt Thy love, though dark the way may be,
Nor murmur, for the sorrow is from God,
And there is comfort also in Thy rod.

I will not seek to know the future years,
Nor cloud to-day with dark to-morrow's fears ;
I will but ask a light from heaven, to show
How, step by step, my pilgrimage should go.

And if the distant perils seem to make
The path impossible that I must take,
Yet as the river winds through mountains lone,
The way will open up — as I go on.

Be still, my heart ; for faithful is thy Lord,
And pure and true and tried His Holy Word ;
Through stormy flood that rageth as the sea,
His promises thy stepping-stones shall be.

—◆—

February 3.

*Simon Peter said unto Him, Lord, whither goest Thou ?
Jesus answered him, Whither I go thou canst not fol-
low me now ; but thou shalt follow me afterwards.*
— JOHN xiii. 36.

FROM the sunlit heights of life, the deep vales and
hollows of its necessities look darkest ; but to the
faithful whose path lies there, there is still light enough to
show the way, and to no other eyes do the everlasting
hills and blue heavens seem so brilliant.

JAMES MARTINEAU.

THE STILL WATERS OF THE VALLEY.

THEIR source is on the mountains,
  The streams of which we drink ;
But we must tread the valleys,
  If we would reach their brink.
Their source is on the mountains,
  Higher than feet can go ;
Yet human lips but touch them,
  In the valleys, still and low.

Once, when the heavenly voices
Did call me on their track,
I wondered why some hindrance
Still drew my footsteps back ;
Some feeble steps to succor,
Some childish feet to lead,
Some wandering lambs to gather,
Some hungred ones to feed ;

Some call of lowly duty,
With low, resistless tone ;
Some weight of others' burdens,
Some burden of my own ;
But now, though heavenly voices
Still bid my spirit soar,
While treading lowly places,
I wonder thus, no more.

Their source is on the mountains,
The streams of which we drink ;
But only in the valleys
Our lips can reach the brink.
Our hearts are on the mountains,
Whither our feet shall go ;
But our path is in the valleys,
Where the still waters flow.

MRS. CHARLES.

—◆—

February 4.

In quietness and in confidence shall be your strength. —
ISA. XXX. 15.

WHEN you undertake to work out your own destiny,
you confide to your own single strength the care
of softening its severity.   God puts consolation only
where He has first put pain, and causes His mercies to
abound nowhere, save in the furrow traced by penitence
and laborious effort.   You are at once too poor and too
great, — too poor in your views, for they do not reach
the true horizon ; too great to be able to be your own
reward.

MADAME SWETCHINE.

"NOT AS I WILL."

BLINDFOLDED and alone I stand
With unknown thresholds on each hand;
The darkness deepens as I grope,
Afraid to fear, afraid to hope;
Yet this one thing I learn to know,
Each day more surely as I go,
That doors are opened, ways are made,
Burdens are lifted or are laid
By some great law unseen and still,
Unfathomed purpose to fulfil,
    "Not as I will."

Blindfolded and alone I wait,
Loss seems too bitter, gain too late;
Too heavy burdens in the load,
And too few helpers on the road;
And joy is weak, and grief is strong,
And years and days so long, so long;
Yet this one thing I learn to know,
Each day more surely as I go,
That I am glad the good and ill
By changeless law are ordered still,
    "Not as I will."

"Not as I will;" the sound grows sweet
Each time my lips the words repeat.
"Not as I will;" the darkness feels
More safe than light when this thought steals
Like whispered voice to calm and bless
All unrest and all loneliness.
"Not as I will," because the One
Who loved us first and best has gone
Before us on the road, and still
For us must all His love fulfil,
    "Not as we will."

                    HELEN HUNT JACKSON

February 5.

Let thine heart keep my commandments ; for length of days and long life and peace shall they add to thee. — PROV. iii. 1, 2.

IF obedience were entire and love were perfect, then would the revelation of the spirit to the soul of man be perfect too. There would be trust expelling care, and enabling one to repose ; there would be a love which could cast out fear ; there would be a sympathy with the mighty all of God. Selfishness would pass, isolation would be felt no longer ; the tide of the universal and eternal life would come with mighty pulsations throbbing through the soul.

F. W. ROBERTSON.

OBEDIENCE.

Oh, thou, so weary of thy self-denials,
    And so impatient of thy little cross,
Is it so hard to bear thy daily trials,
    To count all earthly things a gainful loss ?
Poor wandering soul ! I know that thou art seeking
    Some easier way, as all have sought before,
To silence the reproachful inward speaking,
    Some landward path unto an island shore.
The cross is heavy in thy human measure,
    The way too narrow for thy inward pride ;
Thou canst not lay thine intellectual treasure
    At the low footstool of the Crucified.
In meek obedience to the Heavenly Teacher,
    Thy weary soul can only find its peace ;
Seeking no aid from any human creature,
    Looking to God alone for His release.

February 6.

And He saith unto them, Why are ye fearful, O ye of little faith ? — MATT. viii. 26.

NEVER should we so abandon ourselves to God as when He seems to abandon us. Let us enjoy light and consolation when it is His pleasure to give it to us, but let us not attach ourselves to His gifts, but to Him ; and when He plunges us into the night of Pure Faith, let us still press on through the agonizing darkness.

DOST THOU NOT CARE?

I LOVE and love not ; Lord, it breaks my heart
　　To love and not to love.
Thou veiled within Thy glory, gone apart
　　Into Thy shrine which is above,
Dost Thou not love me, Lord, or care
　　For this mine ill ?
I love thee here or there,
　　I will accept thy broken heart, lie still.

Lord, it was well with me in time gone by
　　That cometh not again,
When I was fresh and cheerful, who but I ?
　　I fresh, I cheerful ; worn with pain
Now, out of sight and out of heart ;
　　O Lord, how long?
I watch thee as thou art,
　　I will accept thy fainting heart, be strong.

" Lie still, be strong," to-day ; but, Lord, to-morrow,
　　What of to-morrow, Lord ?
Shall there be rest from toil, be truce from sorrow,
　　Be living green upon the sward
Now but a barren grave to me,
　　Be joy for sorrow ?
Did I not die for thee ?
　　Do I not live for thee ? leave me to-morrow.

CHRISTINA ROSSETTI

February 7.

And He said, My presence shall go with thee, and I will give thee rest. — Ex. xxxiii. 14.
Also thou shalt lie down, and none shall make thee afraid — Job. xi. 19.

IT is a noble thing, at once to participate in the frailty of man and the security of a god. SENECA.

I KNOW not what men are doing, still at work, when they might better sit still, troubling themselves and all about them, and cannot well tell for what. Oh, the sweet peace of believing and obeying God! They truly conquer, sitting still, — "sedendo vincebant." In all times, they are safe under the shadow of the Almighty; are strong in the Lord and in the power of His might.

EVENING HYMN.

ANOTHER day its course hath run,
 And still, O God! Thy child is blest;
For Thou hast been by day my sun,
 And Thou wilt be by night my rest.

Sweet sleep descends, mine eyes to close;
 And now, when all the world is still,
 give my body to repose,
 My spirit to my Father's will.

JOHN PIERPONT

February 8.

And he said to me, These are they which came out of great tribulation, and have washed their robes, and made them white in the blood of the Lamb. — REV. vii. 14.

IT is the cross that makes the peace so sweet. Amid the tears of grief, peace keeps her silent place like the rainbow upon the spray of the cataract. BONAR.

THE best way to bear crosses, is to consecrate them all in silence to God. FLETCHER.

AFTER THE STORM.

ALL night, in the pauses of sleep, I heard
The moan of the snow-wind and the sea,
Like the wail of Thy sorrowing children, O God!
Who cry unto Thee.

But in beauty and silence the morning broke,
O'erflowing creation the glad light streamed;
And earth stood shining and white as the souls
Of the blessed redeemed.

O glorious marvel in darkness wrought!
With smiles of promise the blue sky bent,
As if to whisper to all who mourned —
Love's hidden intent.

HARRIET McEWEN KIMBALL.

February 9.

Pray without ceasing. — 1 THESS. v. 17.

THAT heart in which the true love of God and true desire exist, never ceases to pray. Love, hid in the bottom of the soul, prays without ceasing, even when the mind is drawn another way. God continually beholds the desire which He has Himself implanted in the soul, though it may at times be unconscious of its existence; His heart is touched by it; it ceaselessly attracts His mercies; it is that spirit, which, according to Saint Paul, helpeth our infirmities and maketh intercession for us with groanings which cannot be uttered. FÉNELON.

PRAYER.

FROM the recesses of a lowly spirit,
Our humble prayer ascends ; O Father ! hear it.
Upsoaring on the wings of awe and meekness,
    Forgive its weakness !

We see Thy hand, — it leads us, it supports us :
We hear Thy voice, — it counsels and it courts us ;
And then we turn away ; and still Thy kindness
    Forgives our blindness.

Oh, how long-suffering, Lord ! but Thou delightest
To win with love the wandering ; Thou invitest,
By smiles of mercy, not by frowns or terrors,
    Man from his errors.

Father and Saviour ! plant within each bosom
The seeds of holiness, and bid them blossom
In fragrance and in beauty bright and vernal,
    And spring eternal.

JOHN BOWRING.

February 10.

*For whether we live, we live unto the Lord; and whether
we die, we die unto the Lord; whether we live therefore, or die, we are the Lord's.* — ROM. xiv. 8.

THEY who are God's without reserve, are in every
state content; for they will only what He wills,
and desire to do for Him whatever He desires them to
do; they strip themselves of everything, and in this naked-
ness find all things restored an hundredfold.

LIVING OR DYING, LORD, I WOULD BE THINE!

OH, what is life?
A toil, a strife,
Were it not lighted by Thy love divine.
I ask not wealth,
I crave not health:
Living or dying, Lord, I would be Thine!

Oh, what is death,
When the poor breath
In parting can the soul to Thee resign!
While patient love
Her trust doth prove,
Living or dying, Lord, I would be Thine!

Throughout my days,
Be constant praise
Uplift to Thee from out this heart of mine;
So shall I be
Brought nearer Thee:
Living or dying, Lord, I would be Thine!

FÉNELON

February 11.

Thou openest Thine hand and satisfiest the desire of every living thing. — Ps. cxlv. 16.

IN our pursuit of the things of this world, we usually prevent enjoyment by expectation; we anticipate our own happiness, and eat out the heart and sweetness of worldly pleasures by delightful forethoughts of them; so that when we come to possess them they do not answer the expectation, nor satisfy the desires which were raised about them, and they vanish into nothing; but the things which are above are so great, so solid, so durable, so glorious, that we cannot raise our thoughts to an equal height with them; we cannot enlarge our desires beyond a possibility of satisfaction. Our hearts are greater than the world; but God is greater than our hearts; and the happiness which He hath laid up for us, is, like Himself, incomprehensibly great and glorious. Let the thoughts of this raise us above the world, and inspire us with greater thoughts and designs, than the care and concernments of this present life.

JOHN TILLOTSON.

MORNING AND NIGHT.

EVERY morn,
When a new day to the earth is born,
The soft light kisses my waking eyes;
The soft winds say, " Awake, arise,
See what glories grow out of the gray.
Behold the day ! "

Every night
The far stars shine with trembling light,
The winds are sighing unsatisfied,
The want of the world is unsupplied,
The glory has faded and died away
Into the gray.

MARY TRIMBLE REILEY.

February 12.

And He saw them toiling in rowing; for the wind was contrary unto them. And about the fourth watch of the night He cometh unto them, walking upon the sea. — MARK vi. 48.

THE heavenly Master has still His eye upon His weary followers, toiling in rowing, and each wave of circumstance bears Him on its crest. We are not required to live above circumstances; they are assigned to us that we may obtain therein a deeper experience of the love and wisdom of Him to whom all power is given in heaven and on earth.

TOILING IN ROWING.

Toiling in rowing! Wind and tide
  Our wearied bark oppose,
As oft, with seams that open wide,
  Upon her course she goes ;
And we have taken nothing yet,
  Though still the watch we keep,
Nor fail to cast an empty net
  Into the boisterous deep.
Toiling in rowing ! Dearest Lord,
  We faint amidst the strife ;
But Thou canst vanquish with a word
  The stormy surge of life ;
And when Thou walkest on the sea,
  With hand outstretched to aid,
Oh, grant us strength to cling to Thee,
  And not to be afraid.

And the dove came in to him in the evening; and, lo, in her mouth was an olive leaf plucked off; so Noah knew that the waters were abated from off the earth. — GEN. viii. 11.

W HEN we plunge ourselves into a difficulty by a neglect of the means or by a misuse of the faculties which God has bestowed upon us, it is to be expected that He will leave us to our own devices. But when in the honest discharge of our duties we find ourselves in circumstances beyond the reach of human aid, we then may look confidently up to God for deliverance. He will always take care of us while we are in the spot where He has placed us. When He appoints for us trials, He also appoints for us the means of escape. The path of duty, though it may seem arduous, is ever the path of safety. We can more easily maintain ourselves in the most difficult position, God being our helper, than in apparent security relying on our own strength. FRANCIS WAYLAND.

THE RETURN OF THE DOVE.

ONLY a waste of waters,
  Only a tideless sea,
Which is not life, which is not death,
  But death in life to me.

Only the years on-coming,
  Rolling their silent waves
Over the by-gone trouble,
  Over life's hidden graves.

Only a drear out-looking
  For a hope that is long delayed,
And a weariful prayer for patience,
  And a wish that may not be prayed.

Why am I ever watching?
  What can I ever see?
Only a dove that is coming
  From a far-off land to me;

Only a branch it is bringing,
Which tells of a clearer day,
And bears me a promise of peace and life,
When the waters have passed away.

——————

February 14.

*I press toward the mark for the prize of the high calling
of God in Christ Jesus.* — PHIL. iii. 14.

STRANGE as it may seem, we, living in a world that is
imperfect, ourselves the very masterpiece of imperfection, are yet haunted continually by an indomitable
love of the perfect. We are not what we may be and
should be, and therefore the soul rises up, exclaiming,
Sometime and *somewhere* I shall be restored, — I shall
clasp my ideal and hold it fast. How this hope has
haunted the world, filling it with dreams of golden ages
and millenniums !

The life here and the life hereafter are one. There is
but one ideal set before us. We are to think by it, work
by it, aspire to it in this world, and then, lest our heart fail
at the sad disparity between us and the divine type, lo ! the
heavens are opened to us, and we see our Lord, putting
His own hand to our work so feebly begun. He presents
us at last faultless to His Father and our Father, before
the presence of His glory with exceeding joy.

JAMES H. ECOB.

"I CLIMB TO REST."

STILL must I climb, if I would rest ;
The bird soars upward to his nest ;
The young leaf on the tree-top high
Cradles itself within the sky.

The streams, that seem to hasten down,
Return in clouds, the hills to crown.
The plant arises from her root
To rock aloft her flower and fruit.

I cannot in the valley stay ;
The great horizons stretch away
The very cliffs that wall me round
Are ladders unto higher ground.

To work, to rest. for each a time ;
I toil, but I must also climb
What soul was ever quite at ease
Shut in by earthly boundaries ?

I am not glad till I have known
Life that can lift me from my own ;
A loftier level must be won,
A mightier strength to lean upon.

And heaven draws near as I ascend ;
The breeze invites, the stars befriend,
All things are beckoning to the Best ;
I climb to Thee, my God, for rest.

LUCY LARCOM.

—◆—

February 15.

With good will doing service, as to the Lord, and not to men. — EPH. vi. 7.

IS the wilderness a loathed and soul-wearying pilgrimage,
or a grand training-ground of God ? Do you cry,
"Oh, for some work which will meet and satisfy the finer
appetites and subtler sympathies of my soul; but this
wholly expends my higher faculty ; it makes life a waste,
and the future a blank" ? Or do you say, "God, my
God, has bound me here, because He knows what
eternity means, and what I have to do there. Because of
the grandeur of my future, He is not ashamed to make
the scene of my present discipline so bare and poor. He
is training me to be faithful in the few things thoroughly ;
to rule the little that is under my power with the bold,
free, royal hand of the heir of a kingdom ; then He will
lift me to a throne. Be my one work here to make the
commonplaces and levels as full of His presence as the
Holy of Holies, where His glory dwells ; so to beautify

earth's dull paths by heavenly patience and joyfulness,
that the angels of God may frequent them ; and to handle
the commonest tools and materials as one who is daily
building up a character and a destiny which will rise,
stately and fair, not among the perishing fabrics that shall
share the wreck of earth's dissolution, but in the calm
heaven of eternity"? J. BALDWIN BROWN.

PATIENCE.

HAVE patience ! the chrysalis lies
　　The lowest of earthly things,
Before, as a butterfly,
　　It rises on outspread wings.
The clouds must part in the sky
　　When summer the sunshine brings.

Have patience ! our feet must rest
　　Where the shade of the valley lies,
Before, with outreaching wings,
　　We flutter towards the skies ;
Before, on the mountain crest,
　　We open our earth-bound eyes.

———◆———

February 16.

*Inasmuch as ye have done it unto one of the least of
these my brethren, ye have done it unto me.* — MATT.
XXV. 40.

NO good that the humblest of us has wrought wholly
dies. If you have served God in serving another,
God remembers it, although he does not. There is one
long unerring memory in the universe out of which nothing good ever fades.

SERVICE.

SOMETHING, my God, for Thee.
　　Something for Thee ;
That each day's setting sun may bring
Some penitential offering ;

In Thy dear name some kindness done;
To Thy dear love some wanderer won ;
Some trial meekly borne for Thee,
Dear Lord, for Thee.

Something, my God, for Thee,
Something for Thee ;
That to Thy gracious throne may rise
Sweet incense from some sacrifice, —
Uplifted eyes undimmed by tears,
Uplifted faith unstained by fears,
Hailing each joy as light from Thee,
Dear Lord, from Thee.   .

Something, my God, for Thee,
Something for Thee ;
For the great love that Thou hast given,
For the great hope of Thee and heaven,
My soul her first allegiance brings,
And upward plumes her heavenward wings,
Nearer, my God, to Thee,
Nearer to Thee.

——◆——

February 17.

See that ye love one another with a pure heart fervently.
— 1 PET. i. 22.

IN love and compassion God hath made us dependent
upon each other to the end that by the use of our
affections we may find true happiness and rest to our
souls. He hath united us so closely with our Fellows,
that they do make, as it were, a part of our being, and in
comforting them we doe most assuredly comfort ourselves.
Therein doth Happiness come to us unawares, and without
seeking, as the servant who goeth on his master's errand
findeth pleasant fruits and sweet flowers overhanging him,
and cool Fountains, which he knew not of, gushing up by
the wayside for his solace and refreshing.

MARGARET SMITH'S JOURNAL (WHITTIER).

TRUE BLESSEDNESS.

IT is not blessedness to know that thou thyself art blessed:
True joy was never yet by one, nor yet by two possessed.

Nor to the many is it given, but only to the all;
The joy that leaves one heart unblessed would be for mine
    too small ;

For when   my spirit   most was   blest, to   know another
    grieved
Would take away the joy from all myself received.

Nor would I seek to blunt that pain, forgetting other's woe ;
From knowledge, not from want of thought, true blessedness
    must grow.

For blessedness I find this earth of ours is then no place,
Where still the happiest man must meet his brother's griev-
    ing face.

And only in one thought I find a joy I never miss,
In faith to know all grief below will grow to final bliss.

And he who holds this faith will strive with firm and ardent
    soul,
And work out his own proper good in working for the whole.

God only sees this perfect good, the way to it is dim ;
God only then is truly blest, man only blest in Him.

RÜCKERT'S WISDOM OF THE BRAHMINS

February 18.

He maketh the storm a calm, so that the waves thereof are still.

Then they are glad because they be quiet; so He bringeth them unto their desired haven. — Ps. cvii. 29, 30.

THE great workman has His eye upon the spiritual faculties of the inner man, disciplining patience until it bring forth experience, and experience hope that maketh not ashamed. Waiting and watching are infinitely more productive of a knowledge of the Lord Himself than any external labor made ready to our hands.

To stay ourselves on God, we must first believe that He who loves us and orders all the events of our lives does not at any time abandon us to be overruled by a counter influence; nor suffer His dear servant, willing to be used in His service and desirous to do His will, to be out of the place designed for him.

ANNA SHIPTON.

UNTO THE DESIRED HAVEN.

PSALM CVII.

WHAT matter how the winds may blow,
  Or blow they east, or blow they west?
What reck I how the tides may flow,
  Since ebb or flood alike is best?
No summer calm, no winter gale,
  Impedes or drives me from my way;
I steadfast toward the haven sail
  That lies, perhaps, not far away.

I mind the weary days of old,
  When motionless I seemed to lie;
The nights when fierce the billows rolled,
  And changed my course, I knew not why.
I feared the calm, I feared the gale,
  Foreboding danger and delay,
Forgetting I was thus to sail
  To reach what seemed so far away.

I measure not the loss and fret
  Which through those years of doubt I bore ;
I keep the memory fresh, and yet
  Would hold God's patient mercy more.
What wrecks have passed me in the gale,
  What ships gone down on summer day ;
While I, with furled or spreading sail,
  Stood for the haven far away.

What matter how the winds may blow,
  Since fair or foul alike are best;
God holds them in His hand, I know,
  And I may leave to Him the rest,
Assured that neither calm nor gale
  Can bring me danger or delay,
As still I toward the haven sail
  That lies, I know, not far away.

—————

February 19.

That which I see not, teach Thou me. — JOB xxxiv. 32.

ANY one who tries as hard as he can to please God is sure of divine guidance. He will get many deep experiences of human helplessness and a Redeemer's strength ; but when God teaches we need not dread the lesson. He may make mistakes ; but God's love holds on to him, and is ready to help him just as far as he is willing to be helped. It may turn him off from the particular track upon which he was going, but it will only be to put him on a higher and straighter one ; for the life of duty is always included in though uplifted by the life of love. Oh, the life of an archangel is only a life of loving service ; and our little bit of mortality has it for its privilege to copy it here in miniature, till we come to the freer, grander sphere above. To do God's will from morn till night ; to bring our hearts into unison with His own ; to grasp the opportunities as they fly ; to plant our earthly seeds for His heavenly harvest, — this is the vocation to which we are called. May He who sees our deep unworthiness and frailty and sin so fill us with Himself that our calling may be our joy !

TEACH me to live! 'T is easier far to die,
    Gently and silently to pass away;
On earth's long night to close the heavy eye
    And waken in the glorious realm of day.

Teach me that harder lesson, — how to live,
    To serve Thee in the darkest paths of life ;
Arm me for conflict now, fresh vigor give,
    And make me more than conqueror in the strife.

Teach me to live Thy purpose to fulfil ;
    Bright for Thy glory let my taper shine ;
Each day renew, remould this stubborn will :
    Closer round Thee my heart's affections twine.

Teach me to live, no idler let me be,
    But in Thy service heart and hand employ,
Prepared to do thy bidding cheerfully, —
    Be this my highest and my holiest joy.

Teach me to live, my daily cross to bear,
    Nor murmur though I bend beneath its load.
Only be with me ; let me feel Thee near ;
    Thy smile sheds gladness on the darkest road.

Teach me to live and find my life in Thee,
    Looking from earth and earthly things away
Let me not falter, but untiringly
    Press on, and gain new strength and power each day

—◆—

February 20.

Wherefore I say unto thee, Her sins, which are many, are forgiven; for she loved much ; but to whom little is forgiven, the same loveth little. — LUKE vii. 47.

GOD never makes us sensible of our weakness except to give us of His strength ; we must not be disturbed by what is involuntary. The great point is, never to act in opposition to the inward light, and to be willing to go as far as God would have us.
                                FÉNELON.

FAILURE.

THE Lord, who fashioned my hands for working,
  Set me a task, and it is not done ;
I 've tried and tried, since the early morning,
  And now to westward sinketh the sun.

Noble the task that was kindly given
  To one so little and weak as I.
Somehow my strength could never grasp it,
  Never, as days and years went by.

Others around me cheerfully toiling
  Showed me their work as they passed away ;
Filled were their hands to overflowing,
  Proud were their hearts and glad and gay.

Laden with harvest spoils they entered
  In at the golden gate of their rest ;
Laid their sheaves at the feet of the Master,
  Found their places among the blest.

Happy be they who strove to help me,
  Failing ever in spite of their aid ;
Fain would their love have borne me with them,
  But I was unready, and sore afraid.

Now I know my task will never be finished,
  And when the Master calleth my name,
The Voice will find me still at my labor,
  Weeping beside it in weary shame.

With empty hands I shall rise to meet Him,
  And when He looks for the fruits of years,
Nothing have I to lay before Him
  But broken efforts and bitter tears,

Yet when He calls I fain would hasten ;
  Mine eyes are dim, and their light is **gone** ;
And I am as weary as though I carried
  A burthen of beautiful work well done.

I will fold my empty hands on my bosom,
  Meekly, thus, in the shape of His cross ;
And the Lord who made them so frail and feeble
  Maybe will pity their strife and loss.

THE MONTH.

February 21.

And when he putteth forth his own sheep, he goeth before them, and the sheep follow him; for they know his voice.

And a stranger will they not follow, but will flee from him; for they know not the voice of strangers. —JOHN X. 4, 5.

THERE is but one way in which God should be loved, and that is to take no step except with Him and for Him, and to follow with a generous self-abandonment everything which He requires.

THE KIND SHEPHERD.

Thou art a shepherd kind,
  That name is ever Thine;
O Jesus, may this faith,
  Sincerely felt. be mine!
Let Thy dear voice be heard,
  That I, awaked thereby,
Obedient as a lamb,
  May follow willingly.

I know Thy gentle voice,
  No stranger's do I hear;
My soul unsummoned turns
  To them a deafened ear.
The hireling's care will fail
  In times of need to stand;
Then will I follow Thee
  And Thy dear shepherd-hand.

Jesus, I would on Thee
  My troubles always throw;
So from Thee in my heart
  A sweet repose shall flow;
Be still, and question not,
  But trust for future need.
His sheep with tender care
  My shepherd safe will lead.

February 22.

I will both lay me down in peace, and sleep; for Thou, Lord, only makest me dwell in safety. — Ps. iv. 8.

PRAYER, to one who lives in daily service of God, oftentimes takes the form of simple communion, the spreading out of our life to one who is worthy, whom we love and trust, not for sake of any special advice or help, but for the heart-rest which there is in the thing itself. For none love confidences so much as they who rarely have them. None love to speak so much, when the mood of speaking comes, as they who are naturally taciturn. None love to lean and recline entirely upon another so much, as strong natures that ordinarily do not lean at all; and so the heart that goes shaded and shut, that hides its thoughts and dreads the knowledge of men's eyes, flings itself wide open to the eye of God.

AT EVENTIDE.

Thou infinitely merciful!
Thy garment's hem in prayer we pull;
Bringing our burdens on our knees,
We take the hand that lends release;
Turn on us one forgiving look
Before this day shall close its book.

So yearningly we seek Thy face
When darkness is our dwelling-place;
Our foolish hearts, that daily roam,
Would nightly come to Thee at home.
Be with us here, and grant that we
Hereafter, Lord, may be with Thee!

God keep our darlings safe this night,
Though scattered, *one* still in Thy sight!
Lead on, by many ways, and past
All perils, till we join at last;
With us the broken links; with Thee
The circle perfect endlessly.

Now take us Father, to Thy breast,
And still all troubled thoughts to rest;
Thy watch and ward about us keep,
That tired souls may smile asleep,
And, having been in heaven awhile,
May wake to-morrow with Thy smile !

February 23.

And as thy days, so shall thy strength be. — DEUT.
xxxiii. 24.

THE lesson of Christianity, urged and enforced by
Nature, is the inestimable worth of common duties,
as manifesting the greatest principles.   It bids us attain
perfection, not by striving to do dazzling deeds, but by
making our experience divine ; it tells us that the Christian hero will ennoble the humblest field of labor ; that
nothing is mean which can be performed as duty ; but
that religious virtue, like the touch of Midas, converts
the humblest call of conscience into spiritual gold.

THOMAS STARR KING.

MY CROSS.

IT is not heavy, agonizing woe
  Bearing me down with hopeless, crushing load,
Not reputation lost, nor friends betrayed, -
  That such is not my cross I thank my God.

It is not sickness, with her withering hand,
  Keeping me low upon a couch of pain,
Longing each morning for the weary night, —
  At night, for weary day to come again.

Mine is a daily cross of petty cares,
  Of daily duties pressing on my heart,
Of little troubles hard to reconcile,
  Of inward struggles — overcome in part.

My feet are weary in their daily round,
    My heart is weary of its daily care,
My sinful nature often doth rebel ;
    I pray for grace my daily cross to bear.

It is not heavy, Lord, yet oft I pine ;
    It is not heavy, but 't is everywhere,
By day and night each hour my cross I bear ;
    I dare not lay it down — Thou keep'st it there.

I dare not lay it down, I only ask
    That, taking up my daily cross, I may
Follow my Master humbly, step by step,
    Through clouds and darkness unto perfect day.

———◆———

February 24.

My peace I give unto you. — JOHN xiv. 27.

DOST thou not know that God is wonderful in His
    people, and placeth His peace in the midst of no
peace ; that is, of all temptations? As it is said, " Reign
Thou in the midst of Thine enemies."

Not he, therefore, hath peace whom none troubleth ;
this is the peace of the world ; but he whom all men and
all things trouble, yet who beareth all these things quietly,
with joy.

MRS. CHARLES.

GOD'S PEACE.

WE bless Thee for Thy peace, O God,
    Deep as the soundless sea,
Which falls like sunshine on the road
    Of those who trust in Thee.

We ask not, Father, for repose
    Which comes from outward rest,
If we may have through all life's woes
    Thy peace within our breast ;

That peace which suffers and is strong,
  Trusts where it cannot see,
Deems not the trial way too long,
  But leaves the end with Thee;

That peace which, though the billows surge,
  And angry tempests roar,
Rings forth no melancholy dirge,
  But joyeth evermore;

That peace which flows serene and deep,
  A river in the soul,
Whose banks a living verdure keep;
  God's sunshine o'er the whole, ---

Such, Father, give our hearts such peace,
  Whate'er the outward be,
Till all life's discipline shall cease,
  And we go home to Thee.

February 25.

Thou wilt keep him in perfect peace, whose mind is stayed on Thee; because he trusteth in Thee. — Isa. xxvi. 3.

WHEN you look at the believer's busy life, you may see no trace of his inward peace of soul. But you know that the ocean under the hurricane is lashed into those huge waves and that wild foam only upon the surface. Not very far down, the waters are as still as an autumn noon; there is not a ripple or breath or motion, and so, my friends, if we had the faith we ought, though there might be ruffles upon the surface of our lot, we should have the inward peace of perfect faith in God.

Amid the dreary noises of this world, amid its cares and tears, amid its hot contentions, ambitions, and disappointments, we should have an inner calm like the ocean depths, to which the influence of the wild winds and waves above can never come.

    GRAVER THOUGHTS OF A COUNTRY PARSON.

REST.

WHEN winds are raging o'er the upper ocean,
    And billows wild contend with angry roar,
'T is said, far down beneath the wild commotion,
    That peaceful stillness reigneth evermore.

Far, far beneath, the noise of tempest dieth,
    And silver waves chime ever peacefully,
And no rude storm, how fierce soe'er he flieth,
    Disturbs the sabbath of that deeper sea.

So to the heart that knows Thy love, O Purest,
    There is a temple, sacred evermore,
And all the babble of life's angry voices
    Dies in hushed silence at its peaceful door.

Far, far away, the roar of passion dieth,
    And loving thoughts rise calm and peacefully,
And no rude storm, how fierce soe'er he flieth,
    Disturbs the soul that dwells, O Lord, in Thee.

Oh, rest of rest! Oh, peace serene, eternal!
    Thou ever livest; and Thou changest never,
And in the secret of Thy presence dwelleth
    Fulness of joy, forever and forever.

HARRIET BEECHER STOWE.

February 26.

*But it shall be one day which shall be known to the Lord,
not day, nor night; but it shall come to pass that at
evening time it shall be light.* — ZECH. xiv. 7.

WHEN the Christian's little day has drawn to its
close, when the Christian's earthly sun has set,
then there should be to him the beginning of a day
whose sun shall never go down, and whose brightness
shall be lessened by no intrusion of the dark. Then a
day shall break in which there shall be no anxiety, no
care, no sorrow, no hiding of God's face, no struggle
with temptation, no fall into sin; not one moment's
darkness to mingle with that unvaried day.

AT evening time let there be light!
  Life's little day draws near its close ;
Around me fall the shades of night,
  The night of death, the grave's repose ;
  To crown my joys, to end my woes,
At evening time let there be light!

At evening time let there be light!
  Stormy and dark hath been my day,
Yet rose the morn benignly bright,
  Dews, birds, and flowers cheered all the way
  Oh, for one sweet, one parting ray !
At evening time let there be light!

At evening time there *shall* be light ;
  For God hath said : "So let it be !"
Fear, doubt, and anguish take their flight,
  His glory now is risen on me ;
  Mine eyes shall His salvation see ;
T is evening time, and there *is* light.

JAMES MONTGOMERY

—◆—

February 27.

*Let us draw near with a true heart in full assurance of
  faith.* — HEB. X. 22.

CHRISTIAN faith is a grand cathedral, with divinely
pictured windows. Standing without, you see no
glory, nor can possibly imagine any. Standing within,
every ray of light reveals a harmony of unspeakable
splendors.

NATHANIEL HAWTHORNE.

THE ETERNAL GOODNESS.

AND so beside the silent sea,
  I wait the muffled oar ;
No harm from Him can come to me
  On ocean or on shore.

I know not where His islands lift
Their fronded palms in air ;
I only know I cannot drift
Beyond His love and care.

Oh, brothers ! if my faith is vain,
If hopes like these betray,
Pray for me that my feet may gain
The sure and safer way.

And Thou, O Lord ! by whom are seen
Thy creatures as they be,
Forgive me if too close I lean
My human heart on Thee !

JOHN G. WHITTIER.

February 28.

And God shall wipe away all tears from their eyes. —
REV. vii. 17.

OBSERVE how He is touched by our infirmities, —
with a separate, special, discriminating love. There
is not a single throb, in a single human bosom, that does
not thrill at once with more than electric speed up to the
mighty heart of God. You have not shed a tear, or
sighed a sigh, that did not come back to you exalted
and purified by having passed through the eternal
bosom.

F. W. ROBERTSON.

COMPASSION.

WE have no tears Thou wilt not dry ;
We have no wounds Thou wilt not heal ;
No sorrows pierce our human hearts
That Thou, dear Saviour, dost not feel !

Thy pity like the dew distils,
And Thy compassion like the light
Our every morning overfills,
And crowns with stars our every night.

March 1.

But they that wait upon the Lord shall renew their strength; they shall mount up with wings as eagles; they shall run and not be weary; they shall walk and not faint. — ISA. xl. 31.

FOR him who aspires, and for him who loves, life may lead through the thorns, but it never stops in the desert.

FIRM must be the will, patient the heart, passionate the aspiration, to secure the fulfilment of some high and lonely purpose, when revery spreads always its beds of roses on the one side, and practical work summons to its treadmill on the other.

STEADFASTNESS.

NAY, never falter, no great deed is done
By falterers who ask for certainty.
No good is certain but the steadfast mind,
The undivided will to seek the good;
'T is that compels the elements, and wrings
A human music from the indifferent air.
The greatest gift a hero leaves his race
Is to have been a hero.

GEORGE ELIOT.

March 2.

Be strong and of a good courage, fear not, nor be afraid of them; for the Lord thy God, He it is that doth go with thee; He will not fail thee, nor forsake thee. — DEUT. xxxi. 6.

GOD should be the object of all our desires, the end of all our actions, the principle of all our affections, and the governing power of our whole souls.

MASSILLON.

THE end of life is to be like unto God; and the soul following God will be like unto him; He being the beginning, middle, and end of all things.

SOCRATES.

FOLLOWING CHRIST.

Jesu, day by day
Lead us on life's way;
Nought of dangers will we reckon,
Simply haste where Thou dost beckon,
Lead us by the hand
To our Fatherland!

Hard should seem our lot,
Let us waver not;
Never murmur at our crosses
In dark days of grief and losses;
'T is through trial here
We must reach Thy sphere.

When the heart must know
Pain for others' woe,
When beneath its own 't is sinking,
Give us patience, hope unshrinking,
Fix our eyes, O Friend,
On our journey's end!

Thus our path shall be
Daily traced by Thee;
Draw Thou nearer when 't is rougher,
Help us most when most we suffer,
And when all is o'er
Ope to us Thy door!

COUNT ZINZENDORF.

March 3.

For I know that in me dwelleth no good thing; for to will is present with me; but how to perform that which is good, I find not. — ROM. vii. 18.

I HAVE to comfort myself with the thought that God is so strong that he can work even with our failures.

ASPIRATION.

My days I offer Thee ; —
No chaplet round and fair,
But broken, stained with tears, and threaded on despair.

How could it be, dear Lord,
A failure so complete
As this my life, which here I lay before Thy feet?

Nothing from me withheld,
Not one good gift of Thine ;
And yet what offering I place upon Thy shrine !

A voice Thou gavest me,
That I should speak Thy praise ;
Hands that should work for Thee, feet that should walk Thy
ways ;

And youth and strength and hope ;
Work for my hands to do :
Days with Thy opportunities filled through and through, —

And no work done for Thee !
My days no chaplet fair,
But broken, stained with tears, and threaded on despair.

And as I offer it,
In deep humility,
My happier fellow-workers everywhere I see,

Through whom Thy glory shines,
With lives all honoring Thee,
And lives not half so rich as this Thou 'st given me.

And yet I too would fain —
Ah God ! Thou dost require
That men should work for Thee, and I — I but aspire.

Too many prayers, and still
Too little work ; I stand
Before Thee, God, to-day, my failure in my hand.

But take it — take it, Lord,
With useless tears though wet ;
So, haply, it may win some use, some beauty yet.

March 4.

Praying always with all prayer and supplication in the Spirit. — EPH. vi. 18.

THE service of the sanctuary is not always carried on in the sight of the multitude, nor in the presence of our brethren. There are those who stand by night in the temple of the Lord. The service consists in the acceptance and faithful performance of the allotted work.

PRAYING IN SPIRIT.

I NEED not leave the jostling world,
    Or wait till daily tasks are o'er
To fold my palms in secret prayer
    Within the close-shut closet door.

There is a viewless, cloistered room
    As high as heaven, as fair as day,
Where, though my feet may join the throng,
    My soul can enter in and pray.

When I have banished wayward thoughts,
    Of sinful works the fruitful seed,
When folly wins my ear no more,
    The closet door is shut indeed.

No human step approaching breaks
    The blissful silence of the place ;
No shadow steals across the light
    That falls from my Redeemer's face.

And never through those crystal walls
    The clash of life can pierce its way,
Nor ever can a human ear
    Drink in the spirit-words I say.

One hearkening, even, cannot know
    When I have crossed the threshold o'er ;
For He, alone. who hears my prayer
    Has heard the shutting of the door.

HARRIET McEWEN KIMBAL]

March 5.

*As one whom his mother comforteth, so will I comfort you;
and ye shall be comforted.* — ISA. lxvi. 13.

CHRIST, as your friend, sympathizes with you at all
times, and in all the moral conditions of your
nature. Do not think that He sympathizes with you and
loves you when in your best moods only; for if you
should, you would wrong Him bitterly. A bird is no
more surely noted by the Father of all when, glancing
upward through the morning light, he pours his liquid
notes upon the fragrant air, than when, stricken by cruelty
or evil chance, he lies fluttering, a bunch of ruffled and
bloody plumage, upon the dewy lawn. And so it is with
us. Our souls are not known and noted of God the most,
when, light and tuneful, they are lifted in ecstasy upward;
but equally watched and as tenderly loved are we, when,
stricken in hope and soiled in spirit, we lie groaning and
stunned, our purposes broken, our virtue stained, our
future dark and forbidding.

ANDREW MURRAY

THE LOVE OF GOD.

LIKE a cradle rocking, rocking,
Silent. peaceful, to and fro,
Like a mother's sweet looks dropping
On the little face below, —
Hangs the green earth, swinging. turning,
Jarless, noiseless, safe, and slow ;
Falls the light of God's face bending
Down and watching us below.

And as feeble babes that suffer,
Toss and cry, and will not rest
Are the ones the tender mother
Holds the closest, loves the best, —
So when we are weak and wretched.
By our sins weighed down, distressed,
Then it is that God's great patience
Holds us closest, loves us best.

O great Heart of God ! whose loving
    Cannot hindered be nor crossed ;
Will not weary, will not even
    In our death itself be lost, —
Love divine ! of such great loving
    Only mothers know the cost, —
Cost of love, which, all love passing,
    Gave a Son to save the lost.

SAXE HOLM

March 6.

Boast not thyself of to-morrow ; for thou knowest not what a day may bring forth. — PROV. xxvii. 1.

WHERE is to-morrow ? In another world
To numbers this is certain ! The reverse
Is sure to none.

YOUNG.

LORD, I do discover a fallacy whereby I have long deceived myself, which is this ; I have desired to begin my amendment from my birthday, or from the first day of the year, or from some eminent festival, so that my repentance might bear some remarkable date. But when those days were come, I have adjourned my amendment to some other time. Thus, whilst I could not agree with myself when to start, I have almost lost the running of the race. I am resolved thus to befool myself no longer. I see no day but to-day ; the instant time is always the fittest time. In Nebuchadnezzar's image, the lower the members, the coarser the metal ; the farther off the time, the more unfit. To-day is the golden opportunity, to-morrow will be the silver season, next day but the brazen one, and so long, till at last I shall come to the toes of clay, and be turned to dust. Grant therefore that to-day I may hear Thy voice ; and if this day be obscure in the calendar, and remarkable in itself for nothing else, give me to make it memorable in my soul, thereupon, by Thy assistance, beginning the reformation of my life.

THOMAS FULLER.

LORD, what am I, that, with unceasing care,
Thou didst seek after me, — that Thou didst wait,
Wet with unhealthy dews, before my gate,
And pass the gloomy nights of winter there?
O strange delusion, that I did not greet
Thy blest approach! and oh, to heaven how lost,
If my ingratitude's unkindly frost
Has chilled the bleeding wounds upon Thy feet!
How oft my guardian angel gently cried,
"Soul, from thy casement look, and thou shalt see
How He persists to knock and wait for thee!"
And oh, how often to that voice of sorrow,
"To-morrow we will open," I replied!
And when the morrow came, I answered still,
   "To-morrow."

LOPE DE VEGA.

March 7.

*For ye have need of patience, that, after ye have done the
will of God, ye might receive the promise.* — HEB.
x. 36.

THE pebbles in our path weary us, and make us footsore, more than the rocks.

It is not the storm which breaks the image of heaven
in the stream, but the million pebbles over which it
chafes.

MRS. CHARLES.

TRIFLES.

THE griefs that fall to every share,
  The heavier sorrows that life brings,
The heart can nerve itself to bear;
  Great sorrows are half holy things.

But for the ills each hour must make,
  The cares with every day renewed,
It seems scarce worth the while to take
  Such little things with fortitude.

And he before whose wakened might
The strongest enemies must fall
Is overcome by foes so slight,
He scorns to hold them foes at all.

———◆———

March 8.

Behold the Lamb of God, which taketh away the sin of the world. — JOHN i. 29.

"WHY," does any one ask, — "why does the battle press hard to the very end? Why is it ordained for man that he shall walk, all through the course of life, in patience and strife, and sometimes in darkness?" Because from patience is to come perfection. Because from strife is to come triumph. Because from the dark cloud is to come the lightning-flash, that opens the way to eternity! ORVILLE DEWEY.

O LAMB of God, who takest away the sins of the world,
  Grant us thy peace.
O Lamb of God, who takest away the sins of the world,
  Have mercy upon us!

The way is long and dreary,
The path is bleak and bare;
Our feet are worn and weary,
But we will not despair.
More heavy was Thy burden,
More desolate Thy way; —
O Lamb of God, who takest
The sin of the world away,
    Have mercy on us!

The snows lie thick around us
In the dark and gloomy night;
And the tempest wails above us,
And the stars have hid their light;
But blacker was the darkness
Round Calvary's cross that day; —
O Lamb of God, who takest
The sin of the world away,
    Have mercy on us!

Our hearts are faint with sorrow,
Heavy and hard to bear ;
For we dread the bitter morrow,
But we will not despair ;
Thou knowest all our anguish,
And Thou wilt bid it cease ; —
O Lamb of God, who takest
The sin of the world away,
        Give us Thy peace !

                    ADELAIDE A. PROCTER.

March 9.

*For now we see through a glass, darkly; but then face to
face : now I know in part; but then shall I know
even as also I am known.* — 1 COR. xiii. 12.

"AH !" said the imprisoned bird, "how unhappy were
I in my eternal night, but for those melodious
tones which sometimes make their way to me like beams
of light from afar, and cheer my gloomy day. But I will
myself repeat those heavenly melodies like an echo, until
I have stamped them in my heart; and then I shall be
able to bring comfort to myself in my darkness ! " Thus
spoke the little warbler, and soon had learned the sweet
airs that were sung to it with voice and instrument. That
done, the curtain was raised ; for the darkness had been
purposely contrived to assist in its instruction.

O man ! how often dost thou complain of overshadow-
ing grief and of darkness resting upon thy days; and
yet what cause of complaint, unless, indeed, thou hast
failed to learn wisdom from suffering? For is not the
whole sum of human life a veiling and an obscuring of
the immortal spirit of man? Then first, when the fleshly
curtain falls away, may it soar upwards into a region of
happier melodies !

                    RICHTER.

A LITTLE BIRD I AM

A LITTLE bird I am,
  Shut from the fields of air ;
And in my cage I sit and sing
  To Him who placed me there ;
Well pleased a prisoner to be
Because, my God, it pleases Thee

Naught have I else to do ;
  I sing the whole day long ;
And He whom most I love to please
  Doth listen to my song ;
He caught and bound my wandering wing,
But still He bends to hear me sing.

Thou hast an ear to hear,
  A heart to love and bless,
And though my notes were e'er so rude,
  Thou wouldst not hear the less ;
Because Thou knowest, as they fall,
That love, sweet love, inspires them all.

My cage confines me round ;
  Abroad I cannot fly ;
But, though my wing is closely bound,
  My heart 's at liberty ;
My prison walls cannot control
The flight, the freedom, of my soul.

Oh! it is good to soar
  These bolts and bars above,
To Him whose purpose I adore, —
  Whose providence I love ;
And in Thy mighty will to find
The joy, the freedom of the mind.

MADAME GUYON

March 10.

For a thousand years in Thy sight are but as yesterday when it is past, and as a watch in the night. — Ps. xc. 4.

As the clock strikes the hour, how often we say
Time flies ; when 't is *we* that are passing away.

TREVILLE

THERE are no hands upon the clock of eternity :
there is no shadow upon its dial.
The very hours of heaven will be measured by the *sunshine,* not by the *shadow.*

THE CIRCLE OF TIME.

THE dial
Receives many shades, and each points to the sun.
The shadows are many, the sunlight is one.
Life's shadows fluctuate ; God's love does not,
And His love is unchanged, when it changes our lot.
Looking up to this light, which is common to all,
And down to these shadows on each side that fall, —
In Time's silent circle, so various for each,
Is it nothing to know that they never can reach
So far, but that light lies beyond them forever ?

OWEN MEREDITH.

—◆—

March 11.

Are they not all ministering spirits, sent forth to minister for them who shall be heirs of salvation ? — HEB. i. 14.

WE must learn that our best and most steadfast friends are invisible, namely, the dear angels, who with faithfulness and love, moreover with all helpfulness and true friendship, far surpass all the friends we have whom we can see. Thus in many ways we enjoy the fellowship of the heavenly spirits.

LUTHER.

EASTER.

Do saints keep holy day in heavenly places?
Does the old joy shine new in angel faces?
Are hymns still sung the night when Christ was born,
And anthems on the Resurrection Morn?

Because our little year of earth is run,
Do they make record there beyond the sun,
And, in their homes of light so far away,
Mark with us the sweet coming of this day?

What is their Easter? For they have no graves :
No shadow there the holy sunrise craves,
Deep in the heart of noontide marvellous
Whose breaking glory reaches down to us.

How did the Lord keep Easter? With His own
Back to meet Mary where she grieved alone,
With face and mien all tenderly the same,
Unto the very sepulchre He came.

Ah, the dear message that He gave her then, —
Said, for the sake of all bruised hearts of men, —
" Go, tell those friends who have believed on Me,
I go before them into Galilee !

" Into the life so poor and hard and plain,
That for a while they must take up again,
My presence passes ! Where their feet toil slow,
Mine, shining swift with love, still foremost go !

" Say, Mary, I will meet them, by the way
To walk a little with them ; where they stay,
To bring My peace. Watch ! For ye do not know
The day, the hour, when I may find you so ! "

And I do think, as He came back to her,
The many mansions may be all astir
With tender steps that hasten in the way,
Seeking their own upon this Easter Day.

Parting the veil that hideth them about,
I think they do come, softly wistful, out
From homes of heaven that only *seem* so far,
And walk in gardens where the new tombs are !

A. D. T. WHITNEY

March 12.

The Lord gave, and the Lord hath taken away; blessed be the name of the Lord. — Job i. 21.

THEREFORE let your grief be such that your consolation shall be more; for ye have not lost them, but sent them before you, that they may be kept forever blessed.

LUTHER

THE LOVED AND LOST.

"THE loved and lost!" Why do we call them lost?
Because we miss them from our onward road?
God's unseen angel o'er our pathway crossed,
Looked on us all, and loving them the most,
Straightway relieved them from life's weary load.

They are not lost; they are within the door
That shuts out loss, and every hurtful thing,
With angels bright, and loved ones gone before,
In their Redeemer's presence evermore,
And God himself their Lord, and Judge, and King

And this we call a "loss"! Oh selfish sorrow
Of selfish hearts! O we of little faith!
Let us look round, some argument to borrow
Why we in patience should await the morrow
That surely must succeed this night of death.

Aye, look upon this dreary desert path,
The thorns and thistles whereso'er we turn;
What trials and what tears, what wrongs and wrath,
What struggles and what strife the journey hath!
They have escaped from these; and lo! we mourn.

A poor wayfarer, leading by the hand
A little child, had halted by the well
To wash from off her feet the clinging sand,
And tell the tired boy of that bright land
Where, this long journey past, they longed to dwell;

When lo ! the Lord, who many mansions had,
  Drew near and looked upon the suffering twain,
Then pitying spake, " Give Me the little lad ;
In strength renewed, and glorious beauty clad,
  I 'll bring him with Me when I come again."

Did she make answer selfishly and wrong, —
  " Nay, but the woes I feel he too must share " ?
No ! rather, bursting into grateful song,
She went her way rejoicing, and made strong
  To struggle on, since he was freed from care.

We will do likewise ; death hath made no breach
  In love and sympathy, in hope and trust ;
No outward sign or sound our ears can reach,
But there 's an inward, spiritual speech,
  That greets us still, though mortal tongues be dust.

It bids us do the work that they laid down, —
  Take up the song where they broke off the strain ;
So journeying till we reach the heavenly town,
Where are laid up our treasures and our crown,
  And our lost loved ones will be found again.

—————

March 13.

They that dwell under His shadow shall return; they shall revive as the corn, and grow as the vine. — HOSEA xiv. 7.

IN the persistence of our Lord's purposes, and the constancy of His love, we have great comfort. His ways are long. His plans are not affected by the events which break our years. What we name death is a change in our life, not in His intention or promise. We are to keep this in mind, that we may understand Him and order our thoughts wisely. One of our greatest mistakes is in attempting to confine His promises within the brief spaces of our life. It is not the highest doctrine, but it is a serviceable principle, — the doctrine of waiting. Let us be honorable with God, and be still while His work is incomplete.   ALEXANDER MCKENZIE.

DECLENSION AND REVIVAL.

Die to thy root, sweet flower!
If God so wills, die, even to thy root.
Live there awhile, an uncomplaining, mute,
Blank life, with darkness wrapt about thy head.
And fear not for the silence round thee spread,
This is no grave, though thou among the dead
Art counted, — but the Hiding-place of Power.
     Die to thy root, sweet flower.

Spring from thy root, sweet flower!
When so God wills, spring even from thy root.
Send through the earth's warm breast a quickened shoot
And lift into the sunny air thy dower
Of bloom and odor ; life is on the plains,
And in the winds a sound of birds and rains
That sing together : lo ! the winter cold
Is past ; sweet scents revive, thick buds unfold ;
Be thou, too, willing in the day of Power.
     Spring from thy root, sweet flower.

                              DORA GREENWELL.

——◆——

March 14.

*Continue in prayer, and watch in the same with thanks-
     giving.* — COL. iv. 2.

Be thou in the fear of the Lord all the day long. — PROV.
     xxiii. 17.

WORK — work — work ! It is the iron ploughshare
that goes over the field of the heart, rooting up
all the pretty grasses and the beautiful, hurtful weeds that
we have taken such pleasure in growing, laying them all
under, fair and foul together, making plain, dull-looking
arable land for our neighbors to peer at ; until at night-
time, down in the deep furrows, the angels come and
sow.
                              DINAH MULOCH CRAIK.

LABOR CONSECRATED.

Through each added day of life,
     Lord, of Thee I'll mindful be,
And with love will bind Thee fast,
     As Thou bindest me to Thee.
When my heart is crushed with care,
Then its light shall still appear ;
With Thy help it nought can fear.
Here to Thee my highest praise

Firmly consecrated is ;
Thine alone my work, my days.
Work, and hope, and smile, and pray ;
   Pass thus manfully the day,
Thanking Him for health, and say,
Earth's rest near and Heaven's rest nearer ;
'T is well that night hath come !

March 15.

Yet will they lean upon the Lord, and say, Is not the Lord
among us ? none evil can come upon us. — MICAH iii. 11.

TO be happy and to feel inward happiness is not the
gift of fate, and comes not from the circumstances
in which we are placed. We must reach it by our own
exertions, if it is to remain. But then it is comforting to
think it is always within our own power. God Himself
cannot make a man happy in his external circumstances,
or at least only to a certain extent, nor yet can He make
him always prosperous and successful in his aims ; for
God has with supreme wisdom placed men in the midst
of ever-changing events, and these do not admit of men
always being happy. But inwardly happy He can always
make him, for He has given us this power in our heart, —
the yearning for Him, the admiration, love, and trust in
Him ; in fact, all those feelings by which His peace comes
to us. HUMBOLDT.

A LIFE OF LIBERTY.

BRIERS beset my every path,
   Which call for patient care ;
There is a cross in every lot.
   An earnest need for prayer ;
But a lowly heart that leans on Thee,
   Is happy everywhere.

In service which Thy love appoints
   There are no bonds for me ;
My secret heart is taught " the truth "
   That makes Thy children "free ; "
A life of self-renouncing love
   Is a life of liberty.

ANNA L. WARING

March 16.

And whatsoever ye do, do it heartily, as to the Lord, and not unto men. — COL. iii. 23.

I T is quite a mistake to fancy that religion belongs only to the highest, and what are called holy, duties of life. While she rises to the highest, she stoops to the meanest, occupations. They are doing the work of the Lord who sweep a floor, or guide a plough, or sit over a desk, with a desire so to do their work that God may thereby be glorified. All work done from such motives, and for such an end, becomes the work of the Lord ; and thus our life, in all its phases, entirely spent in the work of the Lord, should flow on like a river, which, however rough its bed, short or long its course, tame or grand the scene through which it passes, springs from a lofty fountain, and, born of the skies, bears blessings in its waters, and heaven reflected in its bosom.

THOMAS GUTHRIE

THE ELIXIR.

TEACH me, my God and King,
   In all things Thee to see,
And what I do in anything,
   To do it as for Thee.

All may of Thee partake ;
   Nothing can be so mean,
Which, with this tincture, " for Thy sake,"
   Will not grow bright and clean.

A servant, with this clause,
   Makes drudgery divine ;
Who sweeps a room as for Thy laws,
   Makes that and the action fine.

This is the famous stone
   That turneth all to gold :
For that which God doth touch and own
   Cannot for less be told.

GEORGE HERBERT

March 17.

And all things whatsoever ye shall ask in prayer, believ-ing, ye shall receive. — MATT. xxi. 22.

LET us pray the Lord to open to us the whole infini-tude of His paternal Heart, that our own may be there submerged and lost, so that it may make but one with His. Such was the desire of Paul for the faithful, when he longed for them in the bowels of Jesus Christ.

WATCHFULNESS AND PRAYER.

FATHER, how merciful art Thou !
  I pray, and Thou dost strengthen me ;
Trusting the radiance of Thy brow,
  Childlike, I fly in need to Thee.
The Saviour's word I glad obey ;
  He tells me to believe and pray.

When earth's dark sorrows gather round,
  Earth's consolations ever fail ;
But succor is in prayer found ;
  I lift my hands, I lift my wail,
I lift my heart, and Thou dost send
  Solace and strength, Almighty Friend.

Lord, what am I that I should crave,
  Hopeful, my God, in every ill ?
Lord, what am I that Thou shouldst save
  My soul, my yearnings deep fulfil ?
Thanks be to Thee that Thy dear Son
  Taught us the grace by prayer won.

HYMNS OF DENMARK

March 18.

And we know that all things work together for good to them that love God. — ROM. viii. 28.

THE firm persuasion that all things that concern us are completely, every moment, in the hands of our Father above, infinitely wise and merciful; that He disposes all these events in the best possible manner, and that we shall one day bless Him for even His most distressing visitations, — such a sublime persuasion will make the heart and the character sublime. It will enable us to assemble our interests together; our wishes, our prospects, our sorrows, and the circumstances of the persons that are dear to us, and present them in one devout offering to the best Father, the greatest Friend; and it will assure us of being in every scene of life the object of His kind, perpetual care.

JOHN FOSTER.

PRAYER.

FATHER! in Thy mysterious presence kneeling,
  Fain would our souls feel all Thy kindling love,
For we are weak, and need some deep revealing
  Of trust and strength and calmness from above.

Lord! we have wandered forth through doubt and sorrow
  And Thou hast made each step an onward one;
And we will ever trust each unknown morrow —
  Thou wilt sustain us till its work is done.

In the heart's depths a peace serene and holy
  Abides; and when pain seems to have her will,
Or we despair, oh, may that peace rise slowly,
  Stronger than agony, and we be still.

Now, Father, now, in Thy dear presence kneeling.
  Our spirits yearn to feel Thy kindling love;
Now make us strong, we need Thy deep revealing
  Of trust and strength and calmness from above.

March 19.

Let Him do to me as seemeth good unto Him. — 2 SAM. xv. 26.

GOD leads none of us by the rapid and easy path to knowledge, fortune, or happiness. We all of us travel by a path which has long stretches of barren and weary march, and here and there only soft resting-places, flashing like emeralds on the diadem of the desert, where we may wait and sleep and play awhile, before we gird up our loins and pursue our toilsome way. You do not love your daily tasks, whose monotony becomes wearisome; but they must be done before you can ungird and lie down in some oasis of social communion, and live for the moment a life whose sensation is bliss. The oases are few, but they are sure. No true pilgrim can miss them. Not more surely did Israel find sufficient though scanty pasture through the whole desert way, with oases of beauty and plenty at due intervals, than does man find his bread sure under the hardest circumstances, with appointed seasons of joy and even rapture; mounting up, in the holiest and most pilgrim-like way, to "joys unspeakable and full of glory." The short way might bring us to rest and glory sooner, but the rest would relax, and the glory blind us. We travel by a longer, harder path, that muscle may be disciplined by toil, courage assured by conquest, and self-government studied in many a season of shame and pain. Then the crown will fit us, rest will be calm and noble activity, and glory we shall wear like kings.

J. BALDWIN BROWN.

RENUNCIATION.

O WHEREFORE thus, apart with drooping wings,
    Thou stillest, saddest angel,
With hidden face, as if but bitter things
    Thou hadst, and no evangel
        Of good tidings?

Thou know'st that through our tears
 Of hasty, selfish weeping,
Comes surer sun; and for our petty fears
 Of loss, thou hast in keeping
A greater gain than all of which we dreamed.
 Thou knowest that in grasping
The bright possessions which so precious seemed,
 We lose them; but if, clasping
Thy faithful hand, we tread with steadfast feet
 The path of thy appointing.
There waits for us a treasury of sweet
 Delight; royal anointing
With oil of gladness and of strength! O things
 Of Heaven, Christ's evangel
Bearing, call us with shining face and poisèd wings,
 Thou sweetest, dearest angel!

HELEN HUNT JACKSON.

———◆———

March 20.

He that loveth not, knoweth not God; for God is love. —
1 JOHN iv. 8.

AS the best light in the world is the warm light of the
   sun, so the best illumination of life is not from the
moon-like beams of human speculation, but from the love
of God. That love, like the sun, opens the universe,
turns even clouds into glory, and lifts death itself to a
mount of transfiguration.

GOD IS LOVE.

I CANNOT always trace the way
Where Thou, Almighty One, dost move,
But I can always, always say,
 That God is love.

When fear her chilling mantle throws
O'er earth, my soul to heaven above,
As to her native home, upsprings,
 For God is love.

When mystery clouds my darkened path,
I 'll check my dread, my doubt reprove;
In this my soul sweet comfort hath,
    That God is love.

Yes, God is love; — a thought like this
Can every gloomy thought remove,
And turn all tears, all woes, to bliss,
    For God is love.

March 21.

Continue in prayer, and watch in the same with thanks-
giving. — Col. iv. 2.
I will therefore that men pray everywhere, lifting up holy
hands, without wrath and doubting. — 1 Tim. ii. 8.

CONSIDER the dignity of this, — to be admitted into
    so near converse with the highest majesty. Were
there nothing to follow, — no answer at all, — prayer pays
itself in the excellency of its nature, and the sweetness
that the soul finds in it. Poor wretched man, to be admitted into heaven while he is on earth, and there to
come and speak his mind freely to the Lord of heaven
and earth, as his friend, as his Father! to empty all
his complaints into His bosom; when wearied with the
miseries and follies of the world, to refresh his soul in his
God. Where there is anything of His love, this is a
privilege of the highest sweetness; for they who love
find much delight in discoursing together, and count all
hours short, and think the day runs too fast, that is so
spent; and they who are much in this exercise, the Lord
doth impart His secrets much to them.
                                    BISHOP LEIGHTON

PRAYER.

I.

NOT on a prayerless bed, not on a prayerless bed,
    Compose thy weary limbs to rest;
For they alone are blessed with balmy sleep,
        With balmy sleep,
        Whom angels keep;

Nor, though by care oppressed,
  Or anxious sorrow,
Or thought in many a coil perplexed
  For coming morrow,
  Lay not thy head
  On prayerless bed.

For who can tell, when sleep thine eyes shall close,
  That earthly cares and woes
  To thee may e'er return ?
    Arouse, my soul !
    Slumber control,
And let thy lamp burn brightly ;
  So shall thine eyes discern
Things pure and sightly;
    Taught by the Spirit, learn
    Never on prayerless bed
    To lay thine unblest head.

March 22.

Therefore I will look unto the Lord ; I will wait for the God of my salvation ; my God will hear me. — MICAH vii. 7.

WE go to God by prayers, not by steps.

GOD commandeth thee to ask, and teacheth thee how
  to ask, and promiseth that which thou asketh, and
is angry if thou askest not ; and yet, askest thou not ?

ANDREWS.

PRAYER.

II.

HAST thou no pining want, or wish, or care,
  That calls for holy prayer ?
  Has thy day been so bright
    That in its flight
  There is no trace of sorrow ?
  And thou art sure to-morrow
    Will be like this, and more
Abundant ?   Dost thou yet lay up thy store,
    And still make plans for more ?
  Thou fool ! this very night,
  Thy soul may wing its flight.

Hast thou no being than thyself more dear,
  That ploughs the ocean deep,
    And when storms sweep
    The wintry, lowering sky,
  For whom thou wak'st and weepest?
  Oh, when thy pangs are deepest,
Seek then the covenant ark of prayer;
For He that slumbereth not is there;
    His ear is open to thy cry.
  Oh, then on prayerless bed
  Lay not thy thoughtless head.

Arouse thee, weary soul, nor yield to slumber,
  Till in communion blest
    With the elect ye rest, —
Those souls of countless number;
    And with them raise
    The note of praise,
  Reaching from earth to heaven,
  Chosen, redeemed, forgiven;
So lay thy happy head,
Prayer-crowned, on blessed bed.

MARGARET MERCER.

March 23.

That ye sorrow not, even as others which have no hope. —
1 THESS. iv. 13.

THE waves which sorrow lashes up around us stand high between us and the world, and make our ship solitary in the midst of a haven full of vessels.

RICHTER.

FOR a man who knows how to sorrow rightly, knows how to be glad with a holy joy; and when he is happiest, it is as though there were a something of God throbbing in his bosom. It is as souls that we are happiest; and so suffering makes for happiness, because it helps to make the soul. Oh, what good sorrow does us, often! To many a one, while he is happy, the outer world feels eternal; but as soon as he is sorrowful, all worldly existence is only a film, because God and his soul feel so close.

WILLIAM MOUNTFORD.

'T is sorrow builds the shining ladder up,
Whose golden rounds are our calamities,
Whereon our firm feet planting, nearer God
The spirit climbs, and hath its eyes unsealed.
True is it that Death's face seems stern and cold
When he is sent to summon those we love ;
But all God's angels come to us disguised ;
Sorrow and sickness, poverty and death,
One after other, lift their frowning masks,
And we behold the Seraph's face beneath,
All radiant with the glory and the calm
Of having looked upon the front of God.

JAMES RUSSELL LOWELL.

March 24.

All Thy waves and Thy billows are gone over me. — Ps.
xlii. 7.

THOU canst not tell how rich a dowry sorrow gives
the soul, how firm a faith and eagle sight of God.

DEAN ALFORD.

OUR dependence upon God ought to be so entire and
absolute that we should never think it necessary, in any
kind of distress, to have recourse to human consolations.

THOMAS À KEMPIS.

THE BLESSED HEALER.

WHEN across the heart deep waves of sorrow
Break, as on a dry and barren shore :
When hope glistens with no bright to-morrow,
And the storm seems sweeping evermore ;

When the cup of every earthly gladness
Bears no taste of the life-giving stream;
And high hopes, as though to mock our sadness,
Fade and die as in some fitful dream ;

Who shall hush the weary spirit's chiding ?
Who the aching void within shall fill ?
Who shall whisper of a peace abiding,
And each surging billow calmly still ?

Only He whose wounded heart was broken
With the bitter cross and thorny crown ;
Whose dear love glad words of joy had spoken ;
Who His life for us laid meekly down.

Blessed Healer, all our burdens lighten ;
Give us peace, Thine own sweet peace, we pray ;
Keep us near Thee till the morn shall brighten,
And all mists and shadows flee away.

CANTERBURY HYMNAL.

March 25.

And yet I am not alone, because the Father is with me. —
JOHN xvi. 32.

THERE are, within the range of every one's life,
processes of life which must be solitary ; passages
of duty which throw one absolutely upon his individual
moral forces, and admit of no aid whatever from another.
Alone we must stand sometimes ; and if our better nature
is not to shrink into weakness, we must take with us the
thought which was the strength of Christ : " Yet I am not
alone, because the Father is with me." The sense of right
can more readily indurate the tender than melt the rocky
soul, and that is the most finished character which begins
in beauty and ends in power ; that leans on the love of
kindred while it may, and when it may not can stand
erect in the love of God ; that shelters itself amid the
domesticities of life while duty wills, and when it forbids
can go forth under the expanse of immortality, and face
any storm that beats, and traverse any wilderness that
lies beneath that canopy.

JAMES MARTINEAU.

ALONE.

ALONE, yet not alone am I,
Beneath the calm and silent sky;
　'T is still as mountain solitudes,
　Where voice is not, nor step intrudes;
No heart throbs here, gleams out no eye, —
　Alone, yet not alone am I.

A Presence actual as the heart
From whence my own life-motions start;
　A Being real, though unseen,
　More true than trace where form hath been;
A spirit to my soul is nigh, —
　Alone, yet not alone am I.

I ask no favor, feel no want,
Content with bliss nor poor nor scant;
　Serene, submissive, waiting still
　The motion of a sovereign will, —
Attended less if crowds were nigh, —
　Alone, yet not alone am I.

Oh, thus to feel, through every sense,
Omniscience and omnipotence!
　Oh, thus, all other joys above,
　To know that *power is only love!*
My lowly heart, how blest to cry,
　Alone, yet not alone am I.

March 26.

*And He that sent Me is with Me; the Father hath not
left Me alone.* — JOHN viii. 29.

THERE is no lot on earth so lonely, no trouble so
unshared, no fidelity so divorced from human help,
but it may find its counterpart in the life of the Saviour.

EPHRAIM PEABODY.

Is thy path lonely? Fear it not, for He
Who marks the sparrow's fall is guarding thee ;
And not a star shines o'er thy head by night,
But He hath known that it will reach thy sight ;
And not a joy can beautify thy lot,
But tells thee still that thou art unforgot ;
Nay, not a grief can darken or surprise,
Swell in thy heart, or dim with tears thine eyes,
But it is sent in mercy and in love,
To bid thy helplessness seek strength above.

MY REFUGE.

Is there a lone and dreary hour,
When worldly comforts lose their power ?
My Father ! let me turn to Thee,
And set each thought of darkness free.

Is there a time of fear or grief,
Which sees no prospect of relief ?
My Father ! break the cheerless gloom,
And bid my heart its calm resume.

Is there an hour of peace or joy,
When hope is all my soul's employ ?
My Father ! still my hopes will roam
Until they rest with Thee at home.

March 27.

If a man die, shall he live again ? — JOB xiv. 14.

VERY beautiful, is it not? — the picture of the opening
spring-time which we gather from our Bible, catching
here a glimpse and there a glimpse as it lies reflected in
the song of psalmist and prophet, and of Jesus, who had
so often watched it as a boy on the hills of Galilee.
Doubtless He used to go out to gather early lilies, and note
the green garments of the fresh young grass. Ten million
million tiny strugglers on our hills and in our fields to-day
are trying to show us that ours, too, is Holy Land. The
flowers have begun to greet us in our walks, — dumb

angels, with faces all a-shine with the glad tidings that the
Saviour-season hath arisen.   Thank God for the Resurrection thoughts which the spring months bring to us !
We die to live again.   We die *that we may* live again.
Nothing is quickened save it die.   Mortality is the condition of all immortality.   What echoes we have wakened
of this truth !   The opening spring prints it off on every
hill-side in illuminated text of leaf and flower.   We find,
as always with these central facts of Nature, that the best
and highest meaning of the truth belongs to ourselves,
— so completely is man a part of all, so completely is all
represented in man.   Our word " Resurrection " seems to
concentrate the history of the universe, to whisper the
secret of the life of God !   W. C. GANNETT.

A SPRING SONG.

O SPRING-TIME sweet !
Over the hills come thy lovely feet.
The earth's white mantle is cast away,
She clothes herself all in green to-day ;
And the little flowers that hid from the cold
Are springing anew from the warm, fresh mould.

O Spring-time sweet !
The whole earth smiles thy coming to greet ;
Our hearts to their inmost depths are stirred
By the first spring flower and the song of the bird :
Our sweet, strange feelings no room can find,
They wander like dreams through heart and mind.

O Spring-time sweet !
Now the old and the new in thy soft hours meet !
The dear, dead joys of the days long past,
The brightness and beauty that could not last,
Their fair ghosts rise with the ending of snow, —
The springs and the summers of long ago.

O Spring-time sweet !
With silent hope thy coming I greet ;
For all that in winter the bright earth lost
Doth rise, new-born, with the ending of frost ;
Even so shalt thou bring me — at last, at last ! —
All the hope and the joy and the love of the past.

Tr by J. F. CLARKE.

March 28.

Hide Thy face from my sins, and blot out all mine iniqui-
ties. — Ps. li. 9.

BORN of God, attach thyself to Him, as a plant to its
root, that ye may not be withered.   DEMOPHILUS

OH that Christ would break down the old narrow
vessels of these narrow and ebb souls, and make fair,
deep, wide, and broad souls, to hold a sea, and a full tide,
flowing over all its banks, of Christ's love.

SAMUEL RUTHERFORD.

TURNING TO GOD.

IF, gracious God, in life's green, ardent year,
A thousand times Thy patient love I tried;
With reckless heart, with conscience hard and sere,
Thy gifts perverted, and Thy power defied;
Oh, grant me, now that wintry snows appear
Around my brow, and youth's bright promise hide, —
Grant me with reverential awe to hear
Thy holy voice, and in Thy word confide !
Blot from my book of life its early stain !
Since days misspent will never more return,
My future path do Thou in mercy trace ;
So cause my soul with pious zeal to burn,
That all the trust which in Thy name I place,
Frail as I am, may not prove wholly vain !

PIETRO BEMBO

March 29.

Watch ye therefore, and pray always, that ye may be accounted worthy to escape all these things that shall come to pass, and to stand before the Son of man. — LUKE xxi. 36.

LET it be for the encouragement of such among us as are conscious of no high powers, and who sometimes wonder for what service in Christ's church we are fit, that in a great structure all the component portions are not equally great. There are not only the solid and the costly, the rock and timber; not only the precious and ornamental, the gold and silver; but likewise the humble and subsidiary, yea, even the otherwise valueless and the minute; for not even mortar and earth can be spared from the construction. The Great Builder has some lowly crevice in his house, which the meanest and feeblest of us may occupy. We may not be called to bear up buttresses, or to crown turrets, or to adorn the carved work of the sanctuary; but it should satisfy us if, in some remote recess and unknown shade, we fulfil the office which the Master has laid upon us.

JAMES W. ALEXANDER.

THE LOWEST PLACE.

GIVE me the lowest place ; not that I dare
　　Ask for that lowest place, but Thou hast died
That I might live and share
　　Thy glory by Thy side.

Give me the lowest place ; or if for me
　　That lowest place too high, make one more low,
Where I may sit and see
　　My God and love Thee so.

CHRISTINA ROSSETTI.

March 30.

My times are in Thy hand. — Ps. xxxi. 15.

SUDDEN or slow, easy or hard, death advances as God sends it; nay, it is no longer death; it is Jesus who comes to fetch me.

Provided that it be indeed He, and that I feel His presence, and confide my loved ones to His care, the rest matters little. Certainly it will be He.

COUNTESS DE GASPARIN.

WHILE here, to do His will be mine,
And His to fix my time of rest.

WHEN?

IF I were told that I must die to-morrow,
    That the next sun
Which sinks should bear me past all fear and sorrow
    For any one,
All the fight fought, all the short journey through,
    What should I do?

I do not think that I should shrink or falter,
    But just go on,
Doing my work, nor change, nor seek to alter
    Aught that is gone;
But rise, and move, and love, and smile, and pray.
    For one more day; —

And lying down at night for a last sleeping,
    Say in that ear
Which hearkens ever: "Lord, within Thy keeping
    How should I fear?
And when to-morrow brings Thee nearer still,
    Do Thou Thy will."

I might not sleep for awe; but peaceful, tender,
    My soul would lie
All the night long; and when the morning splendor
    Flushed o'er the sky,
I think that I could smile, — could calmly say,
    "It is His day."

But if a wondrous hand, from the blue yonder,
    Held out a scroll
On which my life was writ, and I with wonder
    Beheld unroll
To a long century's end its mystic clew,
    What should I do?

What could I do, O blessed Guide and Master!
    Other than this:
Still to go on as now, not slower, faster,
    Nor fear to miss
The road, although so very long it be,
    While led by Thee?

Step after step, feeling Thee close beside me,
    Although unseen,
Through thorns, through flowers, whether the tempest
    hide Thee,
    Or heavens serene,
Assured Thy faithfulness cannot betray,
    Thy love decay.

I may not know, my God; no hand revealeth
    Thy counsels wise;
Along the path a deepening shadow stealeth,
    No voice replies
To all my questioning thought, the time to tell,
    And it is well.

Let me keep on, abiding and unfearing
    Thy will always,
Through a long century's fruition,
    Or a short day's.
Thou canst not come too soon; and I can wait,
    If Thou come late.
                      SUSAN COOLIDGE

March 31.

For as the heavens are higher than the earth, so are My ways higher than your ways, and My thoughts than your thoughts. — ISA. lv. 9.

WE thank Thee, O Lord, for that perpetual spring-time with which Thou visitest the human soul. We bless Thee for the sun of righteousness which never sets, nor allows any night there, but, with healing in his beams, shakes down perennial day on eyes that open, and on hearts that, longing, lift them up to Thee.

THEODORE PARKER

UNDER THE LEAVES.

OFT have I walked these woodland paths,
  Without the blest foreknowing
That underneath the withered leaves
  The fairest buds were growing.

To-day the south wind sweeps away
  The types of Autumn's splendor,
And shows the sweet Arbutus flowers, —
  Spring's children pure and tender.

O prophet souls, with lips of bloom,
  Outvying in their beauty
The pearly tints of ocean shells,
  Ye teach me faith and duty.

Walk life's dark ways, ye seem to say,
  With Love's divine foreknowing,
That where man sees but withered leaves,
  God sees the sweet flowers growing.

April 1.

Howbeit, that was not first which is spiritual, but that which is natural; and afterward that which is spiritual. — 1 COR. xiii. 46.

CHANGE, surely, as well as growth, is the law of the universe; for nothing is unchangeable but God, who can neither change nor grow.

Oh that we might reach to that fountain of renewing strength which would change us from all that is low and unworthy, from the inordinate love of pleasure, love of possession, and love of the world, into the very image and inward forming of Jesus Christ!

C. A. BARTOL.

GIVE PLACE.

STARRY crowns of heaven
Set in azure night!
Linger yet a little
Ere you hide your light; —
Nay; let starlight fade away,
Heralding the day!

Snow-flakes pure and spotless,
Still, oh, still remain,
Binding dreary winter
In your silver chain; —
Nay; but melt at once and bring
Radiant, sunny spring!

Blossoms, gentle blossoms,
Do not wither yet;
Still for you the sun shines,
Still the dews are wet; —
Nay; but fade and wither fast,
Fruit must come at last!

Joy, so true and tender,
Dare you not abide?
Will you spread your pinions,
Must you leave our side?
Nay; an angel's shining grace
Waits to fill your place!

ADELAIDE A. PROCTER.

April 2.

Shall not God search this out ? for He knoweth the secrets of the heart. ⸪ Ps. xliv. 21.

FAR down in the depths of the forest, under the shadows of gloomy firs, far out on the rolling prairie, springing with the grass, under the full light of the fervid sun, are fair and fragrant blossoms, budding, blossoming, fading, dying, unseen by mortal eye. In millions of homes, scattered over this wide earth of ours, are fairer human blossoms, patient, gentle, thoughtful souls, the fragrance of whose daily sacrifice fills, unheeded, the air ; the flowers of whose offerings wither unseen, on the steps of the altar ; the fruits of whose ceaseless toil are plucked by careless hands. How sweet the thought that there is no lot so low, no care so trifling, no life so hidden, that it escapes a *Father's* eye ! How full of comfort the knowledge that there is no bud of hope, no blossom of joy, no tendril of effort, no leaf of life, that is not fed with the sun of His love, and watered with the dew of His mercy, to the end that it may bring forth fruit unto life eternal.

VON BUHLER.

UNDER THE LEAVES.

THICK green leaves from the soft brown earth,
Happy spring-time hath called them forth ;
First faint promise of summer bloom
Breathes from the fragrant, sweet perfume,
          Under the leaves

Lift them ! what marvellous beauty lies
Hidden beneath, from our thoughtless eyes !
May-flowers, rosy or purest white,
Lift their cups to the sudden light,
          Under the leaves.

Are there no lives whose holy deeds —
Seen by no eye save His who reads
Motive and action — in silence grow
Into rare beauty, and bud and blow
          Under the leaves?

Fair white flowers of faith and trust,
Springing from spirits bruised and crushed ;
Blossoms of love, rose-tinted and bright,
Touched and painted with heaven's own light,
          Under the leaves ;

Full fresh clusters of duty borne,
Fairest of all in that shadow grown ;
Wondrous the fragrance that sweet and rare
Comes from the flower-cups hidden there,
          Under the leaves.

Though unseen by our vision dim,
Bud and blossom are known to Him ;
Wait we content for His heavenly ray, —
Wait till our Master himself one day
          Lifteth the leaves.

April 3.

*Sing unto the Lord with thanksgiving; who covereth the
heaven with clouds, who prepareth rain for the earth,
who maketh grass to grow upon the mountains. —
Ps. cxlvii. 7, 8.*

AS flowers carry dew-drops, trembling on the edges of
the petals, and ready to fall at the first waft of
wind or brush of bird, so the heart should carry its
beaded words of thanksgiving ; and at the first breath
of heavenly favor, let down the shower, perfumed with
the heart's gratitude.

                  HENRY WARD BEECHER.

APRIL.

I HEAR through all the solemn pines
  The south wind's pleasant flow,
And see the clouds, like happy things,
  O'er fields of azure go,
While all the sorrow from the earth
  Seems melting with the snow.

The robin and the bluebird sing
O'er meadows brown and bare ;
They cannot know what wondrous bloom
Is softly budding there ;
But all the joy their hearts outpour
Seems pulsing in the air.

And *we* will sing, though all our days
Seem dark with pain and loss ;
We know that sorrow's furnace-heat
Consumes alone our dross ;
We know that our dear Father's love
Gives both our crown and cross.

Oh, while beneath the snow-drift buds
The flower we love the best,
And on the wind-tossed bough the bird
Still builds its happy nest,
Praise God for all the good we know,
And trust Him for the rest !

—◆—

April 4.

With the ancient is wisdom ; and in length of days under-
standing. — JOB xii. 12.

A WELL-SPENT life ; with its ripened experience,
its mellow wisdom, its remembrances full of peace,
and its hopes full of immortality. It may be useful to
the last, and perhaps more useful as it draws nigh to the
last. Does it not tread closer on the heavenly world?
" At that day shall a man look to his Maker."

HAIL, welcome tide of life, where no tumultuous billows roll,
How wondrous to myself appears this halcyon calm of soul !
The wearied bird blown o'er the deep would sooner quit its
    shore
Than I would cross the gulf again that Time has brought me
    o'er.
                                        CAMPBELL.

THE seas are quiet when the winds give o'er ;
So calm are we when passions are no more ;
For then we know how vain it was to boast
Of fleeting things too certain to be lost.
Clouds of affection from our younger eyes
Concealed that emptiness which age descries.

The soul's dark cottage, battered and decayed,
Lets in new light through chinks that time has made .
Stronger by weakness, wiser men become,
As they draw near to their eternal home !
Leaving the old, both worlds at once they view,
That stand upon the threshold of the new.

WALLER.

—◆—

April 5.

Strengthen Thou me according unto Thy word. — Ps.
cxix. 28.

THOSE who bend and incline toward Him, He bends
and inclines toward them. Between that soul all
sensible of its need, oppressed with its unfitness and
unworthiness, and the blessed, boundless heart of the
Saviour, there is a quick and eager affinity. Christ has
a purpose in that direction, — there is the specific errand
He came for, — to save that lost soul.

GEORGE SHEPARD.

UPWARD.

COME, little snow-drop, struggle on through dark and clinging mould !
Didst hear the great sun calling thee, and bidding thee
unfold ?
Didst feel the spring's refreshing rain, and fragrant, wooing
breath,
Arousing thee to life and light, from out the arms of death ?

Lift up thy slender, fragile stem, though strong the fetters be !
The nearer to the bright warm sun, the more he 'll strengthen
    thee !
Ope wide thy petals ; welcome thou the friendly, cheering
    rays,
And they will nestle at thy heart, to bless thy fleeting days.

Come, earth-bound spirit, leave the depths of sin and doubt
    and care ;
The Saviour calls thee to arise, and pure, white garments
    wear ;
From Him have come the mercy-drops and sunshine of thy
    past,
From Him the winning whisperings of peace and heaven at
    last.

Fear not to lift to Him thy prayer ; strive nobly to be free !
The nearer thou dost come to Him, the more He 'll strengthen
    thee ;
A welcome give Him, and His love will circle thee around,
And raise thee up to life and light, with heavenly beauty
    crowned.

JEANIE A. B. GREENOUGH.

April 6.

And I will pray the Father, and He shall give you another
Comforter, that he may abide with you forever. —
JOHN xiv. 16.

CHRIST seems to delight to lavish His deepest sympathy on "him that has no helper." Comfortless
ones, be comforted ! He often makes you portionless
here, to drive you to Himself, the everlasting portion.
He often dries every drill and fountain of earthly bliss,
that He may lead you to say, " All my springs are in
Thee." He seems intent to fill up every gap love has
been forced to make. How beautifully, in one amazing
verse, does He conjoin the depth and tenderness of His
comfort with the certainty of it, — " As one whom his
mother comforteth, so will I comfort you, and ye shall
be comforted."

COMFORT.

Speak low to me, my Saviour, low and sweet,
From out the hallelujahs, sweet and low,
Lest I should fear and fall, and miss Thee so,
Who art not missed by any that entreat.
Speak to me as to Mary at Thy feet;
And if no precious gums my hands bestow,
Let my tears drop, like amber, while I go
In search of Thy divinest voice, complete
In humanest affection; thus, in sooth,
To lose the sense of losing! As a child,
Whose song-bird seeks the woods forevermore,
Is sung to, in its stead, by mother's mouth,
Till sinking on her breast, love reconciled,
He sleeps the faster that he wept before.

Elizabeth Barrett Browning.

———◆———

April 7.

*In the morning sow thy seed, and in the evening withhold
not thy hand: for thou knowest not whether shall
prosper, either this or that, or whether they both shall
be alike good.* — Eccl. xi. 6.

ALL which happens in the whole world happens
through hope. No husbandman would sow a grain
of corn, if he did not hope it would spring up and bring
forth the ear. How much more are we helped on by
hope in the way to eternal life. Martin Luther.

We reap what we sow, but Nature has love over and
above that justice, and gives us shadow and blossom and
fruit that springs from no planting of ours.

George Eliot.

SEED-TIME.

LABOR and pray, and thou shalt gain
A help in need, a strength in pain.
Thus saith God's word, that law sublime
For all earth's varied clime and time.
We what the Father hath decreed
Fulfil, and hopeful sow the seed.

It lies embosomed in the field ;
Our daily bread rich may it yield.
Father, Thy loving hand we trust,
With spirit soaring from the dust ;
Crown Thou our hopes and diligence ;
Blessings in harvest-tide dispense.

This crave we for the Saviour's sake ;
Thy glory, grace, may we partake.
In Christ Thou, Father, gavest peace,
And heaven's rapture and release ;
But while we wait for things above,
Earth pours the treasures of Thy love.

HYMNS OF DENMARK.

—◆—

April 8.

*My soul thirsteth for God, for the living God ; when shall
I come and appear before God ? — Ps. xlii. 2.*

LIFE, strong life and sound life, — that life which lends
approaches to the Infinite and takes hold on heaven,
— is not so much a progress as it is a resistance.

NORTH BRITISH REVIEW

OH, Christ — He is the fountain,
The deep, sweet well of love !
The streams on earth I 've tasted,
More deep I 'll drink above ;
There to an ocean fulness
His mercy doth expand,
And glory, glory dwelleth
In Immanuel's Land.

SAMUEL RUTHERFORD

"A LITTLE WHILE."

Oh for the peace which floweth as a river!
   Making life's desert places bloom and smile;
Oh for a faith to grasp heaven's bright "forever,"
   Amid the shadows of earth's "little while."

"A little while" for patient vigil keeping,
   To face the storm, to wrestle with the strong;
"A little while" to sow the seed with weeping,
   Then bind the sheaves and sing the harvest song.

"A little while" the earthen pitcher taking
   To wayside brooks from far-off fountains fed;
Then the parched lip its thirst forever slaking
   Beside the fulness of the Fountain-Head.

JANE FOX CREWDSON.

April 9.

Redeeming the time, because the days are evil. — EPH.
v. 16.

WORK is the best birthright which man still retains.
It is the strongest of moral tonics, the most vigorous of mental medicines.

It comes in so many forms in this life of ours, the knowledge that there is something sweetest and noblest of which we despair, and the sense of something present that solicits us with an immediate and easy indulgence.

AROUSE THEE, SOUL!

Arouse thee, soul!
God made not thee to sleep
Thy hour of earth, in doing naught, away;
   He gave thee power to keep.
Oh! use it for His glory while you may.
   Arouse thee, soul!

Arouse thee, soul !
Oh ! there is much to do
For thee, if thou wouldst work for human kind ;
The misty future through
A greatness looms, — 't is mind, awakened mind !
Arouse thee, soul!

Arouse thee, soul!
And let the body do
Some worthy deed for human happiness,
To join, when life is through,
Unto thy name, that angels both may bless !
Arouse thee, soul!

Arouse thee, soul !
Leave nothings of the earth ;
And, if the body be not strong to dare,
To blessed thoughts give birth
High as yon heaven, pure as heaven's air ;
Arouse thee, soul!

ROBERT NICOLL.

—◆—

April 10.

*And let us not be weary in well-doing: for in due season
we shall reap if we faint not.* — GAL. vi. 9.

IF we are poor because we stand true to life and duty,
we are poor only as the sower is poor, because he
has to cast his wheat into the furrow, and then wait for
the sheaves of harvest. If our life is as God will, yet is
bare, it is only as the granary is bare in June, — that very
bareness is the prophecy of plenty. Here or there in the
full time comes the full blessing ; the flower flashing out
glory, the fields laughing with plenty.

ROBERT COLLYER.

SOWING.

Sow with a generous hand ;
Pause not for toil or pain ;
Weary not through the heat of summer,
Weary not through the cold spring rain ;
But wait till the autumn comes
For the sheaves of golden grain.

Scatter the seed, and fear not;
  A table will be spread ;
What matter if you are too weary
  To eat your hard-earned bread?
Sow while the earth is broken,
  For the hungry must be fed.

Sow; while the seeds are lying
  In the warm earth's bosom deep,
And your warm tears fall upon it,
  They will stir in their quiet sleep ;
And the green blades rise the quicker,
  Perchance, for the tears you weep.

Then sow ; for the hours are fleeting,
  And the seed must fall to-day ;
And care not what hands shall reap it,
  Or if you shall have passed away
Before the waving corn-fields
  Shall gladden the sunny day.

ADELAIDE A. PROCTER.

April 11.

*Behold, I stand at the door and knock : if any man hear
My voice, and open the door, I will come in to him, and
will sup with him, and he with Me.* — REV. iii. 20.

CHRIST knocks by the trials and afflictions of our
mortal lot. We cannot always be dealt with softly.
Pain will sting. Calamity will strike. Events and feelings
of this kind have a holy intent in them. They should
not be sent in vain. And is it not their natural effect to
make us tender and receptive, to scatter vain thoughts,
to break up selfish reliances, to sober the views and
chasten the affections, to lead up towards the higher

sources of content, and to let in the contemplations of a better world than this?   Do they not teach us to aspire above the things that we feel to be insufficient?   Should they not make us prudent, patient, and strong?

THE GUEST.

SPEECHLESS Sorrow sat with me;
I was sighing wearily;
Lamp and fire were out; the rain
Wildly beat the window-pane;
In the dark we heard a knock,
And a hand was on the lock;
One in waiting spake to me,
   Saying sweetly,
" I am come to sup with thee ! "

All my room was dark and damp;
" Sorrow," said I, " trim the lamp ;
Light the fire, and cheer thy face ;
Set the guest-chair in its place."
And again I heard the knock;
In the dark I found the lock:
" Enter, I have turned the key ! —
   Enter, stranger !
Who art come to sup with me."

Opening wide the door, He came ;
But I could not speak His name ;
In the guest-chair took His place,
But I could not see His face ;
When my cheerful fire was beaming,
When my little lamp was gleaming,
   Lo ! my Master
Was the guest that supped with me !

HARRIET MCEWEN KIMBALL.

April 12.

I am the good shepherd; the good shepherd giveth his life for the sheep. — JOHN x. 11.

WHAT has the world always needed? Not the help of friends as powerless as themselves; not the frozen and uncertain precepts of philosophy; but faith that God has compassion on them, the assurance that He is pitiful and merciful, and will hear their prayer out of the dust and will help them in their sore need, — the assurance that He does not look coldly on us from the sky, but that He looks in love; and all language is weak to express this assurance compared with the cross of Christ. The heavens might break forth into articulate voices of revelation, and they would be meaningless compared with that great sacrifice. For what is it but saying in the words of the Apostle, "He that spared not His own Son, but delivered Him up for us all, how shall He not with Him also freely give us all things"?

COME, WANDERING SHEEP.

COME, wandering sheep, oh. come!
　I'll bind thee to my breast,
I'll bear thee to thy home,
　And lay thee down to rest.

I saw thee stray forlorn,
　And heard thee faintly cry,
And on the tree of scorn,
　For thee, I deigned to die.
　What greater proof could I
Give, than to seek the tomb?
Come, wandering sheep, oh, come!

I shield thee from alarms,
　And wilt thou not be blest?
I bear thee in My arms, —
　Thou bear Me in thy breast!
　Oh, this is love! — Come, rest!
This is a blissful doom.
Come, wandering sheep, oh, come!

GÓNGORA.

April 13.

He that is faithful in that which is least, is faithful also
in much. — LUKE xvi. 10.

> EACH spirit weaves the robe it wears
> From out life's busy loom ;
> And common tasks and daily cares
> Make up the threads of doom.

FLAVEL compares Providence to "a curious piece of
arras, made up of a thousand shreds, which singly
we know not what to make of, but put together and
stitched up orderly, they represent a beautiful history to
the eye." And we may imagine in like manner the web
of human life with all its varied and wonderful patterns
woven out of separate existences, and rejoice to know
and believe that warp, woof, and loom are all in the hands
of our Heavenly Father.

WEAVING.

> BETTER to weave in the web of life
> A bright and golden filling,
> And to do God's will with a ready heart,
> And hands that are swift and willing,
> Than to snap the slender, delicate threads
> Of our curious life asunder,
> And then blame Heaven for the tangled ends.
> And sit and grieve and wonder.

———◆———

April 14.

Lord, I have called daily upon Thee. — Ps. lxxxix. 8.

MEN err in despising these *little days*. They love
to send their thoughts over years and ages. They
defer their good intentions to further periods. They
praise anniversaries. They would make the intervals
wide between the serious tasks of self-communion. But
these little ones are the chief of all, if we will look at

them as they are, and if we will make them what they should be. Resolve, when you awake, that it shall be to some faithful purpose, and that your renovated powers shall be obedient to Him who has renewed them. And throw a glance backward, before your eyes are weighed down, to see how well you have kept the morning's resolution.

N. L. FROTHINGHAM.

Look upon every day, O youth, as the whole of life, not merely as a section, and enjoy the present without wishing, through haste to spring on to another [lying] before the section.

RICHTER.

EVERY DAY.

EVERY day hath its dawn,
    Its soft and silent eve,
Its noontide hours of bliss or bale ,
    Why should we grieve ?

Why do we heap huge mounds of years
    Before us and behind,
And scorn the little days that pass
    Like angels on the wind ?

Each turning round a small, sweet face
    As beautiful as near :
Because it is so small a face
    We will not see it clear ;

We will not clasp it as it flies,
    And kiss its lips and brow ;
We will not bathe our wearied souls
    In its delicious Now.

And so it turns from us, and goes
    Away in sad disdain ;
Though we would give our lives for it,
    It never comes again.

Yet, every day has its dawn,
    Its noontide and its eve ;
Live while we live, giving God thanks ;
    He will not let us grieve.

DINAH MULOCH CRAIK.

April 15.

Although the fig-tree shall not blossom, neither shall fruit be in the vines; . . . Yet I will rejoice in the Lord, I will joy in the God of my salvation. — HAB. iii. 17, 18.

WINTER, no doubt, is not the pleasant season that summer brings, with her songs and flowers and long bright summer days. Bitter medicines, no doubt, are not savory meat ; yet he who believes that all things shall work together for good will be ready to thank God for the winter frost that kills the weeds and breaks up the soil, as for the dewy nights and sunny days that ripen the fields of corn. May God give us such a faith ! With nature weak, and grace imperfect, when there is no lifting of the cloud, and trials are severe and long-protracted, oh ! though it may be easy for an onlooker to preach patience, it is not easy for a sufferer to practise it. How ready are we to cry, " How long, O Lord, how long ? " Yet let me have a firm faith in God's truth and love ; let me be confident that He will do what He has said, and perform all that He has promised, and I shall discover mercy's bow bent on fortune's blackest cloud, and, under the most trying providences, shall enjoy in my heart, and exhibit to others in my temper, the blessed difference between a sufferer that mourns and a spirit that murmurs.

THOMAS GUTHRIE

AFTER MANY DAYS.

THE land was still ; the skies were gray with weeping ;
  Into the soft brown earth the seed she cast ;
"Oh ! soon," she cried, " will come the time of reaping,
  The golden time when clouds and tears are past ! "
There came a whisper through the autumn haze,
" Yea, thou shalt find it after many days."

Hour after hour she marks the fitful gleaming
  Of sunlight glancing through the cloudy rift ;
Hour after hour she lingers, idly dreaming,
  To see the rain fall and the dead leaves drift :
"Oh! for some small green signs of life," she prays,
" Have I not watched and waited ' many days ' ? "

At early morning, chilled and sad, she hearkens
　　To stormy winds that through the poplars blow;
Far over hill and plain the heaven darkens,
　　Her field is covered with a shroud of snow :
" Ah, Lord ! " she sighs, " are these Thy loving ways ? "
He answers, " Spake I not of *many* days ? "

The snow-drop blooms ; the purple violet glistens
　　On banks of moss that take the sparkling showers ;
Half-cheered, half-doubting yet, she strays and listens
　　To finches singing to the shy young flowers ;
A little longer still His love delays
The promised blessing — "after many days."

" O happy world ! " she cries, "the sun is shining !
　　Above the soil I see the springing green ;
I could not trust His word without repining,
　　I could not wait in peace for things unseen :
Forgive me, Lord, my soul is full of praise :
My doubting heart prolonged Thy ' many days.' "

—◆—

April 16.

Whatsoever a man soweth, that shall he also reap. — GAL.
　vi. 7.

THE seed sown in the ground contains in itself the
future harvest. The harvest is but the development
of the germ of life in the seed. A holy act strengthens
the inward holiness. It is a seed of life growing into
more life. He that sows much thereby becomes more
conformed to God than he was before, in heart and spirit.
That is his reward and harvest. And just as among
the apostles there was one whose spirit, attuned to love,
made him emphatically the disciple whom Jesus loved, so
shall there be some who, by previous discipline of the
Holy Ghost, shall have more of His mind, and understand
more of His love, and drink deeper of His joy, than
others, — they that have sowed bountifully.

F. W. ROBERTSON

THE SOWERS.

THERE be those who sow beside
The waters that in silence glide,
Trusting no echo will declare
Whose footsteps ever wandered there.

The noiseless footsteps pass away ;
The stream flows on as yesterday ;
Nor can it for a time be seen
A benefactor there had been.

Yet think not that the seed is dead
Which in the lonely place is spread ;
It lives, it lives ; the spring is nigh,
And soon its life shall testify.

That silent stream, that desert ground,
No more unlovely shall be found ;
But scattered flowers of simplest grace
Still spread their beauty round the place.

And soon or late a time will come
When witnesses that now are dumb
With grateful eloquence shall tell
From whom the seed, now scattered, fell.

BERNARD BARTON.

April 17.

The Lord direct your hearts into the love of God, and into the patient waiting for Christ. — 2 THESS. iii. 5.

SCHILLER, the poet of grand thoughts, has said, "Those only love that love without hope." There is in those few words more than poetry : they contain a whole religious philosophy, that we do not yet well understand, but that futurity will. Life is a mission : its end is not the search after happiness, but knowledge and fulfilment of duty. Love is not enjoyment, it is devotedness. If on the path of duty and devotedness God sends us some beams of happiness, let us bless God, and bask our

limbs, enfeebled by the fatigues of the journey ; but let us
not suspend it for long.   Let us not say, We have found
the secret of existence, for the action of the law of our
existence cannot be pursued from without.   And if we
meet only suffering, still march on.   Suffer and act.   God
will measure our progress toward Him, not by what we
have suffered, but by how much we have desired to
diminish the sufferings of others ; by how much our efforts
have been directed to the saving and perfecting of our
brethren.

MAZZINI.

TWO DAYS.

A PERFECT day !   I tried to hold it fast ;
To make each hour my own, and sip its sweets,
As if it were a flower, and I its bee.
No one should come between me and my joy,
My will should rule my actions for one day.
Ah, yes ! it slipped away, its secret kept,
And hid from me behind the sunset clouds.

Another day : " God help me use the hours ! "
I said, " And let Thy will be done, not mine."
I watched if might be some one needed help,
If I might speak a word of cheer, or give
A hand, or even softly step where wounds
Were aching.   Day of sweet revealing ! when
It passed, it left its perfume in my heart.

M. F. BUTTS

April 18.

Now Jesus loved Martha, and her sister, and Lazarus. —
JOHN xi. 5.

NO one of my fellows can do that special work for me
which I have come into the world to do ; he may
do a higher work, a greater work, but he cannot do my
work.   I cannot hand my work over to him, any more
than I can hand over my responsibilities or my gifts.

Nor can I delegate my work to any association of men, however well-ordered and powerful. They have their own work to do, and it may be a very noble one. But they cannot do my work for me. I must do it with these hands or with these lips which God has given me. I may do little or I may do much. That matters not. It must be my own work. And by doing my own work, poor as it may seem to some, I shall better fulfil God's end in making me what I am, and more truly glorify His name, than if I were either going out of my own sphere to do the work of another, or calling in another into my sphere to do my proper work for me.

JOHN RUSKIN

MARTHA.

YES, Lord! — Yet some must serve !
  Not all with tranquil heart,
Even at Thy dear feet,
Wrapped in devotion sweet,
  May sit apart !

Yes, Lord ! — Yet some must bear
  The burden of the day,
Its labor and its heat,
While others at Thy feet
  May muse and pray !

Yes, Lord ! — Yet some must do
  Life's daily task-work ; some
Who fain would sing must toil
Amid earth's dust and moil,
  While lips are dumb !

Yes, Lord ! — Yet man must earn
  And woman bake the bread ;
And some must watch and wake
Early for others' sake,
  Who pray instead !

Yes, Lord ! — Yet even Thou
  Hast need of earthly care :
I bring the bread and wine
To Thee, a guest divine —
  Be this my prayer !

JULIA C. R. DORR.

April 19.

Take therefore no thought for the morrow. — MATT. vi. 34.

CHARACTER requires a still air. There may be storm and upheaval around, but there must be peace within for the soul to thrive. But anxiety is the reverse of peace. It teases the mind with questions that it cannot answer; it broods over possible evil; it peoples the future with dark shapes; it frets the sensibilities with worrying conjecture. It spoils the present by loading it with the evil of to-morrow. Its tendency is, by dwelling on evil, to make us cowardly and selfish. Character cannot grow in such an atmosphere. Hence, as a matter of fact, we seldom find any great height and sweetness of character in an anxious-minded person, for the simple reason that it has no chance to grow; all the forces go in other directions. But when one in wise and righteous ways has learned to trust in God, and so has come into peace, then the seeds of all grace and beauty spring up, and spread out their leaves in the calm, warm air, and blossom out into full beauty, fed from beneath and above. It was to secure such an atmosphere, for an end so eternally important as this, that Christ spoke these words: "Take no thought." Oh, how wise the teaching! How blessed to be able to receive it!

T. T. MUNGER.

FEELING THE WAY.

FEELING the way — and all the way up hill;
But on the open summit, calm and still,
The feet of Christ are planted; and they stand
    In view of all the quiet land.

Feeling the way — and though the way is dark,
The eyelids of the morning yet shall mark
Against the east the shining of His face,
    At peace upon the lighted place.

Feeling the way — and if the way is cold,
What matter? since upon the fields of gold
His breath is melting; and the warm winds sing
    While rocking summer days for Him.

April 20.

For the Lamb which is in the midst of the throne shall feed them, and shall lead them unto living fountains of waters : and God shall wipe away all tears from their eyes. — REV. vii. 17.

CONSIDER the kindness and helpfulness of Time. We speak of him as the destroyer, and picture him with his scythe sweeping away all that man would preserve. But, on the other hand, what a healer and restorer is Time ! As we grow older, we see nothing more plainly than that wounds of the spirit, which to youthful eyes appear incurable, are most gently soothed and made whole by the passing years. Under the old scars flows again the calm, healthful tide of life. Nowhere more plainly than here is it seen how much better God's ways are than man's thoughts. Under a great loss the heart impetuously cries that it can never be happy again, and perhaps in its desperation says that it wishes never to be comforted. But, though angels do not fly down to open the grave and restore the lost, the days and months come as angels with healing in their wings. Under their touch aching regret passes into tender memory ; into hands that were empty new joys are softly pressed ; and the heart, that was like the tree stripped of its leaves, and beaten by winter's tempests, is clothed again with the green of spring.

CHRISTIAN UNION.

THE ABIDING LOVE.

IT singeth low in every heart,
　We hear it each and all, —
A song of those who answer not,
　However we may call.
They throng the silence of the breast,
　We see them as of yore, —
The kind, the true, the brave, the sweet,
　Who walk with us no more.

'T is hard to take the burden up,
When these have laid it down :
They brightened all the joy of life,
They softened every frown.
But, oh ! 't is good to think of them
When we are troubled sore ;
Thanks be to God that such have been,
Although they are no more !

More homelike seems the vast unknown,
Since they have entered there ;
To follow them were not so hard,
Wherever they may fare.
They cannot be where God is not,
On any sea or shore ;
Whate'er betides, Thy love abides,
Our God for evermore !

JOHN W. CHADWICK.

April 21.

*If any man will come after Me, let him deny himself, and
take up his cross, and follow Me.* — MATT. xvii. 24.

BE not content with merely living ; desire to live fruit
fully, joyfully, with an ever-enlarging experience
of the life-giving power of Jesus. Be much with Jesus,
hold fast to His guiding hand, bear the daily cross with
patience, be faithful in duty, and Jesus shall, by and by,
give you a crown of life which fadeth not away.

O SILENT LAMB.

O SILENT Lamb, for me Thou hast endured, —
Jesus, thou holy, perfect, sinless One ;
Thy grief and bitter anguish have secured
My soul's salvation when this race is run.
Then let me, to Thine image true,
Thus meekly suffer, with the crown in view

The narrow way that leads us up to heaven
  Must here through strife and tribulation lie ;
Then on the thorny path may strength be given,
  This sinful flesh, O Lord, to crucify.
Oh, take this feebleness away,
And make me strong to bear each future day.

Here daily crosses come to try our weakness,
  Here every member must some burden bear ;
But oh, my Saviour, if I take with meekness
  The cross appointed by Thy love and care,
Too great, too long, it will not be,
For it is weighed and measured out by Thee.

If thus we journey patiently through sadness,
  Each grief will make us dearer to our Lord ;
But if we flee the cross in search of gladness,
  We cannot shun His dread avenging sword.
Oh, blessed they who hear the call,
Who take the cross and follow, leaving all.

HYMNS FROM THE LAND OF LUTHER.

April 22.

My presence shall go with thee, and I will give thee rest.
— Ex. xxxiii. 14.

THERE may be hours of prostration when we ask only
for *rest ;* we pray for the cessation of suffering ; we
seek repose from conflict with ourselves and with God's
providence. But God gives us more. He is more generous than we have dared to believe. He gives us joy ;
He gives us liberty ; He gives us victory ; He gives us a
sense of self-conquest, and of union with Himself in an
eternal friendship. On the basis of that single experience
of Christ as a reality, because a necessity, there rises an
experience of blessedness in communion with God, which
prayer expresses like a Revelation. Such devotion is a
jubilant Psalm.

AUSTIN PHELPS.

I AM tired. Heart and feet
Turn from busy mart and street ;
I am tired : rest is sweet.

I am tired. I have played
In the sunshine and the shade ;
I have seen the flowers fade.

I am tired. I have had
What has made my spirit glad,
What has made my spirit sad.

I am tired. Loss and gain !
Golden sheaves and scattered grain,
Day has not been spent in vain.

I am tired. Eventide
Bids me lay my cares aside,
Bids me in my hopes abide.

I am tired. God is near ;
Let me sleep without a fear,
. Let me die without a tear.

I am tired. I would rest
As the bird within its nest ;
I am tired. Home is best.

———◆———

April 23.

*If ye abide in Me, and My words abide in you, ye shall
ask what ye will, and it shall be done unto you. —*
JOHN XV. 7.

ABIDE with us, that we may feel that our sins are
forgiven. Abide with us, for we see in the past our
follies and our faults, and would do wrong no more.
Abide with us as we lie down to gentle sleep, that it may
be refreshing to us ; that pure thoughts may keep the
portals of our dreams, and God's blessing hold watch
over us.   E. H. CHAPIN.

ABIDE IN ME.

THAT mystic word of Thine, O sovereign Lord
  Is all too pure, too high, too deep for me ;
Weary with striving, and with longing faint,
  I breathe it back again in prayer to Thee.

Abide in me, o'ershadow by Thy love
  Each half-formed purpose, and dark thought of sin ;
Quench, ere it rise, each selfish, low desire,
  And keep my soul as Thine, calm and divine.

The soul, alone, like a neglected harp,
  Grows out of tune, and needs that Hand divine :
Dwell Thou within it ! tune and touch the chord,
  Till every note and string shall answer Thine !

Abide in me, — there have been moments pure
  When I have seen Thy face and felt Thy power ;
Then evil lost its grasp, and passion, hushed,
  Owned the divine enchantment of the hour.

These were but seasons beautiful and rare;
  Abide in me, and they shall ever be ;
I pray Thee now, fulfil my earnest prayer, —
  Come and abide in me, and I in Thee !

                              HARRIET BEECHER STOWE.

———◆———

April 24.

And where the Spirit of the Lord is, there is liberty. —
2 COR. iii. 17.

THAT we are bound to God is as great a restriction of
  our liberty as it is to a plant's freedom to be held
by the sun ; to the child's liberty that the double-orbed
love of father and mother bears it up from cradled nothingness to manly power ; or to the human heart's liberty,
when, finding another life, two souls move through the
sphere of love, flying now with double wings, but one
spirit.   No man has come to himself who has not known
what it is to be utterly forgetful of self in loving ; and no
man has yet learned to love who has not felt his heart
beat upon the bosom of God.

FATHER ! I know that all my life
  Is portioned out for me ;
The changes that will surely come
  I do not fear to see ;
I ask Thee for a subject mind,
  Intent on pleasing Thee.

I ask Thee for a thoughtful love,
  Through constant watching wise,
To meet the glad with joyful smiles,
  To wipe the weeping eyes ;
A heart at leisure from itself
  To soothe and sympathize.

I would not have the restless will
  That hurries to and fro,
Seeking for some great thing to do,
  Or secret thing to know :
I would be treated as a child,
  And guided where I go.

My God, I ask for daily strength,
  To none that ask denied ;
A mind to blend with outward life,
  While keeping at Thy side,
Content to fill a little space,
  If Thou be glorified.

                          ANNA L. WARING

———◆——

April 25.

Father, . . . not My will, but Thine, be done. — LUKE
xxii. 42.

LET a man come out of the fogs and the mists into the
  clear air of the upper world, and he passes at once
into a serene region of peace. He feels that the Highest
has charge of his life and his fortunes. " Consider the
fowls of the air and the lilies of the field," has then new
meanings for him, for he is trying to live, like them, a life
of trust and of hope. He can rest as they rest in the
fatherly care which is over them. It is self-will, — the
schemes and aims which our own hearts condemn, which

spoil our trust in God. Try what blessed peace will enter into you, if you can but say from the heart, " Father, not my will, but thine, be done." And why? On what does the peace rest? " Your heavenly Father knoweth that ye have need of all these things." He is not trying to train you to a sublime indifference. He knows hunger, thirst, weariness, and heart-ache. He knows the tension of the heart-fibres which cling to the beings whom you most tenderly love. He knows your need of all these, and will not mock the cry of the hunger of your hearts. See, he feeds the birds and clothes the lilies. What rare beauty, what lavish bounty ! And shall he not much more feed and clothe you, O ye of little faith ! on the altar of whose salvation He has laid the life-blood of His only begotten and well-beloved Son?

THE SONG-SPARROW.

In this sweet, tranquil afternoon of spring,
    While the low sun declines in the clear west,
I sit and hear the blithe song-sparrow sing
    His strain of rapture not to be suppressed ;
Pondering life's problem strange, while death draws near
I listen to his dauntless song of cheer.

His shadow flits across the quiet stone.
    Like that brief transit is my space of days ;
For, like a flower's faint perfume, youth has flown
    Already, and there rests on all life's ways
A dimness ; closer my beloved I clasp,
For all dear things seem slipping from my grasp.

Death touches all ; the light of loving eyes
    Goes out in darkness ; comfort is withdrawn ;
Lonely and lonelier still the pathway lies,
    Going toward the fading sunset from the dawn ;
Yet hark ! while those fine notes the silence break
As if all trouble were some grave mistake !

Thou little bird, how canst thou thus rejoice,
    As if the world had known no sin nor curse ?
God never meant to mock us with that voice !
    That is the key-note of the universe, —
That song of perfect trust, of perfect cheer,
Courageous, constant, free of doubt or fear.

My little helper, ah, my comrade sweet,
  My old companion in that far-off time
When on life's threshold childhood's wingèd feet
  Danced in the sunrise! Joy was at its prime
When all my heart responded to thy song,
Unconscious of earth's discords harsh and strong.

Now, grown aweary, sad with change and loss,
  With the enigma of myself dismayed ;
Poor, save in deep desire to bear the cross
  God's hand on his defenceless creatures laid,
With patience, — here I sit this eve of spring,
And listen with bowed head while thou dost sing.

And slowly all my soul with comfort fills,
  And the old hope revives, and courage grows ;
Up the deserted shore a fresh tide thrills,
  And like a dream the dark mood melts and goes,
And with thy joy again will I rejoice ;
God never meant to mock us with that voice !

CELIA THAXTER.

—◆—

April 26.

*Thine eyes shall see the King in His beauty ; they shall
behold the land that is very far off.* — ISA. xxxiii. 17.

WE are embosomed in fearful mysteries. We stand
related to that which is highest and greatest
in the universe ; and though we may be frivolous, we
become conscious that life is not frivolous, but most
serious and in earnest. And, then, too, trailing its dread
shadow across the skies, comes over us the idea of death.
One companion after another is taken away, till we almost look into the open gates of eternity. In a few
years we must pass the dread boundary. What is there
beyond? The eye sees not, the mind falls back appalled
from before the clouded mystery.

We can hear the beating of the surf, the faint murmur
of the sea on whose dark waters we must soon embark.
But what doom is beyond, who shall declare? We feel

that our hope in that untrodden eternity must depend on
having wills and inclinations submitted to the will of Him
who is over all. Whatever is best in the human heart,
and grandest in human relations, and most awful in human
destiny, declares the necessity of the Christian heart and
life.

EPHRAIM PEABODY.

THE LAND THAT IS VERY FAR OFF.

UPON the shore of Evermore,
We stand like children at their play,
    And gather shells,
    Where sinks and swells
The mighty sea from far away.

Upon that beach, nor voice nor speech
Doth things intelligible say,
    But o'er our souls
    A whisper rolls
That comes to us from far away.

Into our ears the voice of years
Comes deeper, deeper, day by day ;
    We stoop to hear,
    As it draws near,
Its awfulness from far away.

And o'er that tide, far out and wide,
The longings of our souls do stray ;
    We long to go,
    We do not know
Where it may be, — but far away.

We 'll trust the wave, and Him to save,
Beneath whose feet as marble lay
    The rolling deep ;
    For He can keep
Our souls, in that dim Far-away.

For ye know how that afterward, when he would have inherited the blessing, he was rejected: for he found no place of repentance, though he sought it carefully with tears. — HEB. xii. 17.

For we have not an high priest which cannot be touched with the feeling of our infirmities: but was in all points tempted like as we are, yet without sin. — HEB. iv. 15.

AS the sun and rain visit all Nature, but it is only where the hand of cultivation has been that the precious grain is reaped, and yet all the labor in the world could not reap a kernel without the sun and rain; so the divine Spirit folds all minds, but the growth is poor without inward industry, though all human struggles could bring forth not one germ of virtue without that Spirit.

MY SEED.

GOD gave to me a seed
Out of His garden, for my plot of earth;
Something He told me of its priceless worth,
    That I might tend and feed;
Yet, when it grew, I counted it a weed.

I left it for the sky
To nourish, or the night-frost to destroy;
Its sprouting for a moment gave me joy,
    But soon I passed it by, —
The plant that God had given, I let it die.

I know the beauty now
That would have grown up brightly from my seed;
And if my tears my perished flower could feed,
    It soon would grow, I trow.
I cannot make it live; my God, wilt Thou?

SUNDAY MAGAZINE

April 28.

How long dost Thou make us to doubt ? — JOHN x. 24.

FAITH, which is the source of so much human happiness, is the mainspring of human activity. It moves more than half the machinery of life. What leads the husbandman, for example, to yoke his horses when, no bud bursting to clothe the naked trees, no bird singing in hedgerows or frosty skies, Nature seems dead? With faith in the regularity of her laws, in the ordinance of her God, he believes that she is not dead but sleepeth ; and so he ploughs and sows in the certain expectation that he shall reap, and that these bare fields shall be green in summer with waving corn, and be merry in autumn with sun-browned reapers. The farmer is a man of faith. So is the seaman. No braver man than he who goes down to see God's wonders in the deep. Venturing his frail bark on a sea ploughed by so many keels, but wearing on its bosom the furrows of none, with neither path to follow nor star to guide, the mariner knows no fear. When the last blue hill has dipped beneath the wave, and he is alone on a shoreless sea, he is calm and confident, — his faith in the compass-needle, which, however his ship may turn, or roll, or plunge, ever points true to the north. An example his to be followed by the Christian with his Bible ; on that faith venturing his all, life, crew, and cargo, he steers his way boldly through darkest nights and stormiest oceans, with nothing but a thin plank between him and the grave. And though metaphysicians and divines have involved this matter of faith in mystery, be assured that there is nothing more needed for your salvation or mine, than that God would inspire us with a belief in the declarations of His word, as real, heartfelt, and practical as that which we put in the laws of Providence, — in the due return of day and night, summer and winter, seedtime and harvest.

THOMAS GUTHRIE.

UNBELIEF.

THERE is no unbelief;
Whoever plants a leaf beneath the sod,
And waits to see it push away the clod,
　　He trusts in God.

Whoever says, when clouds are in the sky,
" Be patient, heart, light breaketh by and by ! "
　　Trusts the Most High.

Whoever sees, 'neath Winter's field of snow,
The silent harvest of the future grow,
　　God's power must know.

Whoever lies down on his couch to sleep,
Content to lock each sense in slumber deep,
　　Knows God will keep.

Whoever says, " To-morrow," " The unknown,'
" The future," trusts unto that power alone
　　He dares disown.

The heart that looks on when the eyelids close,
And dares to live when life has only woes,
　　God's comfort knows.

There is no unbelief;
And day by day and night unconsciously,
The heart lives by that faith the lips deny;
　　God knoweth why.

MRS. LIZZIE YORK CASE.

April 29.

And forgive us our sins. . . . And lead us not into temptation ; but deliver us from evil. — LUKE xi. 4.

HUMAN life is a constant want, and ought to be a constant prayer.
OSGOOD.

THOUGHT and prayer both come from a hidden source ; they go forth to fight with foes and gain victory in the external world ; they return to rest in Him who inspired them. Oh ! how fresh and original will each of our lives become, what flatness will pass from society, what excitement and restlessness from our religious acts, when we understand these secrets ! — when the morning prayer is really a prayer for grace to One whose service is perfect freedom, in knowledge of whom is eternal life ; when at evening we really ask One from whom all good thoughts and holy desires and just works proceed for the peace which the world cannot give.
F. D. MAURICE.

EVENING.

FATHER ! by Thy love and power
Comes again the evening hour ;
Light has vanished, labors cease,
Weary creatures rest in peace.
Thou, whose genial dews distil
  On the lowliest weed that grows,
Father ! guard our couch from ill,
  Lull Thy children to repose.
We to Thee ourselves resign,
Let our latest thoughts be Thine.

Saviour ! to Thy Father bear
This our feeble evening prayer ;
Thou hast seen how oft to-day
We, like sheep, have gone astray ;
Worldly thoughts, and thoughts of pride,
  Wishes to Thy cross untrue,
Secret faults, and undescried,
  Meet Thy spirit-piercing view.
Blessed Saviour ! yet through Thee
Pray that these may pardoned be.

April 30.

The Lord shall preserve thee. from all evil; He shall pre-serve thy soul. — Ps. cxxi. 7.

PRAYER is not eloquence, but earnestness; not the definition of helplessness, but the feeling of it; it is the cry of faith to the ear of mercy.

Each thing lives according to its kind : the heart by love, the intellect by truth, the higher nature of man by intimate communion with God.

E. H. CHAPIN.

Holy Spirit ! breath of balm !
Fall on us in evening's calm !
Yet awhile before we sleep
We with Thee will vigils keep ;
Lead us on our sins to muse,
　　Give us truest penitence,
Then the love of God infuse,
　　Breathing humble confidence ;
Melt our spirits, mould our will,
Soften, strengthen, comfort still !

Blessed Trinity ! be near
Through the hours of darkness drear ;
When the help of man is far,
Ye more clearly present are ;
Father, Son, and Holy Ghost,
　　Watch o'er our defenceless head ;
Let your angels, guardian host,
　　Keep all evil from our bed
Till the flood of morning rays
Wake us to a song of praise !

May 1.

*And other sheep I have, which are not of this fold : them
also I must bring, and they shall hear My voice ; and
there shall be one fold, and one shepherd.* — JOHN
x. 16.

LET us hear, oh, let us hear to-day, the Shepherd's
voice, and, as He knows us in our sin, so let us
go after Him in His sacrifice.   Let us claim that inspiration, that ennobled confidence, that comes of being
truly with Him.   Folded thus in His personal care, and
led by the calling of His voice, for which we always
listen, let us take His promise and follow, going in and
out and finding pasture.

> BEYOND the land, beyond the sea,
> There shall be rest for thee and me,
> For thee and me and those we love.
> I heard a promise gently fall,
> I heard a far-off shepherd call
> The weary and the broken-hearted,
> Promising rest unto each and all.

THE FOLD.

> BLESSED fold ! no foe can enter ;
>   And no friend departeth hence ;
> Jesus is their sun, their centre,
>   And their shield Omnipotence.
> Blessed ! for the Lamb shall feed them,
>   All their tears shall wipe away,
> To the living fountains lead them,
>   Till fruition's perfect day.

JOSIAH CONDER.

May 2.

I will lift up mine eyes unto the hills, from whence cometh my help. My help cometh from the Lord, which made heaven and earth. — Ps. cxxi. 1, 2.

TO those who "wait upon the Lord" there is always given strength adequate to the trials of the day, and there ought to be no anxiety as to the trials of the morrow. They have not already in hand the grace that may be needed for future duties and dangers; but they know it to be in better keeping than their own, and certain to be furnished precisely when required. Oh, the peace which a true Christian might possess, if he would take God at His word, and trust Him to make good His promises. It is hard to say what could then ruffle him, or what, at least, could permanently disturb. Day by day his duties might be more arduous, his temptations stronger, his trials more severe. But he would ascertain that the imparted strength grew at the same rate, so that he was always equal to the duties, victorious over the temptations, and sustained under the trials. Faith ought so to people all the future with the presence, the guardianship, the love, and the faithfulness of God, that the soul in her journeyings and searchings should find no cause for anxiety and no ground for fear.

QUIET.

THE quiver of my fears is empty quite;
And do you ask me whence my confidence?
Whence the unsetting sun which gives me light?
The sure hedge which my helplessness doth fence;
My quiet, which no storm disturbeth? Whence
The hopefulness no terror can affright?

I answer that it is my life which fills
My heart with courage, as the flowing rills
Live from the crystal waters of the sky,
Which hourly hope and joyful strength instils.
My quiet comes from the eternal hills,
Which in the everlasting sunshine lie.

May 3.

For we have great joy and consolation in thy love. —
PHILEMON vii.

GOD will suffer none of us to be robbed by circumstances of that which is essential to the progress of our being. The inner sunlight, like the outer, shines alike for all.

IT is a great thing when our Gethsemane hours come, when the cup of bitterness is pressed to our lips, and when we pray that it may pass away, to feel that it is not fate, that it is not necessity, but divine love for good ends working upon us.

E. H. CHAPIN.

GOD'S PRESENCE.

THOU infinite in love !
  Guide this bewildered mind,
Which, like the trembling dove,
  No resting-place can find,
On the wild waters. God of light,
Through the thick darkness lead me right !

Bid the fierce conflict cease,
  And fear and anguish fly ;
Let there again be peace
  As in the days gone by ;
In Jesus' name I cry to Thee,
Remembering Gethsemane.

Fain would earth's true and dear
  Save me in this dark hour ;
And art not Thou more near ?
  Art Thou not love and power ?
Vain is the help of man ; but Thou
Canst send deliverance even now.

Though through the future's shade
  Pale phantoms I descry,
Let me not shrink dismayed,
  But ever feel Thee nigh.
There may be grief, and pain, and care,
But, O my Father ! Thou art there.

May 4.

Into Thine hand I commit my spirit ; Thou hast redeemed me, O Lord God of truth. — Ps. xxxi. 5.

THERE is no holiness if Thou, Lord, withdraw Thy presence ; no wisdom profiteth if Thy Spirit cease to direct ; no strength availeth without Thy support ; no chastity is safe without Thy protection ; no watchfulness effectual when Thy holy vigilance is not on guard !

THOMAS À KEMPIS.

PRAYER.

LORD, thine eye is closèd never ;
When night casts o'er earth her hood,
Thou remainest wakeful ever,
And art like a shepherd good,
Who, through every darksome hour,
Tends his flock with watchful power.

Grant, O Lord ! that we Thy sheep
May this night in safety sleep ;
And when we again awake,
Give us strength our cross to take,
And to order all our ways
To Thine honor and Thy praise.

Or, if Thou hast willed that I
Must before the morning die,
Into Thy hands to the end,
Soul and body I commend.

Amen.

SONGS FROM THE GERMAN.

May 5.

Blessed are the pure in heart; for they shall see God. —
MATT. V. 8.

THE Christian soul is one that has come unto God,
and rested in the peace of God. It dares to call
Him Father ; it is strong with His strength, having all its
faculties in a glorious play of energy. It turns adversity
into peace, for it sees a friendly hand ministering only
good in what it suffers. In dark times it is never anxious ;
for God is its trust, and God will suffer no harm to befall
it. Having the testimony within that it pleases God, it
approves itself in the holy smile of God, that consciously
rests upon it. Divinely guided, walking in the spirit, it
is raised by a kind of inspiration. It sees God and
knows Him by an immediate and ever-present knowledge ;
according even to the promise, " Blessed are the pure in
heart."

HORACE BUSHNELL.

THE PURE IN HEART.

I ASKED the angels in my prayer,
With bitter tears and pains,
To show mine eyes the kingdom where
The Lord of glory reigns.

I said, My way with doubt is dim,
My heart is sick with fear;
Oh, come, and help me build to Him
A tabernacle here !

The storms of sorrow wildly beat,
The clouds with death are chill ;
I long to hear His voice so sweet,
Who whispered, " Peace, be still ! "

The angels said, God giveth you
His love; what more is ours ?
And even as the gentle dew
Descends upon the flowers,

His grace descends, and, as of old,
  He walks with man apart,
Keeping the promise, as foretold,
  With all the pure in heart.

Thou need'st not ask the angels where
  His habitations be,
Keep thou thy spirit clean and fair,
  And He shall dwell with thee.

ALICE CARY.

May 6.

*Therefore with joy shall ye draw water out of the wells of
salvation.* — ISA. xii. 3.

AMID the strife of systems and the war of words our
souls are thirsting for the living God. We long to
find and know Him, to touch Him with the outstretched
hands of faith and love, to feel Him drawing near to us,
and filling the dry cisterns of our lives with the sweet,
clear waters of Divine communion.   Even as one who
has wandered long in the desert yearns and pants for the
flowing spring, so our heart and flesh cry out for God.
After all, this is the deepest need of humanity.

DRAWING WATER.

I HAD drunk, with lips unsated,
  Where the fonts of pleasure burst ;
I had hewn out broken cisterns,
  And they mocked my spirit's thirst ;

And I said, "Life is a desert,
  Measureless, and ever dry,
And God will not give me water
  Though I pray, and faint, and die."

Spoke there then a friend and brother ·
  " Rise and roll the stone away !
There are wells of water hidden
  In thy pathway every day."

Then I said (my heart was sinful ;
  Very sinful was my speech), —
" All the wells of God's salvation
  Are too deep for me to reach."

And he answered, " Rise and labor !
  Doubt and idleness are death ;
Shape thee out a goodly vessel
  With the strong hands of thy faith."

So I wrought and shaped the vessel,
  Then bent, lowly, kneeling there,
And I drew up living water,
  With the golden chain of prayer.

PHŒBE CARY.

May 7.

*And He went a little farther, and fell on His face, and
prayed, saying, O My Father, if it be possible, let this
cup pass from Me : nevertheless, not as I will, but as
Thou wilt.* — MATT. xxvi. 39.

BUT what can we do?   God has so ordered and
balanced this life, that therein we have to learn
and practise the knowledge of His divine and perfect
will, so that we may prove ourselves whether we love and
esteem His will more than our own selves, and than all He
has given us to love and possess on earth.   LUTHER.

LORD, AS THOU WILT.

IT is so sweet to live
  My little life to-day
That I would never leave it, if
  I might forever stay !
  I sometimes say.

I am so weary, Lord,
  I would lie down for aye,
Could I but hear Thee speak the word,
  " Thy sins are washed away !"
  I sometimes say.

> The better mood that lies
>   These moods between, midway,
> Comes softly, and I lift my eyes,
>   " Lord, as Thou wilt ! " I pray ;
>   And would alway.

———◆———

May 8.

*As for man, his days are as grass: as a flower of the
field, so he flourisheth. For the wind passeth over
it, and it is gone ; and the place thereof shall know it
no more.* — Ps. ciii. 15, 16.

AS emblems of humanity, blossoms are particularly
beautiful and expressive. Tongues of Nature, they
are eloquent with divine teachings, which reach at times
the inner ear with a strange power. Man sees his own
fate reflected in their short-lived beauty. As light a hold
as they has he of the tree of life.   HUGH MACMILLAN.

TO BLOSSOMS.

> FAIR pledges of a fruitful tree,
>   Why do ye fall so fast ?
>   Your date is not so past.
> But you may stay yet here awhile
>   To blush and gently smile,
>   Then go at last.
>
> What, were ye born to be
>   An hour or half's delight,
>   And so to bid good-night ?
> 'T was pity Nature brought ye forth
>   Merely to show your worth,
>   And lose you quite.
>
> But you are lovely leaves, where we
>   May read how soon things have
>   Their end, though ne'er so brave ;
> And after they have shown their pride,
>   Like you, awhile, they glide
>   Into the grave.
>   ROBERT HERRICK

May 9.

I will not leave you comfortless ; I will come to you. —
JOHN xiv. 18.
Lo, I am with you alway. — MATT. xxviii. 20.

AS the same blue sky smiles upon the ruin, which
smiled upon the perfect structure, so the same beneficent Providence bends over our shattered hopes and
our answered prayers. GEORGE S. HILLARD

SORROW AND CONSOLATION.

WHAT lack the valleys and mountains
That once were green and gay?
What lack the babbling fountains?
Their voice is sad to-day.
Only the sound of a voice,
Tender and sweet and low,
That made the earth rejoice
A year ago.

What lack the tender flowers?
A shadow is on the sun.
What lack the merry hours,
That I long that they were done?
Only two smiling eyes
That told of joy and mirth ;
They are shining in the skies,
I mourn on earth!

ADELAIDE A. PROCTER

ALL are not taken ! there yet are left behind
Living beloveds, tender looks to bring
And make the daylight still a happy thing ;
And tender voices, to make soft the wind.
But if it were not so, — if I could find
No love in all the world for comforting,
Nor any path but hollowly did ring,
Where "dust to dust" the love from life disjoined ;
And if before those sepulchres unmoving
I stood alone, as some forsaken lamb
Goes bleating up the moors in weary dearth,
Crying, "Where are ye, O my loved and loving?" —
I know a voice would sound, "Daughter, *I am.*
Can I suffice for Heaven, and not for earth?"

ELIZABETH BARRETT BROWNING.

May 10.

And we know that all things work together for good to them that love God, to them who are the called according to His purpose. — ROM. viii. 28.

PAIN is in some wise the artist of the world which creates us, fashions us, sculptures us with the fine edge of a pitiless chisel. It limits the overflowing life ; and that which remains, stronger and more exquisite, enriched by its very loss, draws thence the gift of a higher being.

MICHELET

THY ROD.

THY rod fell on me, stern at first, then soft
As parents' kisses, till the wound was healed ;
And I went forth a laborer in Thy field ; —
They best can bind who have been bruisèd oft.

And Thou wert pitiful. I came heart-sore,
And drank Thy cup because earth's cups ran dry ;
Thou slewest me not for that impiety,
But mad'st the draught so sweet, I thirst no more.

I came for silence, heavy rest, or death :
Thou gavest instead, life, peace, and holy toil;
My sighing lips from sorrow didst assoil,
And fill with righteous thankfulness each breath.

I thank Thee for all joy and for all pain :
For healèd pangs, for years of calm content :
For blessedness of spending and being spent
In Thy high service where all loss is gain.

DINAH MULOCH CRAIK

May 11.

I will lift up mine eyes unto the hills, from whence cometh my help. — Ps. cxxi. 1.

THE heavy thought is the thought of what we were, of what we hoped and purposed to have been, of what we ought to have been, of what but for ourselves we might have been, set by the side of what we are. This is a thought the crushing weight of which nothing but a strength above our own can lighten.

JULIUS C. HARE.

UNATTAINED.

TIRED, tired and spent, the day is almost run, —
And oh! so little done!
Above, and far beyond, far out of sight,
Height over height,
I know the distant hills I should have trod —
The hills of God —
Lift up their airy peaks, crest over crest,
Where I had prest
My faltering, weary feet, had strength been given,
And found my heaven.
Yet once, ah, once, the place where I now stand
The promised land
Seemed to my young rapt vision, from afar;
The morning star
Shone for my guidance, beckoned me along;
At break of day
The path looked strewn with flowers; in that white light
Each distant height
Smiled at me like a friend, — a faithful friend, —
Sure that the end
Would soon, ah, soon repay with sweet redress
All weariness.
But, when the time wore on, and in the bright
And searching light
Of high noonday, I lifted up my eyes,
The purple dyes,
Through which I had descried my mountain height,
Had vanished quite.
Then suddenly I knew that I did stand
Within the promised land

Of youth's fair dreams and hopes ; but, with a thrill,
      I saw that still
Above, and far beyond, far out of sight,
      Height over height,
Lifted the fairer hills I should have trod, —
      The hills of God !

NORA PERRY.

May 12.

Teach me to do Thy will ; for Thou art my God. — Ps.
cxliii. 10.

LOOK up to God, and say, " Make use of me for
the future as Thou wilt. I am of the same mind ;
I am equal with Thee. I refuse nothing which seems
good to Thee. Lead me whither Thou wilt. Clothe me
in whatever dress Thou wilt. Is it Thy will that I should
be in a public or private condition ; dwell here, or be
banished ; be poor or rich ? Under all these circumstances I will make Thy defence to men. I will show
what the nature of everything is."

EPICTETUS.

PRAYERS.

O Jesu sweet, grant that Thy grace
    Always so work in me,
I may desire the thing to do
    Most pleasing unto Thee.

O Jesu meek, Thy will be mine,
    My will be Thine also ;
And that my will may follow Thine
    In pleasure, pain, and woe.

O Jesu, what is good for me
    Is aye best known to Thee ;
Therefore according to Thy will
    Have mercy now on me.

WILLIAM HUMISS.

May 13.

In the Lord put I my trust ; how say ye to my soul, Flee as a bird to your mountain ? — Ps. xi. 1.

THE lord of the winged race is he who does not rest. The chief of navigators is he who never reaches his bourn. Let us envy nothing. No existence is really free here below, no career is sufficiently extensive, no power of flight sufficiently great, no wing can satisfy. The most powerful is but a temporary substitute. The soul waits, demands, and hopes for others : —

> " Wings to soar above life !
> Wings to soar beyond death ! "

That sublime gift is, upon earth, only the dream and hope of another world. MICHELET.

WINGS.

> WINGS ! wings ! to sweep
> O'er mountain high and valley deep.
> Wings ! that my heart may rest
> In the radiant morning's breast.

> Wings ! to hover free
> O'er the dawn-empurpled sea,
> Wings ! above life to soar,
> And beyond death forevermore.
>
> RÜCKERT

May 14.

The Lord gave, and the Lord hath taken away; blessed be the name of the Lord. — JOB i. 21.

RESIGNATION is putting God between one's self and one's grief.

MADAME SWETCHINE.

OUR blessed Jesus walks among the roses and lilies in the garden of His church, and when He sees a wintry storm coming upon some tender plants of righteousness, He hides them in the earth to preserve life in them, that they may bloom with new glories when they shall be raised from that bed. The blessed God acts like a tender Father, and consults the safety and the honor of His children, when the hand of His mercy snatches them away before that powerful temptation comes which He foresees would have defiled and distressed and almost destroyed them.

They are not lost, but they are gone to rest a little sooner than we are. Peace be to that bed of dust where they are hidden, by the hand of their God, from unknown dangers! Blessed be our Lord Jesus, who has the keys of the grave, and never opens it for His favorites but in the wisest season.

ISAAC WATTS.

PRAYER IN SLEEP.

I SAW our darling in my dreams,
    As patient, weak, and frail
As in those sweet last days, before
    She passed beyond the Veil.

And with an anxious questioning
    I thought of all the care,
The heavy burden of our life
    God giveth us to bear.

How can her feebleness sustain
    This last new stroke of grief?
The storm she dreaded breaks at last;
    God send her soul relief!

So fervently I prayed for her,
  That God would guard and keep
Her dear heart from the touch of woe,
  It woke me from my sleep.

Then I remembered she was gone ;
  I knew she was in heaven,
Beyond the shadow of the cloud
  That o'er our sky hath driven.

No anxious care need wake for her,
  No grief, no fear, no prayer ;
There is no trouble that can reach
  Her gentle spirit there.

Thank God, who took her safely Home
  Before this sorrow fell !
It loses half its sting for us,
  Since she is shielded well.

No wish that love can frame for her,
  Nor heart's most full request
But God hath granted. In her peace,
  Heaven's peace, let love find rest.

May 15.

Fear God, and keep His commandments; for this is the whole duty of man. — ECCL. xii. 13.

WHEN a rose-bud is formed, if the soil is soft and the sky is genial, it is not long before it bursts ; for the life within is so abundant that it can no longer contain it all, — but in blossomed brightness and swimming fragrance it must needs let forth its joy, and gladden all the air. And if, when thus ripe, it refused to expand, it would quickly decay at heart, and die. And Christian charity is just piety with its petals fully spread, developing itself, and making it a happier world.

JAMES HAMILTON

MASTER, whose life-long work was doing good,
  Keep, first of all, my body out of pain ;
Then, whether of myself, or not, I would,
  Make me within the universal chain
    A link, whereby
There shall have been accomplished some slight gain
For men and women when I come to die.

ALICE CARY

THE MINISTRY OF LOVE.

I HEARD the wavelet kiss the shore, ere lost within the sea,
And the ripple of the silvery tide seemed as a psalm to me ;
Contented with God's holy will, its feeble voice to raise,
To hymn His glory, and be lost, nor thirst for human praise.
Lord, make me, like the ocean's voice, obedient to Thy will,
Thy purpose work as faithfully, and at Thy word be still.

I marked the soft dew silently descend o'er plain and hill,
On each parched herb and drooping flower the heavenly
  cloud distil.
As noiseless as the sun's first beams, it vanished with the
  day ;
But the waving fields told where it fell, when the dew had
  passed away.
Lord, make me like the gentle dew, that other hearts may
  prove,
E'en through Thy feeblest messenger, Thy ministry of love !

ANNA SHIPTON.

—◆—

May 16.

*For I am now ready to be offered, and the time of my
departure is at hand.* — 2 TIM. iv. 6.

IT is recorded of the Grecian army under Xenophon,
that when, after incredible difficulties and trials en-
countered in their perilous retreat, they had finally gained
an eminence from which, in the distance, the blue waves

of the Euxine could be faintly descried, a thrill of indescribable delight ran with electrical suddenness through
all their wearied ranks, and they burst out into one wild,
tumultuous shout, "The sea, the sea!" That tranquil
expanse of azure spoke not merely to their imaginations
as a thing of beauty to be admired ; it spoke also more
powerfully to their hearts as an object of affection to
be loved. It was to them at once a harbinger of rest, a
symbol of security, a promise of home. For that placid
wave was all that remained to divide them from their
native land, and on its remoter shores sat the peaceful and
smiling cities of Greece ; and it is with a feeling not un-
like this, that the hopeful and pious Christian, drawing
near to the close of an anxious and troubled life, approaches the limit which, like a narrow sea, divides him
from that happy home for which his spirit was created,
and for which its trials here have taught him day by day
more longingly to yearn. The tempest-tossed voyager
beholds his haven at last ; the tired wanderer of the desert
sees the land of promise at his feet ; the scarred and
weather-beaten warrior is permitted at length to lay down
his arms.

F. A. P. BARNARD

SITTING ON THE SHORE.

THE tide has ebbed away ;
No more wild dashing 'gainst the adamant rocks,
Nor swayings amidst sea-weed false that mocks
The hues of gardens gay ;
No laugh of little wavelets at their play ;
No lucid pools reflecting heaven's clear brow
Both storm and calm alike are ended now.

The rocks sit gray and lone ;
The shifting sand is spread so smooth and dry,
That not a tide might ever have swept by
Stirring it with rude moan ;
Only some weedy fragments idly thrown
To rot beneath the sky, tell what has been ;
But Desolation's self has grown serene.

Afar the mountains rise,
And the broad estuary widens out,
All sunshine; wheeling round and round about
Seaward, a white bird flies.
A bird? Nay, seems it rather in these eyes
A spirit, o'er Eternity's dim sea
Calling —" Come thou where all we glad souls be."

O life! O silent shore
Where we sit patient! O great sea beyond
To which we turn with solemn hope and fond,
But sorrowful no more!
A little while, and then we too shall soar
Like white-winged sea-birds into the Infinite Deep;
Till then, Thou, Father, wilt our spirits keep.

DINAH MULOCH CRAIK.

May 17.

*And there shall in no wise enter into it anything that de-
fileth, neither whatsoever worketh abomination or maketh a lie; but they which are written in the Lamb's
book of life.* — REV. xxi. 27.

THE soul that shuts itself and holds its peace while the
world is near grows securer in silence of contemplation, and lets out its gentle thoughts and whispering
joys, its hopes or sad fears, unto the listening ear and
before the kindly eye of God! But in souls which have
caught something of the beauty of the divine life, prayer
in many of its moods becomes more than this. There
are times of yearning and longing, far beyond the help
of the most hopeful. There is a prayer which is the voice
of the soul pleading its birthright, crying out for its immortality; it is heavenly homesickness.

HENRY WARD BEECHER.

LIGHT.

SHE thought by heaven's high wall that she did stray,
   Till she beheld the everlasting gate;
And she climbed up to it to long and wait,
Feel with her hands (for it was night), and lay
Her lips to it with kisses; thus to pray
   That it might open to her, desolate.
And lo! it trembled; lo! her passionate
Crying prevailed. A little, little way
It opened; there fell out a thread of light,
   And she saw winged wonders move therein.
Also she heard sweet talking, as they meant
To comfort her. They said, "Who comes to-night
   Shall certainly an entrance win."
Then the gate closed, and she awoke content.

JEAN INGELOW

May 18.

*Come unto me, all ye that labor and are heavy laden, and
I will give you rest.* — MATT. xi. 28.

IT is rest first, and after that all else that He holds for
us. Our rest should be like our Sabbath, — a beginning of the days. Under the Law the order was,
work at the first, and day after day until the seventh,
when labor shall end in rest. But when Christ rose from
the dead, that first day of the week became the hallowed
one, consecrated to life and rest and joy. And from that
living, joyful rest in Him, the whole being energized and
fitted for its task, the soul can go on to serve Him to the
end. It has found rest because it has ceased from working in its own strength, ceased from its own will, and now
God worketh in it to will and to do of His good pleasure.
Practically, it makes the widest possible difference whether
we work up *to* rest or from it.   SARAH F. SMILEY.

THOU hast made us for Thyself, and the heart never
resteth till it findeth rest in Thee.

SAINT AUGUSTINE.

REST.

MADE for Thyself, O God !
Made for Thy love, Thy service, Thy delight ;
Made to show forth Thy wisdom, grace, and might ;
Made for Thy praise, whom veiled archangels laud !
Oh, strange and glorious thought ! that we may be
    A joy to Thee !

Yet the heart turns away
From the grand destiny of bliss, and deems
'T was made for its poor self, for passing dreams,
Chasing illusions melting day by day,
Till, *for ourselves*, we read on this world's best :
    " This is not rest ! "

Nor can the vain toil cease,
Till in the shadowy maze of life we meet
One who can guide our aching, wayward feet
To find Himself, — our way, our life, our peace.
In Him the long unrest is soothed and stilled ;
    Our hearts are filled.

O rest so true, so sweet !
Would it were shared by all the weary world !
'Neath shadowing banner of His love unfurled
We bend to kiss the Master's piercèd feet,
Then lean our love upon His boundless breast,
    And know God's rest.

———◆———

May 19.

He will be very gracious unto thee at the voice of thy cry :
when He shall hear it, He will answer thee. — ISA.
XXX. 19.

NO cloud can overshadow a true Christian but his
faith will discern a rainbow in it.

BISHOP HORNE.

Pain and pleasure, good and evil, come to us from unexpected sources. It is not there where we have gathered up our brightest hopes that the dawn of happiness breaks. It is not there where we have glanced our eyes with affright that we find the deadliest gloom. What should this teach us? To bow to the great and only Source of light, and live humbly and with confiding resignation.

Goethe.

WEAKNESS.

We will not weep ; for God is standing by us,
And tears will blind us to the blessed sight.
We will not doubt ; if darkness still doth try us,
Our souls have promise of serenest light.

We will not faint : if heavy burdens bind us,
They press no harder than our souls can bear ;
The thorniest way is lying still behind us,
We shall be braver for the past despair.

Oh, not in doubt shall be our journey's ending !
Sin, with its fears, shall leave us at the last !
All its best hopes in glad fulfilment blending,
Life shall be with us when the death is past.

Help us, O Father ! When the world is pressing
On our frail hearts, that faint without their friend,
Help us, O Father ! let Thy constant blessing
Strengthen our weakness, till the joyful end.

May 20.

My times are in Thy hand. — Ps. xxxi. 15.

WE want a guide who knows us, whether we be self-willed and over-confident, or despondent and over-sensitive, or worldly and aspiring. We want a guide who knows our frame and pities us, is not vexed

with our ignorance or mistakes, but is tender towards us
and patient. We want a guide who values character and
knows how to train while he guides ; who guides for the
purpose of training, sometimes into very hard paths, but
profitable for the soul.

THEODORE D. WOOLSEY.

LIFE'S ANSWER.

I KNOW not if the dark or bright
    Shall be my lot ;
If that wherein my hopes delight
    Be best, or not.

It may be mine to drag for years
    Toil's heavy chain ;
Or day and night my meat be tears,
    On bed of pain.

Dear faces may surround my hearth
    With smiles and glee ;
Or I may dwell alone, and mirth
    Be strange to me.

My bark is wafted to the strand
    By breath divine ;
And on the helm there rests a hand
    Other than mine.

One who has known in storms to sail
    I have on board :
Above the raving of the gale
    I hear my Lord.

He holds me when the billows smite ;
    I shall not fall.
If sharp, 't is short ; if long, 't is light ;
    He tempers all.

Safe to the land, safe to the land, —
    The end is this :
And then with Him go hand in hand
    Far into bliss.

HENRY ALFORD, DEAN OF CANTERBURY.

May 21.

Peace I leave with you, My peace I give unto you ; not as the world giveth, give I unto you. Let not your heart be troubled, neither let it be afraid. — JOHN xiv. 27.

THERE is a spiritual proportion where every power does its work, every feeling fills its measure ; all knowledge, desire, and will, playing gently into each other, make a common current to bear the soul along to ever-new freedom and joy. The peaceful heart is quiet, not because inactive, but through intense, harmonious working. For human good, then, as for private joy, let us seek to receive the peace of Jesus, by being like Him, — active, sinless, and holy. The heavenly proportion of His spirit, a harmony in itself, was alive in gladness to every touch of the Divinity, and made His life loving to all mankind.

I WONDER many times that ever a child of God should have a sad heart, considering what the Lord is preparing for Him.

SAMUEL RUTHERFORD.

THE PEACE OF GOD.

O JESUS, why should I complain?
And why fear aught but sin ?
Distractions are but outward things ;
Thy peace dwells far within !·

These surface troubles come and go
Like rufflings of the sea ;
The deeper depth is out of reach
To all, my God, but Thee !

FREDRIC W. FABER

May 22.

Keep thy heart with all diligence; for out of it are the issues of life. — PROV. iv. 23.

H E is already half false who speculates on truth, and does not do it. Truth is given not to be *contemplated*, but to be *done*. Life is an *action*, not a *thought;* and the penalty paid by him who speculates on truth is, that by degrees the very truth he holds becomes to him a falsehood. There is no truthfulness, therefore, except in the witness borne to God by doing His will, — to live the truths we hold, or else they will be no truths at all. It was thus that He witnessed the truth. He lived it.

F. W. ROBERTSON.

TRUTH.

THOU must be true thyself,
   If thou the truth wouldst teach;
Thy soul must overflow, if thou
   Another's soul would reach;
It needs the overflow of heart
   To give the lips full speech.

Think truly, and thy thoughts
   Shall the world's famine feed;
Speak truly, and each word of thine
   Shall be a fruitful seed;
Live truly, and thy life shall be
   A great and noble Creed.

May 23.

Why art thou cast down, O my soul? and why art thou disquieted within me? hope thou in God: for I shall yet praise Him, who is the health of my countenance and my God. — Ps. xlii. 11.

THE soul which God truly leads by the hand ought to watch its path, but with a simple, tranquil vigilance confined to the present moment, and without restlessness from love of self. Its attention should be continually directed to the will of God, in order to fulfil it every instant, and not be engaged in reflex acts upon itself in order to be assured of its state, when God prefers it should be uncertain. Thus the Psalmist exclaims, " Mine eyes are ever toward the Lord ; for He shall pluck my feet out of the net."

CHILDREN OF GOD.

CHILDREN of God, who, faint and slow.
　Your pilgrim-path pursue,
In strength and weakness, joy and woe,
　To God's high calling true ! —

Why move ye thus, with lingering tread,
　A doubting, mourning band ?
Why faintly hangs the drooping head ?
Why fails the feeble hand ?

Oh, weak to know a Saviour's power,
　To feel a Father's care !
A moment's toil, a passing shower,
　Is all the grief ye share.

The orb of light, though clouds awhile
　May hide his noontide ray,
Shall soon in lovelier beauty smile
　To gild the closing day ;

And bursting through the dusky shroud
  That dared his power invest,
Ride throned in light, o'er every cloud,
  Triumphant to his rest.

Then, Christian, dry the falling tear,
  The faithless doubt remove :
Redeemed at last from guilt and fear,
  Oh, wake thy heart to love !

BOWDIER.

May 24.

Blessed are they that mourn, for they shall be comforted.
— MATT. v. 4.

HOW many a Christian pilgrim would never have seen anything of the spiritual manna, and the spiritual stream from the rock, had God listened to him when, with fear and trembling, he besought him not to lead him into a desert !

KRUMMACHER.

BLESSED ARE THEY THAT MOURN.

OH, deem not they are blessed alone
  Whose lives a peaceful tenor keep :
The Power who pities man has shown
  A blessing for the eyes that weep.

The light of smiles shall fill again
  The lids that overflow with tears ;
And weary hours of woe and pain
  Are promises of happier years.

There is a day of sunny rest
  For every dark and troubled night ;
And grief may bide an evening guest,
  But joy shall come with early light.

And thou, who o'er thy friend's low bier
  Sheddest the bitter drops like rain,
Hope that a brighter, happier sphere,
  Will give him to thy arms again.

Nor let the good man's trust depart,
  Though life its common gifts deny, —
Though with a pierced and bleeding heart,
  And spurned of men, he goes to die.

For God hath marked each sorrowing day,
  And numbered every secret tear,
And heaven's long age of bliss shall pay
  For all His children suffer here.

WILLIAM CULLEN BRYANT.

May 25.

Trust in the Lord with all thine heart; and lean not unto thine own understanding. — PROV. iii. 5.

ETERNAL God, who committest to us the swift and solemn trust of life, since we know not what a day may bring forth, but only that the hour for serving Thee is always present, may we wake to the instant claims of Thy holy will ; not waiting for to-morrow, but yielding to-day. Lay to rest, by the persuasion of Thy spirit, the resistance of our passion, indolence, or fear. Consecrate with Thy presence the way our feet may go ; and the humblest work will shine, and the roughest places be made plain. Lift us above unrighteous anger and mistrust into faith and hope and charity, by a simple and steadfast reliance on Thy sure will : and so may we be modest in our time of wealth, patient under disappointment, ready for danger, serene in death. In all things, draw us to the mind of Christ, that Thy lost image may be traced again, and Thou mayst own us at one with Him and Thee.

MARTINEAU'S SERVICE BOOK.

TRUST.

I CANNOT see, with my small, human sight,
Why God should lead this way or that for me ;
I only know He saith, " Child, follow Me ; "
  But I can trust.

I know not why my path should be at times
So straitly hedged, so strangely barred before ;
I only know God could keep wide the door ;
    But I can trust.

I find no answer, often, when beset
With questions fierce and subtle on my way,
And often have but strength to faintly pray.
    But I can trust.

I often wonder, as with trembling hand
I cast the seed along the furrowed ground,
If ripened fruit will there be found ;
    But I can trust.

I cannot know why suddenly the storm
Should rage so fiercely round me in its wrath ;
But this I know, God watches all my path,
    And I can trust.

I may not draw aside the mystic veil
That hides the unknown future from my sight ;
Nor know if for me waits the dark or light;
    But I can trust.

I have no power to look across the tide,
To see, while here, the land beyond the river ;
But this I know, I shall be God's forever ;
    So I can trust.

May 26.

*He leadeth me in the paths of righteousness for His name's
sake. — Ps. xxiii. 3.*

THERE is no uncertainty as to *what* path the Lord
has undertaken to direct; for He has written, " All
thy paths." Not only in the dark way, when we are perplexed ; not only when the heart is in heaviness through
manifold temptations ; but also when we tarry in the
pleasant shade of Elim's palm-trees, as well as by Marah's
bitter waters, — yea, all our ways He will direct and guide,
as every day's need requires.

THY WAY, O LORD.

THY way, not mine, O Lord,
   However dark it be!
Lead me by Thine own hand;
   Choose out the path for me.

Smooth let it be or rough,
   It will be still the best;
Winding or straight it matters not,
   It leads me to Thy rest.

I dare not choose my lot,
   I would not if I might;
Choose Thou for me, my God,
   So shall I walk aright.

The kingdom that I seek
   Is Thine; so let the way
That leads to it be Thine,
   Else I must surely stray.

Not mine, not mine the choice
   In things or great or small;
Be Thou my guide, my strength,
   My wisdom, and my all.

                      HORATIUS BONAR.

May 27.

*For lo, the winter is past, the rain is over and gone; The
flowers appear on the earth; the time of the singing of
birds is come.* — SONG OF SOLOMON, ii. 11, 12.

SEEING what appear to us the most irregular currents
obey a fixed and eternal law, we may be sure that
that Spirit of Truth will work as He has always worked;
that He will change nothing and yet will make all things
new.   That mighty wonder which we behold every year
when the self-same roots and stems, which were the
symbols of all that is hard and dry and separate become
clothed with verdure, full of life and joy and music, will

be exhibited in the moral world. No form will be cast away, no ordinance will be treated as worthless, nothing which has expressed the thought or belief of any man will be found unmeaning, because the Spirit of the living God will call forth every sleeping and latent power into activity; everything that has been dead, into life; all that has been divided, into harmony.

F. D. MAURICE.

THE SONG OF A SUMMER STREAM.

A FEW months ago
I was singing through the snow!
But now the blessed sunshine is filling all the land!
And the memories are lost
Of the winter fog and frost,
In the presence of the summer with her full and glowing hand.

Now the woodlark comes to drink,
At my cool and pearly brink,
And the lady-fern is bending to kiss my rainbow foam;
And the wild-rose buds entwine
With the dark-leaved bramble vine,
And the centuried oak is green around the bright-eyed squirrel's home.

Oh, the full and glad content
That my little song is blent
With the all-melodious mingling of the choristers around!
I no longer sing alone,
Through a chill, pervading moan,
For the very air is trembling with its wealth of summer sound.

Though the hope seem long deferred
Ere the south wind's whisper heard
Gave a promise of the passing of the weary winter days,
Yet the blessing was secure,
For the summer-time was sure,
When the lonely songs are gathered in a mighty choir of praise.

FRANCES RIDLEY HAVERGAL.

May 28.

The watchman said, The morning cometh, and also the night. — ISA. xxi. 12.

And it came to pass in those days, that He went out into a mountain to pray, and continued all night in prayer to God. — LUKE vi. 12.

IF one hour can be endowed with a sacredness above its fellows, it must be the hour when the Lord looseth the bands of Orion, and leadeth forth Arcturus and his sons ; then voices from worlds afar call us to contemplation and adoration, and the stillness of the lower world prepares an oratory for the devout soul.   He surely never prays at all who does not end the day — as all men wish to end their lives — in prayer.

CHARLES H. SPURGEON

NIGHT.

NIGHT is the time for rest ;
How sweet, when labors close,
To gather round the aching breast
The curtain of repose,
Stretch the tired limbs, and lay the head
Upon our own delightful bed !

Night is the time to weep ;
To wet with unseen tears
Those graves of memory, where sleep
The joys of other years ;
Hopes that were angels in their birth,
But perished young, like things on earth !

Night is the time to muse ;
Then from the eyes the soul
Takes flight, and with expanding views
Beyond the starry pole,
Descries athwart the abyss of night
The dawn of uncreated light.

Night is the time to pray ;
Our Saviour oft withdrew
To desert mountains far away ;
So will His followers do, —
Steal from the throng to haunts untrod,
And hold communion there with God.

JAMES MONTGOMERY.

May 29.

Because your sins are forgiven you for His name's sake.
— 1 JOHN ii. 12.

OUR great and most difficult duty as social beings is to
derive constant aid from society without taking its
yoke ; to open our minds to the thoughts, reasonings, and
persuasions of others, and yet to hold fast the sacred right
of private judgment ; to receive impulses from our fellow-
beings, and yet to act from our own souls ; to sympathize
with others, and yet to determine our own feelings ; to
act with others, and yet to follow our own consciences ;
to unite social deference and self-dominion ; to join
moral self-subsistence with social dependence ; to respect
others without losing self-respect ; to love our friends and
to reverence our superiors, whilst our supreme homage is
given to that moral perfection which no friend and no
superior has realized, and which, if faithfully pursued,
will often demand separation from all around us. Such
is our great work as social beings ; and to perform it we
should look habitually to Jesus Christ, who was distin-
guished by nothing more than by moral independence, —
than by resisting and overcoming the world.

THE NAME OF JESUS

To offer prayer I never durst presume,
Did not dear Jesu's name my prayer perfume ;
'T is, O my God, for the loved Jesu's sake
That day by day address to Thee I make ,
That, sinful. I dare Thee my Father own,
With humble confidence approach Thy throne.
Oh wondrous love ! which gives us free recourse
To drink our fill at love's unbounded source,
Our sorrow to unbosom, and our need,
And a rich promise for each want to plead ;
With heaven while here below to keep commerce,
Familiarly with Godhead to converse ;
To intercede for blessings on mankind, —
The pleasure of a charitable mind ;
To beg all graces, deprecate all bane,
Heaven for ourselves and others to obtain.

BISHOP KEN

May 30.

Who comforteth us in all our tribulation, that we may be able to comfort them which are in any trouble by the comfort wherewith we ourselves are comforted of God. — 2 COR. i. 4.

IS there anything more touching and pathetic in the history of man than to see how absolutely, without exception, the men and women who start out with only the need of tasks, of duties, of something which can call out their powers, and of the smile of God stimulating and encouraging them, — how they all come, one by one, certainly up to the place in life where they need consolation?

.   .   .   .

It is the lives like the stars, which simply pour down on us the calm light of their bright and faithful being, up to which we look, and out of which we gather the deepest calm and courage. No man or woman of the humblest sort can really be strong, gentle, pure, and good, without the world being better for it, without somebody being helped and comforted by the very existence of that goodness.

PHILLIPS BROOKS

COMFORT.

IF there should come a time, as well there may,
  When sudden tribulation smites thine heart,
And thou dost come to me for help, and stay,
  And comfort, how shall I perform my part?
How shall I make my heart a resting-place,
  A shelter safe for thee when terrors smite?
How shall I bring the sunshine to thy face,
  And dry thy tears in bitter woe's despite?
How shall I win the strength to keep my voice
  Steady and firm, although I hear thy sobs?
How shall I bid thy fainting soul rejoice,
  Nor mar the counsel of mine own heart-throbs?
Love, my love teaches me a certain way;
So, if thy dark hour come, I am thy stay.

I must live higher, nearer to the reach
  Of angels in their blessed trustfulness,
Learn their unselfishness, ere I can teach
  Content to thee whom I would greatly bless.
Ah me ! what woe were mine if thou shouldst come,
  Troubled, but trusting, unto me for aid,
And I should meet thee powerless and dumb, —
  Willing to help thee, but confused, afraid !
It shall not happen thus : for I will rise,
  God helping me, to higher life, and gain
Courage and strength to give thee counsel wise,
  And deeper love to bless thee in thy pain.
Fear not, dear love ! thy trial hour shall be
The dearest bond between my heart and thee.

ALL THE YEAR ROUND

May 31.

In Thee is my trust; leave not my soul destitute. — Ps. cxli. 8.

WE are not only permitted, we are commanded, to cast all our care upon God ; and that, too, upon the very principle of His caring for us. All our care ! Oh that we might learn to keep no care to ourselves, to commit our least anxieties to God, to lean upon His assistance in the performance of our least duties, upon His strength in the endurance of our least trials, upon His comforts for the soothing of our least sorrows ! If we would not exclude God from anything little, we should find Him with us in everything great. If we thought nothing beneath God, we should find nothing above Him.

HENRY MELVILL.

TRUST.

THE child leans on its parent's breast,
Leaves there its cares, and is at rest ;
The bird sits singing by its nest,
  And tells aloud
His trust in God, and so is blest
  'Neath every cloud.

He hath no store, he sows no seed,
Yet sings aloud, and doth not need ;
By flowing streams or grassy mead,
    He sings to shame
Men, who forget, in fear of need,
    A Father's name.

The heart that trusts forever sings,
And feels as light as it had wings;
A well of peace within it springs ;
    Come good or ill,
Whate'er to-day, to-morrow, brings,
    It is His will !

ISAAC WILLIAMS.

June 1.

Casting all your care upon Him ; for He careth for you.
— 1 PET. V. 7.

AND thou, when thou seest the sparrow fall and many a goodly ship suffer wreck, do not forget that we see merely a portion of the history, — that its last chapter rests in the bosom of Eternal Love ! Let us meekly wait.

FAITH can supply the want of temporal things, and faith is the grave of care.

FRIEDRICH ADOLF KRUMMACHER.

GOD CARETH.

ONE of the sweet old chapters,
    After a day like this.
The day brought tears and troubles,
    The evening brings no kiss,
Nor rest in the arms I long for, —
    Rest and refuge and home ;
Grieved and lonely and weary,
    Unto the book I come.

One of the sweet old chapters, —
The love that blossoms through
His care of the birds and lilies
Out in the meadow dew.
His evening lies soft around them,
Their faith is only *to be;*
Ah! hushed by the tender lesson,
My God, let me rest in Thee!

June 2.

Awake, thou that sleepest, and arise from the dead, and Christ shall give thee light. — EPH. V. 14.

THE heart has reasons that reason does not understand.

BISHOP JACQUES B. BOSSUET.

HEAVEN may have happiness as utterly unknown to us as the gift of perfect vision would be to a man born blind. . . . Mutual love, pure and exalted, founded on charms both mental and corporeal, as it constitutes the highest happiness on earth, may, for anything we know to the contrary, also form the lowest happiness of heaven. And it would appear consonant with the administration of Providence in other matters that there should be such a link between earth and heaven; for in all cases a chasm seems to be purposely avoided, *prudente Deo.* Thus, the material world has its links, by which it is made to shake hands, as it were, with the vegetable, the vegetable with the animal, the animal with the intellectual, and the intellectual with what we may be allowed to hope of the angelic.

C. C. COLTON.

HEAVEN is the opening of a door; it is the finding of a long-sought good, the renewal of a long-lost communion, the restoration to a favor which is in itself the fulness of joy.

A PRESENT HEAVEN.

THE HEAVENLY SPRING.

GOD does not send us strange flowers every year ;
When the spring winds blow o'er the pleasant places,
The same dear things lift up the same fair faces, —
    The violet is here.

It all comes back, — the odor, grace, and hue,
Each sweet relation of its life repeated ;
Nothing is lost, no looking-for is cheated ;
    It is the thing we knew.

So after the death-winter it will be ;
God will not put strange sights in heavenly places ;
The old love will look out from the old faces ;
    Veilchen, I shall have thee.

                    A. D. T. WHITNEY.

June 3.

They that sow in tears shall reap in joy. — Ps. cxxvi. 5.

AH, Gracious One, we toil to reap;
The soil is hard, the way is steep !

                PEARLS OF THE FAITH.

AS roots of plants, by mysterious forces, draw in the materials of life from the earth and throw them upward, and, themselves lying in darkness, minister to shining glory of blossom and leaf in the sunlight above, so prayers uttered here in darkness and tears, and with no seen results, shall in heaven disclose fruits whose transcendent loveliness the utmost wishes of earth did not measure.

REPOSE.

THERE is an hour of hallowed peace
  For those with sins oppressed,
When sighs and sorrowing tears shall cease,
  And all be hushed to rest.

'T is then the soul is freed from fears,
  And doubts that here annoy ;
There they that oft have sown in tears
  Shall reap again in joy.

There is a home of sweet repose,
  Where cares assail no more ;
The waves of endless pleasure roll
  On that celestial shore.

There purity with love appears,
  And bliss without alloy ;
There they that oft have sown in tears
  Shall reap eternal joy.

———◆———

June 4.

Remember not the sins of my youth, nor my transgressions ; according to Thy mercy remember Thou me for Thy goodness' sake, O Lord. — Ps. xxv. 7.

M Y sins are many and great ; yet if they were more, they are far below the mercy of Him that hath remitted them, and the value of His ransom that hath paid for them. We cannot do God a greater wrong than to despair of forgiveness. It is a double injury to God, first, that we offend His justice by sinning ; then, that we wrong His mercy by despairing.

BISHOP HALL.

REMEMBER NOT THE SINS OF MY YOUTH.

COULD I recall the years that now are flown
        Forevermore,
Revive my early visions, — long o'erthrown, —
        And hope restore,
How blest it were to mould my life anew,
And all my broken vows of youth renew !

Oh ! were I once again but free to choose
        As in past days,
How oft the sunlit path I would refuse
        For sterner ways !
Content to turn aside from every road
Save that which kept me in the smile of God !

But vain the dream; the strife is o'er with me ;
        Dark days remain ;
I could not trust my heart if I were free
        To choose again ;
The dazzling morning might again deceive,
Life be misspent, and age be left to grieve.

I would not, if I could, recall the years
        That now are fled :
Their cares and pleasures, labors, hopes, and fears
        For me are dead ;
I ask but mercy for the weary past,
And grace to guide me gently home at last.

                      GOOD WORDS.

June 5.

Surely I come quickly. Amen. Even so, come, Lord Jesus. — REV. xxii. 20.

LORD, I have viewed this world over in which Thou hast set me ; I have tried how this and that thing will fit my spirit, and the design of my creation, and can find nothing on which to rest ; for nothing here doth itself rest ; but such things as please me for a while in

some degree, vanish and flee as shadows from before me.
Lo! I come to Thee, the Eternal Being, the Spring of
Life, the Centre of Rest, the Stay of the Creation, the Fulness of all things.   I join myself to Thee ; with Thee I
will lead my life and spend my days, with whom I am
to dwell forever, expecting, when my little time is over,
to be taken up into Thine own eternity.

NORTH BRITISH REVIEW
(Account of ARTHUR H. HALLAM), for February, 1851.

VESPERS.

WHEN I have said my quiet say,
　　When I have sung my little song,
How sweet, methought, shall die the day
　　The valley and the hill along !
How sweet the summons. " Come away ! "
　　That calls me from the busy throng !

I thought beside the water's flow
　　Awhile to lie beneath the leaves ;
I thought in autumn's harvest glow
　　To rest my head upon the sheaves.
But lo ! methinks the day is brief
　　And cloudy ; flower, nor fruit, nor leaf,
I bring ; and yet, accepted, free,
　　And blest, my Lord, I come to Thee !

What matter now for promise lost
　　Through blast of spring or summer rains ?
What matter now for purpose crossed,
　　For broken hopes, and wasted pains ?
What if the olive little yields ?
　　What if the vine be blasted ?   Thine
The corn upon a thousand fields,
　　Upon a thousand hills the vine !

Thou lovest still the poor, — oh, blest
　　In poverty beloved to be !
Less lowly is my choice confessed. —
　　I love the rich in loving Thee.
My spirit bare before Thee stands ;
　　I bring no gift, I ask no sign ;
I come to Thee with empty hands,
　　The surer to be filled from Thine !

AUTHOR OF "THE PATIENCE OF HOPE."

June 6.

For this God is our God for ever and ever ; He will be our guide even unto death. — Ps. xlviii. 14.

THIS bodily life which we think so sacred, and which is such a mystery, as it waits on the beating pulse and runs through the throbbing, tingling veins, is unutterably less precious than the other life of God in the soul. The life of the body wastes like the dropping sand, and is daily swept away, as the dust of the floor, into the tomb, whose door swings in a thousand turnings while we speak. But the other life, that Christ gives, is not consumed. The language of Scripture lament was not taken up over that. It is no vapor, no fleeing shadow, or withering flower, but firm, bright, and blooming with immortal vigor and increase.

CYRUS A. BARTOL.

DEATH.[1]

I.

THE dew is on the summer's greenest grass
  Through which the modest daisy blushing peeps;
The gentle wind. that like a ghost doth pass,
  A waving shadow on the corn-field keeps ;
But I, who love them all, shall never be
Again among the woods, or on the moorland lea !

The sun shines sweetly, — sweeter may it shine, —
  Blessed is the brightness of a summer's day ;
It cheers lone hearts ; and why should I repine,
  Although among green fields I cannot stray ?
Woods ! I have grown, since last I heard you wave,
Familiar with death, and neighbor to the grave !

These words have shaken mighty human souls ;
  Like a sepulchre's echo drear they sound, —
E'en as the owl's wild whoop at midnight rolls
  The ivied remnants of old ruins round.
Yet wherefore tremble ? Can the soul decay ? —
Or that which thinks and feels in aught e'er fade away ?

[1] This poem is among the last of Elliott's compositions.

Are there not aspirations in each heart
    After a better, brighter world than this ?
Longings for beings nobler in each part,
    Things more exalted — steeped in deeper bliss ?
Who gave us these ? What are they ? Soul ! in thee
The bud is budding now for immortality !

ROBERT NICOLL.

———◆———

June 7.

If a man keep My saying, he shall never taste of death. —
JOHN viii. 52.

FOR when he dies, life shall so lift itself up before him,
    that for this life which he sees, he shall not be able
to see death.   For the night becomes clear light, and
bright as day, because the light and the shining of that
rising, dawning, new life, altogether quenches and shines
away this dying and self-destroying death.   LUTHER.

DEATH.

II.

DEATH comes to take me where I long to be ;
    One pang, and bright blooms the immortal flower ;
Death comes to lead me from mortality,
    To lands which know not one unhappy hour : —
I have a hope — a faith ; — from sorrow here
I 'm led by death away ; why should I start and fear ?

If I have loved the forest and the field,
    Can I not love them deeper, better, there ?
If all that power hath made, to me doth yield
    Something of good and beauty, something fair, —
Freed from the grossness of mortality,
May I not love them all, and better all enjoy ?

A change from woe to joy, from earth to heaven, —
    Death gives me this ; it leads me calmly where
The souls that long ago from mine were riven
    May meet again ! Death answers many a prayer.
Bright day, shine on ; be glad. Days brighter far
Are stretched before my eyes than those of mortal are !

I would be laid among the wildest flowers,
   I would be laid where happy hearts can come.
The worthless clay I heed not ; but in hours
   Of gushing noontide joy, it may be some
Will dwell upon my name ; and I will be
A happy spirit there, affection's look to see.

Death is upon me, yet I fear not now ; —
   Open my chamber window — let me look
Upon the silent vales, the sunny glow
   That fills each alley, close, and copsewood nook ; —
I know them — love them — mourn not them to leave ;
Existence and its change my spirit cannot grieve !

ROBERT NICOLL.

June 8.

That the Lord thy God may bless thee in all the work of thine hand which thou doest. — DEUT. xiv. 29.

BLESSED is he who has found his work ; let him ask no other blessedness. He has a work, a life-purpose ; he has found it, and will follow it ! How, as a free-flowing channel, dug and torn by noble force through the sour mud-swamp of one's existence, like an ever-deepening river there, it runs and flows ; draining off the sour, festering water gradually from the root of the remotest grass-blade ; making, instead of pestilential swamp, a green, fruitful meadow with its clear-flowing stream, — how blessed for the meadow itself, let the stream and its value be great or small ! Labor is life ; from the inmost heart of the Worker rises his God-given force, the sacred celestial life-essence, breathed into him by Almighty God ; from his inmost heart awakens him to all nobleness, to all knowledge, "self-knowledge," and much else, so soon as Work fitly begins. Knowledge ! the knowledge that will hold good in working, cleave thou to that ; for Nature herself accredits that, says Yea to that.

Properly, thou hast no other knowledge but what thou hast got by working; the rest is yet all an hypothesis of knowledge, — a thing to be argued of in schools, a thing floating in the clouds, in endless logic vortices, till we try it and fix it. "*Doubt, of whatever kind*, can be ended by Action alone." All true work is sacred; in all true Work, were it but true hand-labor, there is something of divineness. Labor, wide as the earth, has its summit in heaven.

THOMAS CARLYLE: *Past and Present.*

I AM a stream of Time, running to God my sea,
But once I shall myself the eternal ocean be.

CHERUBIC PILGRIM.

BROOK AND LIFE

I TRACED a little brook to its well-head,
Where, amid quivering weeds, its waters leap
From the earth, and hurrying into shadow, creep
   Unseen but vocal in their deep-worn bed.
   Hawthorns and hazels, interlacing, wed
With roses sweet. and overhang the steep
Mossed banks, while through the leaves stray sunbeams peep,
   And on the whispering stream faint glimmerings shed.
Thus let my life flow on, through green fields gliding,
   Unnoticed, not unuseful, in its course,
Still fresh and fragrant, though in shadow hiding,
   Holding its destined way with quiet force,
Cheered with the music of a peace abiding,
   Drawn daily from its ever-springing source.

RICHARD WILTON: *Good Words.*

June 9.

What! Could ye not watch with Me one hour? — MATT. xxvi. 40.

THE love of the things that perish can only be driven out by the strength of a superior love. Love is the pure and perfect discipline. He who is perfect in love, the love of the divinely beautiful and good, is perfect in life. He wno loves finds sacrifice holy, battle joyous, toil easy; pain nas even a sweetness when love imposes it, and tender touches purge all the anguish away. Commence your self-discipline by that which alone can complete it. Open your heart to the love of the Lord Jesus. Loving Him, all lovely things fall into their just proportion, their true relation to your being; while all unlovely things fall into their true contempt and shame. It is the one regnant principle in the free creation. It will make such order in your nature as reigns in the bright universe around you. It shines resplendent as the essential glory in the saints and angels who bow before the eternal throne.

J. BALDWIN BROWN.

TWO THAT SLEEP AND ONE THAT WATCHETH.

[Suggested by the picture by S. Solomon.]

" COULD ye not watch one hour? " The hour is late,
　And the chill air is drowsy, and they sleep, —
Two, but one sleeps not; he whose love was great,
　And who was greatly loved, his watch will keep.
The stars are clear, but not to them his eyes
　Turn to win patience from their patient light;
　Still on the earth he keeps his steadfast sight,
And bid to watch, so watches for surprise.
And so to his unsleeping eyes was given
　To see his Master's agony, that drew
　That sweat of blood; to hear that cry of woe!
'T is thus with the three priceless gifts of Heaven:
　Hope sleeps, and faith may slumber, but the few
　Who really love, nor sleep nor slumber know.

F. W. BOURDILLON

June 10.

*By Him, therefore, let us offer the sacrifice of praise to God
continually; that is, the fruit of our lips, giving
thanks to His name.* — HEB. xiii. 15.

IF one should give me a dish of sand, and tell me there
were particles of iron in it, I might look for them
with my eyes, and search for them with my clumsy fingers,
and be unable to detect them; but let me take a magnet
and sweep through it, and how would it draw to itself the
most invisible particles, by the mere power of attraction!
The unthankful heart, like my finger in the sand, discov-
ers no mercies; but let the thankful heart sweep through
the day, as the magnet finds the iron, so it will find in
every hour some heavenly blessings; only the iron in
God's sand is gold.
                          OLIVER WENDELL HOLMES.

THANKFULNESS.

My God, I thank Thee, who hast made
    The earth so bright;
So full of splendor and of joy,
    Beauty and light;
So many glorious things are here,
    Noble and right!

I thank Thee, too, that Thou hast made
    Joy to abound;
So many gentle thoughts and deeds
    Circling us round,
That in the darkest spot of earth
    Some love is found.

I thank Thee *more* that all our joy
    Is touched with pain;
That shadows fall on brightest hours;
    That thorns remain;
So that earth's bliss may be our guide,
    And not our chain.

I thank Thee, Lord, that here our souls,
    Though amply blest,
Can never find, although they seek,
    A perfect rest;
Nor ever shall, until they lean
    On Jesus' breast!

                ADELAIDE A. PROCTER.

June 11.

For whom the Lord loveth He chasteneth, and scourgeth every son whom He receiveth. — HEB. xii. 6.

IF quiet and peace could only be had by withdrawing from the duties and occupations of active life, then quiet and peace for most of us could never be. It is not in our power to fly to some far and still retreat in whose quiet we may escape the evils and troubles here. And the corner will never be found in this world where care and evil shall be unknown by human beings. But the peace which the Saviour gives His own is peace of heart and mind amid daily duties. It is that "central peace" which may subsist at the heart of endless agitation.

A. K. H. BOYD, D.D.

THY WILL BE DONE.

I PRAY not, "take my troubles all away;"
It is for love to bear them that I pray,
    And firm belief that all is for my good ;
That every trouble must be kindly meant,
Since from the hands of Him it has been sent,
    Who is my loving Father and my God.

I pray not that my days may smoothly run ;
Ah no ! I pray, Thy will alone be done !
    Yet give a childlike, trusting heart to me ;
Should the earth seek to draw my spirit down,
Oh. let my heart continue still Thine own,
    And draw me upward from the earth to Thee.

June 12.

Man goeth forth into his work, and to his labor until the evening. — Ps. civ. 23.

LIFE runs not smoothly at all seasons, even with the happiest; but after a long course the rocks subside, the views widen, and it flows on more equably at the end.

LANDOR.

Is there a doubt that a God dwells in our breast, and that souls return to heaven and reach it?

MARCUS MANILIUS.

AT THE LAST.

THE stream is calmest when it nears the tide,
And flowers are sweetest at the eventide,
And birds most musical at close of day,
And saints divinest when they pass away.

Morning is lovely, but a holier charm
Lies folded close in evening's robe of balm;
And weary man must ever love her best,
For morning calls to toil, but night to rest.

She comes from heaven, and on her wings doth bear
A holy fragrance, like the breath of prayer;
Footsteps of angels follow in her trace,
To shut the weary eyes of day in peace.

All things are hushed before her, as she throws
O'er earth and sky her mantle of repose;
There is a calm, a beauty, and a power
That morning knows not, in the evening hour.

" Until the evening " we must weep and toil,
Plough life's stern furrow, dig the weary soil,
Tread with sad feet our rough and thorny way,
And bear the heat and burden of the day.

Oh! when our sun is setting, may we glide,
Like summer evening, down the golden tide;
And leave behind us, as we pass away,
Sweet, starry twilight round our sleeping clay.

June 13.

Come, ye blessed of My Father, inherit the kingdom pre-
pared for you from the foundation of the world. —
MATT. XXV. 34.

WHEN we shall come home and enter into the possession of our Brother's fair kingdom, and when
our heads shall find the weight of the eternal crown of
glory, and when we shall look back to pains and suffering, then shall we see life and sorrow to be less than one
step or stride from a prison to glory, and that our little
inch of time-suffering is not worthy of our first night's
welcome home to heaven.

SAMUEL RUTHERFORD.

UP-HILL.

" Does the road wind up-hill all the way ? "
    " Yes, to the very end ! "
" Will the day's journey take the whole long day ? "
    " From morn to night, my friend ! "

" But is there for the night a resting-place ? "
    " A roof for all when the dark hours begin ! "
" May not the darkness hide it from my face ? "
    " You cannot miss that inn ! "

" Shall I meet other wayfarers at night ? "
    " Those who have gone before ! "
" Then must I knock or call when just in sight ? "
    " They will not keep you standing at that door ! "

" Shall I find comfort, travel-sore and weak ? "
    " Of labor you shall find the sum ! "
" Will there be beds for me and all who seek ? "
    " Yea, — beds for all who come ! "

CHRISTINA ROSSETTI.

June 14.

Yea, I have loved thee with an everlasting love; there-
fore with loving-kindness have I drawn thee. — JER.
xxxi. 3.

AS a countenance is made beautiful by the soul's
shining through it, so the world is beautiful by the
shining through it of a God.   JOHANN GEORG JACOBI.

THOSE glorify God most who look with keen eye and
loving heart on His works, who catch in all some glimpses
of beauty and power, who have a spiritual sense for good
in its dimmest manifestations, and who can so interpret the
world that it becomes a bright witness to the divinity.

CHANNING.

UNCHANGING LOVE.

FATHER, it is enough ! my full soul drank
   Such a deep draught of beauty and delight
   From this fair day, just fading into night,
How shall my lips Thy goodness ever thank ?
All is so fair; the clover-dappled bank,
The tendrilled branches drooping from the vine,
Through whose lapped leaves the glowing clusters shine,
The giants of the forest, rank on rank,
   Into the misty distance far withdrawn ;
And through them all, around, below, above,
Felt like a presence, Thy unchanging love.

June 15.

Acquaint now thyself with Him, and be at peace; thereby good shall come unto thee. — JOB xxii. 21.

PRAYER is the peace of our spirit, the stillness of our thoughts, the evenness of our recollection, the seat of our meditation, the rest of our cares, and the calm of our tempest. Prayer is the issue of a quiet mind, of untroubled thoughts; it is the daughter of charity and the sister of meekness. He that prays to God with a troubled and discomposed spirit is like him that retires into a battle to meditate, and sets up his closet in the out-quarters of an army, and chooses a frontier garrison to be wise in.

For so have I seen a lark soaring upwards, beaten back by the sighings of an eastern wind, and descending more at every breath of the tempest than it could recover by the libration and frequent weighing of his wings, till the little creature was forced to sit down and pant, and stay till the storm was over; and then it made a prosperous flight, and did rise and sing as if it had learned music and motion from an angel.

JEREMY TAYLOR

EVENING.

ONE star is trembling into sight,
   And soft as sleep the darkness falls.
   The wood-dove from the forest calls,
The bat begins his wayward flight.

Streams, murmuring in the ear of night,
   Within the woody hollows wind,
   Whose dusky boughs are intertwined
Above their music and their light.

The woodland range is dimly blue
   With smoke, that creeps from cots unseen,
   And briery hedge and meadow green
Put on their white night-robe of dew.

And every sound that breaks the calm
   Is like a lullaby to rest;
   All is at peace — except the breast
That needs the most its soothing balm.

CHAMBERS'S JOURNAL.

June 16.

It is a good thing to give thanks unto the Lord, and to sing praises unto Thy name, O Most High. To shew forth Thy loving-kindness in the morning, and Thy faithfulness every night. — Ps. xcii. 1, 2.

AS the fading coals are rekindled by a breath, so prayer refresheth the hopes of the heart.

I AM persuaded that after earnest prayer the mind is clearest and the will is freest and the judgment is wisest, and that then thoughts come to us most nearly like Divine messages. And after kneeling to God our first few steps are almost certainly in the way of eternal life. It is after having drawn nigh to God, that our feelings are most nearly like Divine guidance. WILLIAM MOUNTFORD.

EVENING SONG OF THE WEARY.

FATHER of Heaven and Earth !
I bless Thee for the night,
The soft, still night !
The holy pause of care and mirth,
Of sound and light.

Now far in glade and dell
Flower-cup and bud and bell
Have shut around the sleeping woodlark's nest;
The bee's long murmuring toils are done,
And I the o'er-wearied one,
O'er-wearied and o'erwrought.
Bless Thee, O God, O Father of the oppressed,
With my last waking thought,
In the still night !

Yes, ere I sink to rest,
By the fire's dying light,
Thou Lord of Earth and Heaven !
I bless Thee, who hast given
Unto Life's fainting travellers the night,
The soft, still, holy night !

FELECIA HEMANS.

June 17.

For He shall give His angels charge over thee, to keep thee in all thy ways. — Ps. xci. 11.

THE life of the angels is the love of uses. Selfishness and death are with them synonymous. Their offices, employments, and duties, all for the good of others, are of infinite variety. Many of them are engaged in secret and constant services to the human race. There are angels of birth and death; angels who comfort in sickness and sorrow; angels who instruct and enlighten; angels who defend from evil spirits; angels who lead the sweet thoughts of innocent children; angels who inspire conjugial love; and a thousand other genera and species of heavenly ministers.

SWEDENBORG.

THE CARE OF ANGELS.

AND is there care in heaven? And is there love
In heavenly spirits to these creatures base,
That may compassion of their evils move?
There is; else much more wretched were the case
Of men than beasts. But oh, the exceeding grace
Of highest God, that loves His creatures so,
And all His works with mercy doth embrace,
That blessed angels He sends to and fro,
To serve to wicked man to serve his wicked foe!

How oft do they their silver bowers leave,
To come to succor us who succor want!
How oft do they with golden pinions cleave
The fleeting skies, like flying pursuivant
Against foul fiends to aid us militant!
They for us fight, they watch and duly ward,
And their bright squadrons round about us plant;
And all for love, and nothing for reward.
Oh, why should heavenly God to men have such regard?

SPENSER

June 18.

Blessed are the undefiled in the way, who walk in the law of the Lord. — Ps. cxix. 1.

THERE are saint-like lives and martyr-deaths which are not recorded, and are worth all the more in Heaven's sight because unsustained by human admiration : men that have given up ambitious hopes because the paths of success were crooked and evil ; they who out of their necessities have still found something with which in Christ's name to help those still poorer ; gentle and believing hearts that bear for others what they would not for themselves ; energetic and heroic hearts that do for others what they would not for themselves,— the multitudes scattered among a myriad homes, whose lives, however imperfect, are governed by an habitual reference to the Christian law.

IN this dim world of clouding cares
We rarely know, till 'wildered eyes
See white wings lessening up the skies,
The angels with us unawares.

GERALD MASSEY.

EARTH'S ANGELS.

YES ; Earth hath angels, though their forms are moulded
    But of such clay as fashions all below ;
Though harps are wanting, and bright pinions folded,
    We know them by the love-light on the brow.

Oh, many a spirit walks the world unheeded,
    Who, when its robe of sadness is laid down,
Will soar aloft with pinions unimpeded,
    And wear its glory like a starry crown.

And if my sight, by earthly dimness hindered,
    Behold no hovering cherubim in air,
I doubt it not, for spirits know their kindred,
    They smile upon the wingless watchers there.

June 19.

When thou art in tribulation, and all these things are come upon thee, even in the latter days, if thou turn to the Lord thy God, and shalt be obedient unto His voice; (For the Lord thy God is a merciful God;) He will not forsake thee, neither destroy thee, nor forget the covenant of thy fathers, which He sware unto them. — DEUT. iv. 30, 31.

AS long as we set up our own will and our own wisdom against God's, we make that wall between us and His love which I have spoken of just now. But as soon as we lay ourselves entirely at His feet, we have enough light given us to guide our own steps; as the foot soldier who hears nothing of the councils that determine the course of the great battle he is in, hears plainly enough the word of command which he must himself obey.

GEORGE ELIOT.

HE DOETH ALL THINGS WELL.

I HOPED that with the brave and strong
  My portioned task might lie;
To toil amid the busy throng
  With purpose pure and high;
But God has fixed another part,
  And He has fixed it well;
I said so with my breaking heart
  When first this anguish fell.

These weary hours will not be lost,
  These days of misery,
These nights of darkness, tempest-tossed.
  Can I but turn to Thee;   .
With secret labor to sustain
  In patience every blow,
To gather fortitude from pain,
  And holiness from woe.

If Thou shouldst bring me back to life,
  More humble I should be,
More wise, more strengthened for the strife,
  More apt to lean on Thee.
Should death be standing at the gate,
  Thus should I keep my vow ;
But, Lord ! whatever be my fate,
  Oh, let me serve Thee now !

ANNE BRONTË

——•——

June 20.

*Behold, the Lord's hand is not shortened, that it cannot
save ; neither His ear heavy, that it cannot hear. —*
ISA. lix. 1.

SEND me that which Thou knowest is blessing, though
it may not seem blessing to me ; and deny me that
which Thou knowest is not blessing, however ready I, in
my ignorance, may be to think it so.   That is the spirit
of prayer.   When we are praying for blessings, we ought
never to pray for them absolutely ; we ought always to
pray for them if they be truly good for us ; if not, God in
answering our prayer would not be blessing us indeed.

A. K. H. BOYD.

PRAYER.

GOD liveth still !
Trust, my soul, and fear no ill ;
God is good ; from His compassion
  Earthly help and comfort flow ;
Strong is His right hand to fashion
  All things well for men below ;
Trial, oft the most distressing,
In the end has proved a blessing ;
  Wherefore then, my soul, despair ?
God still lives, who heareth prayer.

God liveth still!
Trust, my soul, and fear no ill;
He who gave the ear its mission,
　　Shall He slumber once or sleep?
He who gave the eye its vision,
　　Sees He not when mortals weep?
God is God : His ear attendeth,
When the sigh our bosom rendeth ;
　　Wherefore then, my soul, despair?
God still lives, who heareth prayer.

F. E. Cox, from the German of ZIHN.

June 21.

My soul, wait thou only upon God. — Ps. lxii. 5.

THE divine miracle *par excellence* consists surely in the apotheosis of grief, the transfiguration of evil by good. The work of creation finds its consummation, and the eternal will of the Infinite Mercy finds its fulfilment, only in the restoration of the free creature to God and of an evil world to goodness, through love. Every soul in which conversion has taken place is a symbol of the history of the world. To be happy, to possess eternal life, to be in God, to be saved, — all these are the same. All alike mean the solution of the problem, the aim of existence. And happiness is cumulative, as misery may be. An eternal growth in an unchangeable peace, an ever profounder depth of apprehension, a possession constantly more intense and more spiritual of the joy of heaven, — this is happiness. Happiness has no limits, because God has neither bottom nor bounds, and because happiness is nothing but the conquest of God through love.

HENRI FRÉDÉRIC AMIEL.

VESPER HYMN.

THE day is done ; the weary day of thought and toil is past;
Soft falls the twilight cool and gray on the tired earth at last ;
By wisest teachers wearied, by gentlest friends oppressed,
In Thee alone the soul, outworn, refreshment finds, and rest.

Bend, Gracious Spirit, from above, like these o'erarching
skies,
And to Thy firmament of love lift up these longing eyes ;
And folded by Thy sheltering hand, in refuge still and deep,
Let blessed thoughts from Thee descend, as drop the dews
of sleep.

And when refreshed the soul once more puts on new life and
power ;
Oh, let Thine image, Lord, alone, gild the first waking hour !
Let that dear Presence dawn and glow, fairer than morn's first
ray,
And Thy pure radiance overflow the splendor of the day.

So in the hastening evening, so in the coming morn,
When deeper slumber shall be given, and fresher life be
born,
Shine out, true light ! to guide my way amid that deepening
gloom ;
And rise, O Morning Star ! the first that dayspring to illume.

I cannot dread the darkness where Thou wilt watch o'er me,
Nor smile to greet the sunrise unless Thy smile I see ;
Creator, Saviour, Comforter ! on Thee my soul is cast.
At morn, at night, in earth, in heaven, be Thou my first and
last !

ELIZA SCUDDER.

June 22.

*I shewed before Him my trouble. When my spirit was
overwhelmed within me, then Thou knewest my path.*
— Ps. cxlii. 2, 3.

WHAT we need in adversity is an idea, as part of our
being, intertwined with our feeling, that God is
just as much revealed in trials as in blessings ; that His
goodness is shown in putting our moral fibre to hard
tasks that will make it athletic, and so make us permanently nobler ; as the teacher's friendship is shown in
putting the scholar to a tough lesson that makes the

mind sinewy and wise. With that principle as part of our spiritual constitution, we triumph over adversities, because the soul lives with God. When evil seems to gain wider sway, we can be calm and strong if we have the idea, as a broad, rich light around us, that God is stronger than evil, and is unspeakably more opposed to it than we are, and completely committed, now and forever, to the good.

THOMAS STARR KING.

GOD KNOWS.

GOD knows, not I, the devious way
   Wherein my faltering feet must tread,
Before, into the light of day,
   My steps from out this gloom are led ;
And since my Lord the path doth see,
What matter if 't is hid from me ?

God knows, not I, how sweet accord
   Shall grow at length from out this crash
Of earthly discords, which have jarred
   On soul and sense. I hear the clash,
Yet feel and know that on His ear
Breaks harmony, full, deep, and clear.

God knows, not I, why, when I 'd fain
   Have walked in pastures green and fair,
The path He pointed me hath lain
   Through rocky deserts, bleak and bare.
I blindly trust, since 't is His will ;
This way lies safety, that way ill.

His perfect plan I cannot grasp ;
   Yet I can trust Love Infinite,
And with my feeble fingers clasp
   The Hand that leads me to the light.
My soul upon His errand goes ;
The end I know not, but God knows.

June 23.

A new commandment I give unto you, that ye love one another; as I have loved you, that ye also love one another. — JOHN xiii. 34.

THE only preservative from this withering of the heart is love. Love is its own perennial fount of strength. The strength of affection is a proof, not of the worthiness of the object, but of the largeness of the soul which loves. Love descends, not ascends. The might of a river depends, not on the quality of the soil through which it passes, but on the inexhaustibleness and depth of the spring from which it proceeds. The greater mind cleaves to the smaller with more force than the other to it. A parent loves the child more than the child the parent, — and partly because the parent's heart is larger, not because the child is worthier. The Saviour loved His disciples infinitely more than His disciples Him, because His heart was infinitely larger. Love trusts on, ever hopes and expects better things; and this, a trust springing from itself, and out of its own deeps alone. And more than this: it is this *trusting* love that makes men what they are trusted to be, so realizing itself. Would you make men *trustworthy?* Trust them! Would you make them true? Believe them.

F. W. ROBERTSON.

FAITH.

BETTER trust all and be deceived,
   And weep that trust and that deceiving,
Than doubt one heart that, if believed,
   Had blessed one's life with true believing.

Oh, in this mocking world too fast
   The doubting fiend o'ertakes our youth!
Better be cheated to the last
   Than lose the blessed hope of truth.

FANNY KEMBLE.

June 24.

Man is like to vanity ; his days are as a shadow that passeth away. — Ps. cxliv. 4.

O BLESSED God, who neither slumberest nor sleepest, take us into Thy gracious keeping for this night, and make us mindful of that night when the noise of this busy world shall be heard by us no more. O Lord, in whom we trust, help us by Thy grace so to live that we may never be afraid to die, and grant that at the last, as now, our even-song may be : " I will lay me down in peace and sleep ; for Thou, Lord, makest me to dwell in safety."

JAMES MARTINEAU.

EVENING PRAYER.

HEAVENLY Father, hear our prayer,
  Offered through Thy holy Son ;
Evening shadows fill the air ;
  Day, with all its cares, is done.
Soon shall sleep our eyelids close ;
Let our souls in Thee repose.

Lord, Thou knowest all our ways,
  All our life is in Thy hand ;
Few and evil are our days,
  Soon cut off at Thy command ;
Like a flower at morning bright,
Broken, withered, ere the night.

Keep us, Lord, while here we stay,
  Safe beneath Thy sheltering wing ;
Let our nightly rest, we pray,
  Strength for daily labor bring ;
Ever guide us, till at last
Earthly nights and days are past.

From the French of REV. DR. CÆSAR MALAN.

June 25.

GREAT effort from great motives is the best definition of a happy life.

CHANNING.

IF there be no enemy, no fight; if no fight, no victory; if no victory, no crown.

SAVONAROLA.

BUT perhaps life is one long struggle against evil, and that he may find mercy before Thee who has had courage enough not to shrink from the combat, but carry it on to the best of his power.

ZSCHOKKE.

SAY NOT THE STRUGGLE.

SAY not, the struggle naught availeth,
    The labor and the wounds are vain,
The enemy faints not, nor faileth,
    And as things have been they remain.

If hopes were dupes, fears may be liars;
    It may be, in yon smoke concealed,
Your comrades chase e'en now the fliers,
    And, but for you, possess the field.

For while the tired waves, vainly breaking,
    Seem here no painful inch to gain,
Far back, through creeks and inlets making,
    Comes, silent, flooding in, the main.

And not by eastern windows only,
    When daylight comes, comes in the light;
In front, the sun climbs slow, how slowly!
    But westward, look, the land is bright!

ARTHUR HUGH CLOUGH.

June 26.

And now abideth faith, hope, charity, these three; but the greatest of these is charity. — 1 COR. xiii. 13.

THE flights of the human mind are not from enjoy-ment to enjoyment, but from hope to hope.

JOHNSON.

HE who despairs wants love, wants faith ; for faith, hope, and love are three torches which blend their light together nor does the one shine without the other.

METASTASIO.

EVERY Calvary has an Olivet.   To every place of cruci-fixion there is likewise a place of ascension.   The sun that was shrouded is unveiled, and heaven opens with hopes eternal to the soul which was nigh unto despair.

HENRY GILES

TRUST.

WHAT can we do, o'er whom the unbeholden
  Hangs in a night with which we cannot cope ?
What but look sunward, and with faces golden,
  Speak to each other softly of a hope ?

Can it be true, the grace He is declaring?
  Oh, let us trust Him, for His words are fair !
Man, what is this, and why art thou despairing ?
  God shall forgive thee all but thy despair.

F. W. H. MYERS

June 27.

They go from strength to strength, every one of them in Zion appeareth before God. — Ps. lxxxiv. 7.

THE child opens his eyes upon the wonder of the world, and comes to a knowledge of his powers little by little. In myself, I was never more a child, never more on the threshold of all possible good, than I am to-day. That which I have attained gives me no greater sense of completeness than that which I had as a child. The power to comprehend only reveals more and more to comprehend. The power to enjoy but reveals more and more to enjoy. The little country town of my childhood was as much to me as all New England to-day; and the New England of my childhood was as much as all the world of to-day. Slowly, by toil and pain, there has come to me a more sacred friendship, a deeper worship, a vaster thought, a more abundant delight. If this may continue; if the way may still conduct me into higher sensations, into greater knowledge, into more divine love; if the future shall open and open and open; if I may ever pursue something, as I have here; if joy shall forever go with good, and pain with evil, as here; if I may draw closer to better hearts, and draw out more of the fathomlessness of my being, — if this may be, just this, step by step, little by little, I shall not ask, for I cannot conceive, a more glorious destiny.

HERMAN BISBEE.

ETERNAL LIGHT.

SLOWLY, by God's hand unfurled,
Down around the weary world,
Falls the darkness ; oh how still
Is the working of His will !

Mighty Spirit, ever nigh,
Work in me as silently.
Veil the day's distracting sights ;
Show me heaven's eternal lights.

Living stars to view be brought,
In the boundless realms of thought;
High and infinite desires,
Flaming like those upper fires.

Holy Truth, Eternal Right,
Let them break upon my sight;
Let them shine serene and still,
And with light my being fill.

WILLIAM H. FURNESS.

June 28.

*I am come that they might have life, and that they might
have it more abundantly.* — JOHN x. 10.

THAT to the eye of Christian faith the love of our
Father shines on uneclipsed by our sorrows, that
the clouds and darkness round His throne do not mount
to His bosom, that His chastenings are affectionate, what
we call His anger only the faithfulness of His regard, and
all our various disappointment and trouble but His way
of weaning us from the world, — this belief of our religion
fills the soul with a satisfaction so deep and distending
that waves and storms, chafing and weltering by its vessel
of mortality, find no room for a drop of the threatened
anguish to come in.

CYRUS A. BARTOL.

MY HEART IS FIXED.

HAPPY are they that learn in Thee,
Though patient suffering teach,
The secret of enduring strength
And praise too deep for speech, —
Peace that no pressure from without,
No strife within, can reach.

My heart is fixed, O God my strength!
My heart is strong to bear;
I will be joyful in Thy love,
And peaceful in Thy care.
Deal with me, for my Saviour's sake,
According to His prayer.

No suffering, while it lasts, is joy,
  How blest soe'er it be ;
Yet may the chastened child be glad
  His Father's face to see.
And oh ! it is not hard to bear
  What must be borne in Thee !

Deep unto deep may call ; but I,
  With peaceful heart, will say,
Thy loving-kindness hath a charge
  No waves can take away ;
And let the storm that speeds me home
  Deal with me as it may.

ANNA L. WARING.

---◆---

June 29.

*And the peace of God, which passeth all understanding,
shall keep your hearts and minds through Christ
Jesus. —* PHIL. iv. 7.

THIS peace is the highest and most strenuous action
of the soul, but an entirely harmonious action, in
which all our powers and affections are blended in a
beautiful proportion, and sustain and perfect one another.
It is more than silence after storms. It is as the concord
of all melodious sounds ; a season when, in the fullest
flow of thought and feeling, in the universal action of the
soul, an inward calm, profound as midnight silence, yet
bright as the still summer noon, full of joy, but unbroken
by one throb of tumultuous passion, is breathed through
the spirit, and a glimpse and presage given of the serenity
of a happier world. Of this character is the peace of
religion. It is a conscious harmony with God and the
creation, an alliance of love with all beings, a sympathy
with all that is pure and happy, a surrender of every
separate will and interest, a participation of the spirit and
life of the universe, an entire concord of purpose with its
Infinite Original. Human nature has never lost sight of
this its great end. It has always sighed for a repose in
which energy of thought and will might be tempered with
an all-pervading tranquillity.

WILLIAM ELLERY CHANNING.

PEACE.

Is this the peace of God, this strange, sweet calm ?
   The weary day is at its zenith still ;
   Yet 't is as if, beside some cool, clear rill,
Through shadowy stillness, rose an evening psalm,
   And all the noise of life were hushed away,
And tranquil gladness reigned with gently soothing sway

It is not that I feel less weak, but Thou
   Wilt be my strength ; it is not that I see
   Less sin, but there is pardoning love with Thee,
And all-sufficient grace.   Enough ! and now
   I do not think or pray ; I only rest
And feel that Thou art near, and know that I am blest.

———◆———

June 30.

*Wherefore, seeing we also are compassed about with so
great a cloud of witnesses, let us lay aside every weight,
and the sin which doth so easily beset us, and let us run
with patience the race that is set before us.   Looking
unto Jesus, the author and finisher of our faith ; who,
for the joy that was set before Him, endured the cross,
despising the shame, and is set down at the right hand
of the throne of God.* — HEB. xii. 1, 2.

O LORD God, give peace unto us (for Thou hast
   given us all things) : the peace of rest, the peace of
the Sabbath, which hath no evening ; yea, give us rest in
Thee, the Sabbath of eternal life.   For Thou shalt rest in
us, as now Thou workest in us ; and Thy rest shall be
through us, as Thy works are through us.

Amen.

SAINT AUGUSTINE.

PEACE.

My soul, there is a country
  Afar beyond the stars,
Where stands a wingèd sentry
  All skilful in the wars.
There, above noise and danger,
  Sweet peace sits crowned with smiles,
And One born in a manger
  Commands the beauteous files
He is thy gracious friend,
  And (O my soul awake!)
Did in pure love descend
  To die here for thy sake.
If thou canst get but thither,
  There grows the flower of peace, —
The rose that cannot wither, —
  Thy fortress, and thy ease.
Leave, then, thy foolish ranges;
  For none can thee secure
But One who never changes, —
  Thy God, thy life, thy cure.

HENRY VAUGHAN (1621).

July 1.

*And he saw that rest was good, and the land that it was
pleasant. —* GEN. xlix. 15.

LET your rest be perfect in its season, like the rest of
waters that are still. If you will have a model for
your living, take neither the stars, for they fly without
ceasing; nor the ocean, that ebbs and flows; nor the
river, that cannot stay; but rather let your life be like
that of the summer air, which has times of noble energy
and times of perfect peace. It fills the sails of the ships
upon the sea, and the miller thanks it on the breezy
uplands; it works generally for the health and wealth of
all men, yet it claims its hours of rest.

PHILIP GILBERT HAMERTON.

IDLENESS is sweet and sacred.
When you have found a day to be idle, be idle for a day.

LANDOR.

SUMMER REST.

SOAR with the birds, and flutter with the leaf ;
  Dance with the seeded grass in fringy play ;
Sail with the cloud ; wave with the dreaming pine,
  And float with nature all the livelong day.

Call not such hours an idle waste of life ;
  Land that lies fallow gains a quiet power;
It treasures from the brooding of God's wings
  Strength to unfold the future tree and flower.

So shall it be with thee if, restful still,
  Thou rightly studiest in the summer hour ;
Like a deep fountain which a brook doth fill,
  Thy mind in seeming rest shall gather power.

MRS. HARRIET BEECHER STOWE.

July 2.

In returning and rest shall ye be saved. — ISA. xxx. 15.

A FIRM, assured patience grows upon the Christian,
enabling him to hold upon his way undeterred,
unchilled, by whatever he may meet upon it ; enabling him
also, I know not to what inner music, to build up his
spirit to a strength of calm, reliant conviction, even with
the stones he finds there ; as a brook lifts up a more clear
and rapid voice for flowing over pebbles.   The strain
upon the inner life has passed over from self to Christ.
The heart has grown wise, instructed, tolerant, tender
with weakness, patient of imperfection.

How quiet such a life is ! how fruitful ! fruitful because it is so quiet ; it works not, but lives and grows.
The uneasy effort has passed out of it.   *Unresting because
it rests always*, it has done with task-work and anxiety ;
it serves, yet is not cumbered with much serving ; it has
ceased from that sad complaint, — "Thou hast left me
to serve alone."

THE QUIET HOUR.

THE quiet of a shadow-haunted pool
  Where light breaks through in glorious tenderness,
Where the hushed pilgrim in the shadow cool
  Forgets the way's distress, —

Such is this hour, this silent hour with Thee !
  The trouble of the restless heart is still ;
And every swaying wish breathes reverently
  The whisper of Thy will.

———◆———

July 3.

*Not that we are sufficient of ourselves to think anything
as of ourselves; but our sufficiency is of God.* —
2 COR. iii. 5.

THE crucial moment is ever the present. The wise
man has not far to look to find his future. And
when the experience of to-day is deepened and lifted to
its limit of current blessedness, from that lofty altitude
the mysteries of the Highest will not be too distant.
Jesus' consciousness of divine things stands ever in from
our commoner circumference of knowledge, drawing us
to the heart of the great reality. From the centre
streams the light that makes our object and our way
plain. It is the illumination of true, perfect life shining
into and shaming all poorer experience.

EDWARD F. HAYWARD.

AL-MUGHNI.

He is sufficient, and He makes suffice ;
  Praise thus again thy Lord, mighty and wise.

God is enough ! Thou who in hope and fear
  Toilest through desert-sands of life, sore tried,
Climb trustful over Death's black ridge, for near
  The bright wells shine ; thou wilt be satisfied.

God doth suffice ! Oh thou, the patient one,
　Who puttest faith in Him, and none beside,
Bear yet thy load ; under the setting sun
　The glad tents gleam ; thou wilt be satisfied.

By God's gold Afternoon ! peace ye shall have ;
　Man is in loss except he live aright,
And help his fellow to be firm and brave,
　Faithful and patient ; then the restful night !

　　Al-Mughni ! best Rewarder ! we
　　Endure; putting our trust in Thee.
　　　　EDWIN ARNOLD: *Pearls of the Faith.*

----◆----

July 4.

*Even the youths shall faint and be weary, and the young
men shall utterly fall. But they that wait upon the
Lord shall renew their strength ; they shall mount up
with wings as eagles ; they shall run and not be weary ;
and they shall walk and not faint.*—ISA. xl. 31.

WITH an habitual sense of the Divine presence and
　　care, the trials of life are lightened. That cloud
which, drifting alone in the heavens, was so black, when
seen in the light of a merciful Providence, shines with
celestial radiance.　　　　EPHRAIM PEABODY.

　　WITH mercy and with judgment
　　　My web of time He wove,
　　And aye the dews of sorrow
　　　Were lustred with His love.
　　I 'll bless the hand that guided,
　　　I 'll bless the heart that planned,
　　When throned where glory dwelleth
　　　In Immanuel's land.

IF the way of heaven be narrow, it is not long ; and if
the gate be strait, it opens into endless life.
　　　　　　　BISHOP BEVERIDGE

SONNET.

I THINK we are too ready with complaint
In this fair world of God's. Had we no hope
Indeed beyond the zenith and the slope
Of yon gray blank of sky, we might be faint
To muse upon Eternity's constraint
Round our aspirant souls. But since the scope
Must widen early, is it well to droop,
For a few days consumed in loss and taint?
O pusillanimous heart, be comforted, —
And, like a cheerful traveller, take the rod,
Singing, beside the hedge. What if the bread
Be bitter in thine inn, and thou unshod
To meet the flints? At least it may be said,
Because the way is *short*, I thank Thee, God!

ELIZABETH BARRETT BROWNING.

—◆—

July 5.

*All things are yours ; and ye are Christ's ; and Christ is
God's.* — 1 COR. iii. 23.

IN harmony with the great centre, you will be in harmony with all things in His universe. Nature will
serve him who serves her God ; and all her varied powers
and agencies will rejoice to obey the behests and minister to the welfare of one who is the loved and loving
child of their great Master and Lord. For you the morning will dawn, and the evening descend. For you "the
winds will blow, earth rest, heavens move, and fountains
flow." You will be able to claim a peculiar property in
the works of your Father's hand, and the bounties of your
Father's providence. You have become "heir of God,
and joint heir with Christ." And so "the world" and the
fulness thereof will become "yours," because "ye are
Christ's, and Christ is God's."

DR. BAIRD.

GO FORTH, MY HEART.

Go forth, my heart, and seek delight
In all the gifts of God's great might,
   These pleasant summer hours ;
Look how the plains for thee and me
Have decked themselves most fair to see,
   All bright and sweet with flowers.

The trees stand thick and dark with leaves,
And earth o'er all her dust now weaves
   A robe of living green ;
Nor silks of Solomon compare
With glories that the tulips wear,
   Or lilies' spotless sheen.

Thy mighty working, mighty God,
Wakes all my powers ; I look abroad
   And can no longer rest ;
I too must sing when all things sing,
And from my heart the praises ring
   The Highest loveth best.

LYRA GERMANICA (Tr. Catherine Winkworth).

—◆—

July 6.

Justice and judgment are the habitation of Thy throne ; mercy and truth shall go before Thy face. — Ps. lxxxix. 14.

GOD has a definite life-plan set for every man ; one that, being accepted and followed, will conduct him to the best and noblest end possible. And so, as you pass on, stage by stage, in your courses of experience, it is made clear to you that whatever you have laid upon you to do or suffer, whatever to want, whatever to surrender or conquer, is exactly best for you. Your life is a school, exactly adapted to your lesson, and that to the best, last end of your existence. No room for a

discouraged or depressed feeling, therefore, is left you.
Enough that you exist for a purpose high enough to give
meaning to life, and to support a genuine inspiration.
If your sphere is outwardly humble, God understands it
better than you do, and it is a part of His wisdom to
bring out great sentiments in humble conditions, great
characters under great adversities and heavy loads of
incumbrance.

HORACE BUSHNELL.

COMFORT.

WHATE'ER my God ordains is right;
   His will is ever just;
Howe'er He orders now my cause,
   I will be still and trust.
     He is my God;
     Though dark my road,
He holds me that I shall not fall;
Wherefore to Him I leave it all.

Whate'er my God ordains is right;
   He never will deceive;
He leads me by His own right path;
   And so to Him I cleave,
     And take, content,
     What He hath sent.
His hand can turn my griefs away,
And patiently I wait His day.

Whate'er my God ordains is right;
   Though I the cup must drink
That bitter seems to my faint heart,
   I will not fear nor shrink;
     Tears pass away
     With dawn of day;
Sweet comfort yet shall fill my heart,
And pain and sorrow all depart.

July 7.

And I will bring the blind by a way that they knew not;
I will lead them in paths that they have not known :
I will make darkness light before them, and crooked
things straight.   These things will I do unto them,
and not forsake them. — Isa. xlii. 16.

WHEN the song 's gone out of your life, you can't start another while it 's a-ringing in your ears ; it 's best to have a bit o' silence, and out 'o that maybe a psalm 'll come, by-and-by.

Edward Garrett.

RELIGION is to be estimated chiefly by experience. We know little, in such affairs, that we have not lived. Sorrow is sanctified only to those who have summoned their highest energies to live above it. Bereavement is changed to gain only when we turn from our loss to cling more closely to the life in God and humanity. Death is hallowed only when it makes us think and feel more deeply on everlasting life.

LOSS.

AND after He has come to hide
Our lambs upon the other side,
We know our Shepherd and our Guide.

And thus, by ways not understood,
Out of each dark vicissitude
God brings us compensating good.

For faith is perfected by fears,
And souls renew their youth with years,
And Love looks into heaven through tears

July 8.

Suffer the little children to come unto Me, and forbid them not ; for of such is the kingdom of God. — MARK x. 14.

WHEN little children were brought into the presence of the Son of God, his disciples proposed to send them away ; but He said, "Suffer little children to come unto Me." Unto *Me ;* he did not send them first for lessons in morals to the school of the Pharisees, or to the unbelieving Sadducees, nor to read the precepts and lessons phylacteried on the garments of the Jewish priesthood ; He said nothing of different creeds nor clashing doctrines ; but He opened at once to the youthful mind the everlasting fountain of living waters, the only source of eternal truths : "Suffer little children to come *unto Me.*" And that injunction is of perpetual obligation. It addresses itself to-day with the same earnestness and the same authority which attended its first utterance to the Christian world. It extends to the ends of the earth, it will reach to the end of time, always and everywhere sounding in the ears of men, with an emphasis which no repetition can weaken, and with an authority which nothing can supersede : "Suffer little children to come unto Me."

DANIEL WEBSTER.

THE ANGEL IN THE HOUSE.

THREE pairs of dimpled arms, as white as snow,
　　Held me in soft embrace ;
Three little cheeks, like velvet peaches soft,
　　Were placed against my face !

Three pairs of tiny eyes, so clear, so deep,
　　Looked up in mine this even ;
Three pairs of lips kissed me a sweet "good-night,"
　　Three little forms from heaven.

Ah ! it is well that "little ones" should love us !
　　It lights our faith, when dim,
To know that once our blessed Saviour bade them
　　Bring "little ones" to Him.

And said He not, " Of such is heaven," and blessed them,
  And held them to His breast ?
Is it not sweet to know that when they leave us,
  'T is then they go to rest ?

And yet, ye tiny angels of my house,
  Three hearts encased in mine,
How 't would be shattered if the Lord should say,
  " Those angels are not thine " !

—◆—

July 9.

Out of the depths have I cried unto Thee, O Lord. My soul waiteth for the Lord more than they that watch for the morning. — Ps. cxxx. 1, 6.

OUR hearts are naturally of another temper than to take the Lord's word and repose upon it, and when it is deferred, yea, and cross appearances come in betwixt, yet still firmly to believe and patiently to wait for the accomplishment. Yet is it not good reason that we wait for Him? Is He not wise enough to choose the fittest times for His own purposes? Well may we wait till He be gracious to us, for He waits to be gracious. He is staying only for the due season; His love is waiting for the time that His wisdom hath appointed.

ARCHBISHOP LEIGHTON

VERSION OF PSALM CXXX.

FROM the deeps of grief and fear,
O Lord ! to Thee my soul repairs;
From Thy heaven bow down Thine ear ;
Let Thy mercy meet my prayers.
      Oh, if Thou mark'st
      What 's done amiss,
      What soul so pure,
      Can see Thy bliss ?

But with Thee sweet mercy stands,
Sealing pardons, working fear ;
Wait, my soul, wait on His hands ;
Wait mine eye, oh, wait mine ear ;
    If He His eye
    Our tongue affords,
    Watch all His looks,
    Catch all His words.

As a watchman waits for day,
And looks for light, and looks again ;
When the night grows cold and gray,
To be relieved he calls amain ;
    So look, so wait,
    So long mine eyes,
    To see my Lord,
    My sun, arise.

PHINEAS FLETCHER (1584.)

July 10.

And where is the place of my rest ? — ISA. lxvi. 1.

THOU mad'st us for Thyself, and our hearts are restless until they find rest in Thee.

SAINT AUGUSTINE.

IF we were all *one* here on earth there would be great peace ; but God makes it otherwise, and suffers this world to be so strangely entangled and confused, that we may long and sigh for the future Fatherland, and be weary of this toilsome life.

LUTHER

THE GIFTS OF GOD.

WHEN God at first made man,
Having a glass of blessings standing by,
Let us (said He) pour on him all we can ;
Let the world's riches, which dispersèd lie,
    Contract into a span.

So strength first made a way,
Then beauty flowed, then wisdom, honor, pleasure ;
When almost all was out, God made a stay,
Perceiving that alone of all his treasure
Rest in the bottom lay.

For if I should (said He)
Bestow this jewel also on my creature.
He would adore my gifts instead of Me,
And rest in Nature, not the God of Nature ;
So both should losers be.

Yet let him keep the rest,
But keep them with repining restlessness ;
Let him be rich and weary, that at least,
If goodness lead him not, yet weariness
May toss him to My breast.

GEORGE HERBERT.

—◆—

July 11.

*In all their affliction He was afflicted, and the angel of
His presence saved them : in His love and in His pity
He redeemed them ; and He bare them, and carried
them all the days of old.* — ISA. lxiii. 9.

GOD claims a long day and a wide space in dealing
with humanity and with men. Nay, this is my
infirmity, — to think that His day is brief as mine in this
sphere of my mortality, and that the seed-sowing and the
harvest must both fall within the span of a life which is
but as a moment compared with the ages through which
my being shall endure. " But I will remember the years
of the right hand of the Most High." I will get me up
into His serene and lofty tabernacle. I will learn to look
down on life from the height, not up from the depth.
Then I shall see how all the varied movements of His
Providence — the cloud and the sunlight, the calm and
the storm, the want and the fulness, the easy career
before prospering breezes, the stern beating before the
gale, the tempest, the breakers, the wreck, and the

rescue — are but stages in the great order of progress, whose path is forecast by the clearest intelligence and ruled by the dictates of a guardian and fostering love.

CHRISTIAN POLICY OF LIFE.

THE KINGDOM OF GOD.

I SAY to thee, do thou repeat
To the first man thou mayest meet
In lane, highway, or open street, —

That he, and we, and all men move
Under a canopy of love
As broad as the blue sky above;

That doubt and trouble, fear and pain
And anguish, all are shadows vain;
That death itself shall not remain;

That weary deserts we may tread,
A dreary labyrinth may thread,
Through dark ways underground be led,

Yet if we will one Guide obey,
The dreariest path, the darkest way,
Shall issue out in heavenly day.

And we, on divers shores now cast,
Shall meet, our perilous voyage past,
All in our Father's house at last.

And ere thou leave him, say thou this
Yet one word more : they only miss
The winning of that final bliss,

Who will not count it true that Love,
Blessing, not cursing, rules above,
And that in it we live and move.

And one thing further make him know:
That to believe these things are so, —
This firm faith never to forego,

Despite of all which seems at strife
With blessing, all with curses rife, —
That this is blessing, this is life.

RICHARD CHENEVIX TRENCH.

July 12.

*There is no fear in love ; but perfect love casteth out fear.
. . . He that feareth is not made perfect in love. —*
1 JOHN iv. 18.

LIFE is another thing when once a great love has
entered it. Who has not known how love turned
pain to pleasure and made sacrifices sweet? Love never
talks of crosses and of losses. It calls its losses gains and
its crosses crowns. *For my sake* makes even death a
delight. When we so love the Lord with all the heart,
then to follow Him fully is our own choice. There comes
an end to all mere theoretical consecration, in which we
recognize solemnly the claims of God and pass on our
own way. There comes an end, also, to all testing of
ourselves by suppositions of future claims. But another
work begins, — the constant cultivation of the conscience
to see those claims. It is a little thing for Love to re-
spond to an uttered wish. It studies and anticipates the
pleasure of the Beloved. The loving heart escapes a
thousand difficulties which others meet, and a truly devoted life is not often puzzled by details of duty. Such
perplexities are often the simple result of a discordant
will, seeking at once to please itself and avoid displeasing
God. The soul that so loves walks in holy law, but
moves in perfect freedom. When the Lord has enlarged the heart, then it "runs" in the way of His
commandments.

SARAH F. SMILEY,

JULY ON THE MOUNTAINS.

THERE is sultry gloom on the mountain brow,
    And a sultry glow beneath.
Oh for a breeze from the western sea,
Soft and reviving, sweet and free,
Over the shadowless hill and lea,
    Over the barren heath.

There are clouds and darkness around God's ways,
　　And the noon of life grows hot ;
And though His faithfulness standeth fast
As the mighty mountains, a shroud is cast
Over its glory, solemn and vast,
　　Veiling, but changing it not.

Send a sweet breeze from Thy sea, O Lord,
　　From Thy deep, deep sea of love ;
Though it lift not the veil from the cloudy height,
Let the brow grow cool and the footstep light,
As it comes with holy and soothing might,
　　Like the wing of a snowy dove.

FRANCES RIDLEY HAVERGAL.

July 13.

*But the path of the just is as the shining light, that
shineth more and more unto the perfect day.* — PROV.
iv. 18.

ALL things are literally better, lovelier, and more
beloved for the imperfections which have been
divinely appointed, that the law of human life may be
effort, and the law of human judgment mercy.

JOHN RUSKIN.

INCOMPLETENESS.

NOTHING resting in its own completeness
　　Can have worth or beauty ; but alone
Because it leads and tends to further sweetness,
　　Fuller, higher, deeper than its own.

Spring's real glory dwells not in the meaning,
　　Gracious though it be, of her blue hours,
But is hidden in her tender leaning
　　To the summer's richer wealth of flowers.

Dawn is fair, because the mists fade slowly
　　Into day, which floods the world with light;
Twilight's mystery is so sweet and holy
　　Just because it ends in starry night.

Childhood's smiles unconscious graces borrow
From strife that in a far-off future lies ;
And angel glances (veiled now by Life's sorrow)
Draw our hearts to some belovèd eyes.

Life is only bright when it proceedeth
Towards a truer, deeper Life above ;
Human love is sweetest when it leadeth
To a more divine and perfect Love.

Learn the mystery of progression duly ;
Do not call each glorious change, decay ;
But know we only hold our treasures truly
When it seems as if they passed away.

Nor dare to blame God's gifts for incompleteness ;
In that want their beauty lies ; they roll
Towards some infinite depth of love and sweetness,
Bearing onward man's reluctant soul.

ADELAIDE A. PROCTER.

July 14.

Like as a father pitieth his children, so the Lord pitieth them that fear Him. For He knoweth our frame; He remembereth that we are dust. — Ps. ciii. 13, 14.

HIMSELF the " Man of sorrows," he understands what sorrow is, and how it may perform a blessed ministry. Why, then, should we abandon ourselves to sorrow, or fly to human comforters, when there is such a blessed Healer ever nigh and ever merciful, who can be touched with a feeling of our infirmities?

HE KNOWETH ALL.

THE twilight falls, the night is near ;
I fold my work away,
And kneel to One who bends to hear
The story of the day.

The old, old story; yet I kneel
　　To tell it at Thy call;
And cares grow lighter as I feel
　　That Jesus knows them all.

Yes, all! The morning and the night,
　　The joy, the grief, the loss,
The roughened path, the sunbeam bright,
　　The hourly thorn and cross.

Thou knowest all. I lean my head,
　　My weary eyelids close;
Content and glad awhile to tread
　　This path, since Jesus knows!

So here I lay me down to rest,
　　As nightly shadows fall,
And lean, confiding, on His breast
　　Who knows and pities all!

———◆———

July 15.

Pray without ceasing. — 1 THESS. v. 17.

BY far the largest proportion of our daily experience is invested in apparently trifling concerns. We encounter few great problems of heroic duty between sun and sun. Our journey of the day is a succession of moderate steps, so that the greatest breadth of our progressive story were kept in shadow and silence if it might not be lifted, by our pleading, to the light of the Divine countenance. We cannot tell what is large and what is small in the daily questions calling for our decision and action.

The oldest and wisest of us may be as little children in our communion with a prayer-hearing God. No errand to that mercy-seat is too trivial to lead our footsteps thither. We may connect all the issues of life with the control of that overruling Will. We may put our hand in that paternal Hand, no matter how narrow the chasm, how gentle the activity, and look trustfully and hopefully for that availing guidance. Ah! if we could learn this lesson of filial trust at *every step* of our way along our earthly pilgrimage, no matter how steep or rough or obscure the path, it would guide us safely and surely home to our Father's house.

A. L. STONE.

PRAYER.

BE not afraid to pray — to pray is right.
Pray, if thou canst, with hope; but ever pray,
Though hope be weak, or sick with long delay;
Pray in the darkness, if there be no light.
Far is the time, remote from human sight,
When war and discord on the earth shall cease;
Yet every prayer for universal peace
Avails the blessèd time to expedite.
Whate'er is good to wish, ask that of Heaven,
Though it be what thou canst not hope to see;
Pray to be perfect, though material leaven
Forbid the spirit so on earth to be;
But if for any wish thou darest not pray,
Then pray to God to cast that wish away.

HARTLEY COLERIDGE.

July 16.

Oh that I had wings like a dove! for then would I fly away and be at rest. — Ps. lv. 6.

OH that we could really feel that it is as vain a fancy to believe that future years will bring rest with them, as the Psalmist's, that once far away in the wilderness, he would be at rest! The days to come will do no more for us than the dove's wing and the desert would do for him. Coming days may and will do for us just what the wings would have done for the wearied monarch; they will no doubt bear us away from the trials and troubles that now surround us, but they will only bear us to other trials that are awaiting us then. Oh that we could lay it to heart, that the day will never come in which there will not be something to vex and weary; the day will never come in this world that will make the soul happy and complete, — and all this just because God does not intend that such a day should ever come; all because this world was never meant for our rest, and whenever it is beginning to grow too like our rest, God will send us something to remind us that it is not; all this because these immortal souls within us are not to be put off with any worldly aim or enjoyment, but will ever reach and blindly long after something as immortal as themselves!

A. K. H. BOYD, D.D.

LEISURE.

SWEET is the leisure of the bird:
She craves no time for work deferred;
Her wings are not to aching stirred,
    Providing for her helpless ones.
Fair is the leisure of the wheat;
All night the damps about it fleet,
All day it basketh in the heat,
    And grows, and whispers orisons.

Grand is the leisure of the Earth;
She gives her happy myriads birth,
And after harvest fears not dearth,
    But goes to sleep in snow-wreaths dim.
Dread is the leisure up above,
The while He sits whose name is Love,
And waits, as Noah did for the dove,
    To wit if she would fly to him.

He waits for us while, houseless things,
We beat about with bruisèd wings
On the dark floods and water-springs,
    The ruined world, the desolate sea;
With open windows from the prime,
All night, all day, He waits sublime,
Until the fulness of the time
    Decreed from His eternity.

JEAN INGELOW.

July 17.

*But thou, when thou prayest, enter into thy closet, and
when thou hast shut thy door, pray to thy Father which
is in secret; and thy Father, which seeth in secret, shall
reward thee openly.* — MATT. vi. 6.

WE hold to earth and earthly things by so many more
links of thought, if not affection, that it is far
harder to keep our view to heaven clear and strong; when
this life is so busy, and therefore so full of reality to us,
another life seems by comparison unreal. This is our
condition and its peculiar temptations, but we must endure it and strive to overcome them, for I think we may
not try to flee from it.
THOMAS ARNOLD.

WHEN THOU HAST SHUT THY DOOR, PRAY.

LORD, I have shut my door, —
Shut out life's busy cares and fretting noise;
Here in this silence they intrude no more;
Speak Thou, and heavenly joys
Shall fill my heart with music sweet and calm, —
A holy psalm.

Yes, I have shut my door
Even on all the beauty of thine earth,
To its blue ceiling from its emerald floor
Filled with spring's bloom and mirth.
From these Thy works I turn, Thyself I seek,
To Thee I speak.

And I have shut my door
On earthly passion, all its yearning love,
Its tender friendships, all the priceless store
Of human ties. Above
All these my heart aspires. O Heart Divine,
Stoop Thou to mine!

Lord, I have shut my door!
Come Thou and visit me. I am alone!
Come, as when doors were shut Thou cam'st of yore
And visitedst Thine own.
My Lord! I kneel with reverent love and fear,
For Thou art here!
M. E. ATKINSON.

July 18.

He that spared not His own Son, but delivered Him up for us all, how shall He not with Him also freely give us all things? — ROM. viii. 32.

H E that loveth little, prayeth little ; but he that loveth much, prayeth much.
SAINT AUGUSTINE.

PRAYER is so mighty an instrument that no one ever thoroughly mastered all its keys. They sweep along the infinite scale of man's wants and God's goodness.
HUGH MILLER

A PRAYER.

I ASK not wealth, but power to take
  And use the things I have aright ;
Not years, but wisdom that shall make
  My life a profit and delight.

I ask not that for me the plan
  Of good and ill be set aside,
But that the common lot of man
  Be nobly borne and glorified.

I know I may not always keep
  My steps in places green and sweet,
Nor find the pathway of the deep
  A path of safety for my feet ;

But pray that when the tempest's breath
  Shall fiercely sweep my way about,
I make not shipwreck of my faith
  In the unbottomed sea of doubt;

And that, though it be mine to know
  How hard the stoniest pillow seems,
Good angels still may come and go
  On the bright ladder of my dreams.

I do not ask for love below —
  That friends shall never be estranged;
But for the power of loving, so
  My heart may keep its youth unchanged.

Youth, joy, wealth — Fate, I give thee these ;
  Leave faith and hope till life is past ;
And leave my heart's best impulses
  Fresh and unfailing to the last.

For this I count, of all sweet things,
  The sweetest out of heaven above ;
And loving others surely brings
  The fullest recompense of love !

CHAMBERS'S JOURNAL.

July 19.

Casting all your care upon Him, for He careth for you. —
1 PETER v. 7.

O LORD God, Thou art our refuge and our hope ;
on Thee alone we rest, for we find all to be weak
and insufficient but Thee.   Many friends cannot profit,
nor strong helpers assist, nor prudent counsellors advise,
nor the books of the learned afford comfort, nor any precious substance deliver, nor any place give shelter, unless
Thou Thyself dost assist, strengthen, console, instruct, and
guard us.

JAMES MARTINEAU.

EVEN-TIDE.

HOLD Thou my hand, my Father, I am weak ;
Hush me to sleep, for I am sore afraid ;
Yet as Thy child I should be undismayed,
For in the silence I should hear Thee speak.

I could not climb the mountains of Thy love,
But in the valleys do Thy rivers flow ;
The bitter herbs beside those waters grow,
And lo ! they teem with sweetness from above.

I will not trust my thoughts which trouble me,
I will not answer all that they would say ;
I cast my cares and my regrets away,
And leave my spirit all alone with Thee.

July 20.

Behold, He that keepeth Israel shall neither slumber nor sleep. — Ps. cxxi. 4.

EVERY pious heart must feel that God in the very arrangements of Nature, and in the ordinances of the heavens, says to us : " In the morning think of Me, in that calm hour which I send you before the din and toil of life commences ; and in the evening think of Me ; after it is over, when the holy stars pour quiet upon the earth, then remember Me."

J. F. CLARKE.

EVENING HYMN.

Now rest the woods again ;
Man, cattle, town, and plain, —
  The world all sleeping lies.
But sleep not yet, my soul,
For He who made this whole
  Loves that thy prayers to Him arise.

The long bright day is past ;
The golden stars at last
  Bestud the dark-blue heaven ;
And like a star shall I
Forever shine on high,
  When my release from earth is given.

My heavy eyes must close,
Sealed up in deep repose ;
  Where is my safety then ?
Do Thou Thy mercy send.
My helpless hours defend,
  Thou sleepless Eye, that watchest over men.

LYRA GERMANICA

July 21.

Wait on the Lord; be of good courage, and He shall strengthen thy heart; wait, I say, on the Lord. — Ps. xxvii. 14.

WAITING hours are seed-times of blessing.

HOW many are there who by reason of poverty, obscurity, infirmity of mind or body, can never hope to do much by action, and who often sigh at the contemplation of their want of power to effect anything! But it is given to them, as to all, to suffer ; let them only suffer well, and they will give a testimony for God which all who know them will deeply feel and profoundly respect. It is not necessary for all men to be great in action. The greatest and sublimest power is often simple patience ; and for just that reason we need sometimes to see its greatness alone, that we may embrace the solitary, single idea of such greatness, and bring it into our hearts unconfused with all other kinds of power. Let this be remembered ; and let it be your joy, in every trial and grief and pain and wrong you suffer, that to suffer well is to be a true advocate and apostle and pillar of the faith.

HORACE BUSHNELL.

ON HIS BLINDNESS.

WHEN I consider how my light is spent
Ere half my days, in this dark world and wide,
And that one talent which is death to hide,
Lodged with me useless, though my soul more bent
To serve therewith my Maker, and present
My true account, lest He returning chide ;
"Doth God exact day-labor, light denied?"
I fondly ask ; but Patience, to prevent
That murmur, soon replies, "God doth not need
Either man's work or his own gifts; who best
Bear His mild yoke, they serve Him best ; His state
Is kingly ; thousands at His bidding speed,
And post o'er land and ocean without rest ;
They also serve who only stand and wait.

MILTON.

July 22.

His Lord said unto him, well done, thou good and faithful servant; thou hast been faithful over a few things, I will make thee ruler over many things; enter thou into the joy of thy Lord. — MATT. xxv. 21.

NOT man's judgment of what the Lord requires from His weak ones, but God's own requirement, constitutes our true service. SECRET OF THE LORD.

THE more difficulties one has to encounter, within and without, the more significant and the higher in inspiration his life will be. The very troubles that others look on with pity, as if he had taken up a kind of piety more perilous and burdensome than was necessary, will be his fields of victory, and his course of life will be just as much happier as it is more consciously heroic. He has something great to live for, nay, something worthy to die for, if he must, — that which makes it glorious to live, and not less glorious to die.

SPINNING.

LIKE a blind spinner in the sun,
　I thread my days;
I know that all the threads will run
　Appointed ways;
I know each day will bring its task,
And, being blind, no more I ask.

I do not know the use or name
　Of that I spin;
I only know that some one came,
　And laid within
My hand the thread, and said, "Since you
Are blind, but one thing can you do."

Sometimes the threads so rough and fast
　And tangled fly,
I know wild storms are sweeping past,
　And fear that I
Shall fall; but dare not try to find
A safer place, since I am blind.

I know not why, but I am sure
   That tint and place,
In some great fabric to endure
   Past time and race,
My threads will have ; so, from the first,
Though blind, I never felt accursed.

I think, perhaps, this trust has sprung
   From one short word
Said over me when I was young, —
   So very young, I heard
It, knowing not that God's name signed
My brow, and sealed me His, though blind.

But whether this be seal or sign
   Within, without,
It matters not.   The bond divine
   I never doubt.
I know He set me here, and still
Am glad, and, blind, I wait His will ;

But listen, listen day by day
   To hear their tread,
Who bear the finished web away,
   And cut the thread,
And bring God's message in the sun,
" Thou poor blind spinner, work is done."

HELEN HUNT JACKSON

July 23.

And sorrow is turned into joy before Him. — JOB xli. 22.

FROM the long dim tracts of the past come strangely blended recognitions of woe and bliss, undistinguishable now to our own heart, nor knows that heart if it be a dream of imagination or of memory. Yet why should we wonder? In our happiest hours there may have been something in common with our most sorrowful, some shade of sadness cast over them by a passing cloud, that now allies them in retrospect with the sombre spirit of grief; and in our unhappiest hours there may have been gleams of gladness that seem now to give the return the calm character of peace. Do not all thoughts and feelings, almost all events, seem to resemble each other when they are dreamt of as all past? All receive a sort of sanctification in the stillness of the time that has

gone by — just like the human being whom they adorned
or degraded — when they too are at last buried together
in the bosom of the same earth.   CHRISTOPHER NORTH.

OH, how sweet, how painful and sweet, it is to stoop
and bend, day after day, with weary care, over the common dust-heap of our past experiences, and humming old
tunes to ourselves, and thinking of our lost hopes and
buried loves, to pick out the little diamonds of memory
and put them into our bosoms !

MEMORY.

THERE'S not a heath, however rude,
But hath some little flower
To brighten up its solitude
And scent the evening hour.

There's not a heart, however cast
By grief or sorrow down,
But hath some memory of the past
To love and call its own.

———◆———

July 24.

The good seed are the children of the kingdom. — MATT.
xiii. 38.
*Whose fan is in His hand, and He will thoroughly purge
His floor, and gather His wheat into the garner.* —
MATT. iii. 12.

The Grain of Wheat. — O Sower, why dost thou forsake me ? Escaped from the hoar frosts of winter and
the storms of summer, how greatly did I suffer when thou
didst pluck me from the ripened ear, when thou didst
confine me within the depths of the dark granary ! Thou
lovest me then no longer ? Alas ! I had hoped to nourish thee one day, that is, to become flesh of thy body, and
blood of thy veins. O Sower, why dost thou abandon me ?
The Sower. — I do not abandon thee ; I but leave thee
for a space. Soon we shall meet again, thou multiplied,
I grateful. Fructify. Wait. Complain not. Do thy work.
Thou must needs be harvested, and I must harvest thee.

The Man. — Sower of beings, why have You cast me away upon the earth, naked and alone? Day, night, winter, summer, I suffer.   Do You know that I am unhappy after nothingness, before heaven? Why have You cast me away upon the earth, naked and alone, O Sower of beings?

God. — I have not cast thee away; I have confided thee to the fecundating soil.   Grow and prosper.   At the time of the harvest I shall gather thee, and thou shalt be served in thy fragrance upon the table of the father of the family.   I have not cast thee away.

JOSEPH ROUX.

THE WINDMILL.

BEHOLD, a giant am I !
  Aloft here in my tower
  With my granite jaws I devour
The maize, the wheat, and the rye,
  And grind them into flour.

I look down over the farms ;
  In the fields of grain I see
  The harvest that is to be ;
And I fling aloft my arms,
  For I know it is all for me.

I hear the sound of the flails
  Far off from the threshing-floors
  In barns with their open doors,
And the wind, the wind in my sails,
  Louder and louder roars.

I stand here in my place,
  With my foot on the rock below,
  And whichever way it may blow,
I meet it face to face,
  As a brave man meets his foe.

And while we wrestle and strive,
  My master the miller stands
  And feeds me with his hands ;
For he knows who makes him thrive,
  Who makes him lord of lands.

On Sundays I take my rest ;
  Church-going bells begin
  Their low, melodious din ;
I cross my arms on my breast,
  And all is peace within.

H. W. LONGFELLOW

July 25.

The statutes of the Lord are right, rejoicing the heart ; the commandment of the Lord is pure, enlightening the eyes. — Ps. xix. 8.

AS the graces of the spirit are advanced in prayer by their actings, so for this further reason, because prayer sets the soul particularly near to God in Jesus Christ. It is then in His presence ; and being much with God in this way, it is powerfully assimilated to Him by converse with Him, — as we readily contract their habits with whom we have much intercourse, especially if they be such as we singularly love and respect. Thus the soul is moulded farther to the likeness of God, is stamped with clearer characters of Him, by being much with Him, — becomes more like God, more holy and spiritual ; and, like Moses, brings back a bright shining from the mount.   ARCHBISHOP LEIGHTON.

TO MYSELF.

LET nothing make thee sad or fretful,
　　Or too regretful ;
　　　Be still.
What God hath ordered must be right ;
Then find in it thine own delight,
　　　My will.

Why shouldst thou fill to-day with sorrow
　　About to-morrow,
　　　My heart?
One watches all with care most true ;
Doubt not that He will give thee too
　　　Thy part.

Only be steadfast ; never waver,
　　Nor seek earth's favor,
　　　But rest.
Thou knowest what God wills must be
For all His creatures, so for thee,
　　　The best.

PAUL FLEMMING : *Christian Singers of Germany.*

July 26.

My days are swifter than a weaver's shuttle. — JOB vii. 6.
They have passed away as the swift ships. — JOB ix. 26.

LINNÆUS, the botanist, once constructed a clock of flowers. In allusion to this beautiful contrivance, Richter says, " It is best to measure thy years, not by the water-clock of falling tears, but by the flower-clock of thankfulness and praise." " Modern skill has invented curious machines and turned them into articles of luxury, for the more perfect accomplishment of this useful and solemn purpose. It has given the hours audible voices as they come and go. It has placed numerously around us, and enabled us to carry everywhere with us, these monitors of our wasting days. The hours ! They all march in one direction, invisible as they are coming, and irrevocable when they are gone ; with an eternity behind them and an eternity before. The hours ! They will never end their journey, though they will soon complete yours and mine. They are making note of human opportunities and performances ; and the inscriptions that they leave will remain after those opportunities have vanished, and when those actions must be judged." I know of no description that sets them forth better than the motto of a public clock on the college wall at Oxford : *Pereunt ei imputantur,* — " They perish and are imputed."

TIME.

TIME flows from instants ; and of these each one
Should be esteemed as if it were alone.
The shortest space which we so highly prize
When it is coming and before our eyes,
Let it but slide into the eternal main,
No realms, no worlds, can purchase it again.
Remembrance only makes the footsteps last
When wingèd time, which fixed the prints, is past !

SIR JOHN BEAUMONT.

July 27.

Many shall be purified, and made white, and tried. —
DAN. xii. 10.

IT is the outward distractions of life, the examples of
the world, and the irresistible influence exerted upon
us by the current of things which make us forget the
wisdom we have acquired and the principles we have
adopted. That is why life is such weariness ! This eternal beginning over again is tedious, even to repulsion. It
would be so good to go to sleep when we have gathered
the fruit of experience, when we are no longer in opposition to the Supreme Will, when we have broken loose
from self, when we are at peace with all men. Instead of
this, the old round of temptations, disputes, *ennuis*, and
forgettings has to be faced again and again ; and we fall
back into prose, into commonplace. How melancholy,
how humiliating ! The poets are wise in withdrawing
their heroes more quickly from the strife, and in not drag-
ging them after the victory along the common rut of
barren days. " Whom the gods love die young," said the
proverb of antiquity. Yes, but it is our secret self-love
which is set upon this favor from on high ; such may be
our desire, but such is not the will of God. We are to
be exercised, humbled, tried, and tormented to the end.
It is our patience which is the touchstone of our virtue.
To bear with life even when illusion and hope are gone ;
to accept this position of perpetual war, while at the same
time loving only peace ; to stay patiently in the world
even when it repels us as a place of low company, and
seems to us a mere arena of bad passions ; to remain
faithful to one's own faith without breaking with the
followers of false gods ; to make no attempt to escape, —
this is duty. When life ceases to be a promise, it does
not cease to be a task ; its true name, even, is trial.

HENRI FRÉDÉRIC AMIEL.

A WATER-LILY AT EVENING.

SLEEP, lily, on the lake,
  Without one troubled dream
Thy hushed repose to break,
  Until the morning beam
Shall open thy glad heart again
To live its life apart from pain.

So still is thy repose,
  So pure thy petals seem,
As heaven would here disclose
  Its peace, and we might deem
A soul in each white lily lay
Passionless, from the lands of day.

Yet but a flower thou art;
  For angel ne'er, or saint,
Though kept on earth apart
  From every earthly taint,
A life so passionless could know
Amid a world of human woe.

F. W. BOURDILLON.

July 28.

*He that goeth forth and weepeth, bearing precious seed,
shall doubtless come again with rejoicing, bringing his
sheaves with him. — Ps. cxxvi. 6.*

THE harvest-time is the time of fulfilled hopes and
realized expectations, when the ruddy gleam of the
ripened fruit succeeds the lavish wealth of blossoms, and
he who went forth weeping, bearing precious seed, returns
with rejoicing, bringing his sheaves with him. The miracle
of the loaves was a sudden putting forth of God's bountiful hand from behind the veil of His ordinary providence ;
the miracle of the harvest is the working of the same
bountiful hand, only unseen, giving power to the tiny
grains to drink the dew and imbibe the sunshine, and

appropriate the nourishment of the soil during the long
bright days of summer. The harvest-fields are the golden
links that connect the ages and the zones, and associate
together the most distant times and the remotest nations
in one common bond of sympathy and dependence.
They make of the earth one great home, of the human
race one great family, and of God the universal Parent,
to whom, day after day, we are encouraged to go with
filial faith and love, not in selfishness and isolation, but
in a fraternal spirit which embraces the whole world, asking not for ourselves only, but for all our brothers of mankind as well, — " Our Father, which art in heaven, give us
this day our daily bread."

HUGH MACMILLAN.

HARVEST.

THE harvest-time is near,
  The year delays not long,
And he who sowed with many a tear
  Shall reap with many a song.

Forth to his toil he goes,
  His seed with weeping leaves,
But he shall come at early dawn,
  And bind his golden sheaves.

BISHOP COXE.

July 29.

His rest shall be glorious. — ISA. xi. 10.
*This is my rest forever; here will I dwell; for I have
  desired it.* — PS. cxxxii. 14.

WE must be somewhat subdued, indeed, by the
    wear and toil of this weary world, and we must
have gained an insight into the deepest wants of our
spiritual nature, such as comes commonly through fuller
experience and longer thought, before we shall appreciate
such words completely. It is the toil-worn man that

knows the worth of repose; it is the jaded pilgrim that
understands best what it must be to sit down at home;
and as we go on, year after year, till our hearts begin to
grow a little weary, there is music, growing always sweeter,
in the ancient words of the patient patriarch, "There the
wicked cease from troubling, and the weary are at rest."

A. K. H. BOYD, D.D.

AFTER SUNSET.

REST — rest — four little letters, one short word,
Enfolding an infinitude of bliss, —
Rest is upon the earth, thank God, no light,
No open-eyed, loud-voiced, quick-motioned light;
Nothing but gloom and rest. Oh, better far,
Better than bliss is rest.

Oh for a soul-sleep, long and deep and still!
To lie down quiet after the weary day,
Dropping all pleasant flowers from the numbed hands,
Bidding good-night to all companions dear.
Drawing the curtains on this darkened world,
Closing the eyes, and with a patient sigh
Murmuring "Our Father," fall on sleep, till dawn!

DINAH MULOCH CRAIK.

July 30.

*I am the light of the world; he that followeth Me shall
not walk in darkness, but shall have the light of life.*
—JOHN viii. 12.

THERE is something sacramental in perfect metre and
rhythm. They are outward and visible signs of an
inward and spiritual grace, namely, of the self-possessed
and victorious temper of one who has so far subdued
nature as to be able to hear that universal sphere-music of
hers, speaking of which Carlyle says that "all deepest
thoughts instinctively vent themselves in song."

CHARLES KINGSLEY.

WHERE there is light on the song, there is no need for darkness on the way. If I had never gone into darkened rooms where the soul stands at the parting of the worlds ; or grasped the hands of strong men when all they had toiled for was gone, — nothing left but honor ; or ministered to men mangled on the battle-field ; and heard, in all those places where darkness was on the way, melodies, — *melodies* that I never heard among the common places of prosperity, — I could not be so sure as I am, that God often darkens the way that the way may grow clear and entire in the soul.

ROBERT COLLYER

THE SONG IN DARKNESS.

I KNOW not why, I know not why,
   My lips will fain be singing,
And through my soul's discordant cry
   One silver chord keep ringing ;
I cannot see the path I tread,
   For eyes that are a-weary ;
No star is shining overhead,
   To cheer the darkness dreary.

As children wait in darkened rooms
   Some friendly hand to guide them,
And shrinking, feel the deepening glooms
   Roll onward to divide them,
To timid lips there steals a cry,
   New hope and comfort bringing ;
They know not why, they know not why,
   But falter into singing.

Thus, as the shadows close around,
   And the dim world grows lonely,
When all outreaching arms can clasp
   Is utter darkness only,
All through the night faint lips repeat
   The music in me ringing ;
I know not why, I know not why,
   But trust is born of singing !

July 31.

O ye that make mention of the Lord, keep not silence, and give Him no rest.

Ask ye of the Lord rain in the time of the latter rain; so the Lord shall make bright clouds, and give showers of rain, to every one grass in the field. — ZECH. X. 1.

THERE is something very beautiful in the terms of this promise. The "bright clouds," or "lightnings," are the harbingers of the rain; and God declares that He will make these, before He sends the showers. Thus He exercises faith: He does not immediately answer the prayer, but requires His people still to "wait" on Him; He will "make bright clouds" for their encouragement, but they must persevere in supplication if they would have showers for their refreshment. Ay, and to them that "wait upon the Lord" there may be clouds, but are they not "bright clouds"? The murkiest cloud which can rise on the firmament of the believer has a gilded side; "the Sun of righteousness" shines on it. God may bring the cloud over His people, and, as Elihu saith, "men see not the bright light which is in the clouds;" but if the world see it not, the believer may; and God brings the cloud that, its brightness being acknowledged, in and through the acknowledgment of His doing all things well, He may then send a gracious rain on His inheritance, and refresh it when it is weary. But how large is the promise, — "To every one grass in the field!" O Spirit of the living God, the parched and stricken earth waits Thy descent; come down, in answer to our prayers, that the valleys and mountains may no longer lie waste.

HENRY MELVILLE.

SUMMER RAIN.

ALL day fierce heat had held the quivering earth
In iron grip. The sky from red to pale
Had turned with fear; and white and still
The clouds had crept away in masses, to the north.
The meadow hazels, 'neath their clustered load

Of satin and green-ruffled nuts, had dropped.
Sweet ferns had knelt to die ; and choked and mute
Since morn had lain the cricket, hid below
The fallen spear of water-flags.   In dumb
Amaze the patient cattle to their bars
Had crowded, waiting help.   All nature gasped;
All life seemed sinking into death!
                              Then rose,
In distant sunset depths, a solemn sound, —
The wheels of God's great chariot, rolling slow !
An instant more, and with sharp blaze and boom,
His signal-guns lit up and shook the sky,
With word of succor on the way ! and then
The still, small voice of rain, in which He was,
And cooled and lulled His fainting world to sleep.
. . . O iron-handed grief, which holds my soul
In searing grasp, and leaves my stifled days
No voice, no life !   Will there a sound of help
Arise in sunset depths for me ?   Does God
Remember ?   Will His chariot-wheels draw near ?
Will He command this cloud to break in rain
Of healing tears ?   And will He give to me
At last, as unto His beloved, sleep ?

———◆———

August 1.

He that feareth is not made perfect in love. — 1 JOHN
iv. 19.

LOVING God is the secret which reconciles all.   This
is the secret of being occupied, with interest, in
the things of earth, without ceasing to love the things of
heaven.   To love God, is to love the life He has made
and the death He has ordained.   But, ye divided hearts,
who have dreamed of a compromise between heaven and
earth, and have appeared tormented with fears and scru-
ples, now know the cause of your condition : ye fear
God, but ye do not love Him.   Love has speedily cut
the difficulty ; everything for God, nothing for self, is its
motto.   Everything for God, provided God is mine.
Then let Him enrich or impoverish my life, let Him
extend or limit my activity, let Him gratify or oppose my
tastes ; if I have my God, I have all things at once.

                              ALEXANDRE R. VINET.

REAPING.

" REAPER," I asked, " among the golden sheaves,
Toiling at noon amid the falling leaves,
What recompense hast thou for all thy toil,
What tithe of all thy Master's wine and oil ?
Or dost thou coin thy brow's hot drops to gold,
Or add to house and land, or flock and fold ? "

The reaper paused from binding close the grain,
And said, while shone his smile through labor's stain,
" I do my Master's work, as He has taught ;
And work of love with gold was never bought.
He knoweth all of which my life hath need ;
His servants reap as they have sown the seed.
With all my heart I bind my Master's grain,
And love makes sweet my labor and my pain."

August 2.

*Thus saith the Lord: Refrain thy voice from weeping,
and thine eyes from tears; for thy work shall be
rewarded, saith the Lord.* — JER. xxxi. 16.

THE man who has, however imperceptibly, helped in
the work of the universe, has lived ; the man who
has been conscious, in however small a degree, of the
cosmical movement, has lived also. The plain man
serves the world by his action, and as a wheel in the
machine ; the thinker serves it by his intellect, and as a
light upon its path. The man of meditative soul, who
raises and comforts and sustains his travelling-compan-
ions, mortal and fugitive like himself, plays a nobler part
still ; for he unites the other two utilities. Action, thought,
speech, are the three modes of human life. The artisan, the
savant, and the orator are all three God's workmen. To
do, to discover, to teach, — these three things are all labor,
all good, all necessary. Will-o'-the-wisps that we are, we
may yet leave a trace behind us ; meteors that we are, we
may yet prolong our perishable being in the memory of

men, or at least in the contexture of after events. Everything disappears, but nothing is lost ; and the civilization
or city of man is but an immense spiritual pyramid, built
up out of the work of all that has ever lived under the
forms of moral being, just as our calcareous mountains
are made of the débris of myriads of nameless creatures
who have lived under the forms of microscopic animal
life.

HENRI FRÉDÉRIC AMIEL.

WORK.

WHAT are we set on earth for ?   Say. to toil ;
Nor seek to leave thy tending of the vines
For all the heat o' the day, till it declines,
And Death's mild curfew shall from work assoil.
God did anoint thee with His odorous oil
To wrestle, not to reign ; and He assigns
All thy tears over, like pure crystallines,
For younger fellow-workers of the soil
To wear for amulets.   So others shall
Take patience, labor, to their heart and hand,
From thy hand and thy heart and thy brave cheer,
And God's grace fructify through thee to all.
The least flower with a brimming cup may stand,
And share its dew-drop with another near.

ELIZABETH BARRETT BROWNING.

August 3.

Consider the lilies of the field. — MATT. vi. 28.

IN such a manhood, the true manhood of the children
of God, full of devout strength and open love, of a
will at the mercy of no tyrant without, and no passion
within, of affections gentle enough for the humblest sorrows of earth, lofty enough for the aspirings of the skies,
let every one that owns a soul see that he stands fast ; in
its spirit, at once humane and heavenly, do the work,
accept the good, and bear the burdens of life.   Oh !
blessed are they who, for the peace and ornament of life,
dare to rely, not on the glories which Solomon affected,

but on those which Jesus loved, — glories which even God may behold with complacency; nay, in which He shines himself, — glories of Nature, richer than of man's device ; genuine graces, resembling the inimitable beauties of the lilies of the field, painted with the hues of heaven, while bending over the soil of earth.

LILIES.

FLOWERS ! when the Saviour's calm benignant eye
Fell on your gentle beauty, when from you
That heavenly lesson for all hearts He drew,
Eternal, universal as the sky;
Then, in the bosom of your purity,
A voice He set, as in a temple-shrine,
That life's quick travellers ne'er might pass you by
Unwarned of that sweet oracle divine.
And though too oft its low, celestial sound
By the harsh notes of work-day Care is drowned,
And the loud steps of vain, unlistening Haste,
Yet the great ocean hath no tone of power
Mightier to reach the soul, in thought's hushed hour,
Than yours, ye lilies ! chosen thus and graced !

FELICIA HEMANS

August 4.

*Be kindly affectioned one to another with brotherly love ;
in honor preferring one another. — ROM. xii. 10.*

LET us act towards our fellow-creatures as God does to us, and be to them what the sun is to the whole universe. As he daily diffuses his benign influence over the whole earth ; as he shines upon the ungrateful as upon the righteous ; and as he gilds the bosom of the valley as well as the lofty summit of the mountain ; so let our lives be useful, beneficent, and consolatory to our fellow-creatures. May each returning day renew the charitable emotions of our heart, and may we do all the good in our power, and endeavor so to live and to act, that our lives shall be a blessing to mankind.

From the German of STURM.

THE opportunity of making happy, is more scarce than
we imagine ; the punishment of missing it is, never to
meet with it again ; and the use we make of it leaves us
an eternal sentiment of satisfaction or repentance.

ROUSSEAU.

THY love
Shall chant itself in its own beatitudes,
After its own life-working.   A child's kiss
Set on thy sighing lips, shall make thee glad ;
A poor man served by thee, shall make thee rich ;
A sick man helped by thee, shall make thee strong ;
Thou shalt be served thyself by every sense
Of service which thou renderest.

ELIZABETH BARRETT BROWNING.

ASK God to give thee skill
    In comfort's art,
That thou mayst consecrated be
    And set apart
Unto a life of sympathy.
For heavy is the weight of ill
    In every heart ;
And comforters are needed much
    Of Christ-like touch.

ANNA E. HAMILTON.

HIDDEN SWEETS.

THE honey-bee that wanders all day long
The field, the woodland, and the garden o'er,
    To gather in his fragrant winter store,
Humming in calm content his quiet song,
Seeks not alone the rose's glowing breast,
    The lily's dainty cup, the violet's lips,
But from all rank and noxious weeds he sips
The single drop of sweetness closely pressed
    Within the poison chalice.   Thus if we
Seek only to draw forth the hidden sweet
In all the varied human flowers we meet,
    In the wide garden of humanity,
And, like the bee, if home the spoil we bear,
Hived in our hearts it turns to nectar there.

A. C. L. BOTTA.

August 5.

*I know, O Lord, that Thy judgments are right, and that
Thou in faithfulness hast afflicted me. —* Ps. cxix. 75.

TO rejoice in having our wills crossed, in being conformed to His likeness through suffering, is a hard
attainment; and yet perhaps true thankfulness oftener
arises under outward privation than when loaded with
what seem to our eyes the greatest benefits. Our nature
seems more especially to show its root of selfish and
ungodly desires in the midst of God's bounty. The moment we are laid low by His chastening hand, our true
relation to Him, and debt of love, is brought home to our
hearts in the sense of our nothingness and of His power
and mercy. MARIA HARE.

THE NIGHT BEFORE THE MOWING.

ALL shimmering in the morning shine
And diamonded with dew,
And quivering in the scented wind
That thrills its green heart through, —
The little field, the smiling field,
With all its flowers a-blowing,
How happy looks the golden field
The night before the mowing.

All still 'neath the departing light,
Twilight, though void of stars,
Save where, low westering, Venus hides
From the red eye of Mars ;
How quiet lies the silent field
With all its beauties glowing;
Just stirring, like a child asleep,
The night before the mowing.

Sharp steel, inevitable hand,
Cut keen, cut kind ! Our field
We know full well must be laid low
Before its wealth it yield ;
Labor and mirth and plenty blest
Its blameless death bestowing ;
And yet we weep, and yet we weep,
The night before the mowing.
DINAH MULOCH CRAIK.

August 6.

The sacrifices of God are a broken spirit; a broken and a contrite heart, O God, Thou wilt not despise. — Ps. li. 17.

NO pain suffered, nor service rendered, nor work done for Christ, is lost; the very shame we bear for Him shall be transformed into immortal laurels; and every tear shed like His over human sorrow, or hers who bent in penitence at His feet, shall be a pearl in the heavenly crown. The poorer we become for Christ, the richer we shall grow. The more we forget ourselves, the more will He remember us.

THOMAS GUTHRIE.

BRINGING OUR SHEAVES WITH US.

THE time for toil is past, and night has come, —
The last and saddest of the harvest eves;
  Worn out with labor long and wearisome,
  Drooping and faint, the reapers hasten home,
    Each laden with his sheaves.

Last of the laborers, Thy feet I gain,
Lord of the harvest! and my spirit grieves
  That I am burdened not so much with grain
  As with a heaviness of heart and brain; —
    Master, behold my sheaves!

Few, light, and worthless, — yet their trifling weight
Through all my frame a weary aching leaves;
  For long I struggled with my hapless fate,
  And stayed and toiled till it was dark and late, —
    Yet these are all my sheaves!

Full well I know I have more tares than wheat, —
Brambles and flowers, dry stalks and withered leaves,
  Wherefore I blush and weep, as at Thy feet
  I kneel down reverently and repeat,
    " Master, behold my sheaves ! "

I know these blossoms, clustering heavily,
With evening dew upon their folded leaves,
 Can claim no value nor utility, —
Therefore shall fragrancy and beauty be
  The glory of my sheaves.

So do I gather strength and hope anew ;
For well I know Thy patient love perceives
 Not what I did, but what I strove to do,
And though the full, ripe ears be sadly few,
  Thou wilt accept my sheaves !

ELIZABETH AKERS ALLEN.

August 7.

But now they desire a better country, that is, an heavenly;
wherefore God is not ashamed to be called their God;
for He hath prepared for them a city. — HEB. xi. 16.

DUTY reaches down ages in its effects, and into eternity ; and when a man goes about it resolutely, it seems to me now as though his footsteps were echoing beyond the stars, though only heard faintly in the atmosphere of this world, because it is so heavy. What then is death ? It will be a concealment of me from the world, but not a hiding of the world from me. Always there will be something of me lasting on in the world ; and to the end of it the world will be known to me in some things, I think. It is not to be estranged from this world utterly. Oh no ! For it is to be taken into the bosom of the Father, and to feel His feelings for this world, and to look back upon it from under the light of His eyes. Death is this, and it is beauty, and it is peace.

EUTHANASY.

"HE leadeth me !"
I shall not take one needless step through all,
 In wind, or heat, or cold ;
And all day long He sees the peaceful end,
 Through trials manifold ;
Up the fair hill-side, like some sweet surprise,
 Waiteth the quiet Fold.

MARY K. A. STONE.

SONG OF THE SILENT LAND.

INTO the Silent Land!
Ah! who shall lead us thither?
Clouds in the evening sky more darkly gather,
And shattered wrecks lie thicker on the strand;
Who leads us with a gentle hand
Thither, oh thither,
Into the Silent Land?

Into the Silent Land!
To you, ye boundless regions
Of all perfection! Tender morning visions
Of beauteous souls! The future's pledge and band!
Who in life's battle firm doth stand
Shall bear Hope's tender blossoms
Into the Silent Land!

O Land! O Land!
For all the broken-hearted!
The mildest herald by our fate allotted
Beckons, and with inverted torch doth stand
To lead us with a gentle hand
Into the land of the great departed,
Into the Silent Land!

JOHANN GAUDENTZ VON SALIS.

———◆———

August 8.

And as thy days, so shall thy strength be. — DEUT.
xxxiii. 25.

OH, by every tear which God hath wiped from your
eyes, by every anxiety which He has soothed, by
every fear which He has dispelled, by every want which
He has supplied, by every mercy which He has bestowed,
strengthen yourselves for all that awaits you through the
remainder of your pilgrimage; look onwards, if it must
be so, to new trials, to increased perplexities, yea, even to
death itself; but look on what is past, as well as what
is to come, and you will be enabled to say of Him in
whose hand are your times, His future dealings will be
what His former have been, — fulfilments of the promise,
" As thy days, so shall thy strength be."

"AS THY DAY, SO SHALL THY STRENGTH BE."

WHEN adverse winds and waves arise,
And in my heart despondence sighs, —
When life her throng of cares reveals,
And weakness o'er my spirit steals, —
Grateful I hear the kind decree,
That, "as my day, my strength shall be."

When, with sad footstep, memory roves
'Mid smitten joys and buried loves, —
When sleep my tearful pillow flies,
And dewy morning drinks my sighs, —
Still to Thy promise, Lord, I flee,
That, "as my day, my strength shall be."

One trial more must yet be past,
One pang, — the keenest and the last;
And when, with brow convulsed and pale,
My feeble, quivering heartstrings fail,
Redeemer, grant my soul to see
That, "as my day, my strength shall be."

LYDIA H. SIGOURNEY.

August 9.

If we suffer, we shall also reign with Him. — 2 TIM. ii. 12.

ALL the other bonds that had fastened down the spirit of the universe to our narrow round of earth were as nothing in comparison to the golden chain of suffering and self-sacrifice which at once riveted the heart of man to one who, like himself, was acquainted with grief. Pain is the deepest thing we have in our nature; and union through pain has always seemed more real and more holy than any other.

ARTHUR H. HALLAM.

THE FLOWER OF PAIN.

SINGING, I pause amid my glowing roses,
   My leaning lilies fair,
And. lo ! my search a hidden stalk discloses
   Of leaves and blossoms bare.

" A poor dull weed ! " I cry, and all unbrooking
   Its plain and flowerless lines,
I struggle to uproot it, never looking
   Beyond its outward signs.

In vain I strive, with weak, impatient fingers.
   Strong set within the mould,
The hardy interloper lives and lingers
   Where beauty's buds unfold.

Ever with jealous thoughts I watch it growing ;
   It robs my life of grace ;
It spreads its dark root fibres, overflowing
   My garden's tiny space.

It puts forth leaves of tropic duskness, drooping
   Between me and the sun.
My roses' pride, my lilies' graceful grouping
   Are all undone ! undone !

     .   .   .

Waking to-day, dim-eyed and heavy-hearted,
   I catch its breath divine, —
I see amid the dusky leaflets parted
   Rich colors throb and shine.

I see it blooming through the years forever,
   Its blessing, ah, how plain ! —
Life's one deep rose whose crimson fadeth never.
   The perfect flower of pain !

HELEN T. CLARK

August 10.

Fear thou not; for I am with thee: be not dismayed;
for I am thy God: I will strengthen thee, yea, I will
help thee. — ISA. xli. 10.

AND let it be remembered that this Divine aid is really
help. It does not supersede human exertion, but
helps to make it effective. It does not *overbear* the
human faculties, but *invigorates* them. It does not substitute a foreign virtue, attaching it like foreign fruit to
dead branches; but it puts life into the trunk that it may
bear fruit of itself.
EPHRAIM PEABODY.

THE SPIRIT OF GOD.

THE prayers I make will then be sweet indeed,
If Thou the spirit give by which I pray;
My unassisted heart is barren clay,
That of its native self can nothing feed;
Of good and pious works Thou art the seed,
That quickens only when Thou say'st it may;
Unless Thou show to us Thine own true way,
No man can find it; Father! Thou must lead.
Do Thou, then, breathe those thoughts into my mind,
By which such virtue may in me be bred
That in Thy holy footsteps I may tread;
The fetters of my tongue do Thou unbind,
That I may have the power to sing of Thee,
And sound Thy praises everlastingly.
MICHAEL ANGELO.

—◆—

August 11.

I have chosen thee in the furnace of affliction. — ISA.
xlviii. 10.

IF a man has a statue decayed by rust and age, and
mutilated in many of its parts, he breaks it up and
casts it into a furnace, and after the melting he receives
it again in more beautiful form. As thus the dissolving

in the furnace was not a destruction, but a renewing of the statue, so the death of our bodies is not a destruction, but a renovation. When, therefore, you see as in a furnace our flesh flowing away to corruption, dwell not on that sight, but wait for the recasting. And advance in your thoughts to a still higher point, — for the statuary casting into the furnace a brazen image but makes a brazen one again. God does not thus; but casting in a mortal body formed of clay, he returns you an immortal statue of gold.

SAINT CHRYSOSTOM.

THE COVENANT AND CONFIDENCE OF FAITH.

MY whole, though broken, heart, O Lord,
  From henceforth shall be Thine ;
And here I do my vow record ;
  This hand, these words are mine.
All that I have, without reserve,
  I offer here to Thee :
Thy will and honour. all, shall serve,
  That Thou bestowedst on me.

All that exceptions save I lose ;
  All that I lose I save ;
The treasure of Thy love I choose ;
  And Thou art all I crave.
My God, Thou hast my heart and hand ;
  I all to Thee resign ;
I 'll ever to this covenant stand,
  Though flesh hereat repine.

Christ leads me through no darker rooms
  Than He went through before ;
He that into God's kingdom comes
  Must enter by this door.
Come, Lord, when grace hath made me meet
  Thy blessed face to see ;
For if Thy work on earth be sweet,
  What will Thy glory be ?

RICHARD BAXTER (1691).

August 12.

*O man, greatly beloved, fear not; peace be unto thee, be
strong, yea, be strong. And when he had spoken unto
me I was strengthened, and said, Let my Lord speak;
for thou hast strengthened me.* — DAN. x. 19.

WITH the sure knowledge that our smallest concerns
are regulated by Him, we may repose in confidence that if it is good for us happiness will be granted;
and if it be hereafter checkered, as we see is often the
case, the support and the comfort will come with the
trial.

MARIA HARE

THINGS which never could have made a man happy,
develop a power to make him strong.   Strength and not
happiness, or rather only that happiness which comes by
strength, is the end of human living.   And with that
test and standard, the best order and beauty reappear.

AN OLD IDEA.

STREAM of my life, dim-banked pale river, flow!
I have no fear to meet the ingulfing seas;
Neither I look before, nor look behind,
But lying mute, with wave-dipped hand float on.

It was not always thus.   My brethren, see
This oar-marked quivering palm, the better sign
Of youth's mad struggle with the wave that drifts
Immutably, eternally along.

I would have had it glide through fields and flowers,
Giving and taking perfume, freshness, joy;
It winds through a blank desert.   Peace, my soul!
The finger of God's Angel drew its line.

So I lean back, and look up to the stars,
And count the ripples circling to the shore,
And watch the silent river rolling on,
Until it widen to the open seas.

NEW YORK MAIL.

August 13.

Now are we sure that Thou knowest all things. — JOHN xvi. 30.

THERE may be many tongues and many languages of men, but the language of prayer is one by itself, in all and above all. It is the inspiration of that Spirit that is now working with our spirit, and constantly lifting us higher than we know, and by our wants, by our woes, by our tears, by our yearnings, by our poverty, urging us, with mightier and mightier force, against those chains of sin which keep us from our God.   H. B. STOWE.

THE SAVIOUR'S KNOWLEDGE.

THOU knowest, Lord, the weariness and sorrow
   Of the sad heart that comes to Thee for rest;
Cares of to-day, and burdens for to-morrow,
   Blessings implored, and sins to be confessed, —
I come before Thee at Thy gracious word,
And lay them at Thy feet; Thou knowest, Lord.

Thou knowest all the present: each temptation,
   Each toilsome duty, each foreboding fear;
All to myself assigned of tribulation,
   Or to beloved ones than self more dear;
All pensive memories as I journey on,
Longings for vanished smiles and voices gone.

Thou knowest all the future: gleams of gladness,
   By stormy clouds too quickly overcast,
Hours of sweet fellowship and parting sadness,
   And the dark river to be crossed at last.
Oh, what could hope and confidence afford
To tread that path, but this, Thou knowest, Lord?

Thou knowest, not alone as God, all-knowing;
   As man, our mortal weakness Thou hast proved;
On earth with purest sympathies o'erflowing,
   O Saviour, Thou hast wept, and Thou hast loved;
And love and sorrow still to Thee may come,
And find a hiding-place, a rest, a home.

Therefore I come, Thy gentle call obeying,
   And lay my sins and sorrows at Thy feet,
On everlasting strength my weakness staying,
   Clothed in Thy robe of righteousness complete;
Then rising and refreshed, I leave Thy throne,
And follow on to know as I am known.
                HYMNOLOGIA CHRISTIANA (Kennedy's).

August 14.

I have loved thee with an everlasting love ; therefore with loving-kindness have I drawn thee. — JER. xxxi. 3.

IT comes to us, if it comes at all, through those years of learning and of waiting in which our human hearts are both humbled and exalted, both made empty and enriched. That knowledge is the knowledge in which all moral experiences sum up their wisdom of life ; and it cannot be taught, for it is a revelation coming through the life of man, through all his affections, needs, trials, satisfactions, — a knowledge of the heart which cannot be taken away. Thus the Bible sums up its revelations of the Father in one intensely human word, — God is love.

NEWMAN SMYTH.

THE LOVE OF GOD.

AT first I prayed for light ; could I but see the way,
How gladly would I walk to everlasting day !
I asked the world's deep law before my eyes to ope,
And let me see my prayer fulfilled, and realize my hope.
    But God was kinder than my prayer,
    And darkness veiled me everywhere.

And next I asked for strength, that I might tread the road
With firm, unfaltering pace to heaven's serene abode ;
That I might never know a faltering, failing heart,
But manfully go on and reach the highest part.
    But God was kinder than my prayer,
    And weakness checked me everywhere.

And then I asked for faith ; could I but trust my God,
I 'd live in heavenly peace, though foes were all abroad.
His light thus shining round, no faltering should I know ;
And faith in heaven above would make a heaven below.
    But God was kinder than my prayer
    And doubts beset me everywhere.

And now I pray for love, deep love to God and man, —
A love that will not fail, however dark His plan ;
That sees all life in Him, rejoicing in His power,
And faithful, though the darkest clouds of gloom and
    doubt may lower.
    And God is kinder than my prayer ;
    Love fills and blesses everywhere.

EDNAH D. CHENEY.

August 15.

Not slothful in business; fervent in spirit, serving the Lord. — ROM. xii. 11.

SORROWS may take from life its delights ; but, thank God ! they can never take its duties. At the lowest ebb of dejection we still have much to do.

F. D. MAURICE.

HAPPINESS, the choice of all, can be directly gained by none. It is the gift of God to him, who, in the spirit of Christ, toils for the good of others.

DOING GOOD, TRUE HAPPINESS.

WOULDST thou from sorrow find a sweet relief ?
  Or is thy heart oppressed with woes untold ?
Balm wouldst thou gather for corroding grief ?
  Pour blessings round thee like a shower of gold.
  'T is when the rose is wrapped in many a fold
Close to its heart, the worm is wasting there
  Its life and beauty ; not when, all unrolled,
Leaf after leaf, its bosom, rich and fair,
Breathes freely its perfumes throughout the ambient air

Some high or humble enterprise of good
  Contemplate, till it shall possess thy mind,
Become thy study, pastime, rest, and food,
  And kindle in thy heart a flame refined.
  Pray Heaven for firmness thy whole soul to bind
To this thy purpose, — to begin, pursue,
  With thoughts all fixed and feelings purely kind ;
Strength to complete and with delight review,
And grace to give the praise where all is ever due.

CARLOS WILCOX

August 16.

Shew me Thy ways, O Lord; teach me Thy paths. —
Ps. xxv. 4.

MY Father, may I ever humbly follow in Thy way;
may I ever trust, with the full assurance of faith,
that it does lead to Thy heavenly kingdom. It is often
very narrow and perplexed, and I cannot see where it is
leading me; yet, though the guiding light of Thy holy
Word may be half obscured by the mists of the valley, if
I fix my eye steadily upon it, it will become brighter and
brighter; I shall see my way clearly in this seemingly
intricate road, and even discern at the end of it the entrance to Thy heavenly mansion.

THE storms of the pilgrimage are there hushed to
silence; fierce tempests cease to blow; all is blessed
sunshine, calm and sweet repose, there in the Land of
Beulah!   PILGRIM'S PROGRESS.

THROUGH THE VALLEY AT SUNRISE.

ON either side the mountains lift their towering summits high;
Alas, their steep and rugged cliffs our human strength defy!
But down between there winds a path that leads at last to
   home,
Where, sheltered from the piercing winds, the tender ones
   may roam.

On either side, on either side, the woods in darkness lie,
And close the tree-tops overlean to hide the bending sky;
But creeping through the quiet shade the timid sunbeams come
To tell of day that dawns afar, to light the pathway home.

On either side, on either side, shut in, we may not see
How near the tide that rolls beyond, our eager hearts may be;
But, as we listen, through the hush we catch the sound once
   more, —
The music of the restless waves that beat upon the shore.

Beneath our feet, beneath our feet, how rugged lies the way!
Footsore and weak we wander on, and weary grows the day;
But through the vista opening how calm the blue hills lie,
Beneath whose shadows we shall sleep in comfort by-and-by!

August 17.

Verily I say unto you, whosoever shall not receive the kingdom of God as a little child, he shall not enter therein. — MARK x. 5.

BUT in too many cases, what might seem so easy of attainment — to trust in and follow Jesus in the sweet simplicity of childhood — is the slow growth of years, the result of a long and painful process. As we look around among the visible members of the church of Christ who profess to have surrendered their will to His, how few appear to be as little children, and to have as a perpetual possession that peace which floweth as a river! We see many seeking to climb, to soar, but few who say with Paul, "Yet not I, but the grace of God which was with me."

THE HAND OF JESUS.

TRUST.

To Him who hears I whisper all ;
   And softlier than the dews of heaven
The tears of Christ's compassion fall ;
   I know I am forgiven.

Wrapped in the peace that follows prayer,
   I fold my hands in perfect trust,
Forgetful of the cross I bear
   Through noonday heat and dust.

No more Life's mysteries vex my thought ;
   No cruel doubts disturb my breast ;
My heavy-laden spirit sought
   And found the promised rest.

HARRIET MCEWEN KIMBALL.

August 18.

If we love one another, God dwelleth in us. — 1 JOHN iv. 12.

IT never troubles the sun that some of his rays fall wide and vain into ungrateful space, and only a small part on the reflecting planet. Thou art enlarged by thine own shining.

R. W. EMERSON.

OH, where are those noble souls to be found, who, all unconscious of themselves, daily pursue their career like the sun, which rises each morning in the heavens, and scatters its gold to the left and to the right, on the mountains and in the valleys, — those noble souls that, by an inward necessity, here create and renew, there beautify and heal, and everywhere bless, like the sun, that cannot but give light? There is but one in whom such an image of high love has appeared to us in its entire purity; and it is only by faith in Him that such self-sacrificing love is produced.

THOLUCK.

THEY ARE NOT LOST.

THE look of sympathy, the gentle word,
Spoken so low that only angels heard;
The secret act of pure self-sacrifice,
Unseen by men, but marked by angels' eyes, —
These are not lost.

The happy dreams that gladdened all our youth,
When dreams had less of self and more of truth;
The childhood's faith, so tranquil and so sweet,
Which sat like Mary at the Master's feet, —
These are not lost.

The kindly plan devised for others' good,
So seldom guessed, so little understood,
The quiet, steadfast love that strove to win
Some wanderer from the ways of sin, —
These are not lost.

Not lost, O Lord! for in Thy city bright
Our eyes shall see the past by clearer light,
And things long hidden from our gaze below
Thou wilt reveal; and we shall surely know
These are not lost.

RICHARD METCALF.

August 19.

Who maketh the clouds His chariot; who walketh upon the wings of the wind. — Ps. civ. 3.

E VEN as that cloudy giant yields, and is shepherded by the slow, unwilling wind, so is each of us borne onward to an unseen destiny, — a glorious one, if we will but yield to the Spirit of God, that bloweth where it listeth, with a grand listing, — coming whence we know not, and going whither we know not. The very clouds of the air are hung up as dim pictures of the thoughts and history of man. Man can imagine nothing, even in the clouds of the air, that God has not done or is not doing.

GEORGE MACDONALD.

THE EVENING CLOUD.

A CLOUD lay cradled near the setting sun;
A gleam of crimson tinged its braided snow ;
Long had I watched the glory moving on
O'er the still radiance of the lake below.
Tranquil its spirit seemed, and floated slow !
Even in its very motion there was rest ;
While every breath of eve that chanced to blow
Wafted the traveller to the beauteous west.
Emblem, methought, of the departed soul,
To whose white robe the gleam of bliss is given
And by the breath of mercy made to roll
Right onwards to the golden gates of heaven,
Where to the eye of faith it peaceful lies,
And tells to man his glorious destinies.

JOHN WILSON.

August 20.

*He maketh the storm a calm, so that the waves thereof are
still.* — Ps. cvii. 29.

When He giveth quietness, who then can make trouble? —
Job xxxiv. 29.

WHEN in the midst of the stormy whirlwind of action
and passion, we are apt to trust to our own frail
barks; and we hear not the voice of God until after the
storm, in the still, small whisper in our souls.   When
the heart is calmed we can feel the power and behold the
brightness of our Father's love; and we can yield ourselves to Him, and desire to be led by Him wherever He
chooseth.   Hill.

CALM ME, MY GOD.

Calm me, my God, and keep me calm
  While these hot breezes blow;
Be like the night-dew's cooling balm
  Upon earth's fevered brow!

Calm me, my God, and keep me calm,
  Soft resting on Thy breast;
Soothe me with holy hymn and psalm,
  And bid my spirit rest.

Calm me, my God, and keep me calm.
  Let thine outstretchèd wing
Be like the shade of Elim's palm
  Beside her desert-spring.

Yes; keep me calm, though loud and rude
  The sounds my ear that greet, —
Calm in the closet's solitude,
  Calm in the bustling street;

Calm in the hour of buoyant health,
  Calm in my hour of pain;
Calm in my poverty or wealth;
  Calm in my loss or gain;

Calm as the ray of sun or star
  Which storms assail in vain, —
Moving unruffled through earth's war,
  The eternal calm to gain.
              Horatius Bonar.

August 21.

OUR home is always where our affections are. We sigh and wander, we vibrate to and fro, till we rest in that special centre where our deepest loves are garnered up. Then the heart fills and brims over with its own happiness, and spreads sweetness and fertility all around it. Very often when the eyes are closing in death, and this world is shutting off the sight from the departing soul, the last wish which is made audible is "to go home." The words break out sometimes through the cloud of delirium; but it is the soul's deepest and most central want groping after its object, haply soon to find it as the clogs of earth clear away and she springs upon the line of swift affection, as the bee with unerring precision shoots through the dusk of evening to her cell.

E. H. SEARS: *Foregleams of Immortality*.

FREEDOM.

THE bird let loose in eastern skies,
  When hastening fondly home,
Ne'er stoops to earth her wing, nor flies
  Where idle warblers roam ;
But high she shoots through air and light,
  Above all low delay,
Where nothing earthly bounds her flight,
  Nor shadow dims her way.

So grant me, God, from every care
  And stain of passion free,
Aloft through virtue's purer air,
  To hold my course to Thee !
No sin to cloud, no lure to stay
  My soul, as home she springs, —
Thy sunshine on her joyful way,
  Thy freedom in her wings !

THOMAS MOORE.

August 22.

For Thou art my rock and my fortress; therefore for Thy name's sake lead me and guide me. — Ps. xxxi. 3.

FOR our guide in life we want something which our passions or fancies cannot alter, our fingers cannot touch; as we need not a mechanical instrument alone, but the north-star and the sidereal time of the heavens, to direct us on an earthly voyage. Conscience, independent of religion, of God's will, is not enough; all history, in every land, shows it is not enough. It is but like a lantern on the vessel's mast, casting a little light around, but swaying and turning with every motion of the waves, or eclipsed by the tempest and incapable of illumining the whole course. The sailor must look beyond his candle to the steady, ever-shining pole. And while we move in the varying light of our own mind, and keep that inner, indispensable lamp carefully trimmed and burning, we must supply its deficiencies from the bright, high oracles of God in Jesus Christ.

CYRUS A. BARTOL.

THE WAY OF LIFE.

JESUS, wilt Thou go before
On life's pathway evermore?
We will not delay, the while,
After Thee in faith to toil.
Lead us by Thy gentle hand
To our blessed Fatherland.

If the way be rough and drear,
Firmly let us persevere,
And in darkest days refrain
At their burdens to complain;
For through sorrows here must lie
Ways that lead to Thee on high!

LOWLY WAYS.

August 23.

The floods have lifted up, O Lord, the floods have lifted up their voice. — Ps. xciii. 3.

HAVE you never stood by some arm of the sea which penetrates far inland, and seen its emptiness and ugliness? There is only the oozy, miry bed of the creek ; the blue line of ocean is far away on the horizon. There is no human power by which it can be filled with water. The little streams from the hillsides could never fill the thousand empty indentations in our coast. But the great unquiet ocean begins to creep in. It spreads slowly over the flat bottom, and winds into every bend of the shore, and fills every crevice of the rocks ; it covers the long grasses, it drives you back step by step ; it surges in lifting itself with quiet strength, until the little gulf is filled to the brim, and the bowing billows come over the surface, and the ships are lifted from their beds and sail away to their appointed havens. The inlet is full ; it is filled with all the fulness of the ocean, and with its mighty power. So we are empty till we are filled with the power of God. The toils and sacrifices and duties of life seem too heavy for us ; but when inspirations from God begin to come in upon us, when His love rises in our hearts, with His grace and inexhaustible power behind it, we can carry all burdens buoyant upon such a strength, and can feel an undercurrent of Divine Power filling our hearts.

GEORGE HARRIS.

EBB AND FLOW.

How easily He turns the tides!
　Just now the yellow beach was dry ;
Just now the gaunt rocks all were bare,
　The sun beat hot and thirstily.
Each sea-weed waved its long brown hair,
　And beat and languished as in pain ;
Then, in a flashing moment's space
　The white foam-feet which spurned the sand
Paused in their joyous outward race,
　Wheeled, wavered, turned them to the land,
And a swift legionary band
　Poured on the waiting shores again.

How easily He turns the tides !
   The fulness of my yesterday
Has vanished like a rapid dream,
   And pitiless and far away
The cool, refreshing waters gleam ;
   Grim rocks of dread and doubt and pain,
Rear their dark fronts where once was sea ;
   But I can smile and wait for Him
Who turns the tides so easily,
   Fills the spent rock-pool to its brim,
And up from the horizon dim
   Leads His bright morning waves again.

SUSAN COOLIDGE.

August 24.

*Give her of the fruit of her hands ; and let her own works
praise her in the gates.* — PROV. xxxi. 31.

I WONDER why we forget so and seem to think the
dream-days belong only to the young, — never having
a thought for the stories written on hearts that are hidden
by wrinkled, care-worn faces ; never seeming to think
of the pathos of lives grown silent and tired with the long
journey, — of the struggles, the noble deeds looking from
dim eyes, sounding in voices from which the music has
gone, in steps grown slow and halting, hands trembling
and strengthless.

ROSE PORTER.

BEAUTIFUL HANDS.

SUCH beautiful, beautiful hands !
   They 're neither white nor small,
And you, I know, would scarcely think
   That they were fair at all.
I 've looked on hands whose form and hue
   A sculptor's dream might be,
Yet are these aged, wrinkled hands
   Most beautiful to me.

Such beautiful, beautiful hands !
   Though heart were weary or sad,
These patient hands kept toiling on
   That the children might be glad.
I almost weep, as looking back
   To childhood's distant day,
I think how these hands rested not,
   When mine were at their play.

Such beautiful, beautiful hands !
   They 're growing feeble now ;
For time and pain have left their work
   On hand and heart and brow.
Alas ! alas ! the nearing time,
   And the sad, sad day to me,
When 'neath the daisies, out of sight,
   These hands will folded be.

But oh ! beyond this shadow land,
   Where all is bright and fair,
I know full well these dear old hands
   Will palms of victory bear.
Where crystal streams, through endless years,
   Flow over golden sands,
And where the old grow young again,
   I 'll clasp my mother's hands.

August 25.

But I have trusted in Thy mercy ; my heart shall rejoice in Thy salvation. — Ps. xiii. 5.

O IMPATIENT ones ! Did the leaves say nothing to you as they murmured to-day? They were not fashioned this spring, but months ago ; and the summer just begun will fashion others for another year. At the bottom of every leaf stem is a cradle, and in it is an infant germ ; and the winds will rock it, and the birds will sing to it all summer long, and next season it will unfold. So God is working for you and carrying forward to the perfect development all the processes of your lives.

HENRY WARD BEECHER.

TRUST IN GOD.

LIFE'S bitter trials, earth's despair,
　The darkest sorrows, crush me not;
To Thee my weight of woe I bear,
　Great God, thou guardian of my lot.
My bosom finds in Thee alone
　Its grandest strength, its sweetest balm;
And sheltered by Thy mighty throne,
　I conquer, I am brave and calm.

I know Thy mercy changeth pain
　To joy and blessedness and peace;
All worldly loss is wholly gain, —
　A rapture that can never cease.
With thanks I taste Thy bounteous store,
　Though oft my cross may heavy be;
I, like a little child, adore,
　For Thou, my Father, leadest me.

Bright hope sustains and comforts all
　Who seek Thee, Lord, in faithfulness;
Not cruel death can them appal,
　Nor make their mystic transports less.
O Father, I shall ever praise
　Thy wisdom, Thy salvation great;
With voice eternal as Thy days
　Proclaim Thou art compassionate.

HJORT: *Hymns of Denmark.*

August 26.

*It is good that a man should both hope and quietly wait
for the salvation of the Lord.* — LAM. iii. 26.

IF to your life, struggling in obedience to Christ, but
not able to clear itself into light about Christ, there
could come, as from the Christ you long for, a command to you to struggle on still in hope because you
must reach the light some day; and yet a command,
while the light is withheld, to find satisfaction and growth
in the ever-deepening struggle, would not that be the
command you need? Patience and struggle, an earnest

use of what we have now, and, all the time, an earnest
discontent until we come to what we ought to be, — are
not these what we need, what in their rich union we
could not get, except in just such a life as this with its
delayed completions?   Jesus does not blame Peter when
he impetuously begs that he may follow Him now.   He
bids him wait and he shall follow Him some day.   But
we can see that the value of his waiting lies in the certainty that he shall follow ; and the value of his following,
when it comes, will lie in the fact that he has waited.   So,
if we take all Christ's culture, we are sure that our life
on eartl. may get already the inspiration of the heaven
for which we are training, and our life in heaven may keep
forever the blessing of the earth in which we were trained.

PHILLIPS BROOKS

SEA-WEED.

NOT always unimpeded can I pray,
Nor, pitying saint, Thine intercession claim ;
Too closely clings the burden of the day,
And all the mint and anise that I pay
But swells my debt and deepens my self-blame.

Shall I less patience have than Thou, who know
That Thou revisit'st all who wait for Thee,
Nor only fill'st the unsounded deeps below,
But dost refresh with punctual overflow
The rifts where unregarded mosses be ?

The drooping sea-weed hears, in night abyssed,
Far and more far the wave's receding shocks,
Nor doubts. for all the darkness and the mist,
That the pale shepherdess will keep her tryst,
And shoreward lead again her foam-fleeced flocks.

For the same wave that rims the Carib shore
With momentary brede of pearl and gold,
Goes hurrying thence to gladden with its roar
Lorn weeds bound fast on rocks of Labrador,
By Love Divine on one sweet errand rolled.

And though Thy healing waters far withdraw,
I, too, can wait and feed on hope of Thee,
And of the dear recurrence of Thy law, —
Sure that the parting grace that morning saw
Abides its time to come in search of me !

JAMES RUSSELL LOWELL.

August 27.

I delight to do Thy will, O my God: yea, Thy law is within my heart. — Ps. xl. 8.

IF there are any two truths in the whole circle of truth which may be called universal, I think they are these, — that every man has one life, and that every man shall make the most of that life by joining it with God's life and God's thought. . . . As I stand with you to-day and see how life promises to repeat its inefficiency, and that many of us are likely to lie down at last defeated, I cannot cease from saying to you and to myself, that there is but one thing which can save us, but one way in which we can glorify God in our heart and our life, and that is, not by simply trying to be good ; not by working hard to do good ; it is by receiving the Spirit into our spirit ; praying God to come to us and take us ; to teach us, to guide us, to use us. Then God's success shall be our success ; life shall be glorified, and God shall be honored.

ALEXANDER McKENZIE.

THE SACRIFICE OF THE WILL.

LAID on Thine altar, O our Lord Divine,
Accept my gift this day, for Jesu's sake.
I have no jewels to adorn Thy shrine,
Nor any world-famed sacrifice to make,
Yet here I bring, within my trembling hand,
This will of mine, — a thing that seemeth small, —
But Thou alone, O Lord, canst understand,
How, when I yield Thee this, I yield Thee all.
Hidden therein, Thy searching eye can see
Struggles of passion, visions of delight,
All that I have, and am, and fain would be,
Fond hope, deep love, and longing infinite.
It hath been wet with tears, and dimmed with sighs,
Clinched in my grasp till beauty hath it none ;
Now, from Thy footstool, where it vanquished lies,
The prayer ascendeth, " May Thy will be done."
Take it, O Father, ere my courage fail,
And merge it so in Thine own will, that e'en
If in some desperate hour my cries prevail,
And Thou give back my will, it may have been
So changed, so purified, so fair have grown,
So one with Thee, so filled with peace divine,
I may not know or feel it as mine own,
But gaining back my will, may find it Thine.

August 28.

Then they cry unto the Lord in their trouble, and He bringeth them out of their distresses. He maketh the storm a calm. Then are they glad because they be quiet; so He bringeth them unto their desired haven.
— Ps. cvii. 28–30.

THE simplest, most living, most genuine Christians of our own time are such as rest their souls, day by day, on this confidence and promise of accruing power, and make themselves responsible, not for what they have in some inherent ability, but for what they can have in their times of stress and peril and in the continual raising of their own personal quantity and power. Instead of gathering in their souls timorously beforehand, upon the little sufficiency they find in possession, they look upon the great world God has made as being friendly and tributary, ready to pour in help, minister light, and strengthen them to victory, just according to their faith. And so they grow in courage, confidence, personal volume, efficiency of every kind. . . . Commit the keeping of your soul to God, as to a faithful Creator. Believe that He is faithful, and love to trust Him for His faithfulness. The moment you can let go your misgiving, spiritless habit, and cast yourself on God, to go into your duty, you are free. If the wind is high, and the water looks deep, and you have no courage to venture on a holy life, behold Jesus coming to you, treading lightly on the crests of the billows; and He comes to say, " It is I." What assurance more do you want?

HORACE BUSHNELL.

PEACE.

FIERCE was the wild billow, dark was the night,
Oars labored heavily, foam glimmered white;
Mariners trembled, peril was nigh;
Then said the God of Gods, " Peace, it is I ! "

Jesu, Deliverer ! come Thou to me;
Soothe Thou my voyaging over life's sea;
Thou, when the storm of death roars sweeping by,
Whisper, O Truth of Truth, " Peace, it is I ! "

SAINT ANATOLIUS, of Constantinople (Fifth Century).

August 29.

Beloved, now are we the sons of God, and it doth not yet appear what we shall be; but we know that, when He shall appear, we shall be like Him; for we shall see Him as He is. — 1 JOHN iii. 2.

IN life there are many things which interfere with a just estimate of the virtues of others. There are veils upon the heart that hide its most secret workings and its sweetest affections from us; there are earthly clouds that come between us and the excellence that we love. So that it is not, perhaps, till a friend is taken from us, that we entirely feel his value, and appreciate his worth. The vision is loveliest at its vanishing away; and we perceive not, perhaps, till we see the parting wing, that an angel has been with us.

ORVILLE DEWEY.

AN ANGEL IN THE HOUSE.

How sweet it were if, without feeble fright,
Or dying of the dreadful, beauteous sight,
An angel came to us, and we could bear
To see him issue from the silent air
At evening in our room, and bend on ours
His divine eyes, and bring us from his bowers
News of dear friends and children who have never
Been dead indeed, as we shall know forever.
Alas! we think not what we daily see
About our hearths, — angels that are to be,
Or may be if they will, and we prepare
Their souls and ours to meet in happy air;
A child, a friend, a wife whose soft heart sings
In unison with ours, breeding its future wings.

LEIGH HUNT

August 30.

Take therefore no thought for the morrow; for the morrow shall take thought for the things of itself. Sufficient unto the day is the evil thereof. — MATT. vi. 34.

ALL day long my God is moved with compassion. Since the beginning of the world, not one sigh has ever lost its way between heaven and earth. If once I belong to God, He will prepare for me whatever is best. I may ask everything. God has told me so. I have the liberty to desire. I have equal confidence in trusting my death to God as in submitting my life to Him. From that moment I have peace, God knows what I wish; if it is good for me, He will give it me.

COUNTESS DE GASPARIN.

TO-MORROW.

'T is late at night, and in the realm of sleep
My little lambs are folded like the flocks;
From room to room I hear the wakeful clocks
Challenge the passing hour, like guards that keep
Their solitary watch on tower and steep;
Far off I hear the crowing of the cocks,
And, through the opening door that time unlocks,
Feel the fresh breathing of To-morrow creep.
To-morrow! the mysterious, unknown guest,
Who cries aloud: " Remember Barmecide,
And tremble to be happy with the rest."
And I make answer: " I am satisfied;
I dare not ask; I know not what is best;
God hath already said what shall betide."

H. W. LONGFELLOW

August 31.

If we walk in the light as He is in the light, we have fellowship one with another, and the blood of Jesus Christ His son cleanseth us from all sin. — 1 JOHN i. 7.

NOW whenever a man hath been made a partaker of the Divine nature, in him is fulfilled the best and noblest life, and the worthiest in God's eyes that hath been or can be. This life is not chosen in order to serve any end, or to get anything by it, but for love of its nobleness, and because God loveth and esteemeth it so greatly. And whoever saith that he hath had enough of it, and may now lay it aside, hath never tasted or known it; for he who hath truly felt or tasted it can never give it up again. And he who hath put on the life of Christ with the intent to win or deserve aught thereby hath taken it up as an hireling, and not for love, and is altogether without it. For he who doth not take it up for love hath none of it at all; he may dream indeed that he hath put it on, but he is deceived.

THEOLOGIA GERMANICA.

BE NOBLE.

" FOR this true nobleness I seek in vain,
In woman and in man I find it not ;
I almost weary of my earthly lot,
My life-springs are dried up with burning pain."
Thou find'st it not ? I pray thee look again,
Look inward, through the depths of thine own soul.
How is it with thee ? Art thou sound and whole ?
Doth narrow search show thee no earthly stain ?
Be noble ! and the nobleness that lies
In other men, sleeping, but never dead,
Will rise in majesty to meet thine own ;
Then wilt thou see it gleam in many eyes,
Then will pure light around thy path be shed,
And thou wilt never more be sad and lone.

JAMES RUSSELL LOWELL.

September 1.

For if through the offence of one many be dead, much more the grace of God, and the gift by grace, which is by one man, Jesus Christ, hath abounded unto many. — ROM. V. 15.

THE first thing is to meditate on life itself: all it means, all it involves, all the stores of joy or love which it is treasuring daily, all that must grow out of it through eternity.

Then surely the next step is to seek to connect ourselves with One who will bring to us a stronger strength than our own, a braver courage, a gladder hope; that the burden may not crush us, but may call forth, strengthen, and brace our powers, develop, sanctify, and finally glorify our life. The central thought of the gospel of grace is this, — God bending beneath and bearing the burden of the world. We are fearfully and wonderfully made and endowed. Life would be terrible if we had to live it alone, and to bear the burden of it through eternity. He has not taken counsel with us before laying this burden on us, and ordaining that we shall bear it forever; but He has come Himself to stand with us as we strain under it, and add His own almighty strength to ours that it may be borne bravely, and with joy. This is what " the grace of God which is in Christ Jesus our Lord " means and promises, — God's fellowship, partnership, with man, with you and me, in working out this high and hard problem to a successful and even glorious issue.

JAMES BALDWIN BROWN,
Minister of Claylands Chapel, London.

GOD OUR STRENGTH.

MAN in his weakness needs a stronger stay
Than fellow-men the holiest and the best.
And yet we turn to them from day to day,
As if in them our spirits could find rest.

Gently untwine our childish hands that cling
To such inadequate supports as these,
And shelter us beneath Thy heavenly wing,
Till we have learned to walk alone with ease.

Help us, O Lord, with patient love to bear
Each other's faults, to suffer with true meekness,
Help us each other's joys and griefs to share,
But let us turn to Thee alone in weakness.

S. V. Powys.

September 2.

*If I take the wings of the morning, and dwell in the utter-
most parts of the sea ; even there shall Thy hand lead me,
and Thy right hand shall hold me.* — Ps. cxxxix. 10, 11.

OH, what joy it brings to me to think that I am not a
lonely wanderer trying to find my way, but that the
vague and inexplicable yearnings which I have, and which
I am following, are the drawing-strings thrown out to lead
me by One who knows just what my necessities are, and
who stands ready to relieve them all !

HENRY WARD BEECHER.

TO A WATERFOWL.

WHITHER, midst falling dew,
While glow the heavens with the last steps of day,
Far through their rosy depths dost thou pursue
Thy solitary way?

Vainly the fowler's eye
Might mark thy distant flight to do thee wrong,
As, darkly limned upon the crimson sky,
Thy figure floats along.

Seek'st thou the plashy brink
Of weedy lake, or marge of river wide,
Or where the rocking billows rise and sink
On the chafed ocean side?

There is a Power whose care
Teaches thy way along that pathless coast, —
The desert and illimitable air, —
Lone wandering, but not lost.

All day thy wings have fanned,
At that far height, the cold, thin atmosphere,
Yet stoop not, weary, to the welcome land,
Though the dark night is near.

And soon that toil shall end ;
Soon shalt thou find a summer home, and rest,
And scream among thy fellows ; reeds shall bend,
Soon, o'er thy sheltered nest.

Thou 'rt gone: the abyss of heaven
Hath swallowed up thy form ; yet on my heart
Deeply hath sunk the lesson thou hast given,
And shall not soon depart.

He who, from zone to zone,
Guides through the boundless sky thy certain flight,
In the long way that I must tread alone
Will lead my steps aright.

                    WILLIAM CULLEN BRYANT.

—◆—

September 3.

*He discovereth deep things out of darkness, and bringeth
out to light the shadow of death. —* JOB xii. 22.
*For God, who commanded the light to shine out of dark-
ness, hath shined in our hearts, to give the light of the
knowledge of the glory of God. —* 2 COR. iv. 6.

THE circumstances of our lives are not unmeaning,
but infinitely otherwise ; but this we very often do
not see for want of vision. High as heaven and wide as
the earth is the atmosphere of holy opportunity in which
our souls have their being. Is it not felt? Then it is
only because it is not wished. Not every hour, nor every
day, perhaps, can generous wishes ripen into kind actions ;
but there is not a moment that cannot be freighted with
prayer.
                              WILLIAM MOUNTFORD.

THE earth is every day overspread with the veil of night, for the same reason as the cages of birds are darkened, — namely, that we may the more readily apprehend the higher harmonies of thought, in the hush and quiet of darkness. Thoughts which day turns into smoke and mist stand about us in the night as lights and flames; even as the column which fluctuates above Vesuvius in the daytime appears a pillar of cloud, but by night a pillar of fire.

RICHTER.

AT NIGHTFALL.

WHEN, in the evening's solitude,
    My thought has leisure to be free,
The purer life, the higher mood,
    The nobler purpose, wakes in me.

But in the cares that through the day
    Constrain the mind from hour to hour,
The nobler purpose fades away,
    Grows faint, and loses all its power.

So some pure star's excelling ray,
    With all the beauty of its light,
Is hidden by the glare of day,
    And only shines with fall of night.

September 4.

He casteth forth His ice like morsels; who can stand before His cold? He sendeth out His word and melteth them; He causeth His wind to blow, and the waters flow. — Ps. cxlvii. 17, 18.

I THINK that the bareness of her life was exaggerated. Because, after all, in all work honestly done there is, to a certain degree, satisfaction; because there are good moments in every life, however joyless, — moments when the sun shines, and winds are warm, and there is solemn meaning in the great marshalling of the clouds; moments

when the soul of the world, the presence of the great Mother Earth, is with us, bringing deep comfort and rest from pain. And Time is inexorable. There is no cry of agony in the world that with Time does not grow first hoarse and then dumb.
GEORGE ELIOT.

THE setting of a great hope is like the setting of the sun. The brightness of our life is gone. Shadows of evening fall around us, and the world seems but a dim reflection, — itself a broader shadow ; we look forward into the coming lonely night. The soul withdraws into itself. Then stars arise, and the night is holy.
H. W. LONGFELLOW : Hyperion.

LONELINESS.

IF loving hearts were never lonely,
  If all things wished might always be,
Accepting what they looked for only,
  They might be glad, but not in Thee.

We need as much the cross we bear.
  As air we breathe, as light we see ;
It draws us to Thy side in prayer,
  It bends us to our strength in Thee.

—♦—

September 5.

And not only so, but we glory in tribulation also : knowing that tribulation worketh patience. — ROM. V. 3.

LIFE has that value, that even misery cannot destroy it. It neutralizes grief, and makes it a source of deep and sacred interest. Ah ! holy hours of suffering and sorrow, hours of communion with the great and triumphant sufferer, who that has passed through your silent moments of prayer and resignation and trust would give you up for all the brightness of prosperity?

BETHINK thee, while the tears do run,
No cloud would rise but for the sun.
GERALD MASSEY.

THE MYSTERY OF CHASTISEMENT.

WITHIN this leaf, to every eye
So little worth, doth hidden lie
Most rare and subtle fragrancy:

Wouldst thou its secret strength unbind?
Crush it, and thou shalt perfume find,
Sweet as Arabia's spicy wind.

In this dull stone, so poor and bare
Of shape or lustre, patient care
Will find for thee a jewel rare.

But first must skilful hands essay,
With file and flint, to clear away
The film which hides its fire from day.

This leaf? this stone? It is thy heart;
It must be crushed by pain and smart,
It must be cleansed by sorrow's art,

Ere it will yield a fragrance sweet,
Ere it will shine, a jewel meet
To lay before thy dear Lord's feet.

S. WILBERFORCE.

September 6.

Beloved, let us love one another; for love is of God. —
1 JOHN iv. 7.

*Before they call, I will answer; and while they are yet
speaking, I will hear.* — ISA. lxv. 24.

TO know that there are some souls, hearts, and minds
here and there who trust us, and whom we trust;
some who know us, and whom we know; some on whom
we can always rely, and who will always rely on us,— makes
a paradise of this great world. The only solid thing in
this universe is love. This makes our life really life. This
makes us immortal while we are here. This makes us
sure that death is no end, but only a beginning, to us and
to all we love. It is only love and insight which show us

all we have ever done.   Cold sagacity misjudges us ; mere
sympathy, feeble good nature, soothes, but does not essentially help us.   But love illuminated by truth, truth warmed
through and through by love, — these perform for us the
most blessed thing that one human being can do for
another.   They show us to ourselves ; they show us what
we really are, what we have been, may be, can be, shall
be.   J. F. CLARKE.

THE years of God are full and satisfying ; each soul
shall have its turn ; it is His good *pleasure* to give us the
kingdom.   There is so much room ; there are such
thronging possibilities ; there is such endless hope !

A. D. T. WHITNEY.

WHAT is excellent,
  As God lives is permanent ;
Hearts are dust, hearts' loves remain,
Heart's love will meet thee again.

R. W. EMERSON.

A GARDEN REVERIE.

ALL silent is the garden
  Where the children used to stray ;
The children, men and women now
  Grown up and gone away,
Amid the strife and toil of life
  Have never time to play !

Here in the rustling beeches
  Once the linnet loved to sing ;
The bird still seeks the old home-nest
  While human hearts take wing ;
For man has less of faithfulness
  Than any living thing.

O heart, grown sour with sorrow
  While the swift years fly apace,
Is there no everlasting love
  That knows not time nor space ?
All loves revive, and grow and thrive
  In God's great resting-place.

The treasures of His kingdom
  Are our old things all made new, —
Old hopes, old scenes, and faded flowers
  Baptized with heavenly dew ;
The sin and doubt He washes out
  And leaves the pure and true.

Wait in the quiet garden
  While the linnet trills its song ;
The other voices, silent now,
  Shall come to thee ere long ;
Earth's weakness past, love's tone at last
  Shall ring out clear and strong !

J. L. COSHAM

September 7.

Every one loveth gifts, and followeth after rewards. —
ISA. i. 23.

GOD'S love gives in such a way that it flows from a
Father's heart, the wellspring of all good. The
heart of the giver makes the gift dear and precious ; as
among ourselves we say of even a trifling gift, " It comes
from a hand we love," and look not so much at the gift
as at the heart. LUTHER.

BUT ah ! when shall we return love for Love ? When
shall we seek Him who seeks us and constantly carries us
in His arms ? When He bears us along in His tender and
paternal bosom, then it is that we forget Him ; in the
sweetness of His gifts, we forget the Giver ; His ceaseless
blessings, instead of melting us into love. distract our
attention and turn it away from Him. FÉNELON.

LIFE.

IT is not life upon Thy gifts to live,
But to grow fixed with deeper roots in Thee ;
And when the sun and shower their bounties give,
To send out thick-leaved limbs, — a fruitful tree

Whose green head meets the eye for many a mile;
Whose moss-grown arms their rigid branches rear,
And full-faced fruits their blushing welcome smile
As to its goodly shade our feet draw near.
Who tastes its gifts shall never hunger more,
For 't is the Father spreads the pure repast,
Who, while we eat, renews the ready store,
Which at His bounteous board must ever last;
For none the Bridegroom's supper shall attend
Who will not hear and make His word their friend.

JONES VERY.

—◆—

September 8.

Arise ye, and depart; for this is not your rest. — MICAH ii. 10.

ARE there times when the world threatens to become too much to us, the near hillocks of time to hide from us the more distant mountains of eternity, earth's tinsel to outshine heaven's gold? It is in God, in the light of His presence, as we press into that presence, that all things assume their due proportions, are seen in their true significance, — the tinsel for tinsel, the gold for gold; that the hillocks subside, and the mountain-tops reappear; that the shadows flee away, and the eternal substances remain.

RICHARD CHENEVIX TRENCH.

AFFLICTION.

FATHER! forgive the heart that clings,
  Thus trembling, to the things of time;
And bid the soul on angel wings
  Ascend into a purer clime.

There shall no doubts disturb its trust,
  No sorrows dim celestial love;
But these afflictions of the dust,
  Like shadows of the night, remove.

That glorious life will well repay
  This life of care and toil and woe;
O Father! joyful on my way,
  To drink Thy bitter cup I go.

September 9.

Jesus therefore, being wearied with His journey, sat thus on the well. — JOHN iv. 6.

OUR Saviour never drove His over-tired faculties. When tired, " He sat by the well." He used to go and rest in the house of Mary and Martha after the fatigues of working in Jerusalem. He tells us all, you and me, to let the morrow take care of itself, and merely to meet the evils of the present day. Real foresight consists in reserving our own forces. If we labor with anxiety about the future, we destroy that strength which will enable us to meet the future. If we take more in now than we can do well, we break up, and the work is broken up with us.

REST.

REST is not quitting
  The busy career;
Rest is the fitting
  Of self to one's sphere.

'T is the brook's motion,
  Clear, without strife,
Fleeting to ocean,
  After this life.

'T is loving and serving
  The highest and best;
'T is onward, unswerving,
  And this is true rest.

GOETHE

September 10.

Thou wilt shew me the path of life; in Thy presence is fulness of joy; at Thy right hand there are pleasures forevermore. — Ps. xvi. 11.

SEE, then, how faithfully the Lord is leading thee to true peace, who surroundeth thee with so many crosses. It is called "the peace of God which passeth all understanding;" that is, which is not known by feeling or perception or thinking. All our thinking cannot attain nor understand it; none but those who of free-will take up the cross laid on them, — these, tried and troubled in all they feel and think and understand, afterward experience this peace.

LUTHER.

PER PACEM AD LUCEM.

I DO not ask, O Lord, that life may be
    A pleasant road;
I do not ask that Thou wouldst take from me
    Aught of its load;

I do not ask that flowers should always spring
    Beneath my feet;
I know too well the poison and the sting
    Of things too sweet.

For one thing only, Lord, dear Lord, I plead, —
    Lead me aright,
Though strength should falter, and though heart should
    bleed,
    Through Peace to Light.

I do not ask, O Lord, that Thou shouldst shed
    Full radiance here;
Give but a ray of peace. that I may tread
    Without a fear.

I do not ask my cross to understand,
    My way to see;
Better in darkness just to feel Thy hand
    And follow Thee.

Joy is like restless day; but peace divine
    Like quiet night;
Lead me, O Lord. till perfect day shall shine,
    Through Peace to Light.

ADELAIDE A. PROCTER.

September 11.

I will feed My flock, saith the Lord. — EZEK. xxxiv. 15.

THOU glorious spirit-land! Oh that I could behold thee as thou art, — the regions of life and light and love, and the dwelling-place of those beloved ones whose being has flowed onward, like a silver-clear stream, into the solemn sounding main, into the ocean of eternity.

H. W. LONGFELLOW.

THE LIFE OF THE BLESSED.

REGION of life and light!
Land of the good whose earthly toils are o'er!
Nor frost nor heat may blight
Thy vernal beauty, fertile shore,
Yielding thy blessèd fruits forevermore!

There, without crook or sling,
Walks the Good Shepherd; blossoms white and red
Round His meek temples cling;
And, to sweet pastures led,
His own loved flock beneath His eye is fed.

He guides, and near Him they
Follow delighted; for He makes them go
Where dwells eternal May,
And heavenly roses blow,
Deathless, and gathered but again to grow.

He leads them to the height
Warned of the infinite and long-sought Good,
And fountains of delight;
And where His feet have stood,
Springs up, along the way, their tender food.

From His sweet lute flow forth
Immortal harmonies, of power to still
All passions born of earth,
And draw the ardent will
Its destiny of goodness to fulfil.

Might but a little part,
A wandering breath, of that high melody
Descend into my heart,
And change it till it be
Transformed and swallowed up, O love! in thee.

Ah! then my soul should know,
Beloved! where thou liest at noon of day;
And from this place of woe
Released, should take its way
To mingle with thy flock, and never stray.

LUIS PONCE DE LEON,
Tr. by LONGFELLOW.

September 12.

As a shepherd seeketh out his flock in the day that he is among his sheep that are scattered; so will I seek out My sheep, and will deliver them out of all places where they have been scattered in the cloudy and dark day. — EZEK. xxxiv. 12.

HERE then is the beauty and glory of Christ, as a Redeemer and Saviour of lost man, that He goes before, always before, and never behind His flock. The works of love that He requires from us, in words, are preceded and illustrated by real deeds of love, to which He gave up all His mighty powers from day to day. He bore the cross Himself that He commanded us to take up and bear after Him. In all which He is our Shepherd, calling, but never driving; bearing all the losses He calls us to bear; meeting all the dangers, suffering all the cruelties and pains which it is given us to suffer, and drawing us to follow where He leads.

HORACE BUSHNELL.

THE GOOD SHEPHERD.

YES, our Shepherd leads with a gentle hand,
Through the dark pilgrim-land,
His flock so dearly bought,
So long and fondly sought.
Hallelujah!

When in clouds and mist the weak ones stray,
  He shows again the way,
  And points to them afar
  A bright and guiding star,
      Hallelujah !

Tenderly He watches from on high,
  With an unwearied eye;
  He comforts and sustains
  In all their fears and pains,
      Hallelujah !

Through the parched, dreary desert will He guide
  To the green fountain-side, —
  Through the dark stormy night
  To a calm land of light,
      Hallelujah !

Yes, His " little flock " are ne'er forgot;
  His mercy changes not;
  Our home is safe above,
  Within His arms of love,
      Hallelujah !

    From the Danish of KRUMMACHER.

September 13.

He brought me forth also into a large place ; He delivered me, because He delighted in me. — Ps. xviii. 19.

AND what is this " large place " — what can it be — but God himself, that infinite Being in whom all other beings and all other streams of life terminate? God is a large place indeed. And it was through humiliation, through abasement, through nothingness, David was brought into it.
      MADAME GUYON.

No good deed dies ; be it a rejoicing river, be it but a tiny rill of human nobleness, yet, so it be pure and clear, never has it been lost in the poisonous marshes or choked in the muddy sands. It flows inevitably into that great river of the water of life, which is not lost save — if *that* be to be lost — in the infinite ocean of God's eternal love.
      CANON FARRAR.

UP IN THE WILD.

UP in a wild, where few men come to look,
There lives and sings a little lonely brook, —
Liveth and singeth in the dreary pines,
Yet creepeth on to where the daylight shines.

Pure from their heaven, in mountain chalice caught,
It drinks the rains, as drinks the soul her thought ;
And down dim hollows where it winds along
Pours its life-burden of unlistened song.

I catch the murmur of its undertone,
That sigheth ceaselessly, Alone ! alone !
And hear afar the rivers gloriously
Shout on their paths towards the shining sea !

The voiceful rivers, chanting to the sun,
And wearing names of honor, every one ;
Outreaching wide, and joining hand with hand
To pour great gifts along the asking land.

Ah, lonely brook !   Creep onward through the pines ;
Press through the gloom to where the daylight shines !
Sing on among the stones, and secretly
Feel how the floods are all akin to thee !

Drink the sweet rain the gentle heaven sendeth ;
Hold thine own path, however-ward it tendeth ;
For somewhere, underneath the eternal sky,
Thou, too, shalt find the rivers by and by.

SUNDAY MAGAZINE

———◆———

September 14.

I will help thee, saith the Lord. — ISA. xli. 14.

OH, how full of briers is this working-day world !

AS YOU LIKE IT.

LIFE in its literal aspect is wearisome enough ; all life,
looked at from day to day as it goes along, is tiresome ; translate any career into prose, and it is stupid
reading.   Take the grandest of human callings and detail

its routine ; people will turn away from it as from a dull story. And yet one may take the smallest calling, the meanest occupation, the most matter-of-course duty, and shed on it this beautiful light of the ideal world, the glory of religion ; and behold, as every dew-drop becomes a diamond when the morning comes over the hills, as every bit of mica flashes like a pearl when the sunshine strikes it, so this little atom of duty, care, toil, trouble, becomes a gem when touched by the light of its principle.

O. B. FROTHINGHAM

EVERY DAY.

O TRIFLING tasks, so often done,
 Yet ever to be done anew !
O cares that come with every sun,
 Morn after morn, the long years through !
We shrink beneath their paltry sway, —
The irksome calls of every day.

The restless sense of wasted power,
 The tiresome round of little things,
Are hard to bear, as hour by hour
 Its tedious iteration brings ;
Who shall evade or who delay
The small demands of every day ?

The bowlder in the torrent's course,
 By tide and tempest lashed in vain,
Obeys the wave-whirled pebble's force,
 And yields its substance, grain by grain ;
So crumble strongest lives away
Beneath the wear of every day.

We rise to meet a heavy blow :
 Our souls a sudden bravery fills ;
But we endure not always so
 The drop-by-drop of little ills ;
We feel our noblest powers decay
In feeble wars with every day.

The heart which boldly faces death
 Upon the battle-field, and dares
Cannon and bayonet, faints beneath
 The needle-points of frets and cares ;
The stoutest spirits they dismay, —
The tiny stings of every day.

Ah, more than martyr's aureole,
And more than hero's heart of fire,
We need the humble strength of soul
Which daily toils and ills require ; —
Sweet Patience ! grant us, if you may,
An added grace for every day !

ELIZABETH AKERS ALLEN.

———◆———

September 15.

Why sleep ye ? — LUKE xxii. 46.
*Awake! thou that sleepest, and arise from the dead, and
Christ shall give thee light.* — EPH. v. 14.

YOU are not here to find happiness directly as the first
thing. You are here to discover truth ; and the
way is dark, and leads to the Cross before it finds the
Resurrection. . . . Happiness, indeed ! What business
have we yet with happiness ? We must win it before we
wear it. Only toil can give us the power of enjoying.
And God knows this, and He puts us through this long
and painful process. He saves us ; but we must work out
our own salvation. He gives light ; but we must conquer
darkness. And if we want the lazy sweets of life, the ease
undignified by any thought, the life untroubled by any dis-
turbing doubt, why, we may have it by throwing ourselves
out of the sphere of God's training, and sinking down into
our native mud. . . . God will not permit that we have
happiness at the expense of spiritual greatness. But if we
will have something better far, — a grave nobility of spirit ;
a life thrilled through and through with august ideas
bravely won ; a vast and practical love for man, in which
self will be forgotten ; an aspiration toward truth untiring
as the eagle's flight, and with his sun-fixed eye ; the enthusiasm of one who loves with passion God and man ;
the temperate reasonableness which rules enthusiasm, so
as to direct it to its work with wisdom, — then there is
something higher than our miserable happiness. It is the
awful blessedness of life with God, the knowledge that we
are growing up into better things, the certain hope of a
life of eternal righteousness and love and joy, the stern
delight of duty done.   STOPFORD BROOKE.

AND WERE THAT BEST.

AND were that best, Love, dreamless, endless sleep?
Gone all the fury of the mortal day;
The daylight gone, and gone the starry ray!
And were that best, Love, rest serene and deep?
Gone labor and desire; no arduous steep
To climb, no songs to sing, no prayers to pray,
No help for those who perish by the way,
No laughter 'midst our tears, no tears to weep!
And were that best, Love, sleep with no dear dream,
Nor memory of anything in life?
Stark death that neither help nor hurt can know?
Oh, rather, Love, the sorrow-bringing gleam,
The living day's long agony and strife!
Rather strong love in pain, — the waking woe!

RICHARD WATSON GILDER.

—◆—

September 16.

As one whom his mother comforteth, so will I comfort you;
and ye shall be comforted in Jerusalem. — ISA. lxvi. 13.

FATHER, we thank Thee that amid the joys of the
flesh, amid the delights of our daily work, and all
the sweet and silent blessedness of mortal friendship and
love upon the earth, Thou givest us the joy of knowing
Thee, the still and calm delight of lying low in Thy hand,
and feeling the breath of Thy Spirit upon us.   Yea, Lord,
we thank Thee that Thou holdest each one of us, yea, all
of Thy children, and the universe itself, as a mother folds
her baby to her bosom, and blessest us all with Thine
infinite loving-kindness and Thy tender mercy.

THE sun drinks in the drop of dew which casts back its
rays, and God absorbs the soul which reflects Him.

JOSEPH ROUX.

O GOD, we are but leaves upon Thy stream,
Clouds on Thy sky.   We do but move across
The silent breast of Thine infinitude
Which bears us all.   We pour out day by day
Our long, brief moan of mutability
To Thine immutable, and cease.
                     Yet still
Our change yearns after Thine unchangedness ;
Our mortal craves Thine immortality ;
Our manifold and multiform and weak
Imperfectness requires the perfect One.
For Thou art One, and we are all of Thee ;
Dropped from Thy bosom, as Thy sky drops down
Its morning dews, which glitter for a space,
Uncertain whence they fell, or whither tend,
Till the great sun arising on his fields
Upcalls them all, and they rejoicing go !
So, with like joy, O Light eterne, we spring
Thee-ward, and leave the pleasant fields of earth,
Forgetting equally its blossomed meads
And its dry, dusty paths which drank us up
Remorseless, — we, poor humble drops of dew,
That only wished to freshen a flower's breast,
And be exhaled to heaven.
                O Thou supreme
All-satisfying and immutable One,
It is enough to be absorbed in Thee.

DINAH MULOCH CRAIK.

September 17.

Blessed are they that do His commandments, that they may
have right to the tree of life, and may enter in through
the gates into the city. — REV. xxii. 14.

LORD, make me to know Thee aright, that I may more
and more love, and enjoy, and possess Thee.   And
since in the life here below I cannot fully attain this
blessedness, let it at least grow in me day by day, until it
all be fulfilled at last in the life to come !   Here be the

knowledge of Thee increased, and there let it be perfected !
Here let my love to Thee grow, and there may it ripen ;
that my joy being here great in hope, may *there* in fruition
be made perfect.

SAINT ANSELM.

HEAVEN.

BEYOND these chilling winds and gloomy skies,
  Beyond death's cloudy portal,
There is a land where beauty never dies,
  Where love becomes immortal.

A land whose life is never dimmed by shade,
  Whose fields are ever vernal ;
Where nothing beautiful can ever fade,
  But blooms for aye eternal.

The city's shining towers we may not see
  With our dim earthly vision,
For Death, the silent warder, keeps the key
  That opes the gates elysian.

But sometimes, when adown the western sky
  A fiery sunset lingers,
Its golden gates swing inward noiselessly,
  Unlocked by unseen fingers.

And while they stand a moment half ajar,
  Gleams from the inner glory
Stream brightly through the azure vault afar
  And half reveal the story.

O land unknown ! O land of love divine !
  Father, all-wise, eternal !
Oh, guide these wandering, wayworn feet of mine
  Into those pastures vernal.

NANCY A. W. PRIEST

September 18.

Lead me to the rock that is higher than I. — Ps. lxi. 2.

WHERE but in Thee have we a covert from storm, or shadow from the heat of life? In our manifold temptations, Thou alone knowest and art ever nigh; in sorrow Thy pity revives the fainting soul; in our prosperity and ease it is Thy spirit only that can wean us from our pride and keep us low.

JAMES MARTINEAU.

I LOVE knowledge; I love intellect; I love faith, — simple faith yet more. I love God's shadow better than man's light.

MADAME SWETCHINE.

THE SHADOW OF THE ROCK.

THE Shadow of the Rock! Stay, pilgrim, stay!
Night treads upon the heels of day;
There is no other resting-place this way.
 The Rock is near,
 The well is clear;
Rest in the Shadow of the Rock!

The Shadow of the Rock! The desert wide
Lies round thee like a trackless tide,
In waves of sand forlornly multiplied.
 The sun is gone,
 Thou art alone;
Rest in the Shadow of the Rock!

The Shadow of the Rock! All come alone;
All, ever since the sun hath shone,
Who travelled by this road have come alone.
 Be of good cheer,
 A home is here;
Rest in the Shadow of the Rock.

FREDERIC W. FABER.

September 19.

Continue in prayer, and watch in the same with thanksgiving. — COL. iv. 2.

CONNECT all the states of your experience with God. Is the shadow over you, no matter how or whence it comes, no matter how deeply it glooms, be sure that God will be found in the heart of it. Seek Him by prayer. Acquaint thyself with Him and be at peace, while the shadow passes over. Is the sunlight glowing on your life, does the air shine, do the dew-drops glisten around, be sure that God's smile is the brightness of that sunlight, the splendor of that atmosphere. Praise and take in all its blessing; make it thus the antepast of the everlasting joy.

J. BALDWIN BROWN.

ALL weary thought and care,
Lord, we resign;
Ours is to do, to bear,
To choose is Thine.

THOUGHTS OF COMFORT.

HAST thou a care whose pressure dread
Expels sweet slumber from thy bed?
To thy Redeemer take that care,
And change anxiety to prayer.

Hast thou a hope with which thy heart
Would almost feel it death to part?
Entreat thy God that hope to crown,
Or give thee strength to lay it down.

Hast thou a friend whose image dear
May prove an idol worshipped here?
Implore the Lord that nought may be
A shadow between Heaven and thee.

Whate'er the care that breaks thy rest,
Whate'er the wish that swells thy breast,
Spread before God that wish, that care,
And change anxiety to prayer.

September 20.

And He hath put a new song into my mouth, even praise unto our God; many shall see it, and fear, and shall trust in the Lord. — Ps. xl. 3.

DUTIES are ours; events are God's. This removes an infinite burden from the shoulders of a miserable, tempted, dying creature. On this consideration only can he securely lay down his head and close his eyes.

CECIL.

MAY God make us patient to live. Not that we should not have aspirations; but till the flying comes let us brood contentedly upon our nests.

GOD makes the blind bird's nest.

TURKISH PROVERB.

SONG.

BE like the bird, that halting in her flight
   Awhile on boughs too slight,
Feels them give way beneath her, and yet sings,
   Knowing that she hath wings.

VICTOR HUGO

THIS pretty bird, oh, how she flies and sings!
How could she do so if she had not wings?
Her wings bespeak my faith, her songs my peace;
When I believe and sing, my doubtings cease.

September 21.

Not as though I had already attained, either were already perfect; but I follow after, if that I may apprehend that for which also I am apprehended of Christ Jesus. — PHIL. iii. 12.

LOOK forward, we sometimes say, a few days, or a few months, and how differently will all things seem. Yes; but look forward a few more years; and how yet more differently will all things seem! From the height of that future to which on the wings of the ancient prophetic belief we can transport ourselves, look back on the present. Think of our troubles, as they will seem when we know their end. Think of those good thoughts and deeds which alone will survive in that unknown world. Think of our controversies, as they will appear when we shall be forced to sit down at the feast with those whom we have known only as opponents here, but whom we must recognize as companions there. To that future of futures which shall fulfil the yearnings of all that the prophets have desired on earth, it is for us, wherever we are, to look onward, upward, and forward in the constant expectation of something better than we see or know. Uncertain as to "the day and hour," and as to the manner of fulfilment, this last of all the predictions still, like those of old, builds itself upon the present. "It doth not yet appear what we shall be ; but we know that when He shall appear, we shall be like Him ; for we shall see Him as He is."

.DEAN STANLEY.

THEN.

WEARY and bruised and bleeding still
　From life's sharp thorns, on, on we come;
Down at our Master's feet we drop,
　And here are heaven and home!

Safe at those feet, where joy and pain,
　And all that made life dark or bright,
Seem but a mist beneath the sun
　Of our supreme delight.

What matter that the world has frowned,
    That fortune ever was unkind,
That plans have failed, and cares have pressed ?
    All, all is far behind !

What matter now the hard, cold words
    That smote us when for love we sought?
What matter now ?   The goal is reached ;
    The bitter past is nought.

And we can smile a bright, calm smile
    At pains whereby our hearts were riven,
And wonder such small things could touch
    A soul bound straight for heaven !

Wake from the dream — our glorious *then*
    Shines like a star above our sight ;
Our patient *now* before us lies,
    And duty gives the light.

                            G. P. : *The Month.*

—◆—

September 22.

*Fear not ; for I have redeemed thee.   I have called thee by
thy name ; thou art Mine.* — ISA. xliii. 1.

MAN belongs to a higher order that has its life under
     a personal Will ; he lives in relations to a superior
Mind and Heart. . . .
    Man is not happy in himself, but only in God.   " Thou
hast made us, and we have no peace till we have it in
Thee."   This ecstatic cry of Augustine is soundest logic.
Being made by God and set in relations to Him, we do
not know ourselves, nor can we adjust ourselves to our
relations, until we know God.   David's life could be
turned into a life of peaceful content, because God was
over it, and a guiding shepherd throughout it.   Such a
fact makes room for the play of trust, without which life
is a sad perplexity.   For I cannot understand life ; I cannot of myself find out why I am, nor whence I came,
nor for what end ; I cannot explain why this and that

happen to me ; I may see some cause, but no full reason or end ; a cause is not a reason. By myself I am lost in this world, without paths except the circles of a clewless labyrinth, without stars of guidance except such as wander across the heavens, without light except that which only deepens darkness. Now in such a state as this, I must either stray through life in sad perplexity, or I must trust God for a way. In such trust the most painful features of life — its mystery, its seeming vanity, its pain and burden and disappointment, its untimely end, its mischance, its inevitable contact with evil — lose their force.

T T. MUNGER.

DOUBT.

O DISTANT Christ ! the crowded, darkening years
  Drift slow between Thy gracious face and me ;
  My hungry heart leans back to look for Thee,
But finds the way set thick with doubts and fears.

My groping hands would touch Thy garment's hem,
  Would find some token Thou art walking near ;
  Instead they clasp but empty darkness drear,
And no diviner hands reach out to them !

Sometimes my listening soul, with bated breath,
  Stands still to catch a footfall by my side.
  Lest, haply, my earth-blinded eyes but hide
Thy stately figure, leading life and death ;

My straining eyes, O Christ ! but long to mark
  A shadow of Thy presence, dim and sweet,
  Or far-off light to guide my wandering feet,
Or hope for hands prayer-beating 'gainst the dark.

O Thou ! unseen by me, that like a child
  Tries in the night to find its mother's heart,
  And weeping wanders only more apart,
Not knowing in the darkness that she smiled.

Thou, all unseen, dost hear my tired cry,
  As I, in darkness of a half belief,
  Grope for Thy heart, in love and doubt and grief ;
O Lord, speak soon to me — " Lo here am I ! "

MARGARET DELAND.

September 23.

I shall be satisfied when I awake in Thy likeness. — Ps.
xvii. 15.

WHEN I read of the weary at rest, of the land
where no night comes, — where "there shall be
no more death, neither sorrow nor sighing," — is it that
my eyes have been tearful so long ; is it that my life is
darkened with shadows heavy and hard to bear, — is it
this that makes me long to be there?   Or is it that I
sigh for that waking, when I shall be "satisfied, *because*
I awake in 'His presence'?"

I SHALL BE SATISFIED.

NOT here ! not here ! not where the sparkling waters
    Fade into mocking sands as we draw near ;
Where in the wilderness each footstep falters.
    "I shall be satisfied," — but oh ! not here !

Not here, where all the dreams of bliss deceive us,
    Where the worn spirit never gains its goal ;
Where, haunted ever by the thoughts that grieve us,
    Across us floods of bitter memory roll.

There is a land where every pulse is thrilling
    With rapture earth's sojourners may not know,
Where heaven's repose the weary heart is stilling,
    And peacefully life's time-tossed currents flow.

Far out of sight, while yet the flesh infolds us,
    Lies the fair country where our hearts abide,
And of its bliss is naught more wondrous told us
    Than these few words, — "I shall be satisfied."

Satisfied ! satisfied ! the spirit's yearning
    For sweet companionship with kindred minds, —
The silent love that here meets no returning, —
    The inspiration which no language finds.

Shall they be satisfied ?   The soul's vague longing, —
    The aching void which nothing earthly fills ?
Oh ! what desires upon my soul are thronging
    As I look upward to the heavenly hills !

Thither my weak and weary steps are tending.
    Saviour and Lord ! with Thy frail child abide !
Guide me toward home where, all my wanderings ending,
    I shall see Thee, and "shall be satisfied."

September 24.

Whom have I in heaven but Thee? and there is none upon earth that I desire beside Thee. — Ps. lxxiii. 25.

AND so now many resign themselves to their low degree of Christian attainment. It is a case of religious sickness. They are spiritual invalids. I want to find some principle, something solid, something on which to stand the strain of life. Why is religion so dishevelled? Why so made up of heterogeneous scraps? Why does every sermon we hear put out of mind every last sermon? It is because the religious life is without foundation, without a sensible, solid, natural principle on which to rest. I will try to point out that principle which may give permanence, stability, vivacity to the religious life of each. It is the principle that every effect produced upon the soul of man is dependent on some pre-existing cause. Therefore there should be more praying over causes and less upon effects. Nature affords ample illustration. Nothing in the world happens by chance. There is a cause for everything we see or hear or feel. Not an action but what can be traced back to a cause. So in religion. If a man possesses a religious joy or peace, there is some definite cause that produces it. Fulfil these causes, and joy or peace follow as sure as day the night. What Christian grace do you want? Perhaps a little more joy. You have been praying for it for years and have not found it. Joy is an effect; it must have a cause. What is this cause? In the parable of the vine Christ stated it clearly : "Abide in me. . . . These things have I written unto you that you may be full." How Christ bases everything upon some cause. If ye love Me (a cause) ye will keep My commandments. "If ye abide in Me and My words abide in you, ye may ask what ye will," etc. The conditionalness of all God's promises is the point here. Where a cause is not stated it must be understood. All the promises are conditioned. Religion is the simplest thing in the world. Things here go on not by caprice, but by law, law absolutely simple, absolutely unerring. It is the everlasting lesson of science : law is sure and inevitable. Let

us get into the Christian life a little science. Nature and
the eternal truths of God are older than religion, and they
pervade religion. Our common, every-day lives are the
means God implies by which we shall build our Christian
lives. A farm or an office are not places to make crops
or money, but men. All the little things about our daily
toil are the framework and scaffolding of our spiritual
life.

HENRY DRUMMOND,

OUR BEST FRIEND.[1]

In the mid silence of the voiceless night,
When, chased by airy dreams, the slumbers flee,
Whom, in the darkness, doth my spirit seek,
　　O God, but Thee?

And if there be a weight upon my breast,
Some vague impression of the day foregone,
Scarce knowing what it is, I fly to Thee
　　And lay it down.

Or if it be the heaviest that comes,
In token of anticipated ill,
My bosom takes no heed of what it is,
　　Since 't is Thy will.

For oh! in spite of past and present care,
Or anything besides, how joyfully
Passes that almost solitary hour,
　　My God, with Thee!

More tranquil than the stillness of the night,
More peaceful than the stillness of that hour,
More blest than anything, my bosom lies
　　Beneath Thy power.

For what is there on earth that I desire,
Of all that it can give or take from me?
Or whom in heaven doth my spirit seek,
　　O God, but Thee?

[1] The authorship of this beautiful hymn of trust is unknown. It was
found treasured up in an humble cottage in England.

September 25.

Our days on the earth are as a shadow, and there is none abiding. — 1 CHRON. xxix. 15.

BUT to my mind, nothing whatever seems of long duration, in which there is any end. For when that arrives, then the time which has passed has flowed away; that only remains which you have secured by virtue and right conduct. Hours indeed depart from us, and days and months and years; nor does past time ever return, nor can it be discovered what is to follow. Whatever time is assigned to each to live, with that he ought to be content; for neither need the drama be performed entire by the actor, in order to give satisfaction, provided he be approved in whatever act he may be; nor need the wise man live till the *plaudite*. For the short period of life is long enough for living well and honorably; and if you should advance further, you need no more grieve than farmers do when the loveliness of springtime hath passed, that summer and autumn have come. For spring represents the time of youth, and gives promise of the future fruits; the remaining seasons are intended for the plucking and gathering in those fruits. Now the harvest of old age is the recollection and abundance of blessings previously secured. In truth, everything that happens agreeably to Nature is to be reckoned among blessings. What, however, is so agreeable to Nature as for an old man to die? — which even is the lot of the young, though Nature opposes and resists. And thus it is that young men seem to me to die just as when the violence of flame is extinguished by a flood of water; whereas old men die as the exhausted fire goes out, spontaneously, without the exertion of any force; and as fruits when they are green are plucked by force from the trees, but when ripe and mellow drop off, so violence takes away their lives from youths, maturity from old men; a state which to me indeed is so delightful that the nearer I approach to death, I seem as it were to be getting sight of land, and at length, after a long voyage, to be just coming into harbor.

MARCUS TULLIUS CICERO.

YES, it is well! The evening shadows lengthen;
    Home's golden gates shine on our ravished sight;
And though the tender ties we strove to strengthen
    Break one by one, at evening-time 't is light.

'T is well! The way was often dull and weary;
    The spirit fainted oft beneath its load;
No sunshine came from skies all gray and dreary,
    And yet our feet were bound to tread that road.

As voyagers, by fierce winds beat and broken,
    Come into port beneath a calmer sky,
So we, still bearing on our brows the token
    Of tempest past, draw to our haven nigh.

A sweet air cometh from the shore immortal,
    Inviting homeward at the day's decline;
Almost we see where from the open portal
    Fair forms stand beckoning with their smiles divine.

'T is well! The earth with all her myriad voices
    Has lost the power our senses to enthrall:
We hear, above the tumult and the noises,
    Soft tones of music, like an angel's call.

'T is well, O friends! We would not turn, retracing
    The long, vain years, nor call our lost youth back;
Gladly, with spirits braced, the future facing,
    We leave behind the dusty, foot-worn track.

———◆———

September 26.

*Ye are not your own; for ye are bought with a price;
therefore glorify God in your body, and in your spirit,
which are God's.* — 1 COR. vi. 19, 20.
*For with Thee is the fountain of life; in Thy light shall
we see light.* — PS. xxxvi. 9.

WHEN we know that our life is engirdled with law,
fortitude will change grief into resignation and
defeat into triumph. If you would help a soul bear its
sorrow, introduce it to a greater one. Put your small

grievances into their proper perspective, and they cease to be grievances, because you have removed the stumbling-block. It is not the province of religion to explain the ways of God to man ; it is not for me to apologize for the universe, — it is for us to recognize the facts. As we discover these, religion helps us to bear or to change them. Would you know the peace of God, realize that you are a part of that infinite majesty ; strive to catch now and then a note of the heavenly melody ; chant a stray chord of the infinite harmony ; remember that everything beautiful springs from a beauty that is behind it, every strong will rises from a strength underneath, and all your loves are fed from the fountains of infinite love. And for yourself you may mar the beautiful or reflect it, you can either enter into the strength or become its victim, know the love or thwart it. We are impatient only when we forget the infinite patience, we are petulant when we turn away from the unresting and unhasting stars that move in their unimpassioned orbits in darkest nights. We are discouraged when we fail to keep step with the solemn tramp of the generations. The wrong judgments of men hurt us not if we remember that the balances of God are justly poised. No thought of ours is insignificant if we reverently cradle it in the thought of God. No plan of ours will be abandoned if we are sure it is a part of the infinite plan. We have a will of our own only when we believe it to be God's will also.

J. Ll. JONES.

OUR LATTER DAYS.

A CLOUDY morning, and a golden eve
  Warm with the glow that never lingers long :
Such is our life ; and who would pause to grieve
  Over a tearful day that ends in song ?

The dawn was gray with mist and rain,
  There was no sweetness in the chilly blast ;
Dead leaves were strewn along the dusky lane
  That led us to the sunset light at last.

'T is an old tale, belovèd ; we may find
  Heart-stories all around us just the same.
Speak to the sad, and tell them God is kind :
  Do they not tread the path through which we came ?

Our youth went by in recklessness and haste,
  And precious things were lost as soon as gained ;
Yet patiently our Father saw the waste
  And gathered up the fragments that remained.

Taught by His love, we learned to love aright ;
  Led by His hand, we passed through dreary ways ;
And now how lovely is the mellow light
  That shines so calmly on our latter days !

SARAH DOUDNEY.

September 27.

*For I am in a strait betwixt two, having a desire to depart,
and to be with Christ ; which is far better.* — PHIL. i. 23.

WHEN a noble life has prepared old age, it is not
the decline that it reveals, but the first days of
immortality.
MADAME DE STAËL.

THE damps of autumn sink into the leaves and prepare
them for the necessity of their fall ; and thus insensibly
are we, as years close round us, detached from our
tenacity of life by the gentle pressure of recorded sorrows.

LANDOR.

LOOKING BACK.

WOULD you be young again ?
    So would not I ;
One tear to mem'ry given,
    Onward I 'd hie.
Life's dark flood forded o'er,
All but at rest on shore, —
Say, would you plunge once more,
    With home so nigh ?

If you might, would you now
    Retrace your way ?
Wander through stormy wilds,
    Faint and astray ?
Night's gloomy watches spread,
Morning all beaming red,
Hope's smiles around us shed,
    Heavenward — away !

Where, then, are those dear ones,
Our joy and delight ?
Dear, and more dear, though now
Hidden from sight.
Where they rejoice to be,
There is the land for me ;
Fly, time — fly speedily !
Come, life and light !

LADY NAIRN

September 28.

Rest in the Lord, and wait patiently for Him. — Ps.
xxxvii. 7.

O THOU, in whase sicht our deith is precious and no
leicht matter ; wha thro' darkness leads to light,
an' thro' death to the greater life ; we canna believe that
Thou wouldst gie us ony guid thing, to tak' the same
again ; for that would be but bairns' play. We believe
that Thou tak's that Thou mayst gie again the same thing
better nor afore, — mair o't, an' better nor we could ha'
received it ither wise ; jest as the Lord took himsel' frae
the sicht of them 'at lo'ed Him weel, that instead o' bein'
visible afore their een, he micht hide himsel' in their verra
hearts. Come then, an' abide in us, an' tak' us to bide
in Thee ; an' syne gin we be a' in Thee, we canna be that
far frae ane anither, tho' some sud be in heaven, an' some
upo' earth. Lord, help us to do Thy wark, like Thy men
an' maidens doun the stair, remin'in' oursel's 'at them 'at
we miss hae only gane up the stair as gin 't war to hand
things to Thy han' in Thy ain presence chamber, whaur
we houp to be called ere lang, an' to see Thee an' Thy
Son, wham we lo'e aboon a' ; an' in His name we say
Amen.

PRAYER OF DAVID ELGINBROD

HYMN.

TAKE the praise we bring Thee, Lord,
Something more than what we speak,
For the love within us feels
Words uncertain, cold, and weak,
Thoughts that rise and tears that fall
Praise Thee better ; take them all !

Looking back the way we 've come,
    What a sight, O Lord, we see !
All the failure in ourselves,
    All the love and strength in Thee.
Yet it seemed so dark before,
Would that we had trusted more !

Use us for Thy glory, Lord,
    In the way that seemeth right,
Whether but to wait and watch,
    Or to gird our limbs and fight.
Marching on or standing still,
Each is best when 't is Thy will.

When at last the end shall come,
    What, O Lord, is Death but this, —
Door of our dear Father's home,
    Entrance into perfect bliss,
Peril past and labor done,
Sorrow over, peace begun !

September 29.

Ye are the temple of the living God. — 2 COR. vi. 16.

GOD is an accommodation to human weakness. When
He would teach truth He must needs set it in the
form of *fact ;* when He would show Himself, it must be
through the tabernacle of our own flesh ; when He would
reveal heaven, He must illustrate His meaning by the
fragments of light and beauty which are scattered on the
higher side of our own inferior world. Everywhere, could
we but see it, He has set up a ladder by which we may
reach the skies.

JOSEPH PARKER.

THE inward influences and illuminations which come to
us through those who have loved us are deeper than any
that we can realize ; they penetrate all our life, and assure
us that there must be a Fountain of Life and Love from
which they and we are continually receiving strength to
bear and to hope.

F. D. MAURICE.

GOD'S NEARNESS.

THE Lord is in His Holy Place
In all things near and far,
Shekinah of the snowflake He,
And Glory of the star;
And Secret of the April-land
That stirs the field to flowers,
Whose little tabernacles rise
To hold Him through the hours.

He hides Himself within the love
Of those that we love best;
The smiles and tones that make our homes
Are shrines by Him possessed.
He tents within the lonely heart
And shepherds every thought;
We find Him not by seeking long,
We lose Him not unsought.

WILLIAM C. GANNETT.

September 30.

*A friend loveth at all times, and a brother is born for
adversity.* — PROV. xvii. 17.

WE often do more good by our sympathy than by
our labors.
CANON FARRAR.

As Nature, with her old mosses and her new spring
foliage, hides the ruins which man has made, and gives to
the fallen tower and broken cloister a beauty scarcely
less than that which belonged to them in their prime, —
so human love may be at work too, "softening and con-
cealing, and busy with her hand in healing" the rents
which have been made in God's nobler temple, — the
habitation of His own spirit.
F. D. MAURICE.

LIKE the ocean, Love embraces the earth; and by
Love, as by the ocean, whatever is sordid and unsound is
borne away.

ASPASIA TO CLEONE.

TOO LATE.

WHAT silences we keep year after year
With those who are most near to us and dear!
　We live beside each other day by day,
　And speak of myriad things, but seldom say
The full, sweet word that lies just in our reach,
Beneath the commonplace of common speech.

Then out of sight and out of reach they go, —
Those close, familiar friends who loved us so;
　And sitting in the shadow they have left,
　Alone with loneliness, and sore bereft,
We think with vain regret of some fond word
That once we might have said, and they have heard.

For weak and poor the love that we expressed
Now seems beside the vast, sweet unexpressed,
　And slight the deeds we did to those undone,
　And small the service spent, to treasure won,
And undeserved the praise for word and deed,
That should have overflowed the simple need.

This is the cruel cross of life, — to be
Full visioned only when the ministry
　Of death has been fulfilled, and in the place
　Of some dear presence is but empty space.
What recollected services can then
Give consolation for the " might have been " ?

NORA PERRY.

—◆—

October 1.

*Lord, make me to know mine end, and the measure of my
days, what it is; that I may know how frail I am.* —
Ps. xxxix. 4.

THERE is an " eventide " in the year, — a season, as
we now witness, when the sun withdraws his pro-
pitious light, when the winds arise, and the leaves fall,
and nature around us seems to sink into decay. It is
said, in general, to be the season of melancholy; and if
by this word be meant that it is the time of solemn and
of serious thought, it is undoubtedly so; yet it is a

melancholy so soothing, so gentle in its approach, and
so prophetic in its influence, that they who have known
it feel, as instinctively, that it is the doing of God, and
that the heart of man is not thus finely touched but to
fine issues. When we go out into the fields in the evening of the year, we regard, even in spite of ourselves,
the still but steady advances of time. A few days ago,
and the summer of the year was grateful, and every element was filled with life, and the sun of heaven seemed
to glory in his ascendant. He is now enfeebled in his
power; the desert no more "blossoms like the rose;"
the song of joy is no more heard among the branches;
and the earth is strewed with that foliage which once be-
spoke the magnificence of summer. Whatever may be
the passions which society has awakened, we pause amid
this apparent desolation of nature. We sit down in the
lodge " of the wayfaring man in the wilderness," and we
feel that all we witness is the emblem of our own fate.
Such also in a few years will be our own condition. The
blossoms of our spring, the pride of our summer, will
also fade into decay; and the pulse that now beats high
with virtuous or with vicious desire will gradually sink,
and then must stop forever. We rise from our meditations with hearts softened and subdued, and we return
into life as into a shadowy scene, where we have " disquieted ourselves in vain."

Yet a few years, we think, and all that now bless, or
all that now convulse humanity, will also have perished.
The mightiest pageantry of life will pass; the loudest
notes of triumph or of conquest will be silent in the
grave; "the wicked," wherever active, will "cease from
troubling," and "the weary," wherever suffering, will "be
at rest." Under an impression so profound we feel our own
hearts better. The cares, the animosities, the hatreds which
society may have engendered, sink unperceived from our
bosoms. In the general desolation of nature we feel the
littleness of our own passions; we look forward to that
kindred evening which time must bring to all; we anticipate the graves of those we hate as of those we love.
Every unkind passion falls with the leaves that fall around
us; and we return slowly to our homes, and to the society
which surround us, with the wish only to enlighten or to

bless them.   If there were no other effects, my brethren, of such appearances of nature upon our minds, they would still be valuable ; they would teach us humility, and with it they would teach us charity.

ARCHIBALD ALISON.

OCTOBER.

AY, thou art welcome, heaven's delicious breath,
  When woods begin to wear the crimson leaf,
  And suns grow meek, and the meek suns grow brief,
And the year smiles as it draws near its death
Wind of the sunny south ! oh, still delay
  In the gay woods, and in the golden air,
  Like to a good old age released from care,
Journeying, in long serenity, away.
In such a bright, late quiet, would that I
  Might wear out life like thee, 'mid bowers and brooks,
  And, dearer yet, the sunshine of kind looks,
And music of kind voices ever nigh ;
And, when my last sand twinkled in the glass,
Pass silently from men, as thou dost pass.

WILLIAM CULLEN BRYANT.

—◆—

October 2.

I have fought a good fight, I have finished my course, I have kept the faith ; henceforth there is laid up for me a crown of righteousness, which the Lord, the righteous Judge, shall give me at that day; and not to me only, but unto all them also that love His appearing. — 2 TIM. iv. 7, 8.

YEARS will make a change.   As the summer grows in fierce heat, the balminess of the violet banks of spring is lost in the odors of a thousand flowers ; the heart, as it gains in age, loses freshness, but wins breadth.

DONALD G. MITCHELL.

THERE is a peculiar simplicity of heart, and a touching singleness of purpose, in Christian old age which has ripened gradually and not fitfully.   It is then that the somewhat austere and sour character of growing strength, moral and intellectual, mellows into the rich ripeness of an old age made sweet and tolerant by experience ; it is then that man returns to first principles. There comes a love more pure and deep than the boy could ever feel ; there comes a conviction, with a strength beyond that which the boy could ever know, that the earliest lesson of life is infinite, — Christ is all in all.

F. W. ROBERTSON

OCTOBER.

OH, what a glory doth this world put on
For him who, with a fervent heart, goes forth
Under the bright and glorious sky, and looks
On duties well performed, and days well spent !
For him the wind, ay, and the yellow leaves
Shall have a voice and give him eloquent teachings.
He shall so hear the solemn hymn that Death
Has lifted up for all, that he shall go
To his long resting-place without a tear.

H. W. LONGFELLOW

October 3.

God is love; and he that dwelleth in love dwelleth in God, and God in him. Herein is our love made perfect. —
I JOHN iv. 16, 17.

GOD has commanded us to be perfect in love ; not because He was unaware that such a command far exceeded our abilities, but because He desired thereby to remind us of our weakness, and to keep before us the prize of righteousness after which we must strive. In thus demanding from man an impossibility, it is not with the view of hurling him into sin, but of compelling him to humility, that "every mouth may be stopped," and all creation subject unto Christ; for "through the works of the law shall no flesh be justified." When, therefore, we hear this command, and are sensible of our inability to fulfil its requirements, our only course is to cry unto Heaven ; then will our gracious Father look down in His mercy and supply the needed strength.

BERNARD.

OH, this is blessing, this is rest!
Into Thine arms, O Lord, I flee;
I hide me in Thy faithful breast,
And pour out all my soul to Thee.
There is a host dissuading me;
But, all their voices far above,
I hear Thy words : "Oh, taste and see
The comfort of a Saviour's love!"
And, hushing every adverse sound,
Songs of defence my soul surround,
As if all saints encamped about
One trusting heart pursued by doubt.
And oh, how solemn, yet how sweet,
Their one assured, persuasive strain!—
"The Lord of Hosts is thy retreat,
The Man who bore thy sin, thy pain.
Still in His hand thy times remain;
Still of His body thou art part:
And He will prove His right to reign
O'er all things that concern thy heart."
O tenderness! O truth divine!
Lord, I am altogether Thine.
I have bowed down; I need not flee;
Peace, peace is mine in trusting Thee.

ANNA L. WARING.

October 4.

I am He that liveth, and was dead; and, behold, I am alive forevermore, Amen; and have the keys of hell and of death. — REV. i. 18.

WE have a Friend and Protector, from whom, if we do not ourselves depart from Him, nor power nor spirit can separate us. In His strength let us proceed on our journey through the storms and troubles and dangers of the world. However they may rage and swell, though the mountains shake at the tempest, our Rock will not be moved; we have one Friend who will never forsake us; one Refuge, where we may rest in peace and stand in our lot at the end of the days. The same is " He that liveth and was dead," who is "alive forevermore," and hath " the keys of hell and of death."

BISHOP HEBER.

A PSALM OF WEARINESS.

OVERBORNE by journeyings far
Where no resting-places are,
Lured by visions of repose
That in fading mock my woes,
Saviour ! may Thy presence be
        Unto me
As the shadow cool and sweet
Of a rock in desert heat.

Shelter of the shelterless,
Cover Thou my weariness ;
With Thy peace, a tent most fair,
Screen me from this earthly glare,
And Thy consolations shed
        On my head,
Sweeter than the balm of sleep
When the eyes forget to weep.

HARRIET McEWEN KIMBALL.

October 5.

I will say of the Lord, He is my refuge and my fortress ; my God; in Him will I trust. — Ps. xci. 2.

THE furnace of afflictions shows upright real faith to be such indeed, remaining still the same, even in the fire, — the same that it was, undiminished, as good gold loses none of its quantity in the fire. The heart's natural strength of spirit and resolution may bear up under outward weakness, or the failing of the flesh ; but when the heart itself fails, which is the strength of the flesh, what shall strengthen it ? Nothing but God, *who is the strength of the heart and its portion forever.*

ARCHBISHOP LEIGHTON

O God! though sorrow be my fate,
And the world's hate
    For my heart's faith pursue me,
My peace they cannot take away :
From day to day
    Thou dost imbue me ;
Thou art not far ; a little while
Thou hid'st Thy face, with brighter smile
    Thy Father-love to show me.

Lord, not my will, but Thine, be done ;
If I sink down
    When men to terrors leave me,
Thy Father-love still warms my breast ;
All's for the best ;
    Shall man have power to grieve me
When bliss eternal is my goal,
And Thou the keeper of my soul,
    Who never will deceive me ?

Thou art my shield, as saith the Word.
Christ Jesus, Lord,
    Thou standest pitying by me,
And lookest on each grief of mine
As if 't were Thine ;
    What then though foes may try me,
Though thorns be in my path concealed ?
World, do thy worst !   God is my shield,
    And will be ever nigh me !
                                TRANSLATION

—◆—

October 6.

I remember the days of old. — Ps. cxliii. 5.

I CANNOT but remember such things were,
That were most precious to me.
                                MACBETH.

PARTING and forgetting? What faithful heart can do
    these? Our great thoughts, our great affections, the
truths of our life, never leave us. Surely they cannot

separate from our consciousness; shall follow it whither-
soever that shall go; and are of their nature divine and
immortal.   THACKERAY.

THE LEAF OF WOODRUFF.

I FOUND a leaf of woodruff in a book;
    Gone was its scent, and lost its pristine glory;
Each slender bladelet wore a dingy look,
    And all was blanched and hoary.

And yet this withered leaf a spell possessed
    Which worked upon me in mysterious measure,
And sent old memories thronging through my breast,
    Of mingled pain and pleasure;

Of childhood's days that knew no thought of care;
    Of hours that passed on wings of rainbow fleetness;
Of odors floating on the wanton air,
    Sad from their very sweetness;

Of woods that wore a garb of summer green;
    Of knee-deep ferns, and nooks of shady stillness;
Of streams that glimmered in the full moon's sheen,
    And mirrored back its fulness;

Of lazy baskings on the lone hillside,
    In the fierce glow of July's sultry weather;
Of twilight wanderings where the enamored tide
    Crept up to kiss the heather;

Of voices still beneath the churchyard sod;
    Bright eyes that glistened from behind long lashes :
Warm beauty early given back to God;
    Red lips that now are ashes,

And many other memories, gay and grave,
    The woodruff brought in life-like guise before me,
Until I marvelled how a leaf could have
    Such magic influence o'er me.

Ah, so it is! All that hath ever been
    Experienced by the spirit is immortal;
Each hope and joy and grief is hid within
    The memory's sacred portal.

And yet the soft glow of a moonlight hour,
    A strain of haunting music, sweet and olden,
A dream, a bird, a bee, a leaf, a flower,
    A sunset, rich and golden,

Can fling that portal open ; and beyond
   Appears the record of each earlier feeling, —
All hopes, all joys, all fears, all musings fond,
   In infinite revealing,

Till all the present passes from our sight, —
   Its cares and woes that make us weary-hearted, —
And leaves us basking in the holy light
   Of golden days departed.

WILLIAM LEIGHTON

October 7.

I must work the works of Him that sent Me, while it is day; the night cometh when no man can work. — JOHN ix. 4.

WE hear it often said that life is but a day. It is said to express the shortness of our stay upon the earth. It is said, for the most part, sorrowfully. Let us reverse it, and say, with more striking truth, that each day is a life. Every day is a life, fresh with reinstated power, setting out on its allotted labor and limited path. Its morning resembles a whole youth. Its eventide is sobering into age. It is rounded at either end by a sleep, — unconsciousness at the outset and oblivion at the close. We are born anew every time that the sun rises, and lights up the world for man to do his part in it. One thing at least may be shown of each day, as it dawns and darkens : it is that every one, short as it may be, embodies the fulness of the past, and indicates what is long afterwards to come.

N. L. FROTHINGHAM : A Day's Duty.

TO-DAY.

A SINGLE sparkling drop of love divine
   Presses my mortal cup : to-day is mine ;

Mine all its fleeting hours, its golden light ;
   Mine with my highest powers its scroll to write;

Mine, ere its moments fly, to toil and pray,
   To lift mine eyes on high, — this brief to-day.

Soon, in the purple light, its beams shall cease ;
   Oh ! happy is my breast to write it peace.

October 8.

As the mountains are round about Jerusalem, so the Lord is round about His people, from henceforth even forever. — Ps. cxxv. 3.

IF we feel assured of the grace of God through the mediation of Christ, we have just reason to hope that futurity will unfold to us with joy and gladness ; and, as there is a just and gracious God, who orders and directs the universe, who knows all the events of our lives, and before whose view is continually present the circle of eternity, we may with safety, when we lie down to sleep, commend ourselves to His care, undisturbed as to what may happen during the night; and when the morning sun summons us to our duties we may trust ourselves to His protection, without anxiety for the events which are to befall us during the day. And in the hour of trial, when dangers threaten and destruction seems to impend, let us still remember the goodness of God, and repose upon His protecting arm, in perfect assurance that whatever happens is for our good.

From the German of CHRISTOPHER CHRISTIAN STURM.

GOOD–NIGHT.

GOOD–NIGHT!
Be thy cares forgotten quite !
Day approaches to its close ;
Weary nature seeks repose.
Till the morning dawns in light,
Good-night!

Go to rest !
Close thine eyes in slumber blest !
Now 't is still and quiet all ;
Hear we but the watchman's call,
And the night is still and blest.
Go to rest !

Good-night !
Slumber till the morning light !
Slumber till the dawn of day
Brings its sorrow with its ray.
Sleep without or fear or fright !
Our Father wakes ! good-night ! good night !

FROM THE GERMAN.

October 9.

Speak unto the children of Israel, that they go forward.
— Ex. xiv. 15.

THE elements of happiness in this present life no man can command, even if he could command himself, for they depend on the action of many wills, on the purity of many hearts ; and by the highest law of God the holiest must ever bear the sins and sorrows of the rest. But over the *blessedness* of his own spirit, circumstance need have no control ; God has therein given an unlimited power to the means of preservation, of grace and growth, at every man's command. We know the Beatitudes of Christian life ; and these are so far from being a product of circumstance, that only against the contradiction and in the conquest of circumstance do they reach their heights.

THORN.

A GERMAN TRUST SONG.

JUST as God leads me I would go ;
  I would not ask to choose my way ;
Content with what He will bestow,
  Assured He will not let me stray.
    So as He leads, my path I make,
    And step by step I gladly take,
        A child in Him confiding.

Just as God leads, I am content ;
  I rest me calmly in His hands ;
That which He has decreed and sent,
  That which His will for me commands,
    I would that He should all fulfil,
    That I should do His gracious will
        In living or in dying.

Just as God leads, I all resign ;
  I trust me to my Father's will ;
When reason's rays deceptive shine,
  His counsel would I yet fulfil ;
    That which His love ordained as right,
    Before He brought me to the light,
        My all to Him resigning.

Just as God leads, I onward go,
  Oft amid thorns and briers keen ;
God does not yet His guidance show ;
  But in the end it shall be seen,
    How by a loving Father's will,
    Faithful and true He leads me still.

LAMPERTUS.

October 10.

Let me depart, that I may go to mine own country. —
1 KINGS xi. 21.

AS prisoners in castles look out of their grated windows
at the smiling landscape where the sun comes and
goes, so we from this life, as from dungeon bars, look
forth to the heavenly land, and are refreshed with sweet
visions of the home that shall be ours when we are free.

HENRY WARD BEECHER.

THE same desire which, planted on earth, will produce
the flowers of a day, sown in heaven, will bear the fruits
of eternity.

JOSEPH ROUX.

MY AIN COUNTRIE.

I 'M far frae my hame, and I 'm weary aftenwhiles
For the langed-for hame-bringing, an' my Father's welcome
  smiles ;
I 'll ne'er be fu' content until my een do see
The gowden gates o' Heaven, an' my ain countrie.
The earth is flecked wi' flowers, — mony-tinted, fresh an' gay, —
The birdies warble blithely, for my Father make them sae ;
But these sichts an' these soun's will as naething be to me
When I hear the angels singing in my ain countrie.

I 've His gude word o' promise, that, some gladsome day, the
  King,
To His ain royal palace His banished hame will bring ;
Wi' een an' wi' hearts running o'wer we shall see
"The King in His beauty," an' our ain countrie.
My sins hae been mony, an' my sorrows hae been sair,
But there they 'll never vex me, nor be remembered mair ;
His bluid hath made me white, His hand shall dry mine e'e,
When He brings me hame at last to my ain countrie.

Like a bairn to its mither, a wee birdie to its nest,
I would fain be ganging noo unto my Saviour's breast ;
For He gathers in His bosom witless, worthless lambs like me,
An' carries them Himsel' to His ain countrie.
He 's faithfu' that hath promised,— He 'll surely come again,—
He 'll keep His tryst wi' me, at what hour I dinna ken ;
But He bids me still to wait, an' ready aye to be
To gang at ony moment to my ain countrie.

MARY LEE DEMAREST

——◆——

October 11.

For I reckon that the sufferings of this present time are not worthy to be compared with the glory which shall be revealed in us. — ROM. viii. 18.

I WONDER many times that ever a child of God should have a sad heart, considering what the Lord is preparing for him.

SAMUEL RUTHERFORD.

[Samuel Rutherford was a Scotch divine, who suffered much during the religious persecution in Scotland, but maintained his strong integrity of character and deep-toned piety to the last. At death, his last words were, "Glory, glory dwelleth in Immanuel's land!" The lines following are made up mostly of expressions of his own.]

IMMANUEL'S LAND.

I.

THE sands of time are sinking,
  The dawn of heaven breaks,
The summer morn I 've sighed for —-
  The fair sweet morn — awakes.
Dark, dark hath been the midnight,
  But dayspring is at hand ;
And glory, glory dwelleth
  In Immanuel's land.

Oh ! well it is forever,
  Oh ! well forevermore :
My nest hung in no forest
  Of all this death-doomed shore ;

Yea, let this vain world vanish
    As from the ship the strand,
While glory, glory dwelleth
    In Immanuel's land.

There the red Rose of Sharon
    Unfolds its heartmost bloom,
And fills the air of heaven
    With ravishing perfume:
Oh! to behold it blossom,
    While by its fragrance fanned,
Where glory, glory dwelleth
    In Immanuel's land!

The King there in His beauty
    Without a veil is seen;
" It were a well-spent journey,
    Though seven deaths lay between."
The Lamb, with His fair army,
    Doth on Mount Zion stand,
And glory, glory dwelleth
    In Immanuel's land.

Oh, Christ — He is the fountain,
    The deep, sweet well of love!
The streams on earth I 've tasted
    More deep I 'll drink above;
There to an ocean fulness
    His mercy doth expand,
And glory, glory dwelleth
    In Immanuel's land.

October 12.

*And he that taketh not his cross, and followeth after Me, is
not worthy of Me.* — MATT. x. 38.

HOLD fast Christ, but take His cross and Himself
cheerfully. Christ and His cross are not separable
in this life, however they part at heaven's door.

SAMUEL RUTHERFORD

II.

Oft in yon sea-beat prison [1]
  My Lord and I held tryst ;
For Anworth [2] was not heaven,
  And preaching was not Christ.
And aye my murkiest storm-cloud
  Was by a rainbow spanned,
Caught from the glory dwelling
  In Immanuel's land.

But that He built a heaven
  Of His surpassing love, —
A little new Jerusalem
  Like to the one above, —
" Lord, take me o'er the water,"
  Had been my loud demand ;
" Take me to love's own country,
  Unto Immanuel's land ! "

But flowers need night's cool darkness,
  The moonlight and the dew ;
So Christ, from one who loved it,
  His shining oft withdrew ;
And then for cause of absence,
  My troubled soul I scanned ;
But glory, shadeless, shineth
  In Immanuel's land.

The little birds of Anworth
  I used to count them blest ;
Now beside happier altars
  I go to build my nest ;
O'er these there broods no silence ;
  No graves around them stand ;
For glory, deathless, dwelleth
  In Immanuel's land.

Fair Anworth by the Solway !
  To me thou still art dear ;
E'en from the verge of heaven
  I drop for thee a tear.
Oh ! if one soul from Anworth
  Meet me at God's right hand,
My heaven will be two heavens,
  In Immanuel's land.

[1] At St. Andrews.   [2] His parish.

October 13.

For the preaching of the cross is to them that perish, foolishness; but unto us which are saved, it is the power of God. — 1 COR. i. 18.

THE cross of Christ is the sweetest burden that ever I bore; it is such a burden as wings are to a bird, or as sails to a ship, to carry me forward to my desired haven. Those who by faith see the invisible God and the fair city, make no account of present losses and crosses.

SAMUEL RUTHERFORD.

III.

I 'VE wrestled on toward heaven
  'Gainst storm and wind and tide;
Now, like a weary traveller
  That leaneth on his guide,
Amid the shades of evening,
  While sinks life's lingering sand,
I hail the glory dawning
  From Immanuel's land.

Deep waters crossed life's pathway,
  The hedge of thorns was sharp;
Now these lie all behind me;
  Oh! for a well-tuned harp!
Oh! to join Hallelujah
  With yon triumphant band,
Who sing where glory dwelleth, —
  In Immanuel's land!

With mercy and with judgment
  My web of time He wove,
And aye the dews of sorrow
  Were lustred with His love.
I 'll bless the hand that guided,
  I 'll bless the heart that planned,
When throned where glory dwelleth,
  In Immanuel's land.

Soon shall the cup of glory
  Wash down earth's bitterest woes;
Soon shall the desert brier
  Break into Eden's rose;
The curse shall change to blessing,
  The name on earth that 's banned
Be graven on the White Stone
  In Immanuel's land.

October 14.

MORE I can neither wish, nor pray, nor desire for you,
than Christ, singled and chosen out from all things,
even though wearing a crown of thorns. I am sure the
saints are at best but strangers to the might and worth of
the incomparable excellence of Christ. We know not half
of what we love, when we love Christ.

SAMUEL RUTHERFORD.

IV.

OH ! I am my Beloved's,
  And my Beloved is mine !
He brings a poor vile sinner
  Into His " house of wine."
I stand upon His merit ;
  I know no safer stand,
Not even where glory dwelleth,
  In Immanuel's land.

I shall sleep sound in Jesus,
  Filled with His likeness rise,
To love and to adore Him,
  To see Him with these eyes ;
'Tween me and resurrection
  But Paradise doth stand,
Then — then for glory, dwelling
  In Immanuel's land !

The bride eyes not her garment,
  But her dear Bridegroom's face ;
I will not gaze at glory,
  But at my King of grace ;
Not at the crown He giveth,
  But on His pierced hand ;
The Lamb is all the glory
  Of Immanuel's land.

I have borne scorn and hatred,
  I have borne wrong and shame,
Earth's proud ones have reproached me.
  For Christ's thrice-blessèd name.
Where God's seals set the fairest,
  They 've stamped their foulest brand ;
But judgment shines like noonday
  In Immanuel's land.

They 've summoned me before them,
 But there I may not come ;
My Lord says, "Come up hither,"
 My Lord says, " Welcome home ! "
My kingly King at His white throne
 My presence doth command,
Where glory, glory dwelleth
 In Immanuel's land.

October 15.

We all do fade as a leaf. — ISA. lxiv. 6.

THE burden of every sound we hear, the moral of
every sight we see, is the old, old truth, which finds
a ready response in every human bosom, " We all do fade
as a leaf." That is the great *commonplace* of the world.
It is so trite and true that it has lost in a great measure
the power of truth ; and therefore God is annually illu-
minating it to us by the many colored lights of autumn,
and investing it, by the aid of Nature's touching pictures,
with new power and impressiveness. Every year, at the
fall of the leaf, He is spreading before us a great parable,
in which our own decay and death are represented. And
Nature, like a loving mother going before her timid and
reluctant child in some difficult task, to show it the way
and inspire it with confidence, is graciously ordained thus
to go before us in her decay every autumn, to show us
that we too must fade as a leaf, and to cheer and encourage us amid the despondency of such a fate by the
assurance that, as with her by a physical law, so with us
by a law of grace, life comes by death, and decay inevitably precedes a new and better growth.

HUGH MACMILLAN.

AUTUMN.

ON the red autumn leaves I ride,
 While, parting from the half-stripped trees,
The flakes of gold and amber glide
 And float on the November breeze.

The larches' hair is golden now,
　　They stand in groves of springing flame ;
Behind them, dark in leaf and bough,
　　The fir-woods stretch their mighty frame.

Ah, splendor of the fading leaf !
　　Ah, kindly glory of decay !
How it would heal both doubt and grief,
　　Did Age thus brightly fade away !

But we are scared by failing breath ;
　　We cannot trust the heavenly spring ;
And shrinking from the touch of Death,
　　The beauties of the soul take wing ;

— Take wing, or veil themselves in awe
　　And bleak regret, and blank amaze,
As though then first the spirit saw
　　The wasted wealth of deeds and days.

Ah, yes ! this rich autumnal gold
　　Is only sunlight in decay, —
But Age, forlorn and sad and cold,
　　The porch of life, the gate of day.

LONDON SPECTATOR.

———◆———

October 16.

Consider the work of God. — ECCL. vii. 13.

AND for that I shall tell you, that, in ancient times, a
debate hath risen, and it remains yet unresolved,
whether the happiness of man in this world doth consist
more in contemplation or action.　Concerning which,
some have endeavored to maintain their opinion of the
first, by saying that the nearer we mortals come to God,
by way of imitation, the more happy we are.　And they
say that God enjoys himself only by a contemplation of
his own Infiniteness, Eternity, Power, and Goodness, and
the like.　And, upon this ground, many cloisteral men of
great learning and devotion prefer contemplation before
action.　And many of the fathers seem to approve this
opinion, as may appear in their commentaries upon the
words of our Saviour to Martha : Luke x. 42.

IZAAK WALTON.

CONTEMPLATION.

HE is the happy man whose life even now
Shows somewhat of that happier life to come ;
Who, doomed to an obscure but tranquil state,
Is pleased with it, and, were he free to choose,
Would make his fate his choice ; whom peace, the fruit
Of virtue, and whom virtue, fruit of faith,
Prepare for happiness ; bespeak him one
Content indeed to sojourn while he must
Below the skies, but having there his home.
The world o'erlooks him in her busy search
Of objects more illustrious in her view ;
And, occupied as earnestly as she,
Though more sublimely, he o'erlooks the world.
She scorns his pleasures, for she knows them not ;
He seeks not hers, for he has proved them vain.
He cannot skim the ground, like summer birds,
Pursuing gilded flies, and such he deems
Her honors, her emoluments, her joys.
Therefore in contemplation is his bliss,
Whose power is such, that whom she lifts from earth
She makes familiar with a heaven unseen,
And shows him glories yet to be revealed.
Not slothful he, though seeming unemployed,
And censured oft as useless. Stillest streams
Oft water fairest meadows, and the bird
That flutters least is longest on the wing.

WILLIAM COWPER : *Winter Walk at Noon.*

———◆———

October 17.

*But let it be the hidden man of the heart, in that which is
not corruptible, even the ornament of a meek and quiet
spirit, which is in the sight of God of great price. —*
1 PET. iii. 4.

YOUR real life is within, ripening and strengthening and
waiting, as through the long geologic ages of night
and incompleteness waited the germs of all that was to
unfold into this actual, green, and bounteous earth.

THE PETRIFIED FERN.

In a valley, centuries ago,
    Grew a little fern-leaf, green and slender, —
    Veining delicate and fibres tender, —
Waving, when the wind crept down so low;
    Rushes tall and moss and grass grew round it,
    Playful sunbeams darted in and found it,
    Drops of dew stole in by night and crowned it,
But no foot of man e'er trod that way;
Earth was young, and keeping holiday.

Monster fishes swam the silent main,
    Stately forests waved their giant branches,
    Mountains hurled their snowy avalanches,
Mammoth creatures stalked across the plain;
    Nature revelled in grand mysteries,
    But the little fern was not of these,
    Did not number with the hills and trees;
Only grew and waved, its sweet wild way, —
No one came to note it day by day.

Earth, one time, put on a frolic mood,
    Heaved the rocks, and changed the mighty motion
    Of the deep, strong currents of the ocean,
Moved the plain, and shook the haughty wood,
    Crushed the little fern in soft, moist clay,
    Covered it, and hid it safe away;
    Oh! the long, long centuries since that day!
Oh, the agony! Oh, life's bitter cost,
Since that useless little fern was lost!

Useless? Lost? There came a thoughtful man,
    Searching Nature's secrets, far and deep;
    From a fissure in a rocky steep
He withdrew a stone, o'er which there ran
    Fairy pencillings, a quaint design,
    Veinings, leafage, fibres clear and fine,
    And the fern's life lay in every line!
So, I think, God hides some souls away,
Sweetly to surprise us the last day.

PUBLIC OPINION.

October 18.

One that prayed to God always. — ACTS x. 2.

CONSTANTLY *look up.* Be on the watch for chances
to rise, like a bird let loose, though but for a
moment, into the upper air. Such is the nature of holiness. Being from God, it is ever seeking to revert to its
source. The heavier the pressure of a mundane life upon
it, the stronger is the force of its compressed aspirations.
Such pressure is like that of the atmosphere on water,
which seeks, through crevices in its enclosure, the level of
its fountain. A spirit like this will demand the habit of
fragmentary prayer for its own holy indulgence ; and will
demand it with an importunity proportioned to the super-
incumbent weight of earthly cares.

AUSTIN PHELPS.

DEVOTION.

As down in the sunless retreats of the ocean
   Sweet flowers are springing no mortal can see,
So, deep in my soul the still prayer of devotion,
   Unheard by the world, rises silent to Thee,
     My God ! silent to Thee, —
     Pure, warm, silent to Thee.

As still to the star of its worship, though clouded,
   The needle points faithfully o'er the dim sea,
So, dark as I roam, in this wintry world shrouded,
   The hope of my spirit turns trembling to Thee,
     My God ! trembling to Thee, —
     True, fond, trembling to Thee.

THOMAS MOORE

October 19.

Because Thou hast been my help, therefore in the shadow of Thy wings will I rejoice. — Ps. lxiii. 7.

" TIME restores all things." Wrong ! Time restores many things, but Eternity alone restores all.

LOOK not mournfully into the Past. It comes not back again. Wisely improve the Present. It is thine. Go forth to meet the shadowy Future, without fear, and with a manly heart.

LONGFELLOW : *Hyperion*

DO YE THINK OF THE DAYS THAT ARE GONE ?

" Do ye think of the days that are gone, Jeanie,
    As ye sit by your fire at night ?
Do ye wish that the morn would bring back the time
    When your heart and your step were so light ? "
" I think of the days that are gone, Robin,
    And of all that I joyed in then ;
But the brightest that ever arose on me
    I have never wished back again ! "

" Do ye think of the hopes that are gone, Jeanie,
    As ye sit by your fire at night ?
Do ye gather them up as they faded fast,
    Like buds with an early blight ? "
" I think of the hopes that are gone, Robin,
    And I mourn not their stay was fleet ;
For they fell as the leaves of the red rose fall,
    And were even in falling sweet ! "

" Do ye think of the friends that are gone, Jeanie,
    As ye sit by your fire at night ?
Do ye wish they were round you again once more,
    By the hearth that they made so bright ? "
" I think of the friends that are gone, Robin,
    They are dear to my heart as then ;
But the best and the dearest among them all
    I have never wished back again ! "

October 20.

And even to your old age I am He. — ISA. xlvi. 4.

YOUTH, however eclipsed for a season, is undoubtedly the proper, permanent, and genuine condition of man ; and if we look closely into this dreary delusion of growing old, we shall find that it never absolutely succeeds in laying hold of our innermost convictions. A sombre garment, woven of life's unrealities, has muffled us from our true self, but within it smiles the young man whom we knew; the ashes of many perishable things have fallen upon our youthful fire, but beneath them lurk the seeds of inextinguishable flame !

HAWTHORNE : *Dolliver Romance.*

HERE we part; in heaven we shall find each other again.

OLD FOLKS.

AH ! don't be sorrowful, darling,
And don't be sorrowful, pray ;
Taking the year together, my dear,
There is n't more night than day.
'T is rainy weather, my darling,
Time's waves, they heavily run ;
But taking the year together, my dear,
There is n't more cloud than sun.

We 're old folks now, companion,
Our heads, they are growing gray ;
But taking the year all round, my dear,
You always will find the May.
We 've had our May, my darling,
And our roses, long ago ;
And the time of the year is come, my dear,
For the silent night and the snow.

And God is God, my darling,
Of night as well as of day,
And we feel and know that we can go
Wherever He leads the way.
Aye ! God of the night, my darling, —
Of the night of death so grim ;
And the gate that from life leads out, good wife,
Is the gate that leads to Him !

October 21.

*Bless the Lord, O my soul; and all that is within me,
bless His holy name.* — Ps. ciii. 1.

EVERY man can build a chapel in his breast, himself
the priest, his heart the sacrifice, and the earth he
treads on the altar.

JEREMY TAYLOR.

"BLESS the Lord, O my soul!" For doth not all
Nature around me praise Him? If I were silent, I should
be an exception to the universe. Doth not the thunder
praise Him as it rolls like drums in the march of the God
of armies? Do not the mountains praise Him when the
woods upon their summits wave in adoration? Does not
the lightning write His name in letters of fire upon the
midnight darkness? Hath not the whole earth a voice,
and shall I, can I, be silent? "Bless the Lord, O my
soul!"

CHARLES H. SPURGEON.

A CALL TO PRAYER.

FROM slender minaret, 'twixt earth and sky,
　　Comes a clear tone,
Quivering, deepening, trilling on the upper air,
　　Like night-bird lone, —
The Faithful to shrined Mecca turn the eye,
Drop on the knee, and list the call to prayer.

It dies away, — the muezzin's prayer-cry, —
　　The spell is riven.
Hurrying, striving, panting in our breathless care,
　　Hath God not given
To *us* some time to pray, and faintly try
To glance us skyward, — some sweet call to prayer?

Yes, swaying tree, and leaf, and yellowing grain,
　　The ruddy sun,
Rising, lightening, paling in the evening air,
　　All these are one;
Nay, e'en the breeze, the dew-drop, and the rain,
The cloud and moonbeam, are God's call to prayer.

The thrill of joy, the speechless throb of pain,
    The sigh, the tear,
Working, thinking, struggling, smiling, — whatsoe'er
    Marks our life here, —
And God's soft whispers, echoing within, —
These be to-day my precious calls to prayer.

                    JEANIE GRACE CRAWFORD.

October 22.

Oh that I knew where I might find Him! that I might come even to His seat! — JOB xxiii. 3.

THESE hours of the soul's communion with truth and God are the precious hours of life. Sacrifice anything rather than these heavenly impulses. Give up anything that interferes with carrying them out into the life. They are the scattered fountains in the desert, at which the fainting traveller revives his strength and courage. Then heavenly voices speak, and happy is he who gives heed to the heavenly vision, which is from God and conducts to God.

                    EPHRAIM PEABODY.

ASPIRATION.

OH, who the speed of bird and wind
    And sunbeam's glance will lend to me,
That, soaring upward, I may find
    My resting-place and home in Thee?
Thou whom my soul, 'midst doubt and gloom.
    Adoreth with a fervent flame, —
Mysterious Spirit! unto whom
    Pertain nor sign nor name!

  .   .   .   .   .   .

O Thou who bidd'st the torrent flow,
    Who lendest wings unto the wind, —
Mover of all things! where art Thou?
    Oh, whither shall I go to find
The secret of Thy resting-place?
    Is there no holy wing for me,
That, soaring, I may search the space
    Of highest heaven for Thee?

Oh, would I were as free to rise
  As leaves on autumn's whirlwind borne,
The arrowy light of sunset skies,
  Or sound, or ray, or star of morn
Which melts in heaven at twilight's close,
  Or aught which soars unchecked and free
Through earth and heaven, that I might lose
  Myself in finding Thee!

LAMARTINE

October 23.

The Lord will perfect that which concerneth me. — Ps.
cxxxviii. 8.

WHY do I disquiet myself, forever asking, What shall
I do with my life? Useless in the world as I
seem, who knows whether God is not drawing from me
some good that I cannot see; whether, unsuspected by
myself, He has not given me some virtue, some secret
influence for the benefit of men? When I am pursued
by the fatal idea of my uselessness and powerlessness,
I will take refuge in this thought, that Providence does
draw from me some profit, does make me serve some
hidden purpose, exacting only my consent and faith in the
mission that it is not His pleasure to reveal to me. This
constant thought — that I know not the work of good to
which the Lord is setting me — shall teach me to respect
all beings, to conduct myself on earth as in a temple,
where every living thing fulfils a sacred ministry; where
the very atoms of dust are Levites, whose innumerable
legions prostrate themselves and pray in the crevices of
the floor.

MAURICE DE GUERIN.

THE FALLOW FIELD.

THE days were bright, and the year was young,
  As the warm sun climbed the sky;
And a thousand flowers their censers swung,
  And the larks were singing high;

For an angel swept on silent wing
  To the grave where the dead earth lay ;
And the Easter dawned as the angel Spring
  Rolled the rugged stone away.

Then the fields grew green with springing corn
  And some with flowers were bright;
And each day came with an earlier dawn,
  And a fuller, sweeter light.

So the year grew older noon by noon,
  Till the reapers came one day,
And in the light of a harvest moon
  They bore the sheaves away.

But one field lay from the rest apart,
  All silent, lone, and dead ;
And the rude share ribbed its quivering heart
  Till all its life had fled.

And never a blade, and never a flower
  On its silent ridges stirred ;
The sunshine called, and the passing shower, —
  It answered never a word.

It seemed as if some curse of ill
  Were brooding in the air ;
Yet the fallow field did the Master's will,
  Though never a blade it bare ;

For it turned its furrowed face to heaven,
  Catching the light and rain :
It was keeping its Sabbath — one in seven —
  That it might grow rich again.

And the fallow field had *its* harvest moon,
  Reaping a golden spoil;
And it learned in its ever-brightening noon
  That rest for God was toil.

GOOD WORDS.

October 24.

I commune with mine own heart. — Ps. lxxvii. 6.

EACH Christian has had his own dark seasons, to which God sent His own light ; and these times of needfulness and of deliverance are known, perhaps, to no one but himself, — not even, it may be, to his very dearest. There is an inner world of thought and feeling in which each of us lives, wherein we are profoundly alone ; and many a light and shadow may sweep over that little world, many a twilight gloominess may come, and many a heaven-sent light may scatter it, of which none save ourselves will ever know.

A. K. H. BOYD, D.D.

EVENING SOLACE.

The human heart hath hidden treasures,
    In secret kept, in silence sealed,
The thoughts, the hopes, the dreams, the pleasures,
    Whose charms were broken if revealed.
And days may pass in gay confusion,
    And nights in noisy riot fly,
While lost in fame's or wealth's illusion
    The memory of the Past may die.

But there are hours of lonely musing,
    Such as in evening silence come,
When, soft as birds their pinions closing,
    The heart's best feelings gather home :
When in our hearts there seems to languish
    A tender grief that is not woe,
And thoughts that once wrung groans of anguish
    Now cause but some mild tears to flow.

Oh, when the heart is freshly bleeding,
    How longs it for that time to be
When, through the mist of years receding,
    Its woes but live in reverie.
There seems a deeper impulse given
    By lonely hour and darkened room
To solemn thoughts that soar to heaven
    Seeking a life and world to come.

CHARLOTTE BRONTË.

October 25.

When I remember these things, I pour out my soul in me.
— Ps. xlii. 4.

THE happy look at things on their own level; the sorrowful look up; our thoughts settle where our hope is fixed.

IT is never wise to live in the past. There are, indeed, some uses of our past which are helpful, and which bring blessing. We should remember our past lost condition to keep us humble and faithful. We should remember past failures and mistakes, that we may not repeat them. We should remember past mercies, that we may have confidence in new needs or trials in the future. We should remember past comforts, that there may be stars in our sky when night comes again. But while there are these true uses of memory, we should guard against living in the past. We should draw our life's inspirations not from memory, but from hope ; not from what is gone, but from what is yet to come. Forgetting the things which are behind, we should reach forward unto those things which are before.   J. R. MILLER.

IF our hearts do but keep fresh, we may still love those who are gone, and may still find happiness in loving them.   JULIUS C. HARE.

REGRET.

OH ! that word regret !
There have been nights and morns when we have sighed,
"Let us alone, Regret ! We are content
To throw thee all our past, so thou wilt sleep
For aye." But it is patient, and it wakes ;
It has not learned to cry itself to sleep,
But plaineth on the bed that it is hard.
We did amiss when we did wish it gone
And over: sorrows humanize our race ;
Tears are the showers that fertilize this world ;

And memory of things precious keepeth warm
The heart that once did fold them.
                              They are poor
Who have lost nothing ; they are poorer far
Who, losing, have forgotten ; they most poor
Of all, who lose and wish they *might* forget.
For life is one, and in its warp and woof
There runs a thread of gold that glitters fair,
And sometimes in the pattern shows most sweet
Where there are sombre colors.   It is true
That we have wept.   But oh ! this thread of gold,
We would not have it tarnish ; let us turn
Oft and look back upon the wondrous web,
And when it shineth sometimes we shall know
That memory is possession.
                              JEAN INGELOW.

WHEN I remember something which I had,
    But which is gone, and I must do without,
I sometimes wonder how I can be glad,
    Even in cowslip time when hedges sprout ;
It makes me sigh to think on it, — but yet
My days will not be better days should I forget.

When I remember something promised me,
    But which I never had, nor can have now,
Because the promiser we no more see
    In countries that accord with mortal vow ;
When I remember this, I mourn, — but yet
My happier days are not the days when I forget.

—◆—

October 26.

And thou shalt be secure, because there is hope. — JOB
    xi. 18.

THE shadow of human life is traced upon a golden
    ground of immortal hope.   GEORGE S. HILLARD.

HOPE is like the sun, which, as we journey towards it,
casts the shadow of our burden behind us.
                              SMILES.

TO THE FRINGED GENTIAN.

THOU blossom bright with autumn dew,
And colored with the heaven's own blue,
That openest when the quiet light
Succeeds the keen and frosty night, —

Thou comest not when violets lean
O'er wandering brooks and springs unseen,
Or columbines in purple drest
Nod o'er the ground-bird's hidden nest.

Thou waitest late and com'st alone,
When woods are bare and birds are flown,
And frosts and shortening days portend
The aged year is near his end.

Then doth thy sweet and quiet eye
Look through its fringes to the sky,
Blue, — blue as if that sky let fall
A flower from its cerulean wall.

I would that thus, when I shall see
The hour of death draw near to me,
Hope, blossoming within my heart,
May look to heaven as I depart.

WILLIAM CULLEN BRYANT

October 27.

For so He giveth His beloved sleep. — Ps. cxxvii. 2.

REST is the deepest want in the soul of man. If you take off covering after covering of the nature which wraps him round, till you come to the central heart of hearts, deep lodged there you find the requirement of repose. All men do not desire pleasure; all men do not crave intellectual food; but all men long for rest. It is this need which sometimes makes the quiet of the grave an object of such deep desire. "There the weary are at rest." And it is this which, consciously or unconsciously, is the real wish that lies at the bottom of all others. Oh ! for tranquillity of heart, — Heaven's profound silence in the soul !

F. W. ROBERTSON.

REST.

Rest ! rest ! shall I not have all Eternity to rest in ? — ARNAULD.

THERE comes a time of rest to thee,
Whose laden boughs droop heavily
Toward earth, thou golden-fruited tree !

A time when wind and tempest cease
To spoil and stain thy fair increase ;
After fruition deepest peace.

Green, leafy, quiet, freed from care,
No heavier weight thy lithe limbs bear
Than dripping rain and sunny air.

But unto man's diviner sense
The strenuous rest of penitence
Remaineth only for defence.

His fruit drops slowly from his hands,
But only with the dropping sands
That fall on Time's slow-gathering strands

The sower in this mortal field
Shall reap no harvest's gracious yield,
The warrior conquers — on his shield.

But after life and fruit and rest,
Thou, tree ! by dust shalt be possessed ;
To him remains a day more blest ;

A newer hope, a summer-time
Renewed forever in its prime,
Where God, his harvest, sits sublime.

ROSE TERRY COOKE

October 23.

Doth not He see my ways, and count all my steps? —.
JOB xxxi. 4.

IT appears to me most important that we should understand that no mere moment, no isolated act of choice,
under a pressure of temptation, settles destinies. The
quiet, undistinguished years decide the matter for the moments when the election is finally and openly made. It
takes years to give a form and bent to a character. Tem-
perament we are born with, character we have to make ;
and that not in the grand moments, when the eyes of men
or of angels are visibly upon us, but in the daily, quiet
paths of pilgrimage, when the work is being done within
in secret which will be revealed in the daylight of eternity.
Habits, like paths, are the result of constant actions. It
is the multitude of daily footsteps which go to and fro
which shapes them. Let it light up your daily wanderings
to know that there, — in the quiet bracing of the soul
to uncongenial duty, the patient bearing of unwelcome
burdens, the loving acceptance of unlovely companionship,
— and not on the grand occasions, you are making your
eternal future. It is the multitude of little actions which
makes the great ones.

J. BALDWIN BROWN

IF WE HAD BUT A DAY.

WE should fill the hours with the sweetest things,
    If we had but a day ;
We should drink alone at the purest springs
    In our upward way :
We should love with a lifetime's love in an hour,
    If the hours were few ;
We should rest, not for dreams, but for fresher power
    To be and do.

We should guide our wayward or wearied wills
    By the clearest light ;
We should keep our eyes on the heavenly hills
    If they lay in sight ;
We should trample the pride and the discontent
    Beneath our feet;
We should take whatever a good God sent,
    With a trust complete.

We should waste no moments in weak regret,
If the day were but one ;
If what we remember and what we forget
Went out with the sun ;
We should be from our clamorous selves set free
To work or to pray,
And to be what the Father would have us be,
If we had but a day.

M. L. DICKINSON.

October 29.

But he that shall endure unto the end, the same shall be saved. — MATT. xxiv. 13.

THERE is a Spirit who " helpeth our infirmities," and in no way more mightily than by stirring us to renew our efforts of self-discipline, reviving our courage when we are disheartened, our strength when we are weary, our hope when we despair. Why should we struggle? we say. Why should we try to conquer and rule ourselves at so much cost and pain? It is but like casting up sand banks against the ocean. The first storm saps the foundation, it crumbles, melts, vanishes, and the sea sweeps on triumphant as at first. The Holy Ghost, the Comforter, is the Being who answers the question, by moving us, stirring us, to endure. He stands by us, and makes us strong. He keeps before us all that hangs on the effort, all that the end is worth, whatever may be its cost. The eternal state in which all our daily habits and actions have their final issues, He keeps before the eye of the spirit ; and One who is the perfect image of our nature, the mark of our every effort and aspiration ; who presents to all whose eye of faith prevails to behold Him, the prophecy and the pledge of the divine perfection which souls established by grace at last may win.

CHRISTIAN POLICY OF LIFE.

VOICES OF THE DEAD.

OH ! there are moments when the cares of life
Press on the wearied spirit; when the heart
Is fainting in the conflict, and the crown,
The bright, immortal crown, for which we strive,
Shines dimly through the gathering mists of earth;
Then voices of the dead, sweet, solemn voices, —
How have I heard ye in my inmost soul ! —
Voices of those, who, while they walked on earth,
Were linked unto my spirit by the ties
Of pure affection, love more strong than death :
Ye cry, frail child of earth, tried, tempted one,
Shrink not, despond not, strive as we have striven,
In the stern conflict, yet a little while,
And thou shalt be as we are, — thou shalt know
How far the recompense transcends the toil.

October 30.

It is more blessed to give than to receive. — ACTS xx. 35.

BUT he that hath found charity to be the Temper of Happiness, which doth put the soul in a natural and easy condition, and openeth it to the solaces of that pure and sublime entertainment which the angels doe spread for such as obey the will of their Creator, hath discovered a more subtle alchemy than anie of which the philosophers did dream, for he transmuteth the enjoyments of others into his own, and his large and open heart partaketh of the satisfaction of all around him.

MARGARET SMITH'S JOURNAL (WHITTIER).

THE UNFAILING CRUSE.

Is thy cruse of comfort wasting ? Rise and share it with another ;
And through all the years of famine it shall serve thee and thy brother.
Love divine will fill thy storehouse, or thy handful still renew ;
Scanty fare for one will often make a royal feast for two.

For the heart grows rich in giving; all its wealth is living
grain :
Seeds which mildew in the garner, scattered, fill with gold
the plain.
Is thy burden hard and heavy ? Do thy steps drag wearily ?
Help to bear thy brother's burden ; God will bear both it and
thee.

Numb and weary on the mountains, wouldst thou sleep
amidst the snow?
Chafe that frozen form beside thee, and together both shall
glow.
Art thou stricken in life's battle ? Many wounded round thee
moan ;
Lavish on their wounds thy balsams, and that balm shall heal
thine own.

Is thy heart a well left empty ? None but God its void can fill ;
Nothing but a ceaseless fountain can its ceaseless longings
still.
Is the heart a living power ? Self-entwined its strength sinks
low ;
It can only live in loving, and, by serving, love will grow.

MRS. CHARLES.

October 31.

*And He looked up and saw the rich men casting their gifts
into the treasury; and He saw also a certain poor
widow casting in thither two mites. And He said,
Of a truth I say unto you that this poor widow hath
cast in more than they all; for all these have of their
abundance cast in unto the offerings of God; but she
of her penury hath cast in all the living that she had.
— LUKE xxi. 1–4.*

WHAT more tender, more solemnly affecting, more
profoundly pathetic, than this charity, this offering
to God of a farthing ! We know nothing of her name, her
family, or her tribe. We only know that she was a poor

woman, and a widow, of whom there is nothing left on record but this sublimely simple story, that when the rich came to cast their proud offerings into the treasury, this poor woman came also and cast in her two mites, which made a farthing ! And that example, thus made the subject of Divine commendation, has been read, and told, and gone abroad everywhere, and sunk deep into a hundred millions of hearts, since the commencement of the Christian era, and has done more good than could be accomplished by a thousand marble palaces, because it was charity mingled with true benevolence, given in the fear, the love, the service, and honor of God ; because it was charity that had its origin in religious feeling ; because it was a gift to the honor of God.

DANIEL WEBSTER.

AS A LEAF.

THE leaf presents to God its finished story,
Receiving at His hand its meed of glory ;
And floating gently down, with mission ended,
Moulders beneath the bough its life defended.

Freely it gave its all the tree to nourish,
That, by its tiny power, the oak might flourish ;
For 't is the blossomed branch whose vital juices,
Fed by the foliage dense, the fruit produces.

So God delights to teach this lesson ever, —
That His success depends on our endeavor ;
That, lovingly performed, each lowly duty
Adds to the inner strength and outer beauty.

Yet are we slow to learn that death is glorious
Only to those who rise o'er self victorious ;
Only to those who find the bliss of living
In ever, like the leaf, receiving, giving.

To such, life's autumn day yields rich completeness,
Whose mellow splendors dim youth's early sweetness :
And when, to false and true, rewards are meted,
With Jesus' sweet " Well done ! " they shall be greeted.

NETTIE M. ARNOLD.

November 1.

Nevertheless I am continually with Thee: Thou hast holden me by my right hand. Thou shalt guide me with Thy counsel, and afterward receive me to glory. — Ps. lxxiii. 23, 24.

THIS is the Christian's privilege, that he lives in a larger world than other men. He sees things that are hid from their eyes. Behind the chaos of good and bad just about us, behind the seeming defeat of the right, behind disaster and loss and doubt, there stands up to his sight the figure of Infinite Love, controlling all things. Beyond the imperfections of life lies the fulness of Heaven.

HOMEWARD TO THEE.

NEVER so fathomless a sea,
But through its depths there reacheth me
    His still supporting hand;
Never so drear can desert be —
But there His love grows green for me
    Amid the scorching sand.

For He who over sea and land
Doth homeward guide from farthest strand
    The bird's unerring way,
Can surely safe my pathway steer;
Then let me never yield to fear,
    Nor once in darkness stray.

Though I am weak and wayward still,
Lord, do for me Thy chosen will;
    But this my prayer shall be, —
Wherever wings my wandering way,
Oh, steer it so at last it may
    Safe homeward lead to Thee.

Tr. from the Swedish, by LYDIA M. MILLARD.

November 2.

He shall see of the travail of His soul, and shall be satisfied.
— ISA. liii. 11.

IT would seem that by our sorrows only are we called to a knowledge of the Infinite. Are we happy? The limits of life constrain us on all sides.

MADAME SWETCHINE.

OUT of suffering have emerged the strongest souls; the most massive characters are seamed with scars; martyrs have put on their coronation robes glittering with fire, and through their tears have the sorrowful first seen the gates of Heaven.

E. H. CHAPIN.

SORROW.

UPON my lips she laid her touch divine,
    And merry speech and careless laughter died;
She fixed her melancholy eyes on mine,
    And would not be denied.

I saw the west-wind loose his cloudlets white
    In flocks, careering through the April sky;
I could not sing, though joy was at its height,
    For she stood silent by.

I watched the lovely evening fade away;
    A mist was lightly drawn across the stars.
She broke my quiet dream; I heard her say,
    " Behold your prison bars !

" Earth's gladness shall not satisfy your soul,
    This beauty of the world in which you live;
The crowning grace that sanctifies the whole, —
    That, I alone can give."

I heard and shrank away from her afraid;
    But still she held me and would still abide;
Youth's bounding pulses slackened and obeyed,
    With slowly ebbing tide.

"Look Thou beyond the evening star," she said,
  "Beyond the changing splendors of the day;
Accept the pain, the weariness, the dread,
  Accept and bid me stay!"

I turned and clasped her close with sudden strength,
  And slowly, sweetly, I became aware
Within my arms God's angel stood at length,
  White-robed and calm and fair.

And now I look beyond the evening star,
  Beyond the changing splendors of the day,
Knowing the pain He sends more precious far,
  More beautiful, than they.

CELIA THAXTER

——◆——

November 3.

*My people shall dwell in a peaceable habitation, and in
sure dwellings, and in quiet resting-places.* — Isa. xxxii.
18.

THE weather is rainy, the whole atmosphere gray; it is
a time favorable to thought and meditation. I have
a liking for such days as these : they revive one's converse
with one's self, and make it possible to live the inner life ;
they are quiet and peaceful, like a song in a minor key.
We are nothing but thought, but we feel our life to its very
centre. Our very sensations turn to reverie. It is a strange
state of mind ; it is like those silences of worship which
are not the empty moments of devotion, but the full moments, and which are so because at such times the soul,
instead of being polarized, dispersed, localized in a single
impression or thought, feels her own totality and is conscious of herself. She tastes her own substance. She is
no longer played upon, colored, set in motion, affected,
from without ; she is in equilibrium and at rest. Open-
ness and self-surrender become possible to her ; she con-
templates and she adores. She sees the changeless and

the eternal enwrapping all the phenomena of time. She is in the religious state, in harmony with the general order, — or at least in intellectual harmony. For holiness, indeed, more is wanted, — a harmony of will, a perfect self-devotion, death to self, and absolute submission.

Psychological peace — that harmony which is perfect but virtual — is but the zero, the potentiality of all numbers; it is not that moral peace which is victorious over all ills, which is real, positive, tried by experience, and able to face whatever fresh storms may assail it. The peace of fact is not the peace of principle. There are indeed two happinesses, that of nature and that of conquest; two equilibria, that of Greece and that of Nazareth; two kingdoms, that of the natural man and that of the regenerate man.

HENRI FRÉDÉRIC AMIEL.

LOSS AND GAIN.

How sadly beats the heavy autumn rain;
How mournful drives the wind among the trees;
Along the shore the weary sailor sees
The waves roll in that send him out again;
The birds are restless in the scattered leaves,
The clouds move wildly on in massy fold,
And all the outer world, or earth, or air,
But yesterday so warm, so fair,
Is changed, and in a night, to drear and cold.

Now goes the golden autumn far away;
Now nearer comes the winter to my door;
And thus doth Nature, working evermore,
Create new life from changes and decay.
O Christ! who in the hall of Pilate bore
For me the scourge and mocking, for Thy sake
Fill up the daily loss in life of mine
With Thy life. So shall love divine
Out of the changing the unchanging make.

November 4.

For we know that if our earthly house of this tabernacle were dissolved, we have a building of God, a house not made with hands, eternal in the heavens. — 2 COR. V. I.

WHAT we seek is the immortality that is clothed with disinterestedness rather than with wings. We look for a heaven where there will be more disinterested love, more patience with weakness, more hospitality to truth. If such is to be realized, we ourselves must begin to shape it now. By working in and for the life that now is, we lay hold of the life that never ceases to be. We expect the continued life, because we have more work on hand than we can finish in this. . . . The universal providence, that includes bird and flower, is the providence that is to have continuous use for the soul of man. The simplest movement of grass and flowers through the sod reaches the throne of the Eternal. The lowliest blade has its message and rings its Easter bell in April. There is a prophetic instinct in the soul that carries on the lines of thought suggested by our knowledge of the near beauty and the lowly marvel. We build large hopes upon the great and beautiful laws of the universe. We place generous confidence in the Master Builder who so grandly forms the growing order. We cannot believe that he will allow our lives to remain mocking segments of an incompleted circle. There is some vast meaning in this mystic tide that has arisen in the soul of man in all times. There is some distant attraction, some moon in the heavens of infinite life, that bends this ocean of mortality towards its immortality. Immortality as a mere present from God to man, as a compliment or mark of confidence, an opportunity to sing praises to the Power that gave it, does not find much in the analogies of the universe to justify it. But the expectant life, as successive chapters in a continued story, being wrought out for some higher good than we know of, — immortality as a necessity to that which is already begun, — presses upon us as a responsibility, as a necessity.

J. Ll. JONES.

MORTALITY.

Ye dainty mosses, lichens gray,
   Pressed each to each in tender fold,
And peacefully thus, day by day,
   Returning to their mould;

Brown leaves that with aerial grace
   Slip from your branch like birds a-wing,
Each leaving in th' appointed place
   Its bud of future spring; —

If we, God's conscious creatures, knew
   But half your faith in our decay,
We should not tremble as we do
   When summoned clay to clay.

But with an equal patience sweet
   We should put off this mortal gear,
In whatsoe'er new form is meet
   Content to reappear.

Knowing each germ of life He gives
   Must have in Him its source and rise,
Being that of His being lives
   May change, but never dies.

Ye dead leaves, dropping soft and slow,
   Ye mosses green, and lichens fair,
Go to your graves as I will go,
   For God is also there.
              DINAH MULOCH CRAIK.

—◆—

November 5.

*I wait for the Lord, my soul doth wait, and in His word
do I hope.* — Ps. cxxx. 5.

NOW hope is our *anchor fixed within the veil,* which
stays us against all the storms that beat upon us in
this troublesome sea that we are tossed upon.   The soul
which strongly believes and loves may confidently hope to

see what it believes, and to enjoy what it loves ; and in that
it may rejoice.   It may say, Whatsoever hazards, whether
outward or inward, whatsoever afflictions and temptations
I endure, yet this one thing puts me out of hazard, and in
that I will rejoice, that the salvation of my soul depends
not upon my own strength, but is in my Saviour's hand.
The childish world are hunting shadows, and hoping after
they know not what ; but the believer can say, " I know
whom I have trusted."

ARCHBISHOP LEIGHTON.

HOPING AND WAITING.

To-day sweet hopes within my bosom linger,
  The sweet, pure hopes born of unfaltering trust;
  Though joys be fled, or scattered in the dust,
I read the lesson written by God's finger,
  Not upon stony tablets, as of old,
When on the mountain-top, 'mid smoke and flame,
The word of God unto His children came :
  But in my heart the precious boon I hold,
The daily wisdom for the daily round.
  For trusting, waiting souls God loves to teach,
  The needed lesson gives He unto each ;
As to the Hebrews manna on the ground,
  So to the spirit asking daily food,
He sends it daily, fresh and sweet and good.

And we can well afford to wait a season,
  Till all that now is dark shall be made bright,
  If not with earthly, then with heavenly light,
And we shall come at last to know the reason
  Of all the toil, the seeming loss, the pain,
The silent vanishing of some dear face,
The weary gazing at the vacant place, —
  All this, and more, shall in God's time come plain.
Hope, then, my soul, and let thy trust abound.
  His mercies fail not.   Every morning new
  They come to thee, as to the flowers the dew.
Oh ! in all cares and sorrows thou hast found
  His grace sufficient for thee hitherto ;
It will be to the end, if thou art true.

November 6.

Jesus said unto him, If thou canst believe, all things are possible to him that believeth. — MARK ix. 23.

SINK not to rest or slumber beneath the passing shadows of doubt.   To sink, to sleep, is not thy destination ; but to wake, to rise.   Rise then to the glorious pursuit of truth ; connect with it the work of self-purification ; open thy mind to heavenly hope ; aspire to the life everlasting !   Count it not a strange thing that thou hast difficulties and doubts.   Well has it been said that he who never doubted, never believed.   Shrink not and be not afraid, when that cloud passeth over thee.   *Through* the cloud, still press onward.   Only be assured of this, and with this assurance be of courage ; God made thee to believe.

ORVILLE DEWEY.

A DOUBTING HEART.

WHERE are the swallows fled ?
Frozen and dead
Perchance upon some bleak and stormy shore.
O doubting heart !
Far over purple seas,
They wait in sunny ease,
The balmy southern breeze
To bring them to their northern homes once more.

Why must the flowers die ?
Prisoned they lie
In the cold tomb, heedless of tears or rain.
O doubting heart !
They only sleep below
The soft white ermine snow
While winter winds shall blow,
To breathe and smile upon you soon again.

Fair hope is dead, and light
Is quenched in night.
What sound can break the silence of despair ?
O doubting heart !
The sky is overcast,
Yet stars shall rise at last,
Brighter for darkness past,
And angels' silver voices stir the air.

ADELAIDE A. PROCTER.

November 7.

Neither shall they say, Lo here! or, lo there! for, behold, the kingdom of God is within you. — LUKE xvii. 21.

O BEAUTY of ancient days, ancient but ever new! Too late I sought Thee, too late I found Thee. I sought Thee at a distance, and did not know that Thou wast near. I sought Thee abroad in thy works, and behold, Thou wast within me. CONFESSIONS OF SAINT AUGUSTINE.

THE CITY OF GOD.

O THOU not made with hands,
Not throned above the skies,
Nor walled with shining walls,
Nor framed with stones of price,
More bright than gold or gem,
God's own Jerusalem!

Where'er the gentle heart
Finds courage from above;
Where'er the heart forsook
Warms with the breath of love;
Where faith bids fear depart,
City of God! thou art.

Thou art where'er the proud
In humbleness melts down;
Where self itself yields up;
Where martyrs win their crown;
Where faithful souls possess
Themselves in perfect peace.

Where in life's common ways
With cheerful feet we go;
When in His steps we tread
Who trod the way of woe;
Where He is in the heart,
City of God! thou art.

Not throned above the skies,
Nor golden-walled afar,
But where Christ's two or three
In His name gathered are,
Be in the midst of them,
God's own Jerusalem!

FRANCIS TURNER PALGRAVE

November 8.

Give ear to my words, O Lord; consider my meditation. —
Ps. v. 1.

LET prayer be the *key* of the morning, and the *bolt* of
the evening.

MEDITATION is done in silence. By it we renounce
our narrow individuality, and expatiate into that which is
infinite. Only in the sacredness of inward silence does
the soul truly meet the secret, hiding God. The strength
of resolve, which afterwards shapes life and mixes itself
with action, is the fruit of those sacred, solitary moments.
There is a divine depth in silence. We meet God alone.

PRAYER.

I COME to Thee to-night,
In my lone closet where no eye can see,
And dare to crave an interview with Thee,
Father of love and light.

If I this day have striven
With Thy blest Spirit, or have bowed the knee
To aught of earth in weak idolatry,
I pray to be forgiven.

If I have turned away
From grief or suffering which I might relieve,
Careless the cup of water e'en to give,
Forgive me, Lord, I pray.

And teach me how to feel
My sinful wanderings with a deeper smart,
And more of mercy and of grace impart,
My sinfulness to heal.

Father, my soul would be
Pure as the drops of eve's unsullied dew ;
And as the stars whose nightly course is true,
So would I be to Thee.

Not for myself alone
Would I these blessings of Thy love implore,
But for each penitent the wide earth o'er,
Whom Thou hast called Thine own.

And for my heart's best friends,
Whose steadfast kindness o'er my painful years
Has watched to soothe afflictions, griefs, and tears,
My warmest prayer ascends.

And now, O Father, take
The heart I cast with humble faith on Thee,
And cleanse its depths from each impurity,
For my Redeemer's sake.

———+———

November 9.

For I have satiated the weary soul, and I have replenished
every sorrowful soul. — JER. xxxi. 25.

GENIAL, almost to a miracle, is the soil of sorrow;
wherein the smallest seed of love, timely falling,
becometh a tree, in whose foliage the birds of blessed
song lodge and sing unceasingly. And the doubts of
God's goodness, whence are they? Rarely from the weary
and overburdened, from those broken in the practical
service of grief and toil!

Let there be a constant affiliation with God; and as
He pervadeth all things, a unity is imparted to life which
puts not happiness indeed, but character and will, above
the reach of circumstance; a current of pure and strong
affection, fed by the fount of bliss, pours from hidden
and sunlit heights, and winds through the open plains
and dark ravines of life, until its murmurs fall into the
everlasting deep.

A PROTEST.

WHY press we so against the door that Fate
    Has barred upon our hearts' desire?
Why hold our lives bereft and desolate
    Because God writes their almanac in fire?
Why should we sadden with dark clouded skies,
    When others make a ladder of their love,
And while we deem ourselves too weak to rise,
    They've climbed above?

Why sit and dream in Spring's sweet labor time
 Unreal dreams, whose sadness makes them sweet,
And, since we mar and break our life's full prime,
 Deem that we rest contented at God's feet?
Why cry to Heaven for lost and broken hours,
 For faith and hope that faded long ago,
When still within our hearts new fruitful powers
 Are budding now?

O eyes turned inward on our darkened hearts,
 Open to see God's beauty on the earth;
Self-pitying tears that flow upon His smarts,
 Fructify all our barrenness and dearth;
O folded hands, close clasped in dull despair,
 Grow busy with God's work of love and peace;
O heart, forget to grieve, and rise to where
 Misgivings cease.

CAROLINE NORTH.

November 10.

For what dost thou make request? — NEH. ii. 4.

PRAYER opens to us, as it were, the portals of the spirit-world, in which we also have some right of citizenship. We draw nearer to the Deity, and feel that we belong to Him. We rise on the wings of prayer, above all that is worthless and perishable, and become greater, yea, more divine, as we do so. The conviction becomes ever mightier within us, that we can never cease to exist. We distinguish more clearly between what is everlasting and what is perishable, — between what is real and what is mere appearance. We see the whole universe in a new light. And happy presentiments thrill through us. Heavenly joy pervades all nature. This is the power of prayer; this is the effect of drawing nigh unto God.

ZSCHOKKE.

GOOD-NIGHT.

WHEN thou hast spent the lingering day
 In pleasure and delight,
Or after toil and weary way
 Dost seek to rest at night,

Unto thy pains or pleasures past
  Add this one labor yet:
Ere sleep close up thine eye too fast,
  Do not thy God forget.

And think, how well soe'er it be
  That thou hast spent the day,
It came of God, and not of thee,
  So to direct thy way.
Thus if thou try thy daily deeds,
  And pleasure in this pain,
Thy life shall cleanse thy corn from weeds,
  And thine shall be the gain.

GEORGE GASCOIGNE (1500).

—◆—

November 11.

*The Lord hath prepared His throne in the heavens; and
His kingdom ruleth over all.* — Ps. ciii. 19.
We are His people, and the sheep of His pasture. — Ps.
c. 3.

HE who is Christ's, surveying the wonders of creation,
can say, "Glorious though these things be, to me
belongs that which is more glorious far. The streams are
precious, but I have the Fountain; the vesture is beautiful, but the Wearer is mine; the portrait in its every linea-
ment is lovely, but that great Original whose beauty it
feebly depicts is my own. 'God is my portion, the Lord
is my inheritance.' To me belongs all actual and all possible good, all created and uncreated beauty, all that eye
hath seen or imagination conceived; and more than that,
for 'eye hath not seen, nor ear heard, nor hath it entered
into the heart of man to conceive what God hath prepared
for them that love Him.'"

LORD AND FATHER.

LORD! in whose sight a thousand years but seem
  A fleeting moment, — O Eternal Being!
  Turn towards me Thy clemency,
Lest like a shadow vain my brief existence flee!

Thou who upon the sacred throne of heaven
  In glorious light dost sit, Immutable !
    For Thine eternal rest,
Exchange, my Lord, the thoughts of this unstable breast !

Thou by whose hand the sparrow is sustained,
  Father of all, God of the universe !
    Thy gifts with gracious speed
Scatter upon my head, since I am poor indeed !

Being Eternal, Infinite ! Soul ! Life !
  Father all-knowing ! wise, omniscient Power !
    From Thine exalted throne,
Since I Thy creature am, look down upon Thine own.

JUAN VALDES.

———◆———

November 12.

For with Thee is the fountain of life ; in Thy light shall we see light. — Ps. xxxvi. 9.

PRAYER, praise, thanksgiving, contemplation, are the peculiar privilege and duty of a Christian ; and that for their own sakes, from the exceeding comfort and satisfaction they afford him, and without reference to any definite results to which prayer tends, without reference to the answers which are promised to it, from a general sense of the blessedness of being under the shadow of God's throne.

J. H. NEWMAN

JESUS, THOU JOY.

JESUS, thou joy of loving hearts !
  Thou fount of life ! Thou light of men !
From the best bliss that earth imparts,
  We turn, unfilled, to Thee again.
Thy truth unchanged hath ever stood ;
  Thou savest those that on Thee call ;
To them that seek Thee, Thou art good ;
  To them that find Thee, all in all !

We taste Thee, O Thou Living Bread !
And long to feast upon Thee still ;
We drink of Thee, the Fountain-head,
And thirst from Thee our souls to fill.
Our restless spirits yearn for Thee
Where'er our changeful lot is cast ;
Glad when Thy gracious smile we see,
Blest when our faith can hold Thee fast.
O Jesus, ever with us stay !
Make all our moments calm and bright ;
Chase the dark night of sin away,
Shed o'er the world Thy holy light.

BERNARD.
Tr. by RAY PALMER.

—◆—

November 13.

*They that trust in the Lord shall be as Mount Zion, which
cannot be removed, but abideth forever.* — Ps. cxxv. 1.

IT seems a bold thing to say that, properly understood,
there is no more ambitious and aspiring virtue than
content in the Christian sense, none fuller of true *passion*
in the highest meaning of that great but much-abused
word.   In this sense content is, indeed, something far
higher than the virtue which Dekker apostrophized in the
beautiful lines, "Art thou poor, yet hast thou golden
slumbers, O sweet content?"   In the Christian sense,
content has often no golden slumbers ; it is not only not
apathy, not sluggishness, not passiveness of mind, but in
Saint Paul's sense it is radically inconsistent with any
dwindling tendencies.

In all and every case, the virtue of content does not
consist in shrinking within the limits set you, but in going
out of yourself, so to transform and transmute the conditions in which you find yourself as to make them feed
some of the highest passions of the soul, — gratitude, if
the particular conditions specially call for gratitude ; patience and forbearance and fortitude, if they call for them ;
inextinguishable zeal, persuasiveness, and sympathy, if the
external circumstances seem to cry out for the exercise
of a strong moulding and transforming power to recast and

renovate them. This is what the true content means, — that hearty willingness alike for calamity, or joy, or weighty responsibility, which is inspired by the magic secret that in each condition alike there is some divine spring of help, some opportunity of so dealing that the actual conditions, however apparently calamitous, shall be better, there and then, than any alternative, however bright. This is certainly the sense in which Saint Paul regarded content, — as resourcefulness of the highest kind, involving a spiritual elasticity of the highest kind, a power to transform what often seemed like mere wounds and pangs and fetters into new strength and life and freedom. Surely nothing less like a merely passive virtue can be imagined than the virtue of content as described by Saint Paul: "For I have learned, in whatsoever state I am, therewith to be content."

LONDON SPECTATOR.

WHAT is there in the world to distinguish virtues from dishonor, or that can make anything rewardable, but the labor and the danger, the pain and the difficulty?

JEREMY TAYLOR.

LIFT THINE EYES.

O TROUBLED soul of mine! lift up thine eyes
   Unto the mountains, mighty and serene.
   Full strangely checkered hath their fortune been ;
And they have suffered veriest agonies.
And ofttimes still the tyrant tempest lies
   Heavy upon them ; with the thunder they
   Do wrestle. Yet of fear and of dismay
Nothing they know, still rising to the skies.
With many a thousand battles are they scarred ;
   The floods have broken on each helmless head ;
Yet for all this their beauty is not marred,
   Nor in their hearts are they discomforted.
Still they endure, whatever whirlwinds roll
Around, — still glorious they endure, my soul !

JOHN W. HALES: *Hindscarth Cairn*

November 14.

Keep me as the apple of the eye, hide me under the shadow of Thy wings. — Ps. xvii. 8.

TO the Redeemer of men every believer is as a brother, loved with an individualizing love, — "Who loved and gave Himself for us." When we look on the clear starry sky, we are perplexed by the multitude of lights, and we can only single out and identify the brighter among them. But the astronomer will fix his glass on one far away in the silent depths, and watch it in its movements as if there was not another twinkling sister in all the sky. And so through all the ages, and all the millions of chosen saints, — stars to be in heaven forever, — the eye of the Redeemer, all-seeing, fixes its gaze on each as truly as if there were not another, and settles the plan of his life as if it were the sole object of His care.

JOHN HALL.

ALL THROUGH THE NIGHT.

ALL through the night,
Dear Father, when our trembling eyes explore
In vain Thy heavens, bereft of warmth and light,
When birds are mute, and roses glow no more,
And this fair world sinks rayless from our sight,
O Father, keep us then !

All through the night,
When no lips smile, nor dear eyes answer ours,
Nor well-known voices through the shadows come ;
When love and friends seem dreams of vanished hours,
And darkness holds us pitiless and dumb,
O Father, keep us then !

All through the night,
When lone despairs beset our happy hearts,
And drear forebodings will not let us sleep ;
When every smothered sorrow freshly starts
And pleads for pity till we fain would weep,
O Father, keep us then !

All through the night,
When slumbers deep our weary senses fold,
Protect us in the hollow of Thy hand ;
And when the morn, with glances bright and bold,
Thrills the glad heavens and wakes the smiling land,
O Father, keep us then !

November 15.

The whole earth is at rest, and is quiet. — Isa. xiv. 7.

THE sun sets on some retired meadow, where no house is visible, with all the glory and splendor that it lavishes on the cities, and perchance, as it has never set before, — where there is but a solitary marsh hawk to have his wings gilded by it, or only a musquash looks out from his cabin, and there is only some little black-veined brook in the midst of the marsh, just beginning to meander, winding slowly around a decaying stump. We walked in so pure and bright a light, gilding the withered grass and leaves, so softly and serenely bright, I thought I had never bathed in such a golden flood, without a ripple or a murmur in it. The west side of every wood and rising ground gleamed like the boundary of Elysium, and the sun on our backs seemed like a gentle herdsman driving us home at evening. So we saunter towards the Holy Land, till, one day, the sun shall shine more brightly than ever he has done, shall perchance shine into our minds and hearts, and light up our whole lives with a great awakening light, as warm and serene and golden as on a bankside in autumn.

THOREAU.

HOMEWARD.

THE day dies slowly in the western sky;
    The sunset splendor fades, and wan and cold
The far peaks wait the sunrise; cheerily
    The goatherd calls his wanderers to their fold.
      My weary soul, that fain would cease to roam,
      Take comfort; evening bringeth all things home.

Homeward the swift-winged sea-gull takes its flight:
    The ebbing tide breaks softly on the sand;
The sunlit boats draw shoreward for the night;
    The shadows deepen over sea and land;
      Be still, my soul, thine hour shall also come:
      Behold, one evening God shall lead thee home.

November 16.

For this God is our God forever and ever; He will be our guide even unto death. — Ps. xlviii. 14.

BE willing to live by believing, and neither think nor desire to live in any other way. Be willing to see every outward light extinguished, to see the eclipse of every star in the blue heavens, leaving nothing but darkness and perils around, if God will only leave in the soul the inner radiance, the pure bright lamp which faith has kindled.

THOMAS C. UPHAM.

THE PILGRIM.

THE way is dark, my Father! cloud on cloud
Is gathering quickly o'er my head; and loud
The thunders roar above me. See, I stand
Like one bewildered. Father, take my hand,
And through the gloom lead safely home Thy child.

The way is long, my Father! and my soul
Longs for the rest and quiet of the goal,
While yet I journey through this weary land.
Keep me from wandering! Father, take my hand;
Quickly and straight lead to heaven's gate Thy child.

The cross is heavy, Father! I have borne
It long, and still do bear it. Let my worn
And fainting spirit rise to that blessed land
Where crowns are given. Father, take my hand,
And, reaching down, lead to the crown Thy child.

The way is dark, My child, but leads to light;
I would not have thee always walk by sight.
My dealings now thou canst not understand;
I meant it so; but I will take thy hand,
And through the gloom lead safely home My child.

The way is long, My child! but it shall be
Not one step longer than is best for thee,
And thou shalt know at last, when thou shalt stand
Close to the gate, how I did take thy hand,
And quick and straight led to heaven's gate My child.

The cross is heavy, child! yet there is One
Who bore a heavier for thee: My Son,
My Well-Beloved; with Him bear thine and stand;
With Him at last, and from thy Father's hand,
Thy cross laid down, receive thy crown, My child!

HENRY N. COBB.

November 17.

But the God of all grace, who hath called us unto His eternal glory by Christ Jesus, after that ye have suffered a while, make you perfect, stablish, strengthen, settle you. — 1 PET. v. 10.

A MAN may say, I find in me a spirit which has a large, a royal, range of power, and which seems to be ever aiming and struggling toward a great destiny. It finds both the pain and pleasure essential to its progress. It sees that neither is pain the great evil, nor pleasure the great good. Each is good in its time ; they are twin factors in the husbandry of life. I learn that there is One who made the world, the Father of my spirit, who holds them both as He holds the stars of heaven, and the winds of the earth in His hand.

He seems to use them as His husbandmen for the cultivation and development of the immortal part of my being, that it may know Him, grow like Him, and be fit for His presence and His joy eternally. It is my policy therefore to expand my being to the utmost, to push forth every tentacle, to bring myself into contact with the widest possible variety of scenes, things, and experiences, — not that by wise management I may multiply the pleasures and elude the pains, but that I may gather from both all the fruits which my Lord meant them to bear to me ; that I may grow richer, wiser, stronger daily through my double experience ; having no fear that while He rules the pain will master me ; and then that I may bear a rich treasure with me, the spoil of life's pain and pleasure, through the gates of death, to gladden my life in God eternally.

J. BALDWIN BROWN : *Christian Policy of Life.*

MY BIRTHDAY.

BENEATH the moonlight and the snow
Lies dead my latest year ;
The winter winds are wailing low
Its dirges in my ear.

I grieve not with the wailing wind
As if a loss befell,
Before me, even as behind,
God is, and all is well.

His light shines on me from above,
  His low voice speaks within, —
The patience of immortal love
  Outwearying mortal sin.

Not mindless of the growing years
  Of care, and loss, and pain,
My eyes are wet with thankful tears
  For blessings which remain.

If dim the gold of life has grown,
  I will not count it dross,
Nor turn from treasures still my own
  To sigh for lack and loss.

The years no charm from Nature take :
  As sweet her voices call,
As beautiful her mornings break,
  As fair her evenings fall.

Love watches o'er my quiet ways,
  Kind voices speak my name ;
And lips that find it hard to praise
  Are slow at least to blame.

How softly ebb the tides of will !
  How fields, once lost or won,
Now lie behind me green and still
  Beneath a level sun !

How hushed the hiss of party hate,
  The clamor of the throng !
How old, harsh voices of debate
  Flow into rhythmic song !

Methinks the spirit's temper grows
  Too soft in this still air,
Somewhat the restful heart foregoes
  Of needed watch and prayer

The bark by tempest vainly tossed
  May founder in the calm,
And he who braved the polar frost
  Faint by the isles of balm.

Better than self-indulgent years
  The out-flung heart of youth ;
Than pleasant songs in idle ears
  The tumult of the truth.

Rest for the weary hands is good,
  And love for hearts that pine,
But let the manly habitude
  Of upright souls be mine.

Let winds that blow from heaven refresh
  Dear Lord, the languid air ;
And let the weakness of the flesh
  Thy strength of spirit share.

And if the eye must fail of light,
  The ear forget to hear,
Make clearer still the spirit's sight,
  More fine the inward ear !

Be near me in mine hours of need,
  To soothe, or cheer, or warn,
And down these slopes of sunset lead,
  As up the hills of morn !

JOHN G. WHITTIER.

November 18.

Thou makest darkness, and it is night. — Ps. civ. 20.

MUCH might be said on the wisdom of taking a constantly fresh view of life. It is one of the moral
uses of the night that it gives the world anew to us every
morning, and of sleep that it makes life a daily re-creation.
If we always saw the world we might grow weary of it.
If a third of life were not spent in unconsciousness, the
rest might become tedious. God is thus all the while
presenting the cup of life afresh to our lips. Thus, after
a night of peaceful sleep we behold the world as new
and fresh and wonderful as it was on the first morning of
creation, when God pronounced it "very good." And
sleep itself has a divine alchemy that gives us to ourselves
with our primitive energy of body and mind. The days
are not mere repetitions of themselves : to-morrow will
have another meaning ; I shall come to it with larger
vision than I have to-day.

T. T. MUNGER.

MOON-RISE.

Night, beloved night !
She is coming, she soon will come ;
Slowly is paling the dying light,
Twilight has lost its bloom ;
And a serious hush steals silently over the shadowy earth, —
While faint in the delicate air on high the first new star has
birth.

Against the twilight, their shoulders bare,
The mountains are turning as to sleep ;
And one by one from their chambers deep,
Where from the peering search they hid
Of the day's rude gaze and opened lid,
A myriad worlds come forth.

All sleep ! the tired world sleeps.
A quiet infinite
The soul of man and Nature steeps,
And smooths the brow of night.
.   .   .   .   .

O night of grand repose !
O silent, serious night !
Beside thy pathos infinite,
How vain are daylight's shows !
Thine is the grand dim realm of dream,
Thine the mysterious power whose spell
Leads Fancy on beyond the extreme of this world's
possible.
Thine the soft touch that charms the waking sense,
And woos the troubled soul to confidence.
To thee our secret woes we tell,
To thee our inmost being bare,
With thee our deepest feelings share,
Mother divine, ineffable,
Our hopes, our loves, that in the pride
Of busy daylight are repressed ;
Our doubts, remorses, hidden fears,
As thy great arms thou openest wide
To give us rest.

O night, a secret prophecy
Thou whisperest beneath thy breath
Of that vast, dim infinity,
Where broods the silent shadow, Death.
Listening I seem to hear thee say, —
" As I from out the body steal

For a few brief hours the soul away,
   My passing dream-world to reveal;
So my dark Brother, when your eyes
He in his endless sleep shall close,
Shall bear you — far beyond the woes
Of this short life — to the repose
   Of an eternal Paradise."

W. W. S.

November 19.

And ye have forgotten the exhortation which speaketh unto you as unto children, My son, despise not thou the chastening of the Lord, nor faint when thou art rebuked of Him. — HEB. xii. 5.

HERE on earth it is ever imperfect. We cannot here acknowledge and grasp our true treasure as we would. He has indeed begun in us, and will not give up the work, but if we continue in faith and are not impatient, He will bring us to the true, eternal good things and perfect gifts, where we shall never wander, stumble, be angry, or sin any more.

LUTHER.

Do not despise your situation ; in it you must act, suffer, and conquer. From every point on earth we are equally near to heaven and to the infinite.

HENRI FRÉDÉRIC AMIEL.

WEARY IN WELL-DOING.

I WOULD have gone ; God bade me stay.
   I would have worked ; God bade me rest ;
He broke my will from day to day,
   He read my yearnings unexpressed,
      And said them nay.
Now I would stay ; God bids me go.
   Now I would rest; God bids me work.
He breaks my heart tossed to and fro,
   My soul is wrung with doubts that lurk
      And vex it so.
I go, Lord, where Thou sendest me ;
   Day after day I plod and moil ;
But, Christ my God, when will it be
   That I may let alone my toil
      And rest with Thee?

CHRISTINA ROSSETTI.

November 20.

He shall receive me. — Ps. xlix. 15.

THE soul has caught a new idea of God's love when it has not only been fed, but rescued by Him. The sheep has a new conception of his shepherd's care when he has not merely been made " to lie down in green pastures," but also has heard the voice of Him who had left the ninety-and-nine in the wilderness and gone after that which had wandered astray until He found it. The weakness of our own nature and the strength of that on which we rely ; danger, and its correlative, duty ; watchfulness, and its great privilege, trust, — come in together, and are the new life of the soul, the active power in its restored peace.   PHILLIPS BROOKS.

EVENING BRINGS US HOME.

UPON the hills the wind is sharp and cold,
The sweet young grasses wither on the wold,
And we, O Lord, have wandered from Thy fold ;
    But evening brings us home.

Among the mists we stumble, and our feet
Are cut and bleeding, and the lambs repeat
Their pitiful complaints Oh, rest is sweet
    When evening brings us home.

The darkness gathers. Through the gloom no star
Rises to guide us. We have wandered far.
Without Thy lamp we know not where we are ;
    At evening bring us home.

The clouds are round us, and the snow-drifts thicken.
O Thou, dear Shepherd, leave us not to sicken
In the waste night ; our tardy footsteps quicken.
    At evening bring us home.

November 21.

What is man, that Thou art mindful of him? and the son of man, that Thou visitest him? — Ps. viii. 4.

AS I was surveying the moon walking in her brightness, and taking her progress among the constellations, a thought rose in me which I believe very often perplexes and disturbs men of serious and contemplative natures. David himself fell into it, in that reflection, " When I consider the heavens, the work of Thy fingers, the moon and the stars which Thou hast ordained ; what is man, that Thou art mindful of him, and the son of man, that Thou regardest him?" In the same manner, when I considered that infinite host of stars — or, to speak more philosophically, of suns — which were then shining upon me, with those innumerable sets of planets or worlds which were moving round their respective suns ; when I still enlarged the idea, and supposed another heaven of suns and worlds rising still above this which we discovered, and these still enlightened by a superior firmament of luminaries, which are planted at so great a distance that they may appear to the inhabitants of the former as the stars do to us, — in short, whilst I pursued this thought, I could not but reflect on that little insignificant figure which I myself bore amidst the immensity of God's works. . . .

In this consideration of God Almighty's omnipresence and omniscience, every uncomfortable thought vanishes. He cannot but regard everything that has being, especially such of His creatures who fear they are not regarded by Him. He is privy to all their thoughts, and to that anxiety of heart, in particular, which is apt to trouble them on this occasion ; for as it is impossible He should overlook any of His creatures, so we may be confident that He regards, with an eye of mercy, those who endeavor to recommend themselves to His notice, and in an unfeigned humility of heart think themselves unworthy that He should be mindful of them.

JOSEPH ADDISON.

SHOULD Fate command me to the farthest verge
Of the green earth, to distant barbarous climes,
Rivers unknown to song; where first the sun
Gilds Indian mountains, or his setting beam
Flames on th' Atlantic isles; 't is nought to me;
Since God is ever present, ever felt,
In the void waste, as in the city full;
And where He vital breathes, there must be joy.
When even at last the solemn hour shall come,
And wing my mystic flight to future worlds,
I cheerful will obey; there, with new powers,
Will rising wonders sing; I cannot go
Where Universal Love not smiles around,
Sustaining all yon orbs, and all their suns,
From seeming evil still educing good,
And better thence again, and better still;
In infinite progression. But I lose
Myself in Him, in Light ineffable;
Come, then, expressive silence, muse His praise.

THOMSON.

November 22.

Finally, my brethren, be strong in the Lord, and in the power of His might. — GAL. vi. 10.

WHEN the love of God has taken possession of the soul, and the whole man is consecrated to His service, life loses its fragmentary character, and one guiding stream seems to run through it. Then all varying and apparently disjointed circumstances and duties find a fixed and appointed place, and though, through the weakness of the flesh, the surface of things may seem to be ruffled, there is a strong undercurrent that cannot be diverted from its object, but is ever flowing on to its one point, widening and strengthening as it goes, and so mastering all that opposes its progress. Many a little rock or eddy that early in its course would turn it aside, are, as it becomes more powerful, swept away or passed over. And still more, perhaps, are the very hindrances that thwarted, turned into ministers to help its course. The stronger and more fixedly the soul is set upon one object, so much the more does it find power to overcome all difficulties, and despise all that may be only outward or accidental.

MARIA HARE.

BE STRONG.

BE strong to *hope*, O Heart!
  Though day is bright.
The stars can only shine
  In the dark night.
Be strong, O Heart of mine,
  Look towards the light!

Be strong to *bear*, O Heart!
  Nothing is vain;
Strive not, for life is care,
  And God sends pain;
Heaven is above, and there
  Rest will remain!

Be strong to *love*, O Heart!
  Love knows not wrong;
Didst thou love, creatures even,
  Life were not long;
Didst thou love God in Heaven,
  Thou wouldst be strong.

ADELAIDE A. PROCTER.

———◆———

November 23.

But now they desire a better country, that is, an heavenly; wherefore God is not ashamed to be called their God; for He hath prepared for them a city. — HEB. xi. 16.

THE grand difficulty is to feel the reality of both worlds, so as to give each its due place in our thoughts and feelings, to keep our mind's eye and our heart's eye ever fixed on the Land of Promise, without looking away from the road we are to travel toward it.

AUGUSTUS HARE.

THE Land beyond the Sea!
How close it sometimes seems,
When flushed with evening's peaceful gleams;
My wistful heart looks o'er the strait, and dreams!
It longs to fly to thee,
Calm Land beyond the Sea!

The Land beyond the Sea!
Sometimes across the strait,
Like drawbridge to a castle gate,
The slanting sunbeams lie, and seem to wait
For us to pass to thee,
Calm Land beyond the Sea!

O Land beyond the Sea!
When will our toil be done?
Slow-footed years! more swiftly run
Into the gold of that unsetting sun.
Homesick we are for thee,
Calm Land beyond the Sea!

O Land beyond the Sea!
Sweet is thine endless rest,
But sweeter far that Father's breast,
Upon thy shores eternally possest;
For Jesus reigns o'er thee,
Calm Land beyond the Sea!

November 24.

Unto the upright there ariseth light in the darkness; He is gracious, and full of compassion, and righteous. — Ps. cxii. 4.

MARK that weary disciple, who had a long and sorrowing experience. . . . The hour of redemption at length arrives; the submerging waters are passed, and in an instant the celestial glory stands all revealed. As the darkness settles heavily here, the light opens transportingly there; and, as the body is sending out the last moaning sounds of death, the spirit begins to hear, and even join in those heavenly melodies.

GEORGE SHEPARD.

IN THE EVENING.

ALL day the wind had howled along the leas,
  All day the wind had swept across the plain,
All day on rustling grass and waving trees
  Had fallen the "useful trouble of the rain;"
All day, beneath the low-hung dreary sky,
The dripping earth had cowered sullenly.

At last the wind had sobbed itself to rest,
  At last to weary calmness sank the storm;
A crimson line gleamed sudden in the west,
  Where golden flecks rose wavering into form;
A hushed revival heralded the night,
And with the evening time awoke the light.

The rosy color flushed the long gray waves;
  The rosy color tinged the mountains brown;
And, where the old church watched the village graves,
  Wooed to a passing blush the yew-trees' frown.
Bird, beast, and flower relenting Nature knew,
And one pale star rose shimmering in the blue.

So, to a life long crushed in heavy grief,
  So, to a path long darkened by despair,
The slow, sad hours bring touches of relief,
  Whispers of hope, and strength of trustful prayer.
"Tarry His leisure," God of love and might,
And with the evening time there will be light!

ALL THE YEAR ROUND.

———◆———

November 25.

O that my ways were directed to keep Thy statutes. — Ps. cxix. 5.

With my whole heart have I sought Thee: O let me not wander from Thy commandments. — Ps. cxix. 10.

SOME earnest enthusiasm of life is the effectual cure for all disquiet. There will always be minor cares and troubles for those who are at leisure to attend to them; nor can we be rescued from these except by interests and pursuits that take us out of their region. If a man were to spend his time in watching and correcting his faults of temper, he might give himself up to smallness forever; but if he could be filled with the zest of devoted and instructed work in the service of any large affection, sweetness and goodness would begin to dwell with him, and pettiness vanish away. For despondency and quiet, like all other evils, are not positive things with which you can contend directly; you cannot seize them and destroy them, — they are simply the absence of full and blessed life, and you can dispel them only by happier, richer occupation, as you dispel darkness by letting in the light. Enthusiasm, as a constant working power in life, is perhaps not at our command; but to know God, to love Him altogether, to live in the light of His countenance, to be satisfied with a little in some directions because in others we have so much, to receive all things hopefully because they are from Him, to take the peace of resting in His goodness, to desire all the day long, "Oh that my heart were as Thy heart, and that wholly!" — these are open to us.

J. H. THOM.

O HUMAN soul! so long as thou canst so
Set up a mark of everlasting light,
Above the howling senses' ebb and flow,
To cheer thee, and to right thee if thou roam,
Not with lost toil thou laborest through the night!
Thou mak'st the heaven thou hop'st indeed thy home!

MATTHEW ARNOLD.

PEACE.

WINDS and wild waves in headlong huge commotion
    Scud, dark with tempest, o'er the Atlantic's breast;
While underneath, few fathoms deep in Ocean,
    Lie peace and rest.

Storms in mid-air, the rack before them sweeping,
    Hurry and hiss. like furies hate-possessed;
While over all white cloudlets pure are sleeping
    In peace, in rest.

Heart, O wild heart! why in the storm-world ranging
    Flitt'st thou thus midway, passion's slave and jest,
When all so near above, below. unchanging
    Are Heaven and rest?

A. G. B · London Spectator

November 26.

Thy sun shall no more go down ; neither shall thy moon withdraw itself, for the Lord shall be thine everlasting light, and the days of thy mourning shall be ended. — ISA. lx. 20.

UPON him whose mind is engrossed with care, or ruffled by passion, the most beautiful objects make no impression. To perceive and enjoy them the mind must be calm. The beauties and sublimities of Nature are like the stars, which the storm shuts out ; but when the heavens are serene, they come out, one after another, to the eye that is watching for them, till the firmament glows with their light.

MARK HOPKINS.

THE SUN UPON THE WIERDLAW HILL.

THE sun upon the Wierdlaw-hill,
 In Ettrick's vale, is sinking sweet,
The westland wind is hush and still,
 The lake lies sleeping at my feet.
Yet not the landscape to mine eye
 Bears those bright hues that once it bore ;
Though evening, with her richest dye,
 Flames o'er the hills of Ettrick's shore.

With listless look along the plain
 I see Tweed's silver current glide,
And coldly mark the holy fane
 Of Melrose rise in ruined pride.
The quiet lake, the balmy air,
 The hill, the stream, the tower, the tree, —
Are they still such as once they were,
 Or is the dreary change in me ?

Alas, the warp'd and broken board,
 How can it bear the painter's dye !
The harp, of strained and tuneless chord,
 How to the minstrel's skill reply !
To aching eyes each landscape lowers,
 To feverish pulse each gale blows chill,
And Araby's or Eden's bowers
 Were barren as this moorland hill.

SIR WALTER SCOTT.

November 27.

Where is the way where light dwelleth? — JOB xxxviii. 19..
Jesus said, I am the Light of the World; he that follow-
eth Me shall not walk in darkness, but shall have the
light of life. — JOHN viii. 12.

TURN thus into life — life real and true, the life of the
spirit — all that is within you and which you can
appropriate. Do the good you know. Follow the truth
you see. Not words, not admiration, not inaction, but
appropriation, transformation into life, — this is the first
great lesson of the key to life and fruit.

And the process for us must begin here, where God has
placed us. We are seeds cast into the soil, but by a
Divine Sower. Here, under all the conditions of life, just
as they are now, while it is the spring and seed time, and
we have the light of life, and the Spirit of God is poured
out like the water from the skies.

How the possibilities of our lives open to us under this
conception ; how the very drudgery of existence takes to
itself a nobleness and becomes fraught with an eternal
significance ! Dust and ashes in itself, as life often seems,
and much of it really is, it can all be transmuted into the
imperishable and eternal, — go to fruit that shall be gathered into the heavenly garners. Duty performed is a gain
in character whose force can never be wholly spent. A
sacrifice for righteousness means a larger appropriation
of righteousness. Love freely given, even to the thank-
less or to an enemy, becomes a larger power of loving.
Patience in sickness, endurance in helpfulness, fortitude
in trial, strengthen the stalk that bears the fruit ; and the
very fineness of the grain is from the rigor of the climate
in which it ripens. For this is the divine power of life,
that it can turn its environment into growth and fruitage,
and make even of the life we hate for its meagreness and
perishableness, for its uncongeniality and chill, a good that
abides and is kept unto life eternal.

Our life begins here a single seed, — a tiny seed, it may
be. But if it takes to itself what in the divine ordering is
provided for it, if it transforms what is given to it of God

into its own life, it does not abide alone. It is transplanted to the other world, not as it here began. Its powers, its capacities, its acquisitions and joys are already reduplicated beyond computation, and they go on to multiplied and incalculable harvest. There is, indeed, no conceivable limit to the riches of a soul that has once resolved, with a resolution that cannot be shaken, to be true to itself — that has really begun to live as God would have it, — as Christ came to teach us how to live.

EGBERT C. SMYTH.

MY WINDOW IVY.

OVER my window the Ivy climbs,
　　Its roots are in homely jars,
But all day long it looks at the sun,
　　And at night looks out at the stars.

The dust of the room may dim its green,
　　But I call to the breezy air :
"Come in, come in, good friend of mine!
　　And make my garden fair."

So the Ivy thrives from morn to morn,
　　Its leaves all turned to the light ;
And it gladdens my soul with its tender green,
　　And teaches me day and night.

What though my lot is in lonely place,
　　And my spirit behind the bars ?
All the long day I may look at the sun,
　　And at night look out at the stars.

What though the dust of earth would dim?
　　There's a glorious outer air
That will sweep through my soul if I let it in,
　　And make it fresh and fair.

Dear God! let me grow from day to day,
　　Clinging and sunny and bright!
Though planted in shade, Thy window is near,
　　And my leaves may turn to the light.

MARY MAPES DODGE.

25

November 28.

Whereunto ye do well that ye take heed, as unto a light that shineth in a dark place, until the day dawn, and the day-star arise in your hearts. — 2 PET. i. 19.

SAINT BERNARD has said : "Man, if thou desirest a noble and holy life, and unceasingly prayest to God for it, if thou continue constant in this thy desire, it will be granted unto thee without fail, even if only in the day or hour of thy death ; and if God should not give it thee then, thou wilt find it in Him in eternity ; of this be assured."

Therefore do not relinquish your desire, though it be not fulfilled immediately, or though ye may swerve from your aspirations, or even forget them for a time. But when ye hear the word of God, surrender yourselves to it, as if for eternity, with a full purpose of will to retain it in your mind, and to order your life according to it ; and let it sink down right deep into your heart as into an eternity. If afterward it should come to pass that you let it slip, yet the love and aspiration which once really existed live forever before God, and in Him ye shall find the fruit thereof ; that is, to all eternity it shall be better for you than if you had never felt them. What we can *do* is a small thing ; but we can will and aspire to great things.

JOHN TAULER.

ALL BEFORE US LIES THE WAY.

ALL before us lies the way ;
   Give the past unto the wind ;
All before us is the day,
   Night and darkness are behind.

Eden, with its angels bold,
   Love and flowers and coolest sea,
Is less an ancient story told
   Than a glowing prophecy.

When the soul to sin hath died,
   True and beautiful and sound,
Then all earth is sanctified ;
   Up springs Paradise around.

R. W. EMERSON.

November 29.

The grass withereth, the flower fadeth; because the Spirit of the Lord bloweth upon it.— ISA. xl. 7.

THUS gracefully and gently wanes the dying year. The beauty of the woods lingers ere it finally departs, and each much-loved autumnal flower seems frequently to bid us farewell, in gradually sinking to the earth. In all this, every heart not steeled to natural emotion, must feel a designed goodness, and gratefully acknowledge the unremitting care of a kind and bountiful Father. It were easy to point out, in this gentle decay of the year, many analogies to what we daily witness in human life; as, for example, that which obtains between the decay, and the quiet ebbing of life in the aged and almost ripened Christian, whose gray hairs fall peacefully like the undisturbed leaves, and whose time-worn frame is imperceptibly, and by slow degrees, fitted for the undreaded winter of the grave.

H. DUNCAN.

AUTUMN FLOWERS.

THOSE few pale autumn flowers,
    How beautiful they are!
Than all that went before,
Than all the summer's store,
    How lovelier far!

And why? They are the last —
    The last! — the last! — the last! —
Oh, by that little word,
How many thoughts are stirred!
    That whisper of the past!

Pale flowers! — pale, perishing flowers!
    Ye're types of precious things, —
Types of those bitter moments
That flit, like life's enjoyments,
    On rapid, rapid wings;

Last hours with parting dear ones,
    (That time the fastest spends),
Last tears, in silence shed,
Last words, half uttered,
    Last looks of dying friends!

Who but would fain compress
    A life into a day, —
The last day spent with one
Who, ere the morrow's sun,
    Must leave us, and for aye ?

O precious, precious moments !
    Pale flowers, ye 're types of those —
The saddest ! sweetest ! dearest !
Because, like those, the nearest
    To an eternal close.

Pale flowers ! pale, perishing flowers !
    I woo your gentle breath, —
I leave the summer rose
For younger, blither brows ;
    Tell me of change and death.

MRS. SOUTHEY.

—◆—

November 30.

*If a man die, shall he live again ?   All the days of my
appointed time will I wait, till my change come.* —
JOB xiv. 14.

TO live, to outlive, to live again, should be the whole of
    man.

THE time comes when one feels the need of the slumber of death, as, at the end of a toilsome day, one feels
the need of another sleep.

MEDITATIONS OF A PARISH PRIEST.

THE CLOSING SCENE.

WITHIN his sober realm of leafless trees,
    The russet year inhaled the dreamy air ;
Like some tanned reaper in his hour of ease,
    When all the fields are lying brown and bare.

The gray barns, looking from their hazy hills
    O'er the dim waters widening in the vales,
Sent down the air a greeting to the mills,
    On the dull thunder of alternate flails.

All sights were mellowed, and all sounds subdued,
  The hills seemed further, and the streams sang low,
As in a dream the distant woodman hewed
  His winter log with many a muffled blow.

The embattled forests, erewhile armed in gold,
  Their banners bright with every martial hue,
Now stood, like some sad, beaten host of old,
  Withdrawn afar in Time's remotest blue.

On slumberous wings the vulture tried his flight,
  The dove scarce heard his sighing mate's complaint,
And, like a star slow drowning in the light,
  The village church-vane seemed to pale and faint.

The sentinel cock upon the hillside crew, —
  Crew thrice, and all was stiller than before ; —
Silent till some replying wanderer blew
  His alien horn, and then was heard no more.

Where erst the jay, within the elm's tall crest,
  Made garrulous trouble round her unfledged young ;
And where the oriole hung her swaying nest
  By every light wind like a censer swung ;

Where sang the noisy masons of the eaves,
  The busy swallows circling ever near,
Foreboding, as the rustic mind believes,
  An early harvest and a plenteous year ;

Where every bird which charmed the vernal feast
  Shook the sweet slumber from its wings at morn,
To warn the reapers of the rosy east, —
  All now was songless, empty, and forlorn.

Alone, from out the stubble piped the quail,
  And croaked the crow through all the dreamy gloom ;
Alone, the pheasant, drumming in the vale,
  Made echo to the distant cottage loom.

There was no bud, no bloom upon the bowers ;
  The spiders wove their thin shrouds night by night;
The thistle-down, the only ghost of flowers,
  Sailed slowly by, passed noiseless out of sight.

Amid all this, in this most cheerless air,
  And where the woodbine sheds upon the porch
Its crimson leaves, as if the year stood there,
  Firing the floor with his inverted torch, —

Amid all this, the centre of the scene,
  The white-haired matron, with monotonous tread,
Plied her swift wheel, and with her joyless mien
  Sat like a Fate, and watched the flying thread.

She had known Sorrow. He had walked with her,
  Oft supped, and broke with her the ashen crust;
And in the dead leaves still she heard the stir
  Of his black mantle trailing in the dust.

While yet her cheek was bright with summer bloom,
  Her country summoned, and she gave her all ;
And twice War bowed to her his sable plume, —
  Re-gave the swords to rust upon her wall.

Re-gave the swords — but not the hand that drew,
  And struck for liberty the dying blow ;
Nor him who, to his sire and country true,
  Fell 'mid the ranks of the invading foe.

Long, but not loud, the droning wheel went on,
  Like the low murmur of a hive at noon :
Long, but not loud, the memory of the gone
  Breathed through her lips a sad and tremulous tune.

At last the thread was snapped — her head was bowed ;
  Life dropped the distaff through his hands serene ;
And loving neighbors smoothed her careful shroud,
  While Death and Winter closed the autumn scene.

Thomas Buchanan Read.

———◆———

December 1.

He giveth snow like wool. — Ps. cxlvii. 16.

IT is not only that the snow makes fair what was good
  before, but it is a messenger of love from heaven,
bearing glad tidings of great joy. Hope for the future
comes down in every tiny snowflake. The spring sun
will mount higher and higher in the heavens ; the sweet
snow will sink down into the arms of the violets ; and, at
the word of the Lord, the earth shall come up once more,
as a bride adorned for her husband.

Gail Hamilton.

SNOW.

The heavens were gray and dull and low,
The earth was old and stained and sere,
When God outspread his spotless snow, –
A carpet for the coming year.

Above it, sunshine came again,
Beneath it, many a weary thing
From summer heat and autumn rain
Found rest, and waited for the spring.

Lord, I am clouded like the air,
And withered like the flower and sod;
Oh! spread o'er all my sin and care,
Like snow, the perfect peace of God.

Within its folds I still shall feel
The sun above, the growth below;
And the new spring-time shall reveal
What things were nourished by the snow.

Then peace shall meet to joy and praise
And o'er the fruitful gardens blow,
While heaven and earth one chorus raise
To Him who giveth sun and snow.

———◆———

December 2.

They grow, yea, they bring forth fruit. — JER. xii. 2.

LIFE, to be worthy of a rational being, must be always
in progression; we must always purpose to do more
or better than in past times. The mind is enlarged and
elevated by mere purposes, though they end as they begin,
by airy contemplation. We compare and judge, though
we do not practise.

DR. SAMUEL JOHNSON.

FAINT not; the miles to heaven are few and short.

SAMUEL RUTHERFORD.

IN all the relations of life, as wife to husband, mother
to child, one feels always advancing, striving; one has
always to be growing and progressing with the time; as a
child, alone, one is wholly satisfied and complete; then
alone is one a perfect, satisfied being.

AUERBACH: *On the Heights.*

THE LADDER OF SAINT AUGUSTINE.

WE have not wings, we cannot soar:
But we have feet to scale and climb
By slow degrees, by more and more,
The cloudy summits of our time.

All common things, each day's events,
That with the hour begin and end,
Our pleasures and our discontents,
Are rounds by which we may ascend.

The mighty pyramids of stone
That wedge-like cleave the desert airs,
When nearer seen, and better known,
Are but gigantic flights of stairs.

The distant mountains, that uprear
Their solid bastions to the skies,
Are crossed by pathways, that appear
As we to higher levels rise.

The heights by great men reached and kept
Were not attained by sudden flight,
But they, while their companions slept,
Were toiling upward in the night.

Standing on what too long we bore
With shoulders bent and downcast eyes,
We may discern — unseen before —
A path to higher destinies.

Nor deem the irrevocable past
As wholly wasted, wholly vain,
If, rising on its wrecks at last,
To something nobler we attain.

H. W. LONGFELLOW.

December 3.

*And I will bring the blind by a way that they knew not;
I will lead them in paths that they have not known;
I will make darkness light before them, and crooked
things straight. These things will I do unto them, and
not forsake them.* — Isa. xlii. 16.

WE are led on like the little children, by a way that
we know not.

It is a vain thought to flee from the work that God
appoints us, for the sake of finding a greater blessing to
our own souls, as if we could choose for ourselves where
we shall find the fulness of the Divine Presence, instead
of seeking it where alone it is to be found, in loving
obedience.   GEORGE ELIOT.

GOD'S WAYS.

How few that from their youthful day,
    Look on to what their life may be,
Painting the vision of the way
    In colors soft and bright and free !
How few who to such paths have brought
The hopes and dreams of early thought !
For God, through ways they have not known,
        Will lead His own.

The eager hearts, the souls of fire,
    Who pant and toil for God and man,
And view with eyes of keen desire
    The upland way of toil and pain !
Almost with scorn they think of rest,
Of holy calm of tranquil breast ;
But God, through ways they have not known,
        Will lead His own.

The gentle heart, that thinks, with pain,
    It scarce can lowliest tasks fulfil,
And if it dared its life to scan,
    Would ask but pathway low and still ;
Often such lowly heart is brought
To act with power beyond its thought ;
For God, through ways they have not known,
        Will lead His own.

December 4.

My hope is in Thee. — Ps. xxxix. 7.

WHERE there is a soul there is a hope.

THERE is an influence beneath which man must bend, as trees beneath the invisible wind. Sacred ideals arise and overawe our lower nature. We cannot, we will not, endure the thought that the intimations of our immortality mean nothing, because they mean not the egotism of the vulgar, and that the promise of our heart is false. While we muse, the fire burns. Emotions ascend, and life struggles to ascend with them. From the fair Kosmos whence we have derived a life — how strange, undreamable ! that is real — equally have we derived ideals and cravings that seek their satisfaction in things invisible, — in moral beauty, self-forgetting love, the harmony of the inward and outer worlds ; and even as a seed in its sod may feel the warm, quickening touch of the sun it has never seen, so amid the darkness of the earth the heart may feel stirring within the mystical attraction whose nature it cannot dream, whose sweetness seems to promise a far-off flowering into joy. MONCURE D. CONWAY.

HYMN.

IF that bright world which spreads above
  This dark and lowly vale of tears
Is the fond home where holy love
  Shall stronger grow, with growing years,
If God's own hand shall wipe away
  The tear from every weeping eye,
Why should we tremble to survey
  The portals of Eternity ?

The earth which wraps our mouldering clay
  Can ne'er th' immortal soul confine !
With our last breath it breaks away
  And leaves the sorrowing world behind.
It soars to those untrodden spheres
  Where God and saints and angels are,
And by His holy throne appears
  A deep-devoted worshipper.

Oh, it were good, methinks, to soar,
   From this drear world and all its ties,
To where earth's grief is felt no more,
   And hope, in full fruition dies.
Then, when the welcome hour shall come,
   From these dark graves our dust shall spring,
A heavenly light shall guide us home,
   A heavenly hope sustain our wing.

WILLIAM G. BATES

December 5.

*What shall I say? He hath spoken unto me, and Himself
hath done it.* — ISA. xxxviii. 15.

TEARS are the softening showers which cause the seed
of heaven to spring up in the human heart.

SIR WALTER SCOTT.

THERE is a great want about all Christians who have
not suffered. Some flowers must be broken or bruised
before they emit any fragrance. All the wounds of Christ
sent out sweetness; the sorrows of Christians do the
same. To me there is something sacred and sweet in
suffering; it is so much akin to " the man of sorrows."

PURVIS.

"HIMSELF HATH DONE IT."

" HIMSELF hath done it " all! Oh, how those words
   Should hush to silence every murmuring thought.
" Himself hath done it ! " — He who loves me best, —
   He who my soul with His own blood hath bought.

" Himself hath done it ! " Can it then be aught
   Than full of wisdom, full of tenderest love ?
Not *one* unneeded sorrow will He send,
   To teach this wandering heart no more to rove.

" Himself hath done it." Yes, although severe
   May seem the stroke, and bitter be the cup,
'T is His own hand that holds it ; and I know
   He 'll give me grace to drink it meekly up.

" Himself hath done it."   Oh, no arm but His
    Could e'er sustain beneath earth's dreary lot.
But while I know He doeth all things well,
    My heart His loving-kindness questions not.

" Himself hath done it."   He who 's searched me through
    Sees how I cling to earth's ensnaring ties,
And so He breaks each reed on which my soul
    Too much for happiness and joy relies.

" Himself hath done it."   He would have me see
    What broken cisterns human friends *must* prove ;
That I may turn and quench my burning thirst
    At His own fount of *ever-living* love.

" Himself hath done it."   Then I fain would say, —
    Thy will in *all* things ever more be done ;
E'en though that will remove whom best I love,
    While Jesus lives I cannot be alone.

" Himself hath done it," — precious, precious words !
    Himself, — my Father, Saviour, Brother, Friend,
Whose faithfulness no variation knows ;
    Who, having loved me, loves me *to the end !*

And when in His eternal presence blest,
    I at His feet my crown immortal cast,
I 'll gladly own, with all His ransomed saints,
    " Himself hath done it " all from first to last.

——◆——

December 6.

*My soul thirsteth for God, for the living God ; when shall
I come and appear before God ? —* Ps. xlii. 1, 2.

AN old mystic says somewhere : " God is an unutterable
    sigh in the innermost depths of the soul."   With
still greater justice, we may well reverse the proposition
and say, The soul is a never-ending sigh after God ; be-

cause she is from Him, she is also for Him, and tends to Him. In her deepest recesses there lives or slumbers, however hidden, an inextinguishable longing after God. She knows herself, by an inward sentiment, not merely to be dependent on Him, but at the same time drawn towards Him, and destined for a union with Him. Being essentially "reasonable," she reads God everywhere, both in and without herself, so that she is unable to free herself from His presence, however far removed from Him, as the voice of conscience shows. But the more she seeks and apprehends, the greater is her longing after Him. And the more we consider the nature of this longing, the more we discover that what it aims at is not a mere intellectual apprehension of God, but a vital experience, enjoyment, and communion. The religious need is essentially of a practical nature ; it is an impulse to draw nigh to God, and to place one's self in personal fellowship with Him, proceeding from the presentiment that our spirit can find its abiding rest and satisfaction in nothing but this fellowship, and in the enjoyment of the love and peace of God.

THEODORE CHRISTLIEB.

A SONNET TO HEAVENLY BEAUTY.

IF this our little life is but a day
   In the Eternal ; if the years in vain
   Toil after hours that never come again, —
If everything that hath been must decay, —
Why dreamest thou of joys that pass away,
   My soul, that my sad body doth restrain ?
   Why of the moment's pleasure art thou fain ?
Nay, thou hast wings, — nay, seek another stay.

There is the joy whereto each soul aspires,
And there the rest that all the world desires,
   And there is love and peace and gracious mirth ;
And there in the most highest heavens shalt thou
Behold the Very Beauty, whereof now
   Thou worshippest the shadow upon earth.

From the French of
DU BELLAY (1550), tr. by A. LANG.

December 7.

It is God that girdeth me with strength, and maketh my way perfect. — Ps. xviii. 32.

THE confidence of a power always at work within us, manifesting itself in our powerlessness, a love filling up our lovelessness, a wisdom surmounting our folly, the knowledge of our own right to glory in this love, power, and wisdom, the certainty that we can do all righteous acts by submitting to this Righteous Being, and that we do them best when we walk in a line chosen for us, not of our choosing, — this is the strength, surely, and nothing else, which carries us through earth and lifts us into heaven.

QUIET FROM GOD!

QUIET from God! How beautiful to keep
   This treasure the All-Merciful hath given!
To feel, when we awake and when we sleep,
   This incense round us, like a breath from heaven ;

To sojourn in the world, and yet apart ;
   To dwell with God, and still with man to feel ;
To bear about forever in the heart
   The gladness which His Spirit doth reveal.

Who shall make trouble then? Not evil minds,
   Which like a shadow o'er Creation lower.
The soul which peace hath thus attunèd finds
   How strong within doth reign the Calmer's power.

What shall make trouble? Not slow-wasting pain,
   Nor even the threatening, certain stroke of death ;
These do but wear away, then break, the chain
   Which bound the spirit down to things beneath.

SARAH J. WILLIAMS.

December 8.

Yet the Lord will command His loving-kindness in the day-time, and in the night His song shall be with me, and my prayer unto the God of my life.— Ps. xlii. 8.

IN all the lives of the sainted followers of Christ, we find prayer has been the great weapon whereby they have fought so good a fight, and through which they have been made more than conquerors. And yet longing as I do to follow after them, to make their pattern mine, I find it very difficult to do so in this point. Something is ever at hand to keep me away from this instrument of grace, whereby I might draw down the freedom from self and sin that I so often need. O Lord, help me in this my weakness, that I may not quench Thy Spirit, nor lose the privilege Thou hast granted of drawing near the throne of grace. So shall the oil of my lamp be ever freshly trimmed by Thee, and each day's duty and its toil lightened and guided and hallowed by the influence of Thy council and Thy strength.

MARIA HARE.

ALL'S WELL.

THE day is ended. Ere I sink to sleep
  My weary spirit seeks repose in Thine;
Father! forgive my trespasses, and keep
  This little life of mine.

With loving-kindness curtain Thou my bed,
  And cool in rest my burning pilgrim feet;
Thy pardon be the pillow for my head.
  So shall my sleep be sweet.

At peace with all the world, dear Lord, and Thee,
  No fears my soul's unwavering faith can shake:
All's well! whichever side the grave for me
  The morning light may break.

HARRIET McEWEN KIMBALL.

December 9.

When I remember Thee upon my bed, and meditate on Thee in the night-watches. — Ps. lxiii. 6.

FELLOWSHIP with God must spring from the simple faith of the little child ; and this languishes if, instead of seeking His face, we are so occupied about His business that we can only bring to Him the wearied energies and the drooping spirit. No loving husband would be satisfied with such a return of affection, and though others may admire the zeal and activity of the busy wife, he would miss the companion of his life.

PRAYER is a closing of the eyes on things seen, and opening them on things unseen. It is penitence vocal, faith making its profession, and love kindling into a flame. It is a heart brought to the altar, a flower opening to the benignant eye of Heaven. It is a putting off the shoes at Horeb. It is a walk to Emmaus. It is to be present in the upper chamber ; to sit quietly by the Saviour's side, lean the head on His bosom, and feel the beating of Immanuel's heart.

A. C. THOMPSON.

AT EVENING.

ANOTHER day is numbered with the past ;
  Another night is given us for rest ;
Father, my spirit at Thy feet I cast,
  Oh, gather it unto Thy loving breast.

Nightly Thou sendest rest to all the earth,
  Sendest a time for silence and returning ;
O Father ! teach me all the holy worth
  Of the still hours when Thy clear stars are burning.

December 10.

He that is faithful in that which is least, is faithful also in much. — LUKE xvi. 10.

THE growing good of the world is partly dependent on unhistoric acts; and that things are not so ill with you and me as they might have been, is half owing to the number who lived faithfully a hidden life, and rest in unvisited tombs.

GEORGE ELIOT.

IF we could but live in constant remembrance of the great truth, that to God's infinity no actions are great or small; if we could only give up striving to do something which the *world* shall call great, and simply try to live a· life with divinity in the smallest action of it, thereby making our existence one grand anthem of praise to our Creator, — in other words, if our lives could by reason of their simplicity grow more like Christ's, should we not be much happier?

L. II.

LIFE–MOSAIC.

MASTER, to do great work for Thee, my hand
  Is far too weak ! Thou givest what may suit,
  Some little chips to cut with care minute,
Or tint, or grave, or polish. Others stand
Before their quarried marble, fair and grand,
  And make a life-work of the grand design
  Which Thou hast traced ; or, many-skilled, combine
To build vast temples, gloriously planned,
Yet take the tiny stones which I have wrought
  Just one by one, as they were given by Thee,
Not knowing what came next in Thy wise thought.
Let each stone by Thy master-hand of grace
  Form the mosaic as Thou wilt for me,
And in Thy temple-pavement give it place.

FRANCES RIDLEY HAVERGAL.

December 11.

I will lift up mine eyes unto the hills, from whence cometh my help. — Ps. cxxi. 1.

HOW welcome would it often be to many a child of anxiety and toil, to be suddenly transferred from the heat and din of the city, the restlessness and worry of the mart, to the midnight garden or the mountain-top! And like refreshment does a high faith, with its infinite prospects ever open to the heart, afford to the worn and weary. No laborious travels are needed for the devout mind, for it carries within it Alpine heights and starlit skies, which it may reach with a moment's thought, and feel at once the loneliness of nature and the magnificence of God.

JAMES MARTINEAU.

LIGHT ON THE WHITE HILLS.

A LEADEN sky is bending dark
    Above me as I stand ;
The north wind, cold, and thick with storms,
    Is chilling half the land ;
But, far away, a hundred hills
    Stand bathed in mellow light,
All covered deep with winter's snow,
    All radiant and white.

And so to me, who stand alone
    'Neath threatening heavens furled,
Those far-off mountains seem to be
    Hills of a holier world ;
And old Franconia's ragged sides,
    Letting the glory in,
Like the transparent gates of pearl,
    Shutting out grief and sin.

And other skies will gather dark,
    And other winds blow cold,
And storms of sorrow, fierce and strong,
    Come rushing o'er the wold ;
But, brighter, seen through mists and tears,
    Will gleam the distant light,
God's glory, on those shining hills, —
    His promise still in sight.

JULIA A. EASTMAN.

December 12.

For now is your salvation nearer than when ye believed.

AS a child upon a perilous way clings to its mother, so
do we cling closely to Him who has taken from
death its power through His death, and has brought life
and immortality to light through His resurrection.   Yes,
" we are always confident," whether in life or in death.
With calm longing our glance rests upon the blessed
Home which lies before us, and life appears to us peaceful, and death sweet.   The thorns of our pilgrim-path no
longer wound us, and the entrance to the Father's house
is no more narrow and fearful.   The waste blooms into
a garden of the Lord, and the dark valley becomes a light,
lovely path.   With refreshing peace within, praising God
with heart and mouth, we walk joyfully toward the beloved
Home.
MÜLLER.

DRAWING NEARER.

NEARER ! yes ! we feel it not
    'Mid the rushing of the strife.
As we mourned our changeful lot,
    Toiled beneath our shadowed life,
        By each step our worn feet trod,
        We were drawing near to God.

When the day was all withdrawn,
    When we walked in darkest night,
When we panted for the dawn
    Of the ever-blessed Light, —
        In those hours of darkness dim,
        We were drawing near to Him.

When, beneath the sudden stroke,
    All our joys of life went down,
When our best-beloved broke
    Earthly bounds, to take their crown, —
        By the upward path they trod,
        Nearer drew we to our God.

Through the long and vanished years,
    Doubting, struggling, and depressed,
Shrouded with their mists of tears,
    We were passing to our rest ;
        Tempest-tossed and current-driven,
        Ever drawing nearer heaven.

December 13.

I shall go to him, but he shall not return to me. — 2 SAM.
xii. 13.

NEVER a sigh falls to the ground.
TURKISH PROVERB.

IN our sorrow and sadness we look up to Thee ; and
when mortal friends fail us, and the urn that held our
treasured joys is broken into fragments, and the wine of
life is scattered at our feet, O Lord, we rejoice to know
that Thou understandest our lot, and wilt make every sorrow of our life turn out for our endless welfare and our
continual growth, so that Thou wilt take us home to Thyself, with no stain of weeping on our face.

SONG.

OH, the merry, merry lark was up and singing,
And the hare was out and feeding on the lea ;
And the merry, merry bells below were ringing
As my child's laugh rang through me !

Now, the hare is snared and dead beneath the snow-yard,
And the lark beside the dreary winter sea ;
And my baby in its cradle in the church-yard
Waiteth there until the bells bring me.
CHARLES KINGSLEY.

December 14.

He will teach us of His ways, and we will walk in His paths. — ISA. ii. 3.

WE cannot rightly carry out any true or noble object in life in a spirit of despondency. . . . A depressed life — a life which has ceased to believe in its own sacredness, its own capabilities, its own mission, — a life which contentedly sinks into querulous egotism or vegetating aimlessness — has become, so far as the world is concerned, a maimed and useless life.

All our lives are in some sense a " might have been ; " the very best of us must feel, I suppose, in sad and thoughtful moments, that he might have been transcendently nobler, and greater, and loftier than he is ; but while life lasts every " might have been " should lead, not to vain regrets, but to manly resolutions ; it should be but the dark background to a " may be " and " will be yet."

CANON FARRAR.

THE PATH THROUGH THE SNOW.

BARE and sunshiny, bright and bleak,
Rounded cold as a dead maid's cheek,
Folded white as a sinner's shroud,
Or wandering angel's robe of cloud, —
    Well I know, well I know
Over the fields the path through the snow.

Narrow and rough it lies between
Wastes where the wind sweeps, biting keen ;
Every step of the slippery road
Marks where some weary foot has trod ;
    Who 'll go, who 'll go
After the rest on the path through the snow ?

They who tread it must walk alone,
Silent and steadfast — one by one :
Dearest to dearest can only say,
" My heart ! I 'll follow thee all the way,
    As we go, as we go
Each after each, on this path through the snow."

It may be under that western haze
Lurks the omen of brighter days;
That each sentinel tree is quivering
Deep at its core with the sap of spring,
    And while we go, while we go,
Green grass-blades pierce through the glittering snow.

It may be the unknown path will tend
Never to any earthly end,
Die with the dying day obscure,
And never lead to a human door;
    That none know who did go
Patiently once on this path through the snow.

No matter! no matter! the path shines plain;
These pure snow-crystals will deaden pain:
Above, like stars in the deep blue dark,
Eyes that love us look down and mark.
    Let us go, let us go
Whither heaven leads in the path through the snow.

DINAH MULOCH CRAIK

December 15.

*But if we hope for that we see not, then do we with
patience wait for it.* — ROM. viii. 25.

NEVER think that God's delays are God's denials.
Hold on; hold fast; hold out. Patience is genius.

BUFFON.

THE ills which shorten life lengthen it for the patient.
He who has suffered much has lived long.

PATIENCE is the key of content.   MAHOMET.

THE greatest prayer is patience.   BUDDHA.

BUT Patience was willing to wait!

JOHN BUNYAN.

AN ANGEL OF PATIENCE.

BESIDE the toilsome way,
Lowly and sad, by fruits and flowers unblest,
Which my worn feet tread sadly, day by day,
    Longing in vain for rest,

An angel softly walks,
With pale, sweet face, and eyes cast meekly down,
The while, from withered leaves and flowerless stalks,
    She weaves my fitting crown.

A sweet and patient grace,
A look of firm endurance true and tried,
Of suffering meekly borne, rests on her face,
    So pure, so glorified.

And when my fainting heart
Desponds and murmurs at its adverse fate,
Then quietly the angel's bright lips part,
    Murmuring softly, " Wait ! "

" Patience," she sweetly saith;
"'Thy Father's mercies never come too late;
Gird thee with patient strength and trusting faith
    And firm endurance.   Wait ! "

Angel ! behold, I wait,
Wearing the thorny crown through all life's hours, —
Wait till thy hand shall ope th' eternal gate,
    And change the thorns to flowers.

—⧫—

December 16.

For ye have need of patience, that, after ye have done the will of God, ye might receive the promise. — HEB. x. 36.

INFINITE power, wisdom infinite, infinite love, infinite life, — the God of infinities we would gladly offer ourselves up to, all of us, willing sacrifices.   But many of us shrink from some small offering when we are led up to the altar, if it is in an obscure corner of the world, or lowly in look. For at first our wish is to perform grand service before many witnesses; but this is not what God wants often, and so it is seldom a person is called to it; but what He does wish is the sincerity of the soul. And when a soul does become all His own, it is lit up from within with such Divine light as glorifies everything else. Duty is an angel, reverently beloved, that walks beside the man with solemn steps; and common life is a path shining before him more and more; and the future is a mist which he will pass through, and so be nigher God; and if to-day the world feels round him like a temple to worship in, then to-morrow there will be a further world for him to pass on into, and it will be the holy of holies

WILLIAM MOUNTFORD.

O DREARY LIFE!

"O DREARY life!" we cry, — "O dreary life!"
And still the generations of the birds
Sing through our sighing, and the flocks and herds
Serenely live while we are keeping strife
With Heaven's true purpose in us, as a knife
Against which we may struggle. Ocean girds
Unslackened the dry land : savannah swards
Unweary sweep; hills watch, unworn; and rife,
Meek leaves drop yearly from the forest-trees,
To show above the unwasted stars that pass
In their old glory. O Thou God of old!
Grant me some smaller grace than comes to these!
But so much patience as a blade of grass
Grows by, contented, through the heat and cold.

ELIZABETH BARRETT BROWNING.

December 17.

Beloved, if God so loved us, we ought also to love one another. — 1 JOHN iv. 11.

"WHO hath not lost a friend," and when the grave hath closed over him, and we look back along the track of his life and our own, and think as David did, — "Very pleasant hast thou been to me, my brother Jonathan," — how does the embittered feeling, that he is gone, throw a halo of radiance over his living conduct, bring out into distinct and beautiful recollection a thousand delineations of kindly tenderness ; reveal, in hues of before-unnoticed light, conduct which may have grated harshly upon our own sensibilities ; and blot out forever every trace of unkindness from the records of our heart !   W. G. B.

In the years to come memory will hold precious, not the brief moment of triumph, but the love and sympathy of comrades ; and will seek to recall, not the plaudits of success, but "the touch of a vanished hand, the sound of a voice that is still."   MARIA B. BUCK.

HOW DOES DEATH SPEAK OF OUR BELOVED.

How does Death speak of our beloved
   When it has laid them low ;
When it has set its hallowing touch
   On speechless lip and brow ?

It clothes their every gift and grace
With radiance from the holiest place,
With light as from an angel's face ;

Recalling, with resistless force,
And tracing to their hidden source
Deeds scarcely noticed in their course.

The little loving, fond device,
That daily act of sacrifice,
Of which too late we learn the price ;

Opening our weeping eyes to trace
Simple, unnoted kindnesses,
Forgotten notes of tenderness,

Which evermore to us must be
Sacred as hymns in infancy,
Learned listening at a mother's knee.

Thus does Death speak of our beloved
   When it has laid them low ;
Then let Love antedate the work of Death,
   And do this now.

December 18.

My soul hath them still in remembrance, and is humbled in me. — LAM. iii. 20.

THERE is a voice from the tomb sweeter than song. There is a remembrance of the dead to which we turn even from the charms of the living. Oh, the grave ! — the grave ! It buries every error — covers every defect — extinguishes every resentment ! From its peaceful bosom spring none but fond regrets and tender recollections. . . .

Ay, go to the grave of buried love, and meditate ! There settle the account with thy conscience for every past benefit unrequited, every past endearment unregarded, of that departed being who can never — never — never return to be soothed by thy contrition ! . . .

Then weave thy chaplet of flowers, and strew the beauties of Nature about the grave ; console thy broken spirit, if thou canst, with these tender yet futile tributes of regret ; but take warning by the bitterness of this thy contrite affliction over the dead, and henceforth be more faithful and affectionate in the discharge of thy duties to the living. WASHINGTON IRVING

II.

How does Death speak of our beloved,
    When it has laid them low ;
When it has set its hallowing touch
    On speechless lip and brow ?

It shows how such a vexing deed
Was but a generous nature's weed,
Or some choice virtue run to seed ;

How that small fretting fretfulness
Was but love's over-anxiousness,
Which had not been had love been less.

This failing, at which we repined,
But the dim shade of day declined,
Which should have made us doubly kind.

O Christ, our life ! fore-date the work of Death,
    And do this now !
    And do this now !
Thou who art love, thus hallow our beloved !
    Not Death, but Thou.

December 19.

The heavens declare the glory of God, and the firmament sheweth His handy-work. — Ps. xix. 1.

"HOW is it," said the clouds to the evening star, "that while the sun is here you are but a faint vapor-like spot on the clear blue sky; but no sooner is he gone than you shine out with a splendor that fringes us with silver as we pass by?" "It is thus," said the star: "when the source of all my glory is present, what need is there that I should testify to his light? It is when he is absent that I gratefully pour forth the rays I have received from him, showing to all how glorious he must be from whom they first issued."

O POWERS illimitable! it is but the outer hem of God's great mantle our poor stars do gem.

JOHN RUSKIN.

CONTEMPLATION.

THEY are all up — the innumerable stars —
And hold their place in heaven. My eyes have been
Searching the pearly depths through which they spring
Like beautiful creations, till I feel
As if it were a new and perfect world,
Waiting in silence for the word of God
To breathe it into motion. There they stand,
Shining in order, like a living hymn
Written in light, awaking at the breath
Of the celestial dawn, and praising Him
Who made them with the harmony of spheres
I would I had an angel's ear to list
That melody. I would that I might float
Up in that boundless element, and feel
Its ravishing vibration, like the pulse
Beating in heaven! my spirit is athirst
For music — rarer music! I would bathe
My soul in a serener atmosphere
Than this; I long to mingle with the flock
Led by the "living waters," and to stray
In the "green pastures" of the better land!
When wilt thou break, dull fetter? When shall I
Gather my wings, and like a rushing thought
Stretch onward, star by star, up into heaven?

N. P WILLIS.

December 20.

Thanks be to God who giveth us the victory through our Lord Jesus Christ.

O DEATH ! dark hour to hopeless unbelief ! What art thou to the Christian's assurance ? Great hour of answer to life's prayer ; great hour that shall break asunder the bond of life's mystery ; hour of release from life's burden ; hour of reunion with the loved and lost, — what mighty hopes hasten to their fulfilment in Thee ! What longings, what aspirations, — breathed in the still night beneath the silent stars ; what dread emotions of curiosity ; what deep meditations of joy ; what hallowed imaginings of never experienced purity and bliss ; what possibilities, shadowing forth unspeakable realities to the soul, all verge to their consummation in thee ! O death ! the Christian's death ! what art thou but the gate of life, the portal of heaven, the threshold of eternity ?

ORVILLE DEWEY.

YE GOLDEN LAMPS.

Ye golden lamps of heaven, farewell,
  With all your feeble light ;
Farewell, thou ever-changing moon,
  Pale empress of the night.

And thou, refulgent orb of day,
  In brighter flames arrayed,
My soul, that springs beyond thy sphere,
  No more demands thine aid.

Ye stars are but the shining dust
  Of my divine abode,
The pavement of those heavenly courts
  Where I shall reign with God.

The Father of eternal light
  Shall there His beams display ;
Nor shall one moment's darkness mix
  With that unvaried day.

No more the drops of piercing grief
Shall swell into my eyes ;
Nor the meridian sun decline
Amid those brighter skies.

There all the millions of His saints
Shall in one song unite,
And each the bliss of all shall view
With infinite delight.

PHILIP DODDRIDGE.

December 21.

Blessed be God, which hath not turned away my prayer, nor His mercy from me. — Ps. lxvi. 20.

I HAVE no doubt that the old idea of prayer, as a begging of God to set aside wise laws to accommodate puny and often foolish men, will more and more fade away as men grow wiser. But I think that all this will only prepare the way for *true* prayer, — that prayer which seeks to get the highest spiritual good by conforming to the highest spiritual laws of our nature. This kind of prayer, I think, we shall no more outgrow than we shall outgrow hope, or love, or gratitude, or aspiration, or reverence, or the sense of dependence on a Higher Power, or the need, in our weakness and sorrow, of comfort and strength from some source higher than our poor selves. . . . Thus, I think, as we get away from the old, lower views, and come to understand the higher conception of prayer which corresponds with the higher conception of God, it becomes clear that religion has nothing about it that is more perfectly rational, and certainly nothing about it that is more uplifting, and in the profoundest way helpful, to weak, erring, and sorrow-laden human beings than prayer, — the communion of the earthly child with the heavenly parent ; the carrying of our little cups of heart-need and spirit-need to the great Fountain to get them filled ; the reaching up, when we are weak or sad, and laying hold of the Infinite Source of strength and joy which is forever above us.

J. T. SUNDERLAND.

LOVE DIVINE.

O Love Divine, of all that is
  The sweetest still and best !
Fain would I come and rest to-night
  Upon Thy tender breast :
I pray Thee turn me not away,
  For, sinful though I be,
Thou knowest everything I need
  And all my need of Thee.

And yet the spirit in my heart
  Says, Wherefore should I pray
That Thou shouldst seek me with Thy love,
  Since Thou dost seek alway ;
And dost not even wait until
  I urge my steps to Thee,
But in the darkness of my life
  Art coming still to me ?

I pray not, then, because I would, —
  I pray because I must ;
There is no meaning in my prayer
  But thankfulness and trust.
And Thou wilt hear the thought I mean,
  And not the words I say ;
Wilt hear the thanks among the words
  That only seem to pray.

I would not have Thee otherwise
  Than what Thou still must be :
Yea, Thou art God, and what Thou art
  Is ever best for me.
And so, for all my sighs, my heart
  Doth sing itself to rest,
O Love Divine, most far and near,
  Upon Thy tender breast.

John W. Chadwick

December 22.

All things are yours; whether Paul, or Apollos, or Ce-
phas, or the world, or life, or death, or things present,
or things to come; all are yours; and ye are Christ's;
and Christ is God's. — 1 COR. iii. 21–23.

NOT literally can they who are Christ's understand the
promise, " Life is yours." But there is a sense most
real and true in which they *may* apprehend it. For if the
good do not live longer, they live *more* in the same space
of time than other men. Life is to be reckoned not only
extensively, but also intensively : not merely by the number of its days, but also by the amount of thought and
energy which we infuse into them. Existence is not to
be measured by mere duration. An oak lives for centuries, generation after generation of mortals the mean-
while passing away ; but who would exchange for the life
of a plant, though protracted for ages, a single day of the
existence of a living, conscious, thinking man? It is possible for the longest life to be really briefer than the shortest ; and the child or youth may die older, with more of
life crowded into his brief existence, than he whose dull
and stagnant being drags on to an inglorious old age.

CAIRD

WE live in deeds, not years; in thoughts, not breaths ;
In feelings, not in figures on a dial.
We should count time by heart-throbs. He most lives
Who thinks most, feels the noblest, acts the best.

BAILEY

GROWTH.

IT is not growing, like a tree,
In bulk, doth make man better be ;
Or standing long an oak, three hundred year,
To fall a log at last, dry, bald, and sear ;
A lily of a day
Is fairer far in May,
Although it fall and die that night, —
It was the plant and flower of Light.
In small proportions we just beauties see ;
And in short measures life may perfect be.

BEN JONSON

December 23.

*Commune with your own heart upon your bed, and be
still. —* Ps. iv. 4.
*I commune with mine own heart; and my spirit made dili-
gent search. —* Ps. lxxvii. 6.

SECURE for yourself some privacy of life. As George
Herbert says, "By all means use sometimes to be
alone." God has put each into a separate body. We
should follow the Divine hint, and see to it that we do not
lapse again into the general flood of being. Many people
cannot endure being alone ; they are lost unless there is a
clatter of tongues in their ears. It is not only weak, but
it fosters weakness. The gregarious instinct is animal, —
the sheep and deer living on in us ; to be alone is spiritual.
We can have no clear, personal judgment of things till we
are somewhat separate from them. Mr. Webster used to say
of a difficult question, "Let me sleep on it." It was not
merely for morning vigor, but to get the matter at a distance where he could measure the proportions and see its
relations. So it is well at times to get away from our
world — companions, actions, work — in order to measure it, and ascertain our relations to it. The moral use of
the night is in the isolation it brings, shutting out the
world from the senses, that it may be realized in thought.
It is very simple advice, but worth heeding. Get some
moments each day to yourself; take now and then a solitary walk ; get into the silence of thick woods, or some
other isolation as deep, and suffer the mysterious sense of
selfhood to steal upon you, as it surely will. Pythagoras
insisted upon an hour of solitude every day to meet his
own mind and learn what oracle it had to impart.

T. T. MUNGER: *On the Threshold.*

By all means use sometimes to be alone.
Salute thyself : see what thy soul doth wear.
Dare to look in thy chest, — for 't is thine own, —
And tumble up and down what thou find'st there.
  Who cannot rest till he good fellows finde,
  He breaks up house, turns out of doores his minde.

GEORGE HERBERT.

SELF-EXAMINATION.

LET not soft slumber close your eyes,
Before you 've recollected thrice
The train of action through the day !
Where have my feet chose out their way ?
What have I learnt, where'er I 've been,
From all I 've heard, from all I 've seen ?
What know I more that 's worth the knowing ?
What have I done that 's worth the doing ?
What have I sought that I should shun ?
What duty have I left undone,
Or into what new follies run ?
These self-inquiries are the road
That leads to virtue and to God.

ISAAC WATTS

——◆——

December 24.

A little one shall become a thousand, and a small one a strong nation ; I the Lord will hasten it in his time. — ISA. lx. 22.

GOD gathers around Him all that is most like Him, and suffers nothing that is excellent to die. There are things in His world which are not meant to perish, — works which survive the workmen, and multiply blessings when they are gone, and make all who lend a faithful hand to them, part of the husbandry of God, laborers with Him on that great field of time, whose culture and whose harvests are everlasting. The pains we spend upon our mortal selves, will perish with ourselves ; but the care we give out of a good heart to others, the efforts of disinterested duty, the deeds and thoughts of pure affection, are never lost ; they are liable to no waste ; and are like a force that propagates itself forever, changing its place, but not losing its intensity.

GOD, who prepares His work through ages, accomplishes it, when the hour is come, with the feeblest instruments.

MERLE D'AUBIGNE.

THIS learned I from the shadow of a tree,
That to and fro did sway upon a wall, —
Our shadow-selves, our influence, may fall
Where we can never be.

ANNA E. HAMILTON.

SIMILES.

ONE taper lights a thousand, — yet doth beam
No dimmer, giving all, but losing nought.
By one faint glimmering taper light is brought
To altar-candles, many-branched, that gleam
Against high-vaulted chancel-roofs, and stream
Through painted panes with vivid splendors fraught
And shine on effigies of saints, fair-wrought,
Whose folded hands forever praying seem.
These two things have I known; and this beside, —
Fire kindled by a failing flame, which died
That self-same moment. Lord, my flame burns low —
Great fires are kindled by a feeble spark —
Let my poor taper lighten some, whose glow
Shall bless the world when I am cold and dark!

SUNDAY MAGAZINE.

—◆—

December 25.

And the angel said unto them, Fear not; for, behold, I
bring you good tidings of great joy, which shall be to
all people. For unto you is born this day in the city
of David a Saviour, which is Christ the Lord. —
MATT. ii. 10, 11.

HARK! the herald angels sing,
Glory to the new-born King.

HOW good it is for those who are bereaved and sorrowful that our Christian festivals point forward and
upward as well as backward; that the eternal joy to which
we are drawing ever nearer is linked to the earthly joy
which has passed away.

MRS. CHARLES.

A CHRISTMAS HYMN.

IT was the calm and silent night !
  Seven hundred years and fifty-three
Had Rome been growing up to might,
  And now was queen of land and sea !
No sound was heard of clashing wars,
  Peace brooded o'er the hushed domain;
Apollo, Pallas, Jove, and Mars
  Held undisturbed their ancient reign, —
    In the solemn midnight,
      Centuries ago !

'T was in the calm and silent night !
  The senator of haughty Rome
Impatient urged his chariot's flight,
  From lordly revel rolling home.
Triumphal arches, gleaming, swell
  His breast with thoughts of boundless sway;
What recked the Roman what befell
  A paltry province far away, —
    In the solemn midnight,
      Centuries ago !

Within that province far away
  Went plodding home a weary boor;
A streak of light before him lay,
  Fallen through a half-shut stable door
Across his path.   He paused, for naught
  Told what was going on within;
How keen the stars, his only thought;
  The air how calm, and cold, and thin, —
    In the solemn midnight,
      Centuries ago !

O strange indifference ! — Low and high
  Drowsed over common joys and cares;
The earth was still, but knew not why ;
  The world was listening, — unawares !
How calm a moment may precede
  One that shall thrill the world forever !
To that still moment none would heed,
  Man's doom was linked, no more to sever, —
    In the solemn midnight,
      Centuries ago !

It is the calm and silent night !
  A thousand bells ring out, and throw
Their joyous peals abroad, and smite
  The darkness, charmed and holy now !
The night that erst no name had worn,
  To it a happy name is given ;
For in that stable lay, new-born,
  The peaceful Prince of earth and heaven, —
    In the solemn midnight,
      Centuries ago !

ALFRED DOMETT.

—◆—

December 26.

For Thou desirest not sacrifice, else would I give it : Thou delightest not in burnt-offering. The sacrifices of God are a broken spirit ; a broken and a contrite heart, O God, Thou wilt not despise. — Ps. li. 16, 17.

O GOD, who by the leading of a star didst manifest Thy only-begotten Son to the Gentiles ; mercifully grant that we, who know Thee now by faith, may after this life have the fruition of thy glorious Godhead ; through Jesus Christ our Lord. Amen.

BRIGHTEST AND BEST.

BRIGHTEST and best of the sons of the morning,
  Dawn on our darkness, and lend us thine aid !
Star of the east, the horizon adorning,
  Guide where our infant Redeemer is laid !

Cold on His cradle the dew-drops are shining :
  Low lies His bed with the beasts of the stall ;
Angels adore Him in slumber reclining,
  Maker, and monarch, and Saviour of all.

Say, shall we yield Him, in costly devotion,
  Odors of Edom, and offerings divine, —
Gems of the mountain, and pearls of the ocean,
  Myrrh from the forest, and gold from the mine ?

Vainly we offer each ample oblation,
  Vainly with gold would His favor secure :
Richer by far is the heart's adoration,
  Dearer to God are the prayers of the poor.

Brightest and best of the sons of the morning,
  Dawn on our darkness, and lend us thine aid !
Star of the east, the horizon adorning,
  Guide where our infant Redeemer is laid !

REGINALD HEBER

---◆---

December 27.

Wherefore hidest Thou Thy face ? — JOB xiii. 24.

THE soul that knows the sweetness of His presence
and His face shining on it will account no place
nor condition hard, providing it may be refreshed with
that ; as the saints have been in caves and dungeons enjoying more of that light in those times, when other comforts have been abridged.   Then they have had a beam
from Heaven into their souls in their darkest dungeon far
more worth than the light of the sun, and all the advan-
tages the world can afford.

ARCHBISHOP LEIGHTON.

MY LIGHT, MY LIFE, MY WAY.

WHY dost Thou hide Thy lovely face ?   Oh, why
Does that eclipsing hand so long deny
The sunshine of Thy soul-enlivening eye ?

Without that light, what light remains in me ?
Thou art my Life, my Way, my Light ; in Thee
I live, I move, and by Thy beams I see.

Thou art my Life ; if Thou but turn away,
My life 's a thousand deaths.   Thou art my Way ;
Without Thee, Lord, I travel not, but stray.

My Light Thou art ; without Thy glorious sight,
Mine eyes are darkened with perpetual night.
My God, Thou art my Way, my Life, my Light.

Thou art my Way ; I wander if Thou fly ;
Thou art my Light ; if hid, how blind am I !
Thou art my Life ; if Thou withdraw, I die.

Mine eyes are blind and dark, I cannot see ;
To whom, or whither, should my darkness flee,
But to the Light ? and who 's that light but Thee ?

My path is lost, my wandering steps do stray ;
I cannot safely go, nor safely stay ;
Whom should I seek but Thee, my Path, my Way ?

If I have lost my path, great Shepherd, say,
Shall I still wander in a doubtful way ?
Lord, shall a lamb of Israel's sheepfold stray ?

Thou art the pilgrim's Path, the blind man's Eye,
The dead man's Life ; on Thee my hopes rely ;
If Thou remove, I err, I grope, I die.

Disclose Thy sunbeams, close Thy wings, and stay ;
See, see how I am blind and dead, and stray,
O Thou that art my Light, my Life, my Way.

FRANCIS QUARLES (1592) : *Emblems.*

———◆———

December 28.

We spend our years as a tale that is told. — Ps. xc. 10.

NOTHING more reveals the majestic import of life
than this *ennui*, this heart-sinking sense of the vanity of all present acquisitions and attainments. " Man's
misery," it has been well said, " comes of his greatness."
The sphere of life appears small, the ordinary circle of
its avocations narrow and confined, the common routine
of its cares insipid and unsatisfactory ; why ? Because
he who walks therein demands a boundless range of objects. Why does the body seem to imprison the soul?
Because the soul asks for freedom ; because it looks forth
from the narrow and grated windows of sense, upon the
wide and immeasurable creation ; because it knows that
around and beyond it lie outstretched the infinite and the
everlasting paths.   ORVILLE DEWEY.

YES! THERE ARE TALISMANS.

YES! there are talismans that break
The sleep of visions, and awake
   Long silent recollections;
That kindle in the mental eye
Romantic feelings, long gone by,
   And glowing retrospections.
By them the mind is taught to know
That all is vanity below,
   And that our being only
Is for a day, and that we pass
And are forgotten, and the grass
   Will wave above us lonely.
Yea, all must change! we cannot stay
The spoiler. Time, with onward sway,
   All human pride defaces;
A few brief years revolve, and then
We are no more, — and other men
   Shall occupy our places.

———◆———

December 29.

*When they saw the star, they rejoiced with exceeding great
joy. . . . And when they had opened their treasures,
they presented unto Him gifts; gold, and frankincense,
and myrrh.* — MATT. ii. 10, 11.

*In this was manifested the love of God toward us, because
that God sent His only begotten Son into the world,
that we might live through Him.* — 1 JOHN iv. 9.

O THOU who art calumniated, have patience! God
knows. Thou who art misunderstood, be resigned!
God sees. Thou who art forgotten, have hope! God
remembers.

O LORD Jesus! who wert willing to take our soul and
our flesh, in order to suffer like us, with us, for us; who
didst endure all anxieties, all bitterness, all injustices, all
ingratitudes; who didst ask that the cup of the Passion
might be taken from Thee, and didst cry, "Eloi, eloi,

lama, sabachthani!" . . . Ah! when the combat of life
shall cause me to complain, if men have for me neither
pity nor excuse, do You, at least, Lord Jesus, hear me,
understand me, comfort me, cheer me!

JOSEPH ROUX: *Meditations of a Parish Priest.*

THE CHRISTMAS ROSE.

UNTO the cradle of the wondrous Child
Heaven brought its star, and man his gold and myrrh ;
But Nature brings each year a living gift
To halo the divine event ; a star
Of earth, that once came from the East and sheds
Its silver radiance round our common homes.
It comes, like Him whose birth it celebrates,
To cheer the winter of the world, and make
The very snow to blossom into life.
When earth has reached its darkest hour, this gleam
Of coming dawn appears. We seem to see
The snowdrop's mystic presence on the lawn ;
The crocus kindle where its light went out ;
The copse grow dense with purple haze of buds,
The willow's deck their wands with silken plumes.
Long mute, the birds, whene'er they see this sign,
Take heart to twitter ; and the sunbeams pale
Grow warmer as they shine upon its flowers ;
And where it breathes its subtle fragrance round,
The very air seems conscious of the spring.
Last child of the old year, first of the new,
Ghost of the past, soul of the future rose, —
It links the seasons with its silver clasp,
And blends our memories and hopes in one.
In this pale herald of the flowery year
Are sketched the types of Lily and of Rose,
Which afterwards, from its fair side in death,
Are separated to make the seasons gay.
From roots of ebon darkness, through the mould
Spring up the pure white blossoms, one by one, —
Like human heart, whose roots are dark with woe,
And yet produce the brightest flowers of Heaven.
Its seeming petals — green leaves glorified —
Are moonlike made, through the December gloom,
To light dim insects to their honeyed task,
And so fulfil the higher ends of life.
At first they come up pale, and blanched with cold,
But as the days grow long, a warmer hue,

Like that which deepens in the summer rose,
Or tips the daisy's frill, creeps over them ;
As if they blushed, in a white, flowerless world,
To find themselves the only blooming things.
Unchanged they last until the seed is ripe,
In which the single life dies for the race.
And then, their purpose served, they darken down
Into the dusky green of common leaves.
Transfiguration strange ! a lowly sign
Of Him, whose robe and face shone whiter far
Than Hermon's crest, while of His death He talked !
That which exalts the flower above its wont,
Ennobles everything. The priestly dress
Of beauty and of glory clothes each life
That yields itself a sacrifice to love.

HUGH MACMILLAN.

December 30.

So teach us to number our days, that we may apply our hearts unto wisdom. — Ps. xc. 12.

GOD gives thee a little light that thou mayest know thy duty. But He surrounds thee with much darkness, that thou mayest know thy dependence. He rewards thy efforts after knowledge with some discoveries, to encourage thee to persevere. He meets them with more difficulties, to humble thy vain-glory. He allows thee to ascend higher and higher on the mount of prospect ; but He causes the horizon to recede farther and farther from thy view. He reminds thee perpetually that thy career is to be unending ; that thy improvement is to be eternal ; that thou art to be ever learning, and yet never coming to the knowledge of all truth ; that as thou must always remain finite, so forever and ever it will be true that thy thoughts are not God's thoughts, nor His ways thy ways.

ALONZO POTTER.

THE OLD YEAR'S BLESSING.

I AM fading from you, but one draweth near
Called the angel-guardian of the coming year.

If my gifts and graces coldly you forget,
Let the New Year's Angel bless and crown them yet.

For we work together ; he and I are one ;
Let him end and perfect all I leave undone.

I brought Good Desires, though as yet but seeds ;
Let the New Year make them blossom into Deeds.

I brought Joy to brighte· many happy days ;
Let the New Year's A ·ƺel turn it into Praise.

If I gave you Sickness, if I brought you Care,
Let him make one Patience and the other Prayer.

Where I brought you Sorrow, through his care at length
It may rise triumphant into future Strength.

If I brought you Plenty, all wealth's bounteous charms,
Shall not the new Angel turn them into Alms ?

I gave health and leisure, skill to dream and plan ;
Let him make them nobler, — work for God and man.

If I broke your Idols, showed you they were dust,
Let him turn the Knowledge into heavenly Trust.

If I brought Temptation, let Sin die away
Into boundless Pity for all hearts that stray.

If your list of Errors dark and long appears,
Let this new-born Monarch melt them into Tears.

May you hold this Angel dearer than the last, —
So I bless his Future, while he crowns my Past.

ADELAIDE A. PROCTER.

December 31

The Lord shall preserve thy going out and thy coming in, from this time forth, and even forevermore. — Ps. cxxi. 8.

DO we thirst for God? As the days and months and years pass, do we ever look out of and beyond ourselves upon that vast ocean of Uncreated Life which encircles us, which penetrates our inmost selves? Do we ever think steadily, so as to dwell with a real intellectual interest, upon Him who is the first and highest of Truths, to whose free bounty we ourselves owe the gift of existence, and to whom we must one day account for our use of it? Do we ever sincerely desire to love Him, and to live for Him, or are we hurrying along our solitary path, from one vanishing shape towards another, while we neglect the Alone Unchangeable? Be sure that if we will, in God revealed in Christ, the soul may slake the thirst of the Ages; and the dreariest, and darkest, and most restless existence may find illumination and peace. "This God is our God forever and ever. He will be our Guide even unto death," and beyond it. To each of us now this, if we will; if we will, He will be forever to each the Eternal Truth, wherein thought can never find its limit; the Uncreated Beauty, "Most Ancient, but always Fair," whereof affection can never tire; the Perfect Rule, existing eternally in the Life of the Necessary Moral Being, whereunto each created will may perpetually confirm itself, yet never exhaust its task. Without this Awful and Blessed Being man has no adequate object, even during these days of his brief earthly existence; his thought, his affection, his purpose spring up, and are exercised only that they may presently waste and die. With God the human soul not merely interprets the secret of the universe; it comprehends and is at peace with itself. In God is the satisfaction of its thirst, — He is the Object of religion.

CANON LIDDON.

A PSALM FOR NEW YEAR'S EVE.

A FRIEND stands at the door;
In either tight-closed hand
Hiding rich gifts, three hundred and threescore;
Waiting to strew them daily o'er the land
Even as seed the sower.
Each drops he, treads it in, and passes by:
It cannot be made fruitful till it die.

O good New Year, we clasp
This warm shut hand of thine,
Loosing forever, with half sigh, half gasp,
That which from ours falls like dead fingers' twine:
Ay, whether fierce its grasp
Has been, or gentle, having been, we know
That it was blessed: let the Old Year go.

O New Year, teach us faith!
The road of life is hard:
When our feet bleed, and scourging winds us scathe,
Point thou to Him whose visage was more marred
Than any man's; who saith,
"Make straight paths for your feet," and to the opprest,
"Come ye to Me, and I will give you rest."   .

Yet hang some lamp-like hope
Above this unknown way,
Kind year, to give our spirits freer scope
And our hands strength to work while it is day.
But if that way must slope
Tombward, oh, bring before our fading eyes
The lamp of life, the Hope that never dies.

Comfort our souls with love, —
Love of all human kind;
Love special, close, — in which, like sheltered dove,
Each weary heart its own safe nest may find;
And love that turns above
Adoringly, contented to resign
All loves, if need be, for the Love Divine.

Friend, come thou like a friend,
And whether bright thy face,
Or dim with clouds we cannot comprehend,
We'll hold out patient hands, each in his place,
And trust thee to the end,
Knowing thou leadest onwards to those spheres
Where there are neither days, nor months, nor years.

DINAH MULOCH CRAIK.

INDEX

OF

FIRST LINES OF POETICAL QUOTATIONS.

INDEX OF AUTHORS.

𝔓oetry.

𝔓𝔯𝔬𝔰𝔢.

www.ingramcontent.com/pod-product-compliance
Lightning Source LLC
Chambersburg PA
CBHW031100110726
47900CB00003B/1003